IMMORTA

HAUNTING

Experience the chilling origins of modern horror with these classic, gruesome delights:

"The Bottle Imp"
by Robert Louis Stevenson:
The disarming simplicity of a folktale, turned to surprising resonance and dread . . .

"The Country of the Blind"
by H. G. Wells:
A narrative that plausibly and chillingly reorients the old saying, "In the country of the blind, the one-eyed man is king" . . .

"The Yellow Wallpaper"
by Charlotte Perkins Gilman:
This disturbing narrative takes the reader from feverish hallucination to a hideous reality . . .

"Dracula's Guest"
by Bram Stoker:
Journey to a strange land where normal reality doesn't apply, in an uncanny tale drawn from the original manuscript of the classic novel.

"The Beckoning Fair One"
by Oliver Onions:
A writer rents a secluded apartment—but the rooms are not as empty as they seem . . .

And other great stories in a portable treasury of fiendish imagination!

Other anthologies edited by Leslie Pockell:

The 100 Best Poems of All Time

THE 13 BEST HORROR STORIES OF ALL TIME

EDITED BY
LESLIE POCKELL

WARNER BOOKS

An AOL Time Warner Company

Warner Books, Inc., 1271 Avenue of the Americas, New York, NY 10020
Visit our Web site at www.twbookmark.com.

An AOL Time Warner Company

Printed in the United States of America
First Printing: September 2002
10 9 8 7 6 5 4 3 2 1

Library of Congress Cataloging-in-Publication Data
The 13 best horror stories of all time / edited by Leslie Pockell.
p. cm.
Contents: The tell-tale heart / Edgar Allan Poe — Green tea / J. Sheridan Le Fanu — The yellow wallpaper / Charlotte Perkins Gilman — The bottle imp / Robert Louis Stevenson — Dracula's guest / Bram Stoker — The great god Pan / Arthur Machen — The monkey's paw / W. W. Jacobs — Oh, whistle and I'll come to you, my lad / M. R. James — The country of the blind / H. G. Wells — The willows / Algernon Blackwood — The beckoning fair one / Oliver Onions — The call of Cthulhu / H. P. Lovecraft — The lottery / Shirley Jackson.
ISBN 0-446-67950-X
1. Horror tales, American. 2. Horror tales, English. I. Title: Thirteen best horror stories of all time. II. Pockell, Leslie.

PS648.H6 A13 2002
813'.0873808—dc21

2002016843

Cover design by Brigid Pearson
Cover photo by Steve Nilsson/Getty Images
Book design and text composition by Ellen Gleeson

CONTENTS

INTRODUCTION

The horror story emerged in the late eighteenth century from what appears to have been a witches' brew of influences. The Scientific Revolution undermined traditionally accepted explanations for natural phenomena, sometimes replacing them with pseudoscience such as Mesmerism. At the same time, the emergence of the Romantic Movement in literature in Europe and Great Britain sometimes stimulated hyperemotional responses from those reacting to the world around them. In addition, the Age of Revolution provoked the widespread sentiment that the world was in upheaval, and established values were being transformed by new ways of thinking. The gothic novel, with its quasi-medieval settings and supernatural aura, soon provided room for an entire genre given up to creating a sense of foreboding and fright in its readers. So, in a world of uncertainty and experimentation, of science and sadism, the horror story rose up like some kind of unborn monster.

The stories in this volume span about a century, dating back to the formative years of the genre, the days when on the Continent E. T. A. Hoffman was creating his tales of out-of-control automatons. In America Edgar Allan Poe mixed madness and the supernatural so that they were inextricably confused in the mind of the reader, as in perhaps his most horrifying single story, "The Tell-Tale Heart." In fact, madness is often a prominent element in the best horror stories; physicians, scientists, and those we today identify as psychologists are frequently seen as narrators or protagonists (as in Le Fanu's "Green Tea," Machen's "The Great God Pan," and M. R. James's "Oh, Whistle and I'll Come to You, My Lad."). Charlotte Perkins Gilman's protagonist in "The Yellow Wallpaper" is under a doctor's care, but it is left to the reader to decide if she falls into madness or into another dimension. The novelist whose story is told in Onions's "The Beckoning Fair One" believes he is completely rational, while the horrified reader watches his sanity slip away.

Other characteristics of classic horror include the sense that unseen evil dwells among us and can be rooted out only with great difficulty if at all (again "The Great God Pan" and Lovecraft's "The Call of Cthulhu"); attempts to circumvent fate are doomed (Stevenson's "The Bottle Imp" and Jacobs's "The Monkey's Paw," each a variation on the ancient tale of three wishes). Another popular horror motif involves the protagonist's entry into a strange land or dimension, where what would be considered normal reality no longer applies (Bram Stoker's "Dracula's Guest," H. G. Wells's "The Country of the Blind," Blackwood's "The Willows," and perhaps most memorably Shirley Jackson's classic "The Lottery").

Whatever the nature of its appeal—vicarious fright that reveals itself to be "only a story"; a kind of exorcism of the dread of madness or the fear of death; even the kind of escapism that allows the free, uninhibited range of the imagination without consequence—the horror story continues to flourish in today's world of Peter Straub, Dean Koontz, and of course Stephen King, who mine the trivia of our daily lives to uncover the horror beneath. Yet their work only builds upon the accomplishments of those whose creations are included in this volume, stories by the greatest names in the history of this genre that rose out of the ferment of change in the eighteenth century and has never lost its power to hold its readers.

I'd like to thank Jamie Raab for encouraging this project, and Karen Melnyk and Sarah Rustin for their invaluable editorial contributions.

THE 13 BEST HORROR STORIES OF ALL TIME

THE TELL-TALE HEART

Edgar Allan Poe

(1843)

Besides inventing the modern detective story, Poe brought the gothic horror story into American literature. This brief but bravura work of sustained hysteria creates its powerful effect as much by the unrelieved, almost shrieking, intensity of its tone as by its ghastly subject.

True! Nervous—very, very dreadfully nervous I had been and am! but why will you say that I am mad? The disease had sharpened my senses—not destroyed—not dulled them. Above all was the sense of hearing acute. I heard all things in the heaven and in the earth. I heard many things in hell. How, then, am I mad? Hearken! and observe how healthily—how calmly I can tell you the whole story.

It is impossible to tell how first the idea entered my brain; but once conceived, it haunted me day and night. Object there was none. Passion there was none. I loved the old man. He had never wronged me. He had never given me insult. For his gold I had no desire. I think it was his eye! Yes, it was this! One of his eyes resembled that of a vulture—a pale blue eye, with a film over it. Whenever it fell upon me, my blood ran cold; and so by degrees—very gradually—I made up my mind to take the life of the old man, and thus rid myself of the eye forever.

Now this is the point. You fancy me mad. Madmen know nothing. But you should have seen me. You should have seen how wisely I proceeded—with what caution—with what foresight—with what dissimulation I went to work!

I was never kinder to the old man than during the whole

week before I killed him. And every night, about midnight, I turned the latch of his door and opened it—oh, so gently! And then, when I had made an opening sufficient for my head, I put in a dark lantern, all closed, closed, so that no light shone out, and then I thrust in my head. Oh, you would have laughed to see how cunningly I thrust it in! I moved it slowly—very, very slowly, so that I might not disturb the old man's sleep. It took me an hour to place my whole head within the opening so far that I could see him as he lay upon his bed. Ha!—would a madman have been so wise as this? And then, when my head was well in the room, I undid the lantern cautiously—oh, so cautiously—cautiously (for the hinges creaked)—I undid it just so much that a single thin ray fell upon the vulture eye. And this I did for seven long nights—every night just at midnight—but I found the eye always closed; and so it was impossible to do the work; for it was not the old man who vexed me, but his Evil Eye. And every morning, when the day broke, I went boldly into the chamber, and spoke courageously to him, calling him by name in a hearty tone, and inquiring how he had passed the night. So you see he would have been a very profound old man, indeed, to suspect that every night, just at twelve, I looked in upon him while he slept.

Upon the eighth night I was more than usually cautious in opening the door. A watch's minute hand moves more quickly than did mine. Never before that night had I felt the extent of my own powers—of my sagacity. I could scarcely contain my feelings of triumph. To think that there I was, opening the door, little by little, and he not even to dream of my secret deeds or thoughts. I fairly chuckled at the idea; and perhaps he heard me; for he moved on the bed suddenly, as if startled. Now you may think that I drew back—but no. His room was as black as pitch with the thick darkness (for the shutters were close fastened, through fear of robbers), and so I knew that he could not see the opening of the door, and I kept pushing it on steadily, steadily.

I had my head in, and was about to open the lantern, when my thumb slipped upon the tin fastening, and the old man sprang up in bed, crying out: "Who's there?"

I kept quite still and said nothing. For a whole hour I did not move a muscle, and in the meantime I did not hear him lie down. He was still sitting up in the bed listening;—just as I have done, night after night, hearkening to the death watches in the wall.

Presently I heard a slight groan, and I knew it was the groan of mortal terror. It was not a groan of pain or grief—oh no!—it was the low stifled sound that arises from the bottom of the soul when overcharged with awe. I knew the sound well. Many a night, just at midnight, when all the world slept, it has welled up from my own bosom, deepening, with its dreadful echo, the terrors that distracted me. I say I knew it well. I knew what the old man felt, and pitied him, although I chuckled at heart. I knew that he had been lying awake ever since the first slight noise, when he had turned in the bed. His fears had been ever since growing upon him. He had been trying to fancy them causeless, but could not. He had been saying to himself: "It is nothing but the wind in the chimney—it is only a mouse crossing the floor," or "it is merely a cricket which has made a single chirp." Yes, he had been trying to comfort himself with these suppositions; but he had found all in vain. All in vain; because Death, in approaching him, had stalked with his black shadow before him, and enveloped the victim. And it was the mournful influence of the unperceived shadow that caused him to feel—although he neither saw nor heard—to feel the presence of my head within the room.

When I had waited a long time, very patiently, without hearing him lie down, I resolved to open a little—a very, very little crevice in the lantern. So I opened it—you cannot imagine how stealthily, stealthily—until, at length, a single dim ray, like the thread of the spider, shot from out the crevice and full upon the vulture eye.

It was open—wide, wide open—and I grew furious as I gazed upon it. I saw it with perfect distinctness—all a dull blue, with a hideous veil over it that chilled the very marrow in my bones; but I could see nothing else of the old man's face or person: for I had directed the ray, as if by instinct, precisely upon the damned spot.

And now—have I not told you that what you mistake for madness is but over-acuteness of the senses?—now, I say, there came to my ears a low, dull, quick sound, such as a watch makes when enveloped in cotton. I knew that sound well too. It was the beating of the old man's heart. It increased my fury, as the beating of a drum stimulates the soldier into courage.

But even yet I refrained and kept still. I scarcely breathed. I held the lantern motionless. I tried how steadily I could maintain the ray upon the eye. Meantime the hellish tattoo of the heart increased. It grew quicker and quicker and louder and louder every instant. The old man's terror must have been extreme! It grew louder, I say, louder every moment!—do you mark me well? I have told you that I am nervous: so I am. And now at the dead hour of night, amid the dreadful silence of that old house, so strange a noise as this excited me to uncontrollable terror. Yet, for some minutes longer I refrained and stood still. But the beating grew louder, louder! I thought the heart must burst. And now a new anxiety seized me—the sound would be heard by a neighbor! The old man's hour had come! With a loud yell, I threw open the lantern and leaped into the room. He shrieked once—once only. In an instant I dragged him to the floor, and pulled the heavy bed over him. I then smiled gaily, to find the deed so far done. But, for many minutes, the heart beat on with a muffled sound. This, however, did not vex me; it would not be heard through the wall. At length it ceased. The old man was dead. I removed the bed and examined the corpse. Yes, he was stone, stone dead. I placed my hand upon the heart and held it there many minutes. There was no pulsation. He was stone dead. His eye would trouble me no more.

If still you think me mad, you will think so no longer when I describe the wise precautions I took for the concealment of the body. The night waned, and I worked hastily, but in silence. First of all I dismembered the corpse. I cut off the head and the arms and the legs.

I then took up three planks from the flooring of the chamber, and deposited all between the scantlings. I then replaced the boards so cleverly, so cunningly, that no human eye—not even his—could have detected anything wrong. There was nothing to wash out—no stain of any kind—no blood-spot whatever. I had been too wary for that. A tub had caught all—ha! ha!

When I had made an end of these labors, it was four o'clock—still dark as midnight. As the bell sounded the hour, there came a knocking at the street door. I went down to open it with a light heart—for what had I now to fear? There entered three men, who introduced themselves, with perfect suavity, as officers of the police. A shriek had been heard by a neighbor during the night: suspicion of foul play had been aroused; information had been lodged at the police office, and they (the officers) had been deputed to search the premises.

I smiled—for what had I to fear? I bade the gentlemen welcome. The shriek, I said, was my own in a dream. The old man, I mentioned, was absent in the country. I took my visitors all over the house. I bade them search—search well. I led them, at length, to his chamber. I showed them his treasures, secure, undisturbed. In the enthusiasm of my confidence, I brought chairs into the room, and desired them here to rest from their fatigues, while I myself, in the wild audacity of my perfect triumph, placed my own seat upon the very spot beneath which reposed the corpse of the victim.

The officers were satisfied. My manner had convinced them. I was singularly at ease. They sat, and while I answered cheerily, they chatted familiar things. But, ere long, I felt myself getting pale and wished them gone. My head ached, and I fancied a ringing in my ears: but still they sat and still chatted. The ringing became more distinct:—it continued and became more distinct: I talked more freely to get rid of the feeling: but it continued and gained definiteness—until, at length, I found that the noise was not within my ears.

No doubt I now grew very pale,—but I talked more fluently, and with a heightened voice. Yet the sound increased—and what could I do? It was a low, dull, quick sound—much such a sound as a watch makes when enveloped in cotton. I gasped for breath—and yet the officers heard it not. I talked more quickly—more vehemently; but the noise steadily increased. Why would they not be gone? I paced the floor to and fro with heavy strides, as if excited to fury by the observation of the men—but the noise steadily increased. Oh, God; what could I do? I foamed—I raved—I swore! I swung the chair upon which I had been sitting, and grated it upon the boards, but the noise arose over all and continually increased. It grew louder—louder—louder! And still the men chatted pleasantly, and smiled. Was it possible they heard not? Almighty God!—no, no! They heard!—they suspected—they knew!—they were making a mockery of my horror!—this I thought, and this I think. But anything was better than this agony! Anything was more tolerable than this derision! I could bear those hypocritical smiles no longer! I felt that I must scream or die!—and now—again!—hark! louder! louder! louder! louder!

"Villains!" I shrieked, "dissemble no more! I admit the deed!—tear up the planks!—here, here!—it is the beating of his hideous heart!"

GREEN TEA

J. Sheridan Le Fanu

(1869)

Le Fanu was born and died in Dublin, and his stories are characterized by a certain lightness and Irish wit that provide an unsettling counterpoint to the dark subtext of his narratives. "Green Tea" is a harrowing tale of paranoid obsession told from the point of view of a somewhat self-satisfied physician.

Though carefully educated in medicine and surgery, I have never practised either. The study of each continues, nevertheless, to interest me profoundly. Neither idleness nor caprice caused my secession from the honourable calling which I had just entered. The cause was a very trifling scratch inflicted by a dissecting knife. This trifle cost me the loss of two fingers, amputated promptly, and the more painful loss of my health, for I have never been quite well since, and have seldom been twelve months together in the same place.

In my wanderings I became acquainted with Dr. Martin Hesselius, a wanderer like myself, like me a physician, and like me an enthusiast in his profession. Unlike me in this, that his wanderings were voluntary, and he a man, if not of fortune, as we estimate fortune in England, at least in what our forefathers used to term "easy circumstances." He was an old man when I first saw him; nearly five-and-thirty years my senior.

In Dr. Martin Hesselius, I had found my master. His knowledge was immense, his grasp of a case was an intuition. He was the very man to inspire a young enthusiast, like me, with awe and delight. My admiration has stood the test of time and survived the separation of death. I am sure it was well-founded.

For nearly twenty years I acted as his medical secretary. His immense collection of papers he has left in my care, to be arranged, indexed and bound. His treatment of some of these cases is curious. He writes in two distinct characters. He describes what he saw and heard as an intelligent layman might, and when in his style of narrative he had seen the patient either through his own halldoor, to the light of day, or through the gates of darkness to the caverns of the dead, he returns upon the narrative, and in the terms of his art and with all the force of originality of genius, proceeds to the work of analysis, diagnosis and illustration.

Here and there a case strikes me as of a kind to amuse or horrify a lay reader with an interest quite different from the peculiar one which it may possess for an expert. With slight modifications, chiefly of language, and of course a change of names, I copy the following. The narrator is Dr. Martin Hesselius. I find it among the voluminous notes of cases which he made during a tour in England about sixty-four years ago.

It is related in series of letters to his friend Professor Van Loo of Leyden. The professor was not a physician, but a chemist, and a man who read history and metaphysics and medicine, and had, in his day, written a play.

The narrative is therefore, if somewhat less valuable as a medical record, necessarily written in a manner more likely to interest an unlearned reader.

These letters, from a memorandum attached, appear to have been returned on the death of the professor, in 1819, to Dr. Hesselius. They are written, some in English, some in French, but the greater part in German. I am a faithful, though I am conscious, by no means a graceful translator, and although here and there I omit some passages, and shorten others, and disguise names, I have interpolated nothing.

1. Dr. Hesselius Relates How He Met the Rev. Mr. Jennings

The Rev. Mr. Jennings is tall and thin. He is middle-aged, and dresses with a natty, old-fashioned, high church precision. He is naturally a little stately, but not at all stiff. His features, without being handsome, are well formed, and their expression extremely kind, but also shy.

I met him one evening at Lady Mary Heyduke's. The modesty and benevolence of his countenance are extremely prepossessing.

We are but a small party, and he joined agreeably enough in the conversation. He seems to enjoy listening very much more than contributing to the talk; but what he says is always to the purpose and well said. He is a great favourite of Lady Mary's, who it seems, consults him upon many things, and thinks him the most happy and blessed person on the earth. Little knows she about him.

The Rev. Mr. Jennings is a bachelor, and has, they say, sixty thousand pounds in the funds. He is a charitable man. He is most anxious to be actively employed in his sacred profession, and yet though always tolerably well elsewhere, when he goes down to his vicarage in Warwickshire, to engage in the actual duties of his sacred calling, his health soon fails him, and in a very strange way. So says Lady Mary.

There is no doubt that Mr. Jennings' health does break down in, generally, a sudden and mysterious way, sometimes in the very act of officiating in his old and pretty church at Kenlis. It may be his heart, it may be his brain. But so it has happened three or four times, or oftener, that after proceeding a certain way in the service, he has on a sudden stopped short, and after a silence, apparently quite unable to resume, he has fallen into solitary, inaudible prayer, his hands and his eyes uplifted, and then pale as death, and in the agitation of a strange shame and horror, descended trembling, and got into the vestry-room, leaving his congregation, without explanation, to themselves. This occurred when his curate was absent. When he goes down to Kenlis now, he always takes care to provide a clergyman to share his duty, and to supply his place on the instant should he become thus suddenly incapacitated.

When Mr. Jennings breaks down quite, and beats a retreat from the vicarage, and returns to London, where, in a dark street off Piccadilly, he inhabits a very narrow house, Lady Mary says that he is always perfectly well. I have my own opinion about that. There are degrees of course. We shall see.

Mr. Jennings is a perfectly gentlemanlike man. People, however, remark something odd. There is an impression a little ambiguous. One thing which certainly contributes to it, people I think don't remember; or, perhaps, distinctly remark. But I did, almost immediately. Mr. Jennings has a way of looking sidelong upon the carpet, as if his eye followed the movements of something there. This, of course, not always. It occurs now and then. But often enough to give a certain oddity, as I have said, to his manner, and in this glance travelling along the floor there is something both shy and anxious.

A medical philosopher, as you are good enough to call me, elaborating theories by the aid of cases sought out by himself, and by him watched and scrutinised with more time at command, and consequently infinitely more minuteness than the ordinary practitioner can afford, falls insensibly into habits of observation, which accompany him everywhere, and are exercised, as some people would say, impertinently, upon every subject that presents itself with the least likelihood of rewarding inquiry.

There was a promise of this kind in the slight, timid, kindly, but reserved gentleman, whom I met for the first time at this agreeable little evening gathering. I observed, of course, more than I here set down; but I reserve all that borders on the technical for a strictly scientific paper.

I may remark, that when I here speak of medical science, I do so, as I hope some day to see it more generally understood, in a much more comprehensive sense than its generally material treatment would warrant. I believe the entire natural world is but the ultimate expression of that spiritual world from which, and in which alone, it has its life. I believe that the essential man is a spirit, that the spirit is an organised substance, but as different in point of material from what we ordinarily understand by matter, as light or electricity is; that the material body is, in the most literal sense, a vesture, and death consequently no interruption of the living man's existence, but simply his extrication from the natural body—a process which commences at the moment of what we term death, and the completion of which, at further a few days later, is the resurrection "in power."

The person who weighs the consequences of these positions will probably see their practical bearing upon medical science. This is, however, by no means the proper place for displaying the proofs and discussing the consequences of this too generally unrecognised state of facts.

In pursuit of my habit, I was covertly observing Mr. Jennings, with all my caution—I think he perceived it—and I saw plainly that he was as cautiously observing me. Lady Mary happening to address me by my name, as Dr. Hesselius, I saw that he glanced at me more sharply, and then became thoughtful for a few minutes.

After this, as I conversed with a gentleman at the other end of the room, I saw him look at me more steadily, and with an interest which I thought I understood. I then saw him take an opportunity of chatting with Lady Mary, and was, as one always is, perfectly aware of being the subject of a distant inquiry and answer.

This tall clergyman approached me by-and-by; and in a little time we had got into conversation. When two people, who like reading, and know books and places, having travelled, wish to converse, it is very strange if they can't find topics. It was not accident that brought him near me, and led him into conversation. He knew German and had read my Essays on Metaphysical Medicine which suggest more than they actually say.

This courteous man, gentle, shy, plainly a man of thought and reading, who moving and talking among us, was not altogether of us, and whom I already suspected of leading a life whose transactions and alarms were carefully concealed, with an impenetrable reserve from, not only the world, but his best beloved friends—was cautiously weighing in his own mind the idea of taking a certain step with regard to me.

I penetrated his thoughts without his being aware of it, and was careful to say nothing which could betray to his sensitive vigilance my suspicions respecting his position, or my surmises about his plans respecting myself.

We chatted upon indifferent subjects for a time; but at last he said:

"I was very much interested by some papers of yours, Dr. Hesselius, upon what you term Metaphysical Medicine—I read them in German, ten or twelve years ago—have they been translated?"

"No, I'm sure they have not—I should have heard. They would have asked my leave, I think."

"I asked the publishers here, a few months ago, to get the book for me in the original German; but they tell me it is out of print."

"So it is, and has been for some years; but it flatters me as an author to find that you have not forgotten my little book, although," I added, laughing, "ten or twelve years is a considerable time to have managed without it; but I suppose you have been turning the subject over again in your mind, or something has happened lately to revive your interest in it."

At this remark, accompanied by a glance of inquiry, a sudden embarrassment disturbed Mr. Jennings, analogous to that which makes a young lady blush and look foolish. He dropped his eyes, and folded his hands together uneasily, and looked oddly, and you would have said, guiltily, for a moment.

I helped him out of his awkwardness in the best way, by appearing not to observe it, and going straight on, I said: "Those revivals of interest in a subject happen to me often; one book suggests another, and often sends me back on a wild-goose chase over an interval of twenty years. But if you will care to possess a copy, I shall be only too happy to provide you; I have still got two or three by me—and if you allow me to present one I shall be very much honoured."

"You are very good indeed," he said, quite at his ease again, in a moment: "I almost despaired—I don't know how to thank you."

"Pray don't say a word; the thing is really so little worth that

I am only ashamed of having offered it, and if you thank me any more I shall throw it into the fire in a fit of modesty."

Mr. Jennings laughed. He inquired where I was staying in London, and after a little more conversation on a variety of subjects, he took his departure.

2. The Doctor Questions Lady Mary, and She Answers

"I like your vicar so much, Lady Mary," said I, as soon as he was gone. "He has read, travelled, and thought, and having also suffered, he ought to be an accomplished companion."

"So he is, and, better still, he is a really good man," said she. "His advice is invaluable about my schools, and all my little undertakings at Dawlbridge, and he's so painstaking, he takes so much trouble—you have no idea—wherever he thinks he can be of use; he's so good-natured and so sensible."

"It is pleasant to hear so good an account of his neighbourly virtues. I can only testify to his being an agreeable and gentle companion, and in addition to what you have told me, I think I can tell you two or three things about him," said I.

"Really!"

"Yes, to begin with, he's unmarried."

"Yes, that's right—go on."

"He has been writing, that is he *was*, but two or three years perhaps he has not gone on with his work, and the book was upon some rather abstract subject—perhaps theology."

"Well, he was writing a book, as you say; I'm not quite sure what it was about, but only that it was nothing that I cared for; very likely you are right, and he certainly did stop—yes."

"And although he only drank a little coffee here tonight, he likes tea, at least, did like it extravagantly."

"Yes, that's *quite* true."

"He drank green tea, a good deal, didn't he?" I pursued.

"Well, that's very odd! Green tea was a subject on which we used almost to quarrel."

"But he has quite given that up," said I.

"So he has."

"And, now, one more fact. His mother or his father, did you know them?"

"Yes, both; his father is only ten years dead, and their place is near Dawlbridge. We knew them very well," she answered.

"Well, either his mother or his father—I should rather think his father, saw a ghost," said I.

"Well, you really are a conjuror, Dr. Hesselius."

"Conjuror or no, haven't I said right?" I answered merrily.

"You certainly have, and it *was* his father; he was a silent, whimsical man, and he used to bore my father about his dreams, and at last he told him a story about a ghost he had seen and talked with, and a very odd story it was. I remember it particularly, because I was so afraid of him. This story was long before he died—when I was quite a child—and his ways were so silent and moping, and he used to drop in sometimes, in the dusk, when I was alone in the drawing-room, and I used to fancy there were ghosts about him."

I smiled and nodded.

"And now, having established my character as a conjuror, I think I must say good-night," said I.

"But how *did* you find it out?"

"By the planets, of course, as the gipsies do," I answered, and so, gaily, we said goodnight.

Next morning I sent the little book he had been inquiring after, and a note to Mr. Jennings, and on returning late that evening, I found that he had called at my lodgings, and left his card. He asked whether I was at home, and asked at what hour he would be most likely to find me.

Does he intend opening his case, and consulting me "professionally," as they say? I hope so. I have already conceived a theory about him. It is supported by Lady Mary's answers to my parting questions. I should like much to ascertain from his own lips. But what can I do consistently with good breeding to invite a confession? Nothing. I rather think he meditates one. At all events, my dear Van L., I shan't make myself difficult of access; I mean to return his visit tomorrow. It will be only civil in return for his politeness, to ask to see him. Perhaps something may come of it. Whether much, little, or nothing, my dear Van L., you shall hear.

3. Dr. Hesselius Picks Up Something in Latin Books

Well, I have called at Blank Street.

On inquiring at the door, the servant told me that Mr. Jennings was engaged very particularly with a gentleman, a clergyman from Kenlis, his parish in the country. Intending to reserve my privilege, and to call again, I merely intimated that I should try another time, and had turned to go, when the servant begged my pardon, and asked me, looking at me a little more attentively than well-bred persons of his order usually do, whether I was Dr. Hesselius; and, on learning that I was, he said, "Perhaps then, sir, you would allow me to mention it to Mr. Jennings, for I am sure he wishes to see you."

The servant returned in a moment, with a message from Mr. Jennings, asking me to go into his study, which was in effect his back drawing-room, promising to be with me in a very few minutes.

This was really a study—almost a library. The room was lofty, with two tall slender windows, and rich dark curtains. It was much larger than I had expected, and stored with books on every side, from floor to the ceiling. The upper carpet—for to my tread it felt that there were two or three—was a Turkey carpet. My steps fell noiselessly. The bookcases standing out, placed the windows, particularly narrow ones, in deep recesses. The effect of the room was, although extremely comfortable, and even luxurious, decidedly gloomy, and aided by the silence, almost oppressive. Perhaps, however, I ought to have allowed something for association. My mind had connected peculiar ideas with Mr. Jennings. I stepped into this perfectly silent room, of a very silent house, with a peculiar foreboding; and its darkness, and solemn clothing of books, for except where two narrow looking-glasses were set in the wall, they were everywhere, helped this sombre feeling.

While awaiting Mr. Jennings' arrival, I amused myself by looking into some of the books with which his shelves were laden. Not among these, but immediately under them, with their backs upward, on the floor, I lighted upon a complete set of Swedenborg's *Arcana Cœlestia*, in the original Latin, a very fine folio set, bound in the natty livery which theology affects, pure vellum, namely, gold letters, and carmine edges. There were paper markers in several of these volumes. I raised and placed them, one after the other upon the table, and opening where these papers were placed, I read in the solemn Latin phraseology, a series of sentences indicated by a pencilled line at the margin. Of these I copy here a few, translating them into English.

"When man's interior sight is opened, which is that of his spirit, then there appears the things of another life, which cannot possibly be made visible to the bodily sight . . ."

"By the internal sight it has been granted to me to see the things that are in the other life, more clearly than I see those that are in the world. From these considerations, it is evident that external vision exists from interior vision, and this from a vision still more interior, and so on . . ."

"There are with every man at least two evil spirits . . ."

"With wicked genii there is also a fluent speech, but harsh and grating. There is also among them a speech which is not fluent, wherein the dissent of the thoughts is perceived as something secretly creeping along within it . . ."

"The evil spirits associated with man are indeed from the hells, but when with man they are not then in hell, but are taken out thence. The place where they then are, is in the midst between heaven and hell, and is called the world of spirits—when the evil spirits who are with man, are in that world, they are not in any infernal torment, but in every thought and affection of man, and so, in all that the man himself enjoys. But when they are remitted into their hell, they return to their former state . . ."

"If evil spirits could perceive that they were associated with man, and yet that they were spirits separate from him, and if they could flow in into the things of his body, they would attempt by a thousand means to destroy him; for they hate man with a deadly hatred . . ."

"Knowing, therefore, that I was a man in the body, they were continually striving to destroy me, not as to the body only, but especially as to the soul; for to destroy any man or spirit is the very delight of the life of all who are in hell; but I have been continually protected by the Lord. Hence it appears how dangerous it is for man to be in a living consort with spirits unless he be in the good of faith . . ."

"Nothing is more carefully guarded from the knowledge of associate spirits than their being thus conjoint with a man, for if they knew it they would speak to him, with the intention to destroy him . . ."

"The delight of hell is to do evil to man, and to hasten his eternal ruin."

A long note, written with a very sharp and fine pencil, in Mr. Jennings' neat hand, at the foot of the page, caught my eye. Expecting his criticism upon the text, I read a word or two, and stopped, for it was something quite different, and began with these words, *Deus misereatur mei*—"May God compassionate me." Thus warned of its private nature, I averted my eyes, and shut the book, replacing all the volumes as I had found them, except one which interested me, and in which, as men studious and solitary in their habits will do, I grew so absorbed as to take no cognisance of the outer world, nor to remember where I was.

I was reading some pages which refer to "representatives" and "correspondents," in the technical language of Swedenborg, and had arrived at a passage, the substance of which is, that evil spirits, when seen by other eyes than those of their infernal associates, present themselves, by "correspondence," in the shape of the beast (*fera*) which represents their particular lust and life, in aspect direful and atrocious. This is a long passage, and particularises a number of those bestial forms.

4. Four Eyes Were Reading the Passage

I was running the head of my pencil-case along the line as I read it, and something caused me to raise my eyes.

Directly before me was one of the mirrors I have mentioned, in which I saw reflected the tall shape of my friend, Mr. Jennings, leaning over my shoulder, and reading the page at which I was busy, and with a face so dark and wild that I should hardly have known him.

I turned and rose. He stood erect also, and with an effort laughed a little, saying:

"I came in and asked you how you did, but without succeeding in awaking you from your book; so I could not restrain my curiosity, and very impertinently, I'm afraid, peeped over your shoulder. This is not the first time of looking into those pages. You have looked into Swedenborg, no doubt, long ago?"

"Oh dear, yes! I owe Swedenborg a great deal; you will discover traces of him in the little book on Metaphysical Medicine, which you were so good as to remember."

Although my friend affected a gaiety of manner, there was a slight flush in his face, and I could perceive that he was inwardly much perturbed.

"I'm scarcely yet qualified, I know so little of Swedenborg. I've only had them a fortnight," he answered, "and I think they are rather likely to make a solitary man nervous—that is, judging from the very little I have read—I don't say that they have made me so," he laughed; "and I'm so very much obliged for the book. I hope you got my note?"

I made all proper acknowledgments and modest disclaimers.

"I never read a book that I go with, so entirely, as that of yours," he continued. "I saw at once there is more in it than is quite unfolded. Do you know Dr. Harley?" he asked, rather abruptly.

In passing, the editor remarks that the physician here named was one of the most eminent who had ever practised in England.

I did, having had letters to him, and had experienced from

him great courtesy and considerable assistance during my visit to England.

"I think that man one of the very greatest fools I ever met in my life," said Mr. Jennings.

This was the first time I had ever heard him say a sharp thing of anybody, and such a term applied to so high a name a little startled me.

"Really! and in what way?" I asked.

"In his profession," he answered.

I smiled.

"I mean this," he said: "he seems to me, one half, blind—I mean one half of all he looks at is dark—preternaturally bright and vivid all the rest; and the worst of it is, it seems *wilful*. I can't get him—I mean he won't—I've had some experience of him as a physician, but I look on him as, in that sense, no better than a paralytic mind, an intellect half dead. I'll tell you—I know I shall some time—all about it," he said, with a little agitation. "You stay some months longer in England. If I should be out of town during your stay for a little time, would you allow me to trouble you with a letter?"

"I should be only too happy," I assured him.

"Very good of you. I am so utterly dissatisfied with Harley."

"A little leaning to the materialistic school," I said.

"A *mere* materialist," he corrected me; "you can't think how that sort of thing worries one who knows better. You won't tell anyone—any of my friends you know—that I am hippish; now, for instance, no one knows—not even Lady Mary—that I have seen Dr. Harley, or any other doctor. So pray don't mention it; and, if I should have any threatening of an attack, you'll kindly let me write, or, should I be in town, have a little talk with you."

I was full of conjecture, and unconsciously I found I had fixed my eyes gravely on him, for he lowered his for a moment, and he said:

"I see you think I might as well tell you now, or else you are forming a conjecture; but you may as well give it up. If you were guessing all the rest of your life, you will never hit on it."

He shook his head smiling, and over that wintry sunshine a black cloud suddenly came down, and he drew his breath in, through his teeth as men do in pain.

"Sorry, of course, to learn that you apprehend occasion to consult any of us; but, command me when and how you like, and I need not assure you that your confidence is sacred."

He then talked of quite other things, and in a comparatively cheerful way and after a little time, I took my leave.

5. Dr. Hesselius Is Summoned to Richmond

We parted cheerfully, but he was not cheerful, nor was I. There are certain expressions of that powerful organ of spirit—the human face—which, although I have seen them often, and possess a doctor's nerve, yet disturb me profoundly. One look of Mr. Jennings' haunted me. It had seized my imagination with so dismal a power that I changed my plans for the evening, and went to the opera, feeling that I wanted a change of ideas.

I heard nothing of or from him for two or three days, when a note in his hand reached me. It was cheerful, and full of hope. He said that he had been for some little time so much better—quite well, in fact—that he was going to make a little experiment, and run down for a month or so to his parish, to try whether a little work might not quite set him up. There was in it a fervent religious expression of gratitude for his restoration, as he now almost hoped he might call it.

A day or two later I saw Lady Mary, who repeated what his note had announced, and told me that he was actually in Warwickshire, having resumed his clerical duties at Kenlis; and she added, "I begin to think that he is really perfectly well, and that there never was anything the matter, more than nerves and fancy; we are all nervous, but I fancy there is nothing like a little hard work for that kind of weakness, and he has made up his mind to try it. I should not be surprised if he did not come back for a year."

Notwithstanding all this confidence, only two days later I had this note, dated from his house off Piccadilly:

Dear Sir, I have returned disappointed. If I should feel at all able to see you, I shall write to ask you kindly to call. At present, I am too low, and, in fact, simply unable to say all I wish to say. Pray don't mention my name to my friends. I can see no one. By-and-by, please God, you shall hear from me. I mean to take a run into Shropshire, where some of my people are. God bless you! May we, on my return, meet more happily than I can now write.

About a week after this I saw Lady Mary at her own house, the last person, she said, left in town, and just on the wing for Brighton, for the London season was quite over. She told me that she had heard from Mr. Jennings' niece, Martha, in Shropshire. There was nothing to be gathered from her letter, more than that he was low and nervous. In those words, of which healthy people think so lightly, what a world of suffering is sometimes hidden!

Nearly five weeks had passed without any further news of Mr. Jennings. At the end of that time I received a note from him. He wrote:

I have been in the country, and have had change of air, change of scene, change of faces, change of everything—and in everything—but myself. *I have made up my mind, so far as the most irresolute creature on earth can do it, to tell my case fully to you. If your engagements will permit, pray come to me today, tomorrow, or the next day; but, pray defer as little as possible. You know not how much I need help. I have a quiet house at Richmond, where I now am. Perhaps you can manage to come to dinner, or to luncheon, or even to tea. You shall have no trouble in finding me out. The servant at Blank Street, who takes this note, will have a carriage at your door at any hour you please; and I am always to be found. You will say that I ought not to be alone. I have tried everything. Come and see.*

I called up the servant, and decided on going out the same evening, which accordingly I did.

He would have been much better in a lodging-house, or hotel, I thought, as I drove up through a short double row of sombre elms to a very old-fashioned brick house, darkened by the foliage of these trees, which overtopped, and nearly surrounded it. It was a perverse choice, for nothing could be imagined more triste and silent. The house, I found, belonged to him. He had stayed for a day or two in town, and, finding it for some cause insupportable, had come out here, probably because being furnished and his own, he was relieved of the thought and delay of selection, by coming here.

The sun had already set, and the red reflected light of the western sky illuminated the scene with the peculiar effect with which we are all familiar. The hall seemed very dark, but, getting to the back drawing-room, whose window command the west, I was again in the same dusky light.

I sat down, looking out upon the richly-wooded landscape that glowed in the grand and melancholy light which was every moment fading. The corners of the room were already dark; all was growing dim, and the gloom was insensibly toning my mind, already prepared for what was sinister. I was waiting alone for his arrival, which soon took place. The door communicating with the front room opened, and the tall figure of Mr. Jennings, faintly seen in the ruddy twilight, came, with quiet stealthy steps, into the room.

We shook hands, and, taking a chair to the window, where there was still light enough to enable us to see each other's faces, he sat down beside me, and, placing his hand upon my arm, with scarcely a word of preface began his narrative.

6. How Mr. Jennings Met His Companion

The faint glow of the west, the pomp of the then lonely woods of Richmond, were before us, behind and about us the darkening room, and on the stony face of the sufferer—for the character of his face, though still gentle and sweet, was changed—rested that dim, odd glow which seems to descend and produce, where it touches, lights, sudden though faint, which are lost, almost without gradation, in darkness. The silence, too, was utter: not a distant wheel, or bark, or whistle from without; and within, the depressing stillness of an invalid bachelor's house.

I guessed well the nature, though not even vaguely the particulars of the revelations I was about to receive, from that fixed face of suffering that so oddly flushed stood out, like a portrait of Schalken's, before its background of darkness.

"It began," he said, "on the 15th of October, three years and eleven weeks ago, and two days—I keep very accurate count, for every day is torment. If I leave anywhere a chasm in my narrative, tell me.

"About four years ago I began a work, which had cost me very much thought and reading. It was upon the religious metaphysics of the ancients."

"I know," said I, "the actual religion of educated and thinking paganism, quite apart from symbolic worship? A wide and very interesting field."

"Yes, but not good for the mind—the Christian mind, I mean. Paganism is all bound together in essential unity, and, with evil sympathy, their religion involves their art, and both their manners, and the subject is a degrading fascination and the Nemesis sure. God forgive me!

"I wrote a great deal; I wrote late at night. I was always thinking on the subject, walking about, wherever I was, everywhere. It thoroughly infected me. You are to remember that all the material ideas connected with it were more or less of the beautiful, the subject itself delightfully interesting, and I, then, without a care."

He sighed heavily.

"I believe that every one who sets about writing in earnest does his work, as a friend of mine phrased it, *on* something—tea, or coffee, or tobacco. I suppose there is a material waste that must be hourly supplied in such occupations, or that we should grow too abstracted, and the mind, as it were, pass out of the body, unless it were reminded often enough of the connection by actual sensation. At all events, I felt the want, and I supplied it. Tea was my companion—at first the ordinary black tea, made in the usual way, not too strong; but I drank a good deal, and increased its strength as I went on. I never experienced an uncomfortable symptom from it.

"I began to take a little green tea. I found the effect pleasanter, it cleared and intensified the power of thought so, I had come to take it frequently, but not stronger than one might take it for pleasure. I wrote a great deal out here, it was so quiet, and in this room. I used to sit up very late, and it became a habit with me to sip my tea—green tea—every now and then as my work proceeded. I had a little kettle on my table, that swung over a lamp, and made tea two or three times between eleven o'clock and two or three in the morning, my hours of going to bed.

"I used to go into town every day. I was not a monk, and, although I spent an hour or two in a library, hunting up authorities and looking out lights upon my theme, I was in no morbid state as far as I can judge. I met my friends pretty much as usual and enjoyed their society, and, on the whole, existence had never been, I think, so pleasant before.

"I had met with a man who had some odd old books, German editions in mediæval Latin, and I was only too happy to be permitted access to them. This obliging person's books were in the City, a very out-of-the-way part of it. I had rather out-stayed my intended hour, and, on coming out, seeing no cab near, I was tempted to get into the omnibus which used to drive past this house. It was darker than this by the time the 'bus had reached an old house, you may have remarked, with four poplars at each side of the door, and there the last passenger but myself got out. We drove along rather faster. It was twilight now. I leaned back in my corner next the door ruminating pleasantly.

"The interior of the omnibus was nearly dark. I had observed in the corner opposite to me at the other side, and at the end next the horses, two small circular reflections, as it seemed to me of a reddish light. They were about two inches apart, and about the size of those small brass buttons that yachting men used to put upon their jackets. I began to speculate, as listless men will, upon this trifle, as it seemed. From what centre did that faint but deep red light come, and from what—glass beads, buttons, toy decorations—was it reflected? We were lumbering along gently, having nearly a mile still to go. I had not solved the puzzle, and it became in another minute more odd, for these two luminous points, with a sudden jerk descended nearer and nearer the floor, keeping still their relative distance and horizontal position, and then, as suddenly they rose to the level of the seat on which I was sitting and I saw them no more.

"My curiosity was now really excited, and, before I had time to think, I saw again these two dull lamps, again together near the floor; again they disappeared, and again in their old corner I saw them.

"So, keeping my eyes upon them, I edged quietly up my own side, towards the end at which I still saw these tiny discs of red.

"There was very little light in the 'bus. It was nearly dark. I leaned forward to aid my endeavour to discover what these little circles really were. They shifted position a little as I did so. I began now to perceive an outline of something black, and I soon saw, with tolerable distinctiveness, the outline of a small black monkey, pushing its face forward in mimicry to meet mine; those were its eyes, and I now dimly saw its teeth grinning at me.

"I drew back, not knowing whether it might not meditate a spring. I fancied that one of the passengers had forgot this ugly pet, and wishing to ascertain something of its temper, though not caring to trust my fingers to it, I poked my umbrella softly towards it. It remained immovable—up to it—*through* it! For through it, and back and forward it passed, without the slightest resistance.

"I can't, in the least, convey to you the kind of horror I felt. When I had ascertained that the thing was an illusion, as I then supposed, there came a misgiving about myself and a terror that fascinated me in impotence to remove my gaze from the eyes of the brute for some moments. As I looked, it made a little skip back, quite into the corner, and I, in a panic found myself at the door, having put my head out, drawing deep breaths of the outer air, and staring at the lights and trees we were passing, too glad to reassure myself of reality.

"I stopped the 'bus and got out. I perceived the man look oddly at me as I paid him. I dare say there was something unusual in my looks and manner, for I had never felt so strangely before."

7. The Journey: First Stage

"When the omnibus drove on, and I was alone upon the road, I looked carefully round to ascertain whether the monkey had followed me. To my indescribable relief I saw it nowhere. I can't describe easily what a shock I had received, and my sense of genuine gratitude on finding myself, as I supposed, quite rid of it.

"I had got out a little before we reached this house, two or three hundred steps. A brick wall runs along the footpath, and inside the wall is a hedge of yew, or some dark evergreen of that kind, and within that again the row of fine trees which you may have remarked as you came.

"This brick wall is about as high as my shoulder, and happening to raise my eyes I saw the monkey, with that stooping gait, on all fours, walking or creeping, close beside me, on top of the wall. I stopped, looking at it with a feeling of loathing and horror. As I stopped so did it. It sat up on the wall with its long hands on its knees looking at me. There was not light enough to see it much more than in outline, nor was it dark enough to bring the peculiar light of its eyes into strong relief. I still saw, however, that red foggy light plainly enough. It did not show its teeth, nor exhibit any sign of irritation, but seemed jaded and sulky, and was observing me steadily.

"I drew back into the middle of the road. It was an unconscious recoil, and there I stood, still looking at it; it did not move.

"With an instinctive determination to try something—anything, I turned about and walked briskly towards town with askance look, all the time, watching the movements of the beast. It crept swiftly along the wall, at exactly my pace.

"Where the wall ends, near the turn of the road, it came down, and with a wiry spring or two brought itself close to my feet, and continued to keep up with me, as I quickened my pace. It was at my left side, so close to my leg that I felt every moment as if I should tread upon it.

"The road was quite deserted and silent, and it was darker every moment. I stopped dismayed and bewildered, turning as I did so, the other way—I mean, towards this house, away from which I had been walking. When I stood still, the monkey drew back to a distance of, I suppose, about five or six yards, and remained stationary, watching me.

"I had been more agitated than I have said. I had read, of course, as everyone has, something about 'special illusions,' as you physicians term the phenomena of such cases. I considered my situation, and looked my misfortune in the face.

"These affections, I had read, are sometimes transitory and sometimes obstinate. I had read of cases in which the appearance, at first harmless, had, step by step, degenerated into something direful and insupportable, and ended by wearing its victim out. Still as I stood there, but for my bestial companion, quite alone, I tried to comfort myself by repeating again and again the assurance, 'the thing is purely disease, a well-known physical affection, as distinctly as small-pox or neuralgia. Doctors are all agreed on that, philosophy demonstrates it. I must not be a fool. I've been sitting up too late, and I daresay my digestion is quite wrong, and, with God's help, I shall be all right, and this is but a symptom of nervous dyspepsia.' Did I believe all this? Not one word of it, no more than any other miserable being ever did who is once seized and riveted in this satanic captivity. Against my convictions, I might say my knowledge, I was simply bullying myself into a false courage.

"I now walked homeward. I had only a few hundred yards to go. I had forced myself into a sort of resignation, but I had not got over the sickening shock and the flurry of the first certainty of my misfortune.

"I had made up my mind to pass the night at home. The

brute moved close beside me, and I fancied there was the sort of anxious drawing toward the house, which one sees in tired horses or dogs, sometimes as they come toward home.

"I was afraid to go into town. I was afraid of anyone's seeing and recognising me. I was conscious of an irrepressible agitation in my manner. Also, I was afraid of any violent change in my habits, such as going to a place of amusement, or walking from home in order to fatigue myself. At the hall door it waited till I mounted the steps, and when the door was opened entered with me.

"I drank no tea that night. I got cigars and some brandy-and-water. My idea was that I should act upon my material system, and by living for a while in sensation apart from thought, send myself forcibly, as it were, into a new groove. I came up here to this drawing-room. I sat just there. The monkey then got upon a small table that then stood *there*. It looked dazed and languid. An irrepressible uneasiness as to its movements kept my eyes always upon it. Its eyes were half closed, but I could see them glow. It was looking steadily at me. In all situations, at all hours, it is awake and looking at me. That never changes.

"I shall not continue in detail my narrative of this particular night. I shall describe, rather, the phenomena of the first year, which never varied, essentially. I shall describe the monkey as it appeared in daylight. In the dark, as you shall presently hear, there are peculiarities. It is a small monkey, perfectly black. It had only one peculiarity—a character of malignity—unfathomable malignity. During the first year it looked sullen and sick. But this character of intense malice and vigilance was always underlying that surly languor. During all that time it acted as if on a plan of giving me as little trouble as was consistent with watching me. Its eyes were never off me. I have never lost sight of it, except in my sleep, light or dark, day or night, since it came here, excepting when it withdraws for some weeks at a time, unaccountably.

"In total dark it is visible as in daylight. I do not mean merely its eyes. It is *all* visible distinctly in a halo that resembles a glow of red embers, and which accompanies it in all its movements.

"When it leaves me for a time, it is always at night, in the dark, and in the same way. It grows at first uneasy, and then furious, and then advances towards me, grinning and shaking, its paws clenched, and, at the same time, there comes the appearance of fire in the grate. I never have any fire. I can't sleep in the room where there is any, and it draws nearer and nearer to the chimney, quivering, it seems, with rage, and when its fury rises to the highest pitch, it springs into the grate, and up the chimney, and I see it no more.

"When first this happened, I thought I was released. I was now a new man. A day passed—a night—and no return, and a blessed week—a week—another week. I was always on my knees, Dr. Hesselius, always, thanking God and praying. A whole month passed of liberty, but on a sudden, it was with me again."

8. The Second Stage

"It was with me, and the malice which before was torpid under a sullen exterior, was now active. It was perfectly unchanged in every other aspect. This new energy was apparent in its activity and its looks, and soon in other ways.

"For a time, you will understand, the change was shown only in an increased vivacity, and an air of menace, as if it were always brooding over some atrocious plan. Its eyes, as before, were never off me."

"Is it here now?" I asked.

"No," he replied, "it has been absent exactly a fortnight and a day—fifteen days. It has sometimes been away so long as nearly two months, once for three. Its absence always exceeds a fortnight, although it may be but by a single day. Fifteen days having past since I saw it last, it may return now at any moment."

"Is its return," I asked, "accompanied by any peculiar manifestation?"

"Nothing—no," he said. "It is simply with me again. On lifting my eyes from a book, or turning my head, I see it, as usual, looking at me, and then it remains, as before, for its appointed time. I have never told so much and so minutely before to any one."

I perceived that he was agitated, and looking like death, and he repeatedly applied his handkerchief to his forehead; I suggested that he might be tired, and told him that I would call, with pleasure, in the morning, but he said:

"No, if you don't mind hearing it all now. I have got so far, and I should prefer making one effort of it. When I spoke to Dr. Harley, I had nothing like so much to tell. You are a philosophic physician. You give spirit its proper rank. If this thing is real—"

He paused, looking at me with agitated inquiry.

"We can discuss it by-and-by, and very fully. I will give you all I think," I answered, after an interval.

"Well—very well. If it is anything real, I say, it is prevailing, little by little, and drawing me more interiorly into hell. Optic nerves, he talked of. Ah! well—there are other nerves of communication. May God Almighty help me! You shall hear.

"Its power of action, I tell you, had increased. Its malice became, in a wary, aggressive. About two years ago, some questions that were pending between me and the bishop having been settled, I went down to my parish in Warwickshire, anxious to find occupation in my profession. I was not prepared for what happened, although I have since thought I might have apprehended something like it. The reason of my saying so is that—"

He was beginning to speak with a great deal more effort and reluctance, and sighed often, and seemed at times nearly overcome. But at this time his manner was not agitated. It was more like that of a sinking patient, who has given himself up.

"Yes, but I will first tell you about Kenlis, my parish.

"It was with me when I left this place for Dawlbridge. It was my silent travelling companion, and it remained with me at the vicarage. When I entered on the discharge of my duties, another change took place. The thing exhibited an atrocious determination to thwart me. It was with me in the church—in the reading-desk—in the pulpit—within the communion rails. At last, it reached this extremity, that while I was reading to the congregation, it would spring upon the book and squat there, so that I was unable to see the page. This happened more than once.

"I left Dawlbridge for a time. I placed myself in Dr. Harley's hands. I did everything he told me. He gave my case a great deal of thought. It interested him, I think. He seemed successful. For nearly three months I was perfectly free from a return. I began to think I was safe. With his full assent I returned to Dawlbridge.

"I travelled in a chaise. I was in good spirits. I was more—I was happy and grateful. I was returning, as I thought, delivered from a dreadful hallucination, to the scene of duties which I longed to enter upon. It was a beautiful sunny evening, everything looked serene and cheerful, and I was delighted. I remember looking out of the window to see the spire of my church at Kenlis among the trees, at the point where one has the earliest view of it. It is exactly where the little stream that bounds the parish passes under the road by a culvert, and where it emerges at the roadside, a stone with an old inscription is placed. As we passed this point, I drew my head in and sat down, and in the corner of the chaise was the monkey.

"For a moment I felt faint, and then quite wild with despair and horror. I called to the driver, and got out, and sat down at the roadside, and prayed to God silently for mercy. A despairing resignation supervened. My companion was with me as I re-entered the vicarage. The same persecution followed. After a short struggle I submitted, and soon I left the place.

"I told you," he said, "that the beast had before this become in certain ways aggressive. I will explain a little. It seemed to be actuated by intense and increasing fury, whenever I said my prayers, or even meditated prayer. It amounted at last to a dreadful interruption. You will ask, how could a silent immaterial phantom effect that? It was thus, whenever I meditated praying; it was always before me, and nearer and nearer.

"It used to spring on a table, on the back of a chair, on the chimney-piece, and slowly to swing itself from side to side, looking at me all the time. There is in its motion an indefinable power to dissipate thought, and to contract one's attention to that monotony, till the ideas shrink, as it were, to a point, and at last to nothing—and unless I had started up, and shook off the catalepsy I have felt as if my mind were on the point of losing itself. There are other ways," he sighed heavily; "thus, for instance, while I pray with my eyes closed, it comes closer and closer, and I see it. I know it is not to be accounted for physically, but I do actually see it, though my lids are closed, and so it rocks my mind, as it were, and overpowers me, and I am obliged to rise from my knees. If you have ever yourself known this, you would be acquainted with desperation."

9. The Third Stage

"I see, Dr. Hesselius, that you don't lose one word of my statement. I need not ask you to listen specially to what I am now going to tell you. They talk of the optic nerves, and of spectral illusions, as if the organ of sight was the only point assailable by the influences that have fastened upon me—I know better. For two years in my direful case that limitation prevailed. But as food is taken in softly at the lips, and then brought under the teeth, as the tip of the little finger caught in a mill crank will draw in the hand, and the arm, and the whole body, so the miserable mortal who has been once caught firmly by the end of the finest fibre of his nerve, is drawn in and in, by the enormous machinery of hell, until he is as I am. Yes, Doctor, as *I* am, for while I talk to you, and implore relief, I feel that my prayer is for the impossible, and my pleading with the inexorable."

I endeavoured to calm his visibly increasing agitation, and told him that he must not despair.

While we talked the night had overtaken us. The filmy moonlight was wide over the scene which the window commanded, and I said:

"Perhaps you would prefer having candles. This light, you know, is odd. I should wish you, as much as possible, under your usual conditions while I make my diagnosis, shall I call it—otherwise I don't care."

"All lights are the same to me," he said; "except when I read or write, I care not if night were perpetual. I am going to tell you what happened about a year ago. The thing began to speak to me."

"Speak! How do you mean—speak as a man does, do you mean?"

"Yes; speak in words and consecutive sentences, with perfect coherence and articulation; but there is a peculiarity. It is not like the tone of a human voice. It is not by my ears it reaches me—it comes like a singing through my head.

"This faculty, the power of speaking to me, will be my undoing. It won't let me pray, it interrupts me with dreadful blasphemies. I dare not go on, I could not. Oh! Doctor, can the skill, and thought, and prayers of man avail me nothing!"

"You must promise me, my dear sir, not to trouble yourself with unnecessarily exciting thoughts; confine yourself strictly to the narrative of *facts*; and recollect, above all, that even if the thing that infests you be, you seem to suppose, a reality with an actual independent life and will, yet it can have no power to hurt you, unless it be given from above: its access to your senses depends mainly upon your physical condition—this is, under God, your comfort and reliance: we are all alike environed. It is only that in your case, the *paries*, the veil of the flesh, the screen, is a little out of repair, and sights and sounds are transmitted. We must enter on a new course, sir—be encouraged. I'll give tonight to the careful consideration of the whole case."

"You are very good, sir; you think it worth trying, you don't give me quite up; but, sir, you don't know, it is gaining such an influence over me; it orders me about, it is such a tyrant, and I'm growing so helpless. May God deliver me!"

"It orders you about—of course you mean by speech?"

"Yes, yes; it is always urging me to crimes, to injure others, or myself. You see, Doctor, the situation is urgent, it is indeed. When I was in Shropshire, a few weeks ago" (Mr. Jennings was speaking rapidly and trembling now, holding my arm with one hand, and looking in my face), "I went out one day with a party of friends for a walk: my persecutor, I tell you, was with me at the time. I lagged behind the rest: the country near the Dee, you know, is beautiful. Our path happened to lie near a coal mine, and at the verge of the wood is a perpendicular shaft, they say, a hundred and fifty feet deep. My niece had remained behind with me—she knows, of course, nothing of the nature of my sufferings. She knew, however, that I had been ill, and was low, and she remained to prevent my being quite alone. As we loitered slowly on together, the brute that accompanied me was urging me to throw myself down the shaft.

"I tell you now—oh, sir, think of it!—the one consideration that saved me from that hideous death was the fear lest the shock of witnessing the occurrence should be too much for the poor girl. I asked her to go on and walk with her friends, saying that I could go no further. She made excuses, and the more I urged her the firmer she became. She looked doubtful and frightened. I suppose there was something in my looks or manner that alarmed her; but she would not go, and that literally saved me. You had no idea, sir, that a living man could be made so abject a slave of Satan," he said, with a ghastly groan and shudder.

There was a pause here, and I said, "You *were* preserved nevertheless. It was the act of God. You are in His hands and in the power of no other being: be therefore confident for the future."

10. Home

I made him have candles lighted, and saw the room looking cheery and inhabited before I left him. I told him that he must regard his illness strictly as one dependent on physical, though *subtle* pysical causes. I told him that he had evidence of God's care and love in the deliverance which he had just described, and that I had perceived with pain that he seemed to regard its peculiar features as indicating that he had been delivered over to spiritual reprobation. Than such a conclusion nothing could be, I insisted, less warranted; and not only so, but more contrary to facts, as disclosed in his mysterious deliverance from that murderous influence during his Shropshire excursion.

First, his niece had been retained by his side without his intending to keep her near him; and, secondly, there had been infused into his mind an irresistible repugnance to execute the dreadful suggestion in her presence.

As I reasoned this point with him, Mr. Jennings wept. He seemed comforted. One promise I exacted, which was that should the monkey at any time return, I should be sent for immediately; and, repeating my assurance that I would give neither time nor thought to any other subject until I had thoroughly investigated his case, and that tomorrow he should hear the result, I took my leave.

Before getting into the carriage I told the servant that his master was far from well, and that he should make a point of frequently looking into his room.

My own arrangements I made with a view to being quite secure from interruption.

I merely called at my lodgings, and with a travelling-desk and carpet-bag, set off in a hackney-carriage for an inn about two miles out of town, called The Horns, a very quiet and comfortable house, with good thick walls. And there I resolved, without the possibility of intrusion or distraction, to devote some hours of the night, in my comfortable sitting-room, to Mr. Jennings' case, and so much of the morning as it might require.

(There occurs here a careful note of Dr. Hesselius' opinion upon the case, and of the habits, dietary, and medicines which he prescribed. It is curious—some persons would say mystical. But, on the whole, I doubt whether it would sufficiently interest a reader of the kind I am likely to meet with, to warrant its being here reprinted. The whole letter was plainly written at the inn where he had hid himself for the occasion. The next letter is dated from his town lodgings.)

I left town for the inn where I slept last night at half-past nine, and did not arrive at my room in town until one o'clock this afternoon. I found a letter in Mr. Jennings' hand upon my table. It had not come by post, and, on inquiry, I learned that Mr. Jennings' servant had brought it, and on learning that I was not to return until today, and that no one could tell him my address, he seemed very uncomfortable, and said his orders from his master were that he was not to return without an answer.

I opened the letter and read:

> *Dear Dr. Hesselius.—It is here. You had not been an hour gone when it returned. It is speaking. It knows all that has happened. It knows everything—it knows you, and is frantic and atrocious. It reviles. I send you this. It knows every word I have written—I write. This I promised, and I therefore write, but, I fear, very confused, very incoherently. I am so interrupted, disturbed.*
>
> *Ever yours, sincerely yours,*
> *Robert Lynder Jennings.*

"When did this come?" I asked.

"About eleven last night: the man was here again, and has been here three times today. The last time is about an hour since."

Thus answered, and with the notes I had made upon his case in my pocket, I was in a few minutes driving towards Richmond, to see Mr. Jennings.

I by no means, as you perceive, despaired of Mr. Jennings' case. He had himself remembered and applied, though quite in a mistaken way, the principle which I lay down in my Metaphysical Medicine, and which governs all such cases. I was about to apply it in earnest. I was profoundly interested, and very anxious to see and examine him while the "enemy" was actually present.

I drove up to the sombre house, and ran up the steps, and knocked. The door, in a little time, was opened by a tall woman in black silk. She looked ill, and as if she had been crying. She curtseyed, and heard my question, but she did not answer. She turned her face away, extending her hand towards two men who were coming downstairs; and thus having, as it were, tacitly made me over to them, she passed through a side-door hastily and shut it.

The man who was nearest the hall, I at once accosted, but being now close to him, I was shocked to see that both his hands were covered in blood.

I drew back a little, and the man, passing downstairs, merely said in a low tone, "Here's the servant, sir."

The servant had stopped on the stairs, confounded and dumb at seeing me. He was rubbing his hands in a handkerchief, and it was steeped in blood.

"Jones, what is it? what has happened?" I asked, while a sickening suspicion overpowered me.

The man asked me to come up to the lobby. I was beside him in a moment, and, frowning and pallid, with contracted eyes, he told me the horror which I already half guessed.

His master had made away with himself.

I went upstairs with him to the room—what I saw there I won't tell you. He had cut his throat with his razor. It was a frightful gash. The two men had laid him on the bed, and composed his limbs. It had happened, as the immense pool of blood on the floor declared, at some distance between the bed and the window. There was carpet round his bed, and a carpet under his dressing-table, but none on the rest of the floor, for the man said he did not like a carpet in his bedroom. In this sombre and now terrible room, one of the great elms that darkened the house was slowly moving the shadow of one of its great boughs upon this dreadful floor.

I beckoned to the servant, and we went downstairs together. I turned off the hall into an old-fashioned panelled room, and there standing, I heard all the servant had to tell. It was not a great deal.

"I concluded, sir, from your words, and looks, sir, as you left last night, that you thought my master was seriously ill. I thought it might be that you were afraid of a fit, or something. So I attended very close to your directions. He sat up late, till past three o'clock. He was not writing or reading. He was talking a great deal to himself, but that was nothing unusual. At about that hour I assisted him to undress, and left him in his slippers and dressing-gown. I went back softly in about half-an-hour. He was in his bed, quite undressed, and a pair of candles lighted on the table beside his bed. He was leaning on his elbow, and looking out at the other side of the bed when I came in. I asked him if he wanted anything, and he said no.

"I don't know whether it was what you said to me, sir, or something a little unusual about him, but I was uneasy, uncommon uneasy about him last night.

"In another half hour, or it might be a little more, I went up again. I did not hear him talking as before. I opened the door a little. The candles were both out, which was not usual. I had a bedroom candle, and I let the light in, a little bit, looking softly round.

"I saw him sitting in that chair beside the dressing-table with his clothes on again. He turned round and looked at me. I thought it strange he should get up and dress, and put out the candles to sit in the dark, that way. But I only asked him again if I could do anything for him. He said no, rather sharp, I thought. I asked him if I might light the candles and he said, 'Do as you like, Jones.' So I lighted them, and I lingered about the room, and he said, 'Tell me truth, Jones; why did you come again—you did not hear anyone cursing?' 'No, sir,' I said, wondering what he could mean.

"'No,' said he, after me, 'of course, no'; and I said to him, 'Wouldn't it be well, sir, you went to bed? It's just five o'clock,' and he said nothing, but, 'Very likely; good-night, Jones.' So I went, sir, but in less than an hour I came again. The door was fast, and he heard me, and called as I thought from the bed to know what I wanted, and he desired me not to disturb him again. I lay down and slept for a little.

"It must have been between six and seven when I went up again. The door was still fast, and he made no answer, so I did not like to disturb him, and thinking he was asleep, I left him till nine. It was his custom to ring when he wished me to come, and I had no particular hour for calling him. I tapped very gently, and getting no answer, I stayed away a good while, supposing he was getting some rest then. It was not till eleven o'clock I grew really uncomfortable about him—for at the latest he was never, that I could remember, later than half-past ten. I got no answer. I knocked and called, and still no answer. So not being able to force the door, I called Thomas from the stables, and together we forced it, and found him in the shocking way you saw."

Jones had no more to tell. Poor Mr. Jennings was very gentle, and very kind. All his people were fond of him. I could see that the servant was very much moved.

So, dejected and agitated, I passed from that terrible house, and its dark canopy of elms, and I hope I shall never see it more. While I write to you I feel like a man who has but half waked from a frightful and monotonous dream. My memory rejects the picture with incredulity and horror. Yet I know it is true. It is the story of the process of a poison, a poison which excites the reciprocal action of spirit and nerve, and paralyses the tissue that separates those cognate functions of the senses, the external and the interior. Thus we find strange bed-fellows, and the mortal and immortal prematurely make acquaintance.

Conclusion: A Word for Those Who Suffer

My dear Van L——, you have suffered from an affection similar to that which I have just described. You twice complained of a return of it.

Who, under God, cured you? Your humble servant, Martin Hesselius. Let me rather adopt the more emphasised piety of a certain good old French surgeon of three hundred years ago: "I treated, and God cured you."

Come, my friend, you are not to be hippish. Let me tell you a fact.

I have met with, and treated, as my book shows, fifty-seven cases of this kind of vision, which I term indifferently "sublimated," "precocious," and "interior."

There is another class of affections which are truly termed—though commonly confounded with those which I describe—spectral illusions. These latter I look upon as being no less simply curable than a cold in the head or a trifling dyspepsia.

It is those which rank in the first category that test our

promptitude of thought. Fifty-seven such cases have I encountered, neither more nor less. And in how many of these have I failed? In no single instance.

There is no one affliction of mortality more easily and certainly reducible, with a little patience, and a rational confidence in the physician. With these simple conditions, I look upon the cure as absolutely certain.

You are to remember that I had not even commenced to treat Mr. Jennings' case. I have not any doubt that I should have cured him perfectly in eighteen months, or possibly it might have extended to two years. Some cases are very rapidly curable, others extremely tedious. Every intelligent physician who will give thought and diligence to the task, will effect a cure.

You know my tract on The Cardinal Functions of the Brain. I there, by the evidence of innumerable facts, prove, as I think, the high probability of a circulation arterial and venous in its mechanism, through the nerves. Of this system, thus considered, the brain is the heart. The fluid, which is propagated hence through one class of nerves, returns in an altered state through another, and the nature of that fluid is spiritual, though not immaterial, any more than, as I before remarked, light or electricity are so.

By various abuses, among which the habitual use of such agents as green tea is one, this fluid may be affected as to its quality, but it is more frequently disturbed as to equilibrium. This fluid being that which we have in common with spirits, a congestion found upon the masses of brain or nerve, connected with the interior sense, forms a surface unduly exposed, on which disembodied spirits may operate: communication is thus more or less effectually established. Between this brain circulation and the heart circulation there is an intimate sympathy. The seat, or rather the instrument of exterior vision, is the eye. The seat of interior vision is the nervous tissue and brain, immediately about and above the eyebrow.

You remember how effectually I dissipated your pictures by the simple application of iced eau-de-cologne. Few cases, however, can be treated exactly alike with anything like rapid success. Cold acts powerfully as a repellant of the nervous fluid. Long enough continued it will even produce that permanent insensibility which we call numbness, and a little longer, muscular as well as sensational paralysis.

I have not, I repeat, the slightest doubt that I should have first dimmed and ultimately sealed the inner eye which Mr. Jennings had inadvertently opened. The same senses are opened in delirium tremens, and entirely shut up again when the overaction of the cerebral heart, and the prodigious nervous congestions that attend it, are terminated by a decided change in the state of the body. It is by acting steadily upon the body by a simple process, that this result is produced—and inevitably produced—I have never yet failed.

Poor Mr. Jennings made away with himself. But that catastrophe was the result of a totally different malady, which, as it were, projected itself upon the disease which was established. His case was in the distinctive manner a complication, and the complaint under which he really succumbed, was a hereditary suicidal mania. Poor Mr. Jennings I cannot call a patient of mine, for I had not even begun to treat his case, and he had not yet given me, I am convinced, his full and unreserved confidence. If the patient do not array himself on the side of the disease, his cure is certain.

THE YELLOW WALLPAPER

Charlotte Perkins Gilman

(1892)

Gilman suffered for a time from severe post-childbirth depression, before recovering and eventually becoming a prominent feminist intellectual and author. This disturbing tale takes its departure from a similar situation, but with nightmarish consequences.

It is very seldom that mere ordinary people like John and myself secure ancestral halls for the summer.

A colonial mansion, a hereditary estate, I would say a haunted house and reach the height of romantic felicity—but that would be asking too much of fate!

Still I will proudly declare that there is something queer about it.

Else, why should it be let so cheaply? And why have stood so long untenanted?

John laughs at me, of course, but one expects that.

John is practical in the extreme. He has no patience with faith, an intense horror of superstition, and he scoffs openly at any talk of things not to be felt and seen and put down in figures.

John is a physician, and *perhaps* (I would not say it to a living soul, of course, but this is dead paper and a great relief to my mind)—*perhaps* that is one reason I do not get well faster.

You see, he does not believe I am sick! And what can one do?

If a physician of high standing, and one's own husband, assures friends and relatives that there is really nothing the matter with one but temporary nervous depression—a slight hysterical tendency—what is one to do?

My brother is also a physician, and also of high standing, and he says the same thing.

So I take phosphates or phosphites—whichever it is—and tonics, and air and exercise, and journeys, and am absolutely forbidden to "work" until I am well again.

Personally, I disagree with their ideas.

Personally, I believe that congenial work, with excitement and change, would do me good.

But what is one to do?

I did write for a while in spite of them; but it *does* exhaust me a good deal—having to be so sly about it, or else meet with heavy opposition.

I sometimes fancy that in my condition, if I had less opposition and more society and stimulus—but John says the very worst thing I can do is to think about my condition, and I confess it always makes me feel bad.

So I will let it alone and talk about the house.

The most beautiful place! It is quite alone, standing well back from the road, quite three miles from the village. It makes me think of English places that you read about, for there are hedges and walls and gates that lock, and lots of separate little houses for the gardeners and people.

There is a *delicious* garden! I never saw such a garden—large and shady, full of box-bordered paths, and lined with long grape-covered arbors with seats under them.

There were greenhouses, but they are all broken now.

There was some legal trouble, I believe, something about the heirs and co-heirs; anyhow, the place has been empty for years.

That spoils my ghostliness, I am afraid, but I don't care—there is something strange about the house—I can feel it.

I even said so to John one moonlight evening, but he said what I felt was a draught, and shut the window.

I get unreasonably angry with John sometimes. I'm sure I never used to be so sensitive. I think it is due to this nervous condition.

But John says if I feel so I shall neglect proper self-control; so I take pains to control myself—before him, at least, and that makes me very tired.

I don't like our room a bit. I wanted one downstairs that opened onto the piazza and had roses all over the window, and such pretty old-fashioned chintz hangings! But John would not hear of it.

He said there was only one window and not room for two beds, and no near room for him if he took another.

He is very careful and loving, and hardly lets me stir without special direction.

I have a schedule prescription for each hour in the day; he takes all care from me, and so I feel basely ungrateful not to value it more.

He said he came here solely on my account, that I was to have perfect rest and all the air I could get. "Your exercise depends on your strength, my dear," said he, "and your food somewhat on your appetite; but air you can absorb all the time." So we took the nursery at the top of the house.

It is a big, airy room, the whole floor nearly, with windows that look all ways, and air and sunshine galore. It was a nursery first, and then playroom and gymnasium, I should judge, for the windows are barred for little children, and there are rings and things in the walls.

The paint and paper look as if a boys' school had used it. It is stripped off—the paper—in great patches all around the head of my bed, about as far as I can reach, and in a great place on the other side of the room low down. I never saw a worse paper in my life. One of those sprawling, flamboyant patterns committing every artistic sin.

It is dull enough to confuse the eye in following, pronounced enough constantly to irritate and provoke study, and when you follow the lame uncertain curves for a little distance they suddenly commit suicide—plunge off at outrageous angles, destroy themselves in unheard-of contradictions.

The color is repellent, almost revolting: a smouldering unclean yellow, strangely faded by the slow-turning sunlight. It is a dull yet lurid orange in some places, a sickly sulphur tint in others.

No wonder the children hated it! I should hate it myself if I had to live in this room long.

There comes John, and I must put this away—he hates to have me write a word.

We have been here two weeks, and I haven't felt like writing before, since that first day.

I am sitting by the window now, up in this atrocious nursery, and there is nothing to hinder my writing as much as I please, save lack of strength.

John is away all day, and even some nights when his cases are serious.

I am glad my case is not serious!

But these nervous troubles are dreadfully depressing.

John does not know how much I really suffer. He knows there is no reason to suffer, and that satisfies him.

Of course it is only nervousness. It does weigh on me so not to do my duty in any way!

I meant to be such a help to John, such a real rest and comfort, and here I am a comparative burden already!

Nobody would believe what an effort it is to do what little I am able—to dress and entertain, and order things.

It is fortunate Mary is so good with the baby. Such a dear baby!

And yet I *cannot* be with him, it makes me so nervous.

I suppose John never was nervous in his life. He laughs at me so about this wallpaper!

At first he meant to repaper the room, but afterward he said that I was letting it get the better of me, and that nothing was worse for a nervous patient than to give way to such fancies.

He said that after the wallpaper was changed it would be the heavy bedstead, and then the barred windows, and then that gate at the head of the stairs, and so on.

"You know the place is doing you good," he said, "and really, dear, I don't care to renovate the house just for a three months' rental."

"Then do let us go downstairs," I said. "There are such pretty rooms there."

Then he took me in his arms and called me a blessed little goose, and said he would go down to the cellar, if I wished, and have it whitewashed into the bargain.

But he is right enough about the beds and windows and things.

It is as airy and comfortable a room as anyone need wish, and, of course, I would not be so silly as to make him uncomfortable just for a whim.

I'm really getting quite fond of the big room, all but that horrid paper.

Out of one window I can see the garden—those mysterious deep-shaded arbors, the riotous old-fashioned flowers, and bushes and gnarly trees.

Out of another I get a lovely view of the bay and a little private wharf belonging to the estate. There is a beautiful shaded lane that runs down there from the house. I always fancy I see people walking in these numerous paths and arbors, but John has cautioned me not to give way to fancy in the least. He says that with my imaginative power and habit of storymaking, a nervous weakness like mine is sure to lead to all manner of excited fancies, and that I ought to use my will and good sense to check the tendency. So I try.

I think sometimes that if I were only well enough to write a little it would relieve the press of ideas and rest me.

But I find I get pretty tired when I try.

It is so discouraging not to have any advice and companionship about my work. When I get really well, John says we will ask Cousin Henry and Julia down for a long visit; but he says he would as soon put fireworks in my pillow-case as to let me have those stimulating people about now.

I wish I could get well faster.

But I must not think about that. This paper looks to me as if it *knew* what a vicious influence it had!

There is a recurrent spot where the pattern lolls like a broken neck and two bulbous eyes stare at you upside down.

I get positively angry with the impertinence of it and the everlastingness. Up and down and sideways they crawl, and those absurd unblinking eyes are everywhere. There is one place where two breadths didn't match, and the eyes go all up and down the line, one a little higher than the other.

I never saw so much expression in an inanimate thing before, and we all know how much expression they have! I used to lie awake as a child and get more entertainment and terror out of blank walls and plain furniture than most children could find in a toy-store.

I remember what a kindly wink the knobs of our big old bureau used to have, and there was one chair that always seemed like a strong friend.

I used to feel that if any of the other things looked too fierce I could always hop into that chair and be safe.

The furniture in this room is no worse than inharmonious, however, for we had to bring it all from downstairs. I suppose when this was used as a playroom they had to take the nursery things out, and no wonder! I never saw such ravages as the children have made here.

The wallpaper, as I said before, is torn off in spots, and it sticketh closer than a brother—they must have had perseverance as well as hatred.

Then the floor is scratched and gouged and splintered, the plaster itself is dug out here and there, and this great heavy bed, which is all we found in the room, looks as if it had been through the wars.

But I don't mind it a bit—only the paper.

There comes John's sister. Such a dear girl as she is, and so careful of me! I must not let her find me writing.

She is a perfect and enthusiastic housekeeper, and hopes for no better profession. I verily believe she thinks it is the writing which made me sick!

But I can write when she is out, and see her a long way off from these windows.

There is one that commands the road, a lovely shaded winding road, and one that just looks off over the country. A lovely country, too, full of great elms and velvet meadows.

This wallpaper has a kind of subpattern in a different shade, a particularly irritating one, for you can only see it in certain lights, and not clearly then.

But in the places where it isn't faded and where the sun is just so—I can see a strange, provoking, formless sort of figure that seems to skulk about behind that silly and conspicuous front design.

There's sister on the stairs!

Well, the Fourth of July is over! The people are all gone, and I am tired out. John thought it might do me good to see a little company, so we just had Mother and Nellie and the children down for a week.

Of course I didn't do a thing. Jennie sees to everything now.

But it tired me all the same.

John says if I don't pick up faster he shall send me to Weir Mitchell in the fall.

But I don't want to go there at all. I had a friend who was in his hands once, and she says he is just like John and my brother, only more so!

Besides, it is such an undertaking to go so far.

I don't feel as if it was worthwhile to turn my hand over for anything, and I'm getting dreadfully fretful and querulous.

I cry at nothing, and cry most of the time.

Of course I don't when John is here, or anybody else, but when I am alone.

And I am alone a good deal just now. John is kept in town very often by serious cases, and Jennie is good and lets me alone when I want her to.

So I walk a little in the garden or down that lovely lane, sit on the porch under the roses, and lie down up here a good deal.

I'm getting really fond of the room in spite of the wallpaper. Perhaps *because* of the wallpaper.

It dwells in my mind so!

I lie here on this great immovable bed—it is nailed down, I believe—and follow that pattern about by the hour. It is as good as gymnastics, I assure you. I start, we'll say, at the bottom, down in the corner over there where it has not been touched, and I determine for the thousandth time that I *will* follow that pointless pattern to some sort of a conclusion.

I know a little of the principle of design, and I know this thing was not arranged on any laws of radiation, or alternation, or repetition, or symmetry, or anything else that I ever heard of.

It is repeated, of course, by the breadths, but not otherwise.

Looked at in one way, each breadth stands alone; the bloated curves and flourishes—a kind of "debased Romanesque" with delirium tremens go waddling up and down in isolated columns of fatuity.

But, on the other hand, they connect diagonally, and the sprawling outlines run off in great slanting waves of optic horror, like a lot of wallowing sea-weeds in full chase.

The whole thing goes horizontally, too, at least it seems so, and I exhaust myself trying to distinguish the order of its going in that direction.

They have used a horizontal breadth for a frieze, and that adds wonderfully to the confusion.

There is one end of the room where it is almost intact, and there, when the crosslights fade and the low sun shines directly upon it, I can almost fancy radiation after all—the interminable grotesque seems to form around a common center and rush off in headlong plunges of equal distraction.

It makes me tired to follow it. I will take a nap, I guess.

I don't know why I should write this.

I don't want to.

I don't feel able.

And I know John would think it absurd. But I must say what I feel and think in some way—it is such a relief!

But the effort is getting to be greater than the relief.

Half the time now I am awfully lazy, and lie down ever so much. John says I mustn't lose my strength, and has me take cod liver oil and lots of tonics and things, to say nothing of ale and wines and rare meat.

Dear John! He loves me very dearly, and hates to have me sick. I tried to have a real earnest reasonable talk with him the other day, and tell him how I wish he would let me go and make a visit to Cousin Henry and Julia.

But he said I wasn't able to go, nor able to stand it after I got there; and I did not make out a very good case for myself, for I was crying before I had finished.

It is getting to be a great effort for me to think straight. Just this nervous weakness, I suppose.

And dear John gathered me up in his arms, and just carried me upstairs and laid me on the bed, and sat by me and read to me till it tired my head.

He said I was his darling and his comfort and all he had, and that I must take care of myself for his sake, and keep well.

He says no one but myself can help me out of it, that I must use my will and self-control and not let any silly fancies run away with me.

There's one comfort—the baby is well and happy, and does not have to occupy this nursery with the horrid wallpaper.

If we had not used it, that blessed child would have! What a fortunate escape! Why, I wouldn't have a child of mine, an impressionable little thing, live in such a room for worlds.

I never thought of it before, but it is lucky that John kept me here after all; I can stand it so much easier than a baby, you see.

Of course I never mention it to them any more—I am too wise—but I keep watch for it all the same.

There are things in the wallpaper that nobody knows about but me, or ever will.

Behind that outside pattern the dim shapes get clearer every day.

It is always the same shape, only very numerous.

And it is like a woman stooping down and creeping about behind that pattern. I don't like it a bit. I wonder—I begin to think—I wish John would take me away from here!

It is so hard to talk with John about my case, because he is so wise, and because he loves me so.

But I tried it last night.

It was moonlight. The moon shines in all around just as the sun does.

I hate to see it sometimes, it creeps so slowly, and always comes in by one window or another.

John was asleep and I hated to waken him, so I kept still and watched the moonlight on that undulating wallpaper till I felt creepy.

The faint figure behind seemed to shake the pattern, just as if she wanted to get out.

I got up softly and went to feel and see if the paper *did* move, and when I came back John was awake.

"What is it, little girl?" he said. "Don't go walking about like that—you'll get cold."

I thought it was a good time to talk, so I told him that I really was not gaining here, and that I wished he would take me away.

"Why, darling!" said he. "Our lease will be up in three weeks, and I can't see how to leave before.

"The repairs are not done at home, and I cannot possibly leave town just now. Of course, if you were in any danger, I could and would, but you really are better, dear, whether you can see it or not. I am a doctor, dear, and I know. You are gaining flesh and color, your appetite is better, I feel really much easier about you."

"I don't weigh a bit more," said I, "nor as much; and my appetite may be better in the evening when you are here but it is worse in the morning when you are away!"

"Bless her little heart!" said he with a big hug. "She shall be as sick as she pleases! But now let's improve the shining hours by going to sleep, and talk about it in the morning!"

"And you won't go away?" I asked gloomily.

"Why, how can I, dear? It is only three weeks more and then

we will take a nice little trip for a few days while Jennie is getting the house ready. Really, dear, you are better!"

"Better in body perhaps—" I began, and stopped short, for he sat up straight and looked at me with such a stern, reproachful look that I could not say another word.

"My darling," said he, "I beg you, for my sake and for our child's sake, as well as for your own, that you will never for one instant let that idea enter your mind! There is nothing so dangerous, so fascinating, to a temperament like yours. It is a false and foolish fancy. Can you trust me as a physician when I tell you so?"

So of course I said no more on that score, and we went to sleep before long. He thought I was asleep first, but I wasn't, and lay there for hours trying to decide whether that front pattern and the back pattern really did move together or separately.

On a pattern like this, by daylight, there is a lack of sequence, a defiance of law, that is a constant irritant to a normal mind.

The color is hideous enough, and unreliable enough, and infuriating enough, but the pattern is torturing.

You think you have mastered it, but just as you get well under way in following, it turns a back-somersault and there you are. It slaps you in the face, knocks you down, and tramples upon you. It is like a bad dream.

The outside pattern is a florid arabesque, reminding one of a fungus. If you can imagine a toadstool in joints, an interminable string of toadstools, budding and sprouting in endless convolutions—why, that is something like it.

That is, sometimes!

There is one marked peculiarity about this paper, a thing nobody seems to notice but myself, and that is that it changes as the light changes.

When the sun shoots in through the east window—I always watch for that first long, straight ray—it changes so quickly that I never can quite believe it.

That is why I watch it always.

By moonlight—the moon shines in all night when there is a moon—I wouldn't know it was the same paper.

At night in any kind of light, in twilight, candlelight, lamplight, and worst of all by moonlight, it becomes bars! The outside pattern, I mean, and the woman behind it is as plain as can be.

I didn't realize for a long time what the thing was that showed behind, that dim subpattern, but now I am quite sure it is a woman.

By daylight she is subdued, quiet. I fancy it is the pattern that keeps her so still. It is so puzzling. It keeps me quiet by the hour.

I lie down ever so much now. John says it is good for me, and to sleep all I can.

Indeed he started the habit by making me lie down for an hour after each meal.

It is a very bad habit, I am convinced, for you see, I don't sleep.

And that cultivates deceit, for I don't tell them I'm awake—oh, no!

The fact is I am getting a little afraid of John.

He seems very queer sometimes, and even Jennie has an inexplicable look.

It strikes me occasionally, just as a scientific hypothesis, that perhaps it is the paper!

I have watched John when he did not know I was looking, and come into the room suddenly on the most innocent excuses, and I've caught him several times *looking at the paper!* And Jennie too. I caught Jennie with her hand on it once.

She didn't know I was in the room, and when I asked her in a quiet, a very quiet voice, with the most restrained manner possible, what she was doing with the paper, she turned around as if she had been caught stealing, and looked quite angry—asked me why I should frighten her so!

Then she said that the paper stained everything it touched, that she had found yellow smooches on all my clothes and John's and she wished we would be more careful!

Did not that sound innocent? But I know she was studying that pattern, and I am determined that nobody shall find it out but myself!

Life is very much more exciting now than it used to be. You see, I have something more to expect, to look forward to, to watch. I really do eat better, and am more quiet than I was.

John is so pleased to see me improve! He laughed a little the other day, and said I seemed to be flourishing in spite of my wallpaper.

I turned it off with a laugh. I had no intention of telling him it was *because* of the wallpaper—he would make fun of me. He might even want to take me away.

I don't want to leave now until I have found it out. There is a week more, and I think that will be enough.

I am feeling so much better!

I don't sleep much at night, for it is so interesting to watch developments; but I sleep a good deal during the daytime.

In the daytime it is tiresome and perplexing.

There are always new shoots on the fungus, and new shades of yellow all over it. I cannot keep count of them, though I have tried conscientiously.

It is the strangest yellow, that wallpaper! It makes me think of all the yellow things I ever saw—not beautiful ones like buttercups, but old, foul, bad yellow things.

But there is something else about that paper—the smell! I noticed it the moment we came into the room, but with so much air and sun it was not bad. Now we have had a week of fog and rain, and whether the windows are open or not, the smell is here.

It creeps all over the house.

I find it hovering in the dining-room, skulking in the parlor, hiding in the hall, lying in wait for me on the stairs.

It gets into my hair.

Even when I go to ride, if I turn my head suddenly and surprise it—there is that smell!

Such a peculiar odor, too! I have spent hours in trying to analyze it, to find what it smelled like.

It is not bad—at first—and very gentle, but quite the subtlest, most enduring odor I ever met.

In this damp weather it is awful. I wake up in the night and find it hanging over me.

It used to disturb me at first. I thought seriously of burning the house—to reach the smell.

But now I am used to it. The only thing I can think of that it is like is the *color* of the paper! A yellow smell.

There is a very funny mark on this wall, low down, near the mopboard. A streak that runs round the room. It goes behind every piece of furniture, except the bed, a long, straight, even *smooch*, as if it had been rubbed over and over.

I wonder how it was done and who did it, and what they did it for. Round and round and round—round, and round and round—it makes me dizzy!

I really have discovered something at last.

Through watching so much at night, when it changes so, I have finally found out.

The front pattern *does* move—and no wonder! The woman behind shakes it!

Sometimes I think there are a great many women behind, and sometimes only one and she crawls around fast, and her crawling shakes it all over.

Then in the very bright spots she keeps still, and in the very shady spots she just takes hold of the bars and shakes them hard.

And she is all the time trying to climb through. But nobody could climb through that pattern—it strangles so; I think that is why it has so many heads.

They get through and then the pattern strangles them off and turns them upside down, and makes their eyes white!

If those heads were covered or taken off it would not be half so bad.

I think that woman gets out in the daytime!

And I'll tell you why—privately—I've seen her!

I can see her out of every one of my windows!

It is the same woman, I know, for she is always creeping, and most women do not creep by daylight.

I see her in that long shaded lane, creeping up and down. I see her in those dark grape arbors, creeping all round the garden.

I see her on that long road under the trees, creeping along, and when a carriage comes she hides under the blackberry vines.

I don't blame her a bit. It must be very humiliating to be caught creeping by daylight!

I always lock the door when I creep by daylight. I can't do it at night, for I know John would suspect something at once.

And John is so queer now that I don't want to irritate him. I wish he would take another room! Besides, I don't want anybody to get that woman out at night but myself.

I often wonder if I could see her out of all the windows at once.

But, turn as fast as I can, I can only see out of one at one time.

And though I always see her, she *may* be able to creep faster than I can turn: I have watched her sometimes away off in the open country, creeping as fast as a cloud shadow in a wind.

If only that top pattern could be gotten off from the under one! I mean to try it, little by little.

I have found out another funny thing, but I shan't tell it this time! It does not do to trust people too much.

There are only two more days to get this paper off, and I believe John is beginning to notice. I don't like the look in his eyes.

And I heard him ask Jennie a lot of professional questions about me. She had a very good report to give.

She said I slept a good deal in the daytime.

John knows I don't sleep very well at night, for all I'm so quiet!

He asked me all sorts of questions too, and pretended to be very loving and kind.

As if I couldn't see through him!

Still, I don't wonder he acts so, sleeping under this paper for three months.

It only interests me, but I feel sure John and Jennie are affected by it.

Hurrah! This is the last day, but it is enough. John is to stay in town over night, and won't be out until this evening.

Jennie wanted to sleep with me—the sly thing; but I told her I should undoubtedly rest better for a night all alone.

That was clever, for really I wasn't alone a bit! As soon as it was moonlight and that poor thing began to crawl and shake the pattern, I got up and ran to help her.

I pulled and she shook. I shook and she pulled, and before morning we had peeled off yards of that paper.

A strip about as high as my head and half around the room.

And then when the sun came and that awful pattern began to laugh at me, I declared I would finish it today!

We go away tomorrow, and they are moving all my furniture down again to leave things as they were before.

Jennie looked at the wall in amazement, but I told her merrily that I did it out of pure spite at the vicious thing.

She laughed and said she wouldn't mind doing it herself, but I must not get tired.

How she betrayed herself that time!

But I am here, and no person touches this paper but Me—not *alive*!

She tried to get me out of the room—it was too patent! But I said it was so quiet and empty and clean now that I believed I would lie down again and sleep all I could, and not to wake me even for dinner—I would call when I woke.

So now she is gone, and the servants are gone, and the things are gone, and there is nothing left but that great bedstead nailed down, with the canvas mattress we found on it.

We shall sleep downstairs tonight, and take the boat home tomorrow.

I quite enjoy the room, now it is bare again.

How those children did tear about here!

This bedstead is fairly gnawed!

But I must get to work.

I have locked the door and thrown the key down into the front path.

I don't want to go out, and I don't want to have anybody come in, till John comes.

I want to astonish him.

I've got a rope up here that even Jennie did not find. If that woman does get out, and tries to get away, I can tie her!

But I forgot I could not reach far without anything to stand on!

This bed will *not* move!

I tried to lift and push it until I was lame, and then I got so angry I bit off a little piece at one corner—but it hurt my teeth.

Then I peeled off all the paper I could reach standing on the floor. It sticks horribly and the pattern just enjoys it! All those strangled heads and bulbous eyes and waddling fungus growths just shriek with derision!

I am getting angry enough to do something desperate. To jump out of the window would be admirable exercise, but the bars are too strong even to try.

Besides I wouldn't do it. Of course not. I know well enough that a step like that is improper and might be misconstrued.

I don't like to *look* out of the windows even—there are so many of those creeping women, and they creep so fast.

I wonder if they all come out of that wallpaper as I did!

But I am securely fastened now by my well-hidden rope—you don't get *me* out in the road there!

I suppose I shall have to get back behind the pattern when it comes night, and that is hard!

It is so pleasant to be out in this great room and creep around as I please!

I don't want to go outside. I won't, even if Jennie asks me to.

For outside you have to creep on the ground, and everything is green instead of yellow.

But here I can creep smoothly on the floor, and my shoulder just fits in that long smooch around the wall, so I cannot lose my way.

Why, there's John at the door!

It is no use, young man, you can't open it!

How he does call and pound!

Now he's crying to Jennie for an axe.

It would be a shame to break down that beautiful door!

"John, dear!" said I in the gentlest voice. "The key is down by the front steps, under a plantain leaf!"

That silenced him for a few moments.

Then he said, very quietly indeed, "Open the door, my darling!"

"I can't," said I. "The key is down by the front door under a plantain leaf!" And then I said it again, several times, very gently and slowly, and said it so often that he had to go and see, and he got it of course, and came in. He stopped short by the door.

"What is the matter?" he cried. "For God's sake, what are you doing!"

I kept on creeping just the same, but I looked at him over my shoulder.

"I've got out at last," said I, "in spite of you and Jane. And I've pulled off most of the paper, so you can't put me back!"

Now why should that man have fainted? But he did, and right across my path by the wall, so that I had to creep over him every time!

THE BOTTLE IMP

Robert Louis Stevenson

(1893)

Tales of otherworldly powers granting wishes with troubling consequences go back centuries, at least to the tales of Midas, the Arabian Nights, and the Faust legend. This superb example has the disarming simplicity of a folktale, but the graceful narrative gradually takes on a surprising resonance and dread, until its ironic climax.

There was a man of the island of Hawaii, whom I shall call Keawe; for the truth is, he still lives, and his name must be kept secret; but the place of his birth was not far from Honaunau, where the bones of Keawe the Great lie hidden in a cave. This man was poor, brave, and active; he could read and write like a schoolmaster; he was a first-rate mariner besides, sailed for some time in the island steamers, and steered a whale-boat on the Hamakua coast. At length it came in Keawe's mind to have a sight of the great world and foreign cities, and he shipped on a vessel bound to San Francisco.

This is a fine town, with a fine harbour, and rich people uncountable; and, in particular, there is one hill which is covered with palaces. Upon this hill Keawe was one day taking a walk, with his pocket full of money, viewing the great houses upon either hand with pleasure. "What fine houses these are!" he was thinking, "and how happy must these people be who dwell in them, and take no care for the morrow!" The thought was in his mind when he came abreast of a house that was smaller than some others, but all finished and beautified like a toy; the steps of that house shone like silver, and the borders of the garden bloomed like garlands, and the windows were bright like diamonds; and Keawe stopped and wondered at the excellence of all he saw. So stopping, he was aware of a man that looked forth upon him through a window, so clear that Keawe could see him as you see a fish in a pool upon the reef. The man was elderly, with a bald head and a black beard; and his face was heavy with sorrow, and he bitterly sighed. And the truth of it is, that as Keawe looked in upon the man, and the man looked out upon Keawe, each envied the other.

All of a sudden the man smiled and nodded, and beckoned Keawe to enter, and met him at the door of the house.

"This is a fine house of mine," said the man, and bitterly sighed. "Would you not care to view the chambers?"

So he led Keawe all over it, from the cellar to the roof, and there was nothing there that was not perfect of its kind, and Keawe was astonished.

"Truly," said Keawe, "this is a beautiful house; if I lived in the like of it, I should be laughing all day long. How comes it, then, that you should be sighing?"

"There is no reason," said the man, "why you should not have a house in all points similar to this, and finer, if you wish. You have some money, I suppose?"

"I have fifty dollars," said Keawe; "but a house like this will cost more than fifty dollars."

The man made a computation. "I am sorry you have no more," said he, "for it may raise you trouble in the future; but it shall be yours at fifty dollars."

"The house?" asked Keawe.

"No, not the house," replied the man; "but the bottle. For, I must tell you, although I appear to you so rich and fortunate, all my fortune, and this house itself and its garden, came out of a bottle not much bigger than a pint. This is it."

And he opened a lock-fast place, and took out a round-bellied bottle with a long neck; the glass of it was white like milk, with changing rainbow colours in the grain. Withinsides something obscurely moved, like a shadow and a fire.

"This is the bottle," said the man; and, when Keawe laughed,

"You do not believe me?" he added. "Try, then, for yourself. See if you can break it."

So Keawe took the bottle up and dashed it on the floor till he was weary; but it jumped on the floor like a child's ball, and was not injured.

"This is a strange thing," said Keawe. "For by the touch of it, as well as by the look, the bottle should be of glass."

"Of glass it is," replied the man, sighing more heavily than ever; "but the glass of it was tempered in the flames of hell. An imp lives in it, and that is the shadow we behold there moving; or, so I suppose. If any man buy this bottle the imp is at his command; all that he desires—love, fame, money, houses like this house, ay, or a city like this city—all are his at the word uttered. Napoleon had this bottle, and by it he grew to be the king of the world; but he sold it at the last and fell. Captain Cook had this bottle, and by it he found his way to so many islands; but he, too, sold it, and was slain upon Hawaii. For, once it is sold, the power goes and the protection; and unless a man remain content with what he has, ill will befall him."

"And yet you talk of selling it yourself?" Keawe said.

"I have all I wish, and I am growing elderly," replied the man. "There is one thing the imp cannot do—he cannot prolong life; and, it would not be fair to conceal from you, there is a drawback to the bottle; for if a man die before be sells it, he must burn in hell for ever."

"To be sure, that is a drawback and no mistake," cried Keawe. "I would not meddle with the thing. I can do without a house, thank God; but there is one thing I could not be doing with one particle, and that is to be damned."

"Dear me, you must not run away with things," returned the man. "All you have to do is to use the power of the imp in moderation, and then sell it to someone else, as I do to you, and finish your life in comfort."

"Well, I observe two things," said Keawe. "All the time you keep sighing like a maid in love, that is one; and, for the other, you sell this bottle very cheap."

"I have told you already why I sigh," said the man. "It is because I fear my health is breaking up; and, as you said yourself, to die and go to the devil is a pity for anyone. As for why I sell so cheap, I must explain to you there is a peculiarity about the bottle. Long ago, when the devil brought it first upon earth, it was extremely expensive, and was sold first of all to Prester John for many millions of dollars; but it cannot be sold at all, unless sold at a loss. If you sell it for as much as you paid for it, back it comes to you again like a homing pigeon. It follows that the price has kept falling in these centuries, and the bottle is now remarkably cheap. I bought it myself from one of my great neighbours on this hill, and the price I paid was only ninety dollars. I could sell it for as high as eighty-nine dollars and ninety-nine cents, but not a penny dearer, or back the thing must come to me. Now, about this there are two bothers. First, when you offer a bottle so singular for eighty-odd dollars, people suppose you to be jesting. And second—but there is no hurry about that—and I need not go into it. Only remember it must be coined money that you sell it for."

"How am I to know that this is all true?" asked Keawe.

"Some of it you can try at once," replied the man. "Give me your fifty dollars, take the bottle, and wish your fifty dollars back into your pocket. If that does not happen, I pledge you my honour I will cry off the bargain and restore your money."

"You are not deceiving me?" said Keawe.

The man bound himself with a great oath.

"Well, I will risk that much," said Keawe, "for that can do no harm." And he paid over his money to the man, and the man handed him the bottle.

"Imp of the bottle," said Keawe, "I want my fifty dollars back." And sure enough, he had scarce said the word before his pocket was as heavy as ever.

"To be sure this is a wonderful bottle," said Keawe.

"And now good-morning to you, my fine fellow, and the devil go with you for me," said the man.

"Hold on," said Keawe, "I don't want any more of this fun. Here, take your bottle back."

"You have bought it for less than I paid for it," replied the man, rubbing his hands. "It is yours now; and, for my part, I am only concerned to see the back of you." And with that he rang for his Chinese servant, and had Keawe shown out of the house.

Now, when Keawe was in the street, with the bottle under his arm, he began to think. "If all is true about this bottle, I may have made a losing bargain," thinks he. "But, perhaps the man was only fooling me." The first thing he did was to count his money; the sum was exact—forty-nine dollars American money, and one Chili piece. "That looks like the truth," said Keawe. "Now I will try another part."

The streets in that part of the city were as clean as a ship's decks, and though it was noon, there were no passengers. Keawe set the bottle in the gutter and walked away. Twice he looked back, and there was the milky, round-bellied bottle where he left it. A third time he looked back, and turned a corner; but he had scarce done so, when something knocked upon his elbow, and behold! it was the long neck sticking up; and as for the round belly, it was jammed into the pocket of his pilot-coat.

"And that looks like the truth," said Keawe.

The next thing he did was to buy a corkscrew in a shop, and go apart into a secret place in the fields. And there he tried to draw the cork, but as often as he put the screw in, out it came again, and the cork was as whole as ever.

"This is some new sort of cork," said Keawe, and all at once he began to shake and sweat, for he was afraid of that bottle.

On his way back to the port-side he saw a shop where a man sold shells and clubs from the wild islands, old heathen deities, old coined money, pictures from China and Japan, and all manner of things that sailors bring in their sea-chests. And here he had an idea. So he went in and offered the bottle for a hundred dollars. The man of the shop laughed at him at first, and offered him five; but, indeed, it was a curious bottle, such glass was never blown in any human glass-works, so prettily the colours shone under the milky white, and so strangely the shadow hovered in the midst; so, after he had disputed a while after the manner of his kind, the shopman gave Keawe sixty silver dollars for the thing and set it on a shelf in the midst of his window.

"Now," said Keawe, "I have sold that for sixty which I bought for fifty—or, to say truth, a little less, because one of my dollars was from Chili. Now I shall know the truth upon another point."

So he went back on board his ship, and when he opened his chest, there was the bottle, and had come more quickly than himself. Now Keawe had a mate on board whose name was Lopaka.

"What ails you?" said Lopaka, "that you stare in your chest?"

They were alone in the ship's forecastle, and Keawe bound him to secrecy, and told all.

"This is a very strange affair," said Lopaka; "and I fear you will be in trouble about this bottle. But there is one point very clear—that you are sure of the trouble, and you had better have the profit in the bargain. Make up your mind what you want with it; give the order, and if it is done as you desire, I will buy the bottle myself; for I have an idea of my own to get a schooner, and go trading through the islands."

"That is not my idea," said Keawe; "but to have a beautiful house and garden on the Kona Coast, where I was born, the sun shining in at the door, flowers in the garden, glass in the windows, pictures on the walls, and toys and fine carpets on the tables, for all the world like the house I was in this day—only a story higher, and with balconies all about like the King's palace; and to live there without care and make merry with my friends and relatives."

"Well," said Lopaka, "let us carry it back with us to Hawaii; and if all comes true, as you suppose, I will buy the bottle, as I said, and ask a schooner."

Upon that they were agreed, and it was not long before the ship returned to Honolulu, carrying Keawe and Lopaka, and the bottle. They were scarce come ashore when they met a friend upon the beach, who began at once to condole with Keawe.

"I do not know what I am to be condoled about," said Keawe.

"Is it possible you have not heard," said the friend, "your uncle—that good old man—is dead, and your cousin—that beautiful boy—was drowned at sea?"

Keawe was filled with sorrow, and, beginning to weep and to lament, he forgot about the bottle. But Lopaka was thinking to himself, and presently, when Keawe's grief was a little abated, "I have been thinking," said Lopaka. "Had not your uncle lands in Hawaii, in the district of Kaü?"

"No," said Keawe, "not in Kaü; they are on the mountain side—a little way south of Hookena."

"These lands will now be yours?" asked Lopaka.

"And so they will," says Keawe, and began again to lament for his relatives.

"No," said Lopaka, "do not lament at present. I have a thought in my mind. How if this should be the doing of the bottle? For here is the place ready for your house."

"If this be so," cried Keawe, "it is a very ill way to serve me by killing my relatives. But it may be, indeed; for it was in just such a station that I saw the house with my mind's eye."

"The house, however, is not yet built," said Lopaka.

"No, nor like to be!" said Keawe; "for though my uncle has some coffee and ava and bananas, it will not be more than will keep me in comfort; and the rest of that land is the black lava."

"Let us go to the lawyer," said Lopaka; "I have still this idea in my mind."

Now, when they came to the lawyer's, it appeared Keawe's uncle had grown monstrous rich in the last days, and there was a fund of money.

"And here is the money for the house!" cried Lopaka.

"If you are thinking of a new house," said the lawyer, "here is the card of a new architect of whom they tell me great things."

"Better and better!" cried Lopaka. "Here is all made plain for us. Let us continue to obey orders."

So they went to the architect, and he had drawings of houses on his table.

"You want something out of the way," said the architect. "How do you like this?" and he handed a drawing to Keawe.

Now, when Keawe set eyes on the drawing, he cried out aloud, for it was the picture of his thought exactly drawn.

"I am in for this house," thought he. "Little as I like the way it comes to me, I am in for it now, and I may as well take the good along with the evil."

So he told the architect all that he wished, and how he would have that house furnished, and about the pictures on the wall and the knick-knacks on the tables; and he asked the man plainly for how much he would undertake the whole affair.

The architect put many questions, and took his pen and made a computation; and when he had done he named the very sum that Keawe had inherited.

Lopaka and Keawe looked at one another and nodded.

"It is quite clear," thought Keawe, "that I am to have this house, whether or no. It comes from the devil, and I fear I will get little good by that; and of one thing I am sure, I will make no more wishes as long as I have this bottle. But with the house I am saddled, and I may as well take the good along with the evil."

So he made his terms with the architect, and they signed a paper; and Keawe and Lopaka took ship again and sailed to Australia; for it was concluded between them they should not interfere at all, but leave the architect and the bottle imp to build and to adorn that house at their own pleasure.

The voyage was a good voyage, only all the time Keawe was holding in his breath, for he had sworn he would utter no more wishes, and take no more favours from the devil. The time was up when they got back. The architect told them that the house was ready, and Keawe and Lopaka took a passage in the *Hall*, and went down Kona way to view the house, and see if all had been done fitly according to the thought that was in Keawe's mind.

Now, the house stood on the mountain side, visible to ships. Above, the forest ran up into the clouds of rain; below, the black lava fell in cliffs, where the kings of old lay buried. A garden bloomed about that house with every hue of flowers; and there was an orchard of papaia on the one hand and an orchard of bread-fruit on the other, and right in front, towards the sea, a ship's mast had been rigged up and bore a flag. As for the house, it was three stories high, with great chambers and broad balconies on each. The windows were of glass, so excellent that it was as clear as water and as bright as day. All manner of furniture adorned the chambers. Pictures hung upon the wall in golden frames—pictures of ships, and men fighting, and of the most beautiful women, and of singular places; nowhere in the world are there pictures of so bright a colour as those Keawe found hanging in his house. As for the knick-knacks, they were extraordinary fine: chiming clocks and musical boxes, little men with nodding heads, books filled with pictures, weapons of price from all quarters of the world, and the most elegant puzzles to entertain the leisure of a solitary man. And as no one would care to live in such chambers, only to walk through and view them, the balconies were made so broad that a whole town might have lived upon them in delight; and Keawe knew not which to prefer, whether the back porch, where you got the land breeze and looked upon the orchards and the flowers, or the front balcony, where you could drink the wind of the sea, and look down the steep wall of the mountain and see the *Hall* going by once a week or so between Hookena and the hills of Pele, or the schooners plying up the coast for wood and ava and bananas.

When they had viewed all, Keawe and Lopaka sat on the porch.

"Well," asked Lopaka, "is it all as you designed?"

"Words cannot utter it," said Keawe. "It is better than I dreamed, and I am sick with satisfaction."

"There is but one thing to consider," said Lopaka, "all this may be quite natural, and the bottle imp have nothing whatever to say to it. If I were to buy the bottle, and got no schooner after all, I should have put my hand in the fire for nothing. I gave you my word, I know; but yet I think you would not grudge me one more proof."

"I have sworn I would take no more favours," said Keawe. "I have gone already deep enough."

"This is no favour I am thinking of," replied Lopaka. "It is only to see the imp himself. There is nothing to be gained by that, and so nothing to be ashamed of, and yet, if I once saw him, I should be sure of the whole matter. So indulge me so far, and let me see the imp; and, after that, here is the money in my hand, and I will buy it."

"There is only one thing I am afraid of," said Keawe. "The imp may be very ugly to view, and if you once set eyes upon him you might be very undesirous of the bottle."

"I am a man of my word," said Lopaka. "And here is the money betwixt us."

"Very well," replied Keawe, "I have a curiosity myself. So come, let us have one look at you, Mr. Imp."

Now as soon as that was said, the imp looked out of the bottle, and in again, swift as a lizard; and there sat Keawe and Lopaka turned to stone. The night had quite come, before either found a thought to say or voice to say it with; and then Lopaka pushed the money over and took the bottle.

"I am a man of my word," said he, "and had need to be so, or I would not touch this bottle with my foot. Well, I shall get my schooner and a dollar or two for my pocket; and then I will be rid of this devil as fast as I can. For to tell you the plain truth, the look of him has cast me down."

"Lopaka," said Keawe, "do not you think any worse of me than you can help; I know it is night, and the roads bad, and the pass by the tombs an ill place to go by so late, but I declare since I have seen that little face, I cannot eat or sleep or pray till it is gone from me. I will give you a lantern, and a basket to put the bottle in, and any picture or fine thing in all my house that takes your fancy; and be gone at once, and go sleep at Hookena with Nahinu."

"Keawe," said Lopaka, "many a man would take this ill; above all, when I am doing you a turn so friendly, as to keep my word and buy the bottle; and for that matter, the night and the dark, and the way by the tombs, must be all tenfold more dangerous to a man with such a sin upon his conscience and such a bottle under his arm. But for my part, I am so extremely terrified myself I have not the heart to blame you. Here I go, then; and I pray God you may be happy in your house, and I fortunate with my schooner, and both get to heaven in the end in spite of the devil and his bottle."

So Lopaka went down the mountain; and Keawe stood in his front balcony, and listened to the clink of the horse's shoes, and watched the lantern go shining down the path, and along the cliff of caves where the old dead are buried; and all the time he trembled and clasped his hands, and prayed for his friend, and gave glory to God that he himself was escaped out of that trouble.

But the next day came very brightly, and that new house of his was so delightful to behold that he forgot his terrors. One day followed another, and Keawe dwelt there in perpetual joy. He had his place on the back porch; it was there he ate and lived, and read the stories in the Honolulu newspapers; but when anyone came by they would go in and view the chambers and the pictures. And the fame of the house went far and wide; it was called *Ka-Hale Nui*—the Great House—in all Kona; and sometimes the Bright House, for Keawe kept a Chinaman, who was all day dusting and furbishing; and the glass, and the gilt, and the fine stuffs, and the pictures, shone as bright as the morning. As for Keawe himself, he could not walk in the chambers without singing, his heart was so enlarged; and when ships sailed by upon the sea, he would fly his colours on the mast.

So time went by, until one day Keawe went upon a visit as far as Kailua to certain of his friends. There he was well feasted; and left as soon as he could the next morning, and rode hard, for he was impatient to behold his beautiful house; and, besides, the night then coming on was the night in which the dead of old days go abroad in the sides of Kona; and having already meddled with the devil, he was the more chary of meeting with the dead. A little beyond Honaunau, looking far ahead, he was aware of a woman bathing in the edge of the sea; and she seemed a well-grown girl, but he thought no more of it. Then he saw her white shift flutter as she put it on, and then her red holoku; and by the time he came abreast of her she was done with her toilet, and had come up from the sea, and stood by the track-side in her red holoku, and she was all freshened with the bath, and her eyes shone and were kind. Now Keawe no sooner beheld her than he drew rein.

"I thought I knew every one in this country," said he. "How comes it that I do not know you?"

"I am Kokua, daughter of Kiano," said the girl, "and I have just returned from Oahu. Who are you?"

"I will tell you who I am in a little," said Keawe, dismounting from his horse, "but not now. For I have a thought in my mind, and if you knew who I was, you might have heard of me, and would not give me a true answer. But tell me, first of all, one thing: are you married?"

At this Kokua laughed out aloud. "It is you who ask questions," she said. "Are you married yourself?"

"Indeed, Kokua, I am not," replied Keawe, "and never thought to be until this hour. But here is the plain truth. I have met you here at the road-side, and I saw your eyes, which are like the stars, and my heart went to you as swift as a bird. And so now, if you want none of me, say so, and I will go on to my own place; if you think me no worse than any other young man, say so, too, and I will turn aside to your father's for the night, and tomorrow I will talk with the good man."

Kokua said never a word, but she looked at the sea and laughed.

"Kokua," said Keawe, "if you say nothing, I will take that for the good answer; so let us be stepping to your father's door."

She went on ahead of him, still without speech; only sometimes she glanced back and glanced away again, and she kept the strings of her hat in her mouth.

Now, when they had come to the door, Kiano came out on his verandah, and cried out and welcomed Keawe by name. At that the girl looked over, for the fame of the great house had come to her ears; and, to be sure, it was a great temptation. All that evening they were very merry together; and the girl was as bold as brass under the eyes of her parents, and made a mock of Keawe, for she had a quick wit. The next day he had a word with Kiano, and found the girl alone.

"Kokua," said he, "you made a mock of me all the evening; and it is still time to bid me go. I would not tell you who I was, because I have so fine a house, and I feared you would think too much of that house and too little of the man who loves you. Now you know all, and if you wish to have seen the last of me, say so at once."

"No," said Kokua, but this time she did not laugh, nor did Keawe ask for more.

This was the wooing of Keawe; things had gone quickly; but so an arrow goes, and the ball of a rifle swifter still, and yet both may strike the target. Things had gone fast, but they had gone far also, and the thought of Keawe rang in the maiden's head; she heard his voice in the breach of the surf upon the lava, and for this young man that she had seen but twice she would have left father and mother and her native islands. As for Keawe himself, his horse flew up the path of the mountain under the cliff of tombs, and the sound of the hoofs, and the sound of Keawe singing to himself for pleasure, echoed in the caverns of the dead. He came to the Bright House, and still he was singing. He sat and ate in the broad balcony, and the Chinaman wondered at his master, to hear how he sang between the mouthfuls. The sun went down into the sea, and the night came; and Keawe walked the balconies by lamplight, high on the mountains, and the voice of his singing startled men on ships.

"Here am I now upon my high place," he said to himself. "Life may be no better; this is the mountain top; and all shelves about me toward the worse. For the first time I will light up the chambers, and bathe in my fine bath with the hot water and the cold, and sleep above in the bed of my bridal chamber."

So the Chinaman had word, and he must rise from sleep and light the furnaces; and as he wrought below, beside the boilers, he heard his master singing and rejoicing above him in the lighted chambers. When the water began to be hot the Chinaman cried to his master: and Keawe went into the bathroom; and the Chinaman heard him sing as he filled the marble basin; and heard him sing, and the singing broken, as he undressed; until of a sudden, the song ceased. The Chinaman listened, and listened; he called up the house to Keawe to ask if all were well, and Keawe answered him "Yes," and bade him go to bed; but there was no more singing in the Bright House; and all night long the Chinaman heard his master's feet go round and round the balconies without repose.

Now, the truth of it was this: as Keawe undressed for his bath, he spied upon his flesh a patch like a patch lichen on a rock, and it was then that he stopped singing. For he knew the likeness of that patch, and knew that he was fallen in the Chinese Evil.

Now, it is a sad thing for any man to fall into this sickness. And it would be a sad thing for anyone to leave a house so beautiful and so commodious, and depart from all his friends to the north coast of Molokai, between the mighty cliff and the sea-breakers. But what was that to the case of the man Keawe, he who had met his love but yesterday and won her but that morning, and now saw all his hopes break, in a moment, like a piece of glass?

A while he sat upon the edge of the bath, then sprang, with a cry, and ran outside; and to and fro, to and fro, along the balcony, like one despairing.

"Very willingly could I leave Hawaii, the home of my fathers," Keawe was thinking. "Very lightly could I leave my house, the high-placed, the many-windowed, here upon the mountains. Very bravely could I go to Molokai, to Kalaupapa by the cliffs, to live with the smitten and to sleep there, far from my fathers. But what wrong have I done, what sin lies upon my soul, that I should have encountered Kokua coming cool from the sea-water in the evening? Kokua, the soul ensnarer! Kokua, the light of my life! Her may I never wed, her may I look upon no longer, her may I no more handle with my loving hand; and it is for this, it is for you, O Kokua! that I pour my lamentations!"

Now you are to observe what sort of a man Keawe was, for he might have dwelt there in the Bright House for years, and no one been the wiser of his sickness; but he reckoned nothing of that, if he must lose Kokua. And again he might have wed Kokua even as he was; and so many would have done, because they have the souls of pigs; but Keawe loved the maid manfully, and he would do her no hurt and bring her in no danger.

A little beyond the midst of the night, there came in his mind the recollection of that bottle. He went round to the back porch, and called to memory the day when the devil had looked forth; and at the thought ice ran in his veins.

"A dreadful thing is the bottle," thought Keawe, "and dreadful is the imp, and it is a dreadful thing to risk the flames of hell. But what other hope have I to cure my sickness or to wed Kokua? What!" he thought, "would I beard the devil once, only to get me a house, and not face him again to win Kokua?"

Thereupon he called to mind it was the next day the *Hall* went by on her return to Honolulu. "There must I go first," he thought, "and see Lopaka. For the best hope that I have now is to find that same bottle I was so pleased to be rid of."

Never a wink could he sleep; the food stuck in his throat; but he sent a letter to Kiano, and about the time when the steamer would be coming, rode down beside the cliff of the tombs. It rained; his horse went heavily; he looked up at the black mouths of the caves, and he envied the dead that slept there and were done with trouble; and called to mind how he had galloped by the day before, and was astonished. So he came down to Hookena, and there was all the country gathered for the steamer as usual. In the shed before the store they sat and jested and passed the news; but there was no matter of speech in Keawe's bosom, and he sat in their midst and looked without on the rain falling on the houses, and the surf beating among the rocks, and the sighs arose in his throat.

"Keawe of the Bright House is out of spirits," said one to another. Indeed, and so he was, and little wonder.

Then the *Hall* came, and the whale-boat carried him on board. The after-part of the ship was full of Haoles—who had been to visit the volcano, as their custom is; and the midst was crowded with Kanakas, and the fore-part with wild bulls from Hilo and horses from Kaü; but Keawe sat apart from all in his sorrow, and watched for the house of Kiano. There it sat low upon the shore in the black rocks, and shaded by the cocoa-palms, and there by the door was a red holoku, no greater than a fly, and going to and fro with a fly's busyness. "Ah, queen of my heart," he cried, "I'll venture my dear soul to win you!"

Soon after darkness fell and the cabins were lit up, and the Haoles sat and played at the cards and drank whiskey as their custom is; but Keawe walked the deck all night; and all the next day, as they steamed under the lea of Maui or of Molokai, he was still pacing to and fro like a wild animal in a menagerie.

Towards evening they passed Diamond Head, and came to the pier of Honolulu. Keawe stepped out among the crowd and began to ask for Lopaka. It seemed he had become the owner of a schooner—none better in the islands—and was gone upon an adventure as far as Pola-Pola or Kahiki; so there was no help to be looked for from Lopaka. Keawe called to mind a friend of his, a lawyer in the town (I must not tell his name), and inquired of him. They said he was grown suddenly rich, and had a fine new house upon Waikiki shore; and this put a thought in Keawe's head, and he called a hack and drove to the lawyer's house.

The house was all brand new, and the trees in the garden no greater than walking-sticks, and the lawyer, when he came, had the air of a man well pleased.

"What can I do to serve you?" said the lawyer.

"You are a friend of Lopaka's," replied Keawe, "and Lopaka purchased from me a certain piece of goods that I thought you might enable me to trace."

The lawyer's face became very dark. "I do not profess to misunderstand you, Mr. Keawe," said he, "though this is an ugly business to be stirring in. You may be sure I know nothing, but yet I have a guess, and if you would apply in a certain quarter I think you might have news."

And he named the name of a man, which, again, I had better not repeat. So it was for days, and Keawe went from one to another, finding everywhere new clothes and carriages, and fine new houses and men everywhere in great contentment, although, to be sure, when he hinted at his business their faces would cloud over.

"No doubt I am upon the track," thought Keawe. "These new clothes and carriages are all the gifts of the little imp, and these glad faces are the faces of men who have taken their profit and got rid of the accursed thing in safety. When I see pale cheeks and hear sighing, I shall know that I am near the bottle."

So it befell at last he was recommended to a Haole in Beritania Street. When he came to the door, about the hour of the evening meal, there were the usual marks of the new house, and the young garden, and the electric light shining in the windows; but when the owner came, a shock of hope and fear ran through Keawe; for here was a young man, white as a corpse, and black about the eyes, the hair shedding from his head, and such a look in his countenance as a man may have when he is waiting for the gallows.

"Here it is, to be sure," thought Keawe, and so with this man he noways veiled his errand. "I am come to buy the bottle!" said he.

At the word, the young Haole of Beritania Street reeled against the wall.

"The bottle!" he gasped. "To buy the bottle!" Then he seemed to choke, and seizing Keawe by the arm, carried him into a room and poured out wine in two glasses.

"Here is my respects," said Keawe, who had been much about with Haoles in his time. "Yes," he added, "I am come to buy the bottle. What is the price by now?"

At that word the young man let his glass slip through his fingers, and looked upon Keawe like a ghost.

"The price," says he; "the price! You do not know the price?"

"It is for that I am asking you," returned Keawe. "But why are you so much concerned? Is there anything wrong about the price?"

"It has dropped a great deal in value since your time, Mr. Keawe," said the young man, stammering.

"Well, well, I shall have the less to pay for it," says Keawe. "How much did it cost you?"

The young man was as white as a sheet. "Two cents," said he.

"What?" cried Keawe, "two cents? Why, then, you can only sell it for one. And he who buys it—" The words died upon Keawe's tongue; he who bought it could never sell it again, the bottle and the bottle imp must abide with him until he died, and when he died must carry him to the red end of hell.

The young man of Beritania Street fell upon his knees. "For God's sake, buy it!" he cried. "You can have all my fortune in the bargain. I was mad when I bought it at that price. I had embezzled money at my store; I was lost else; I must have gone to jail."

"Poor creature," said Keawe, "you would risk your soul upon so desperate an adventure, and to avoid the proper punishment of your own disgrace; and you think I could hesitate with love in front of me. Give me the bottle, and the change which I make sure you have all ready. Here is a five-cent piece."

It was as Keawe supposed; the young man had the change ready in a drawer; the bottle changed hands, and Keawe's fingers were no sooner clasped upon the stalk than he had breathed his wish to be a clean man. And, sure enough, when he got home to his room, and stripped himself before a glass, his flesh was whole like an infant's. And here was the strange thing: he had no sooner seen this miracle than his mind was changed within him, and he cared naught for the Chinese Evil, and little enough for Kokua; and had but the one thought, that here he was bound to the bottle imp for time and for eternity, and had no better hope but to be a cinder for ever in the flames of hell. Away ahead of him he saw them blaze with his mind's eye, and his soul shrank, and darkness fell upon the light.

When Keawe came to himself a little, he was aware it was the night when the band played at the hotel. Thither he went, because he feared to be alone; and there, among happy faces, walked to and fro, and heard the tunes go up and down, and saw Berger beat the measure, and all the while he heard the flames crackle and saw the red fire burning in the bottomless pit. Of a sudden the band played *Hiki-ao-ao*; that was a song that he had sung with Kokua, and at the strain courage returned to him.

"It is done now," he thought, "and once more let me take the good along with the evil."

So it befell that he returned to Hawaii by the first steamer, and as soon as it could be managed he was wedded to Kokua, and carried her up the mountain side to the Bright House.

Now it was so with these two, that when they were together Keawe's heart was stilled; but so soon as he was alone he fell into a brooding horror, and heard the flames crackle, and saw the red fire burn in the bottomless pit. The girl, indeed, had come to him wholly; her heart leaped in her side at sight of him, her hand clung to his; and she was so fashioned, from the hair upon her head to the nails upon her toes, that none could see her without joy. She was pleasant in her nature. She had the good word always. Full of song she was, and went to and fro in the Bright House, the brightest thing in its three stories, carolling like the birds. And Keawe beheld and heard her with delight, and then must shrink upon one side, and weep and groan to think upon the price that he had paid for her; and then he must dry his eyes, and wash his face, and go and sit with her on the broad balconies joining in her songs, and, with a sick spirit, answering her smiles.

There came a day when her feet began to be heavy and her songs more rare; and now it was not Keawe only that would weep apart, but each would sunder from the other and sit in opposite balconies with the whole width of the Bright House betwixt. Keawe was so sunk in his despair, he scarce observed the change, and was only glad he had more hours to sit alone and brood upon his destiny, and was not so frequently condemned to pull a smiling face on a sick heart. But one day, coming softly through the house, he heard the sound of a child sobbing, and there was Kokua rolling her face upon the balcony floor, and weeping like the lost.

"You do well to weep in this house, Kokua," he said. "And yet I would give the head off my body that you (at least) might have been happy."

"Happy!" she cried. "Keawe, when you lived alone in your Bright House you were the word of the island for a happy man;

laughter and song were in your mouth, and your face was as bright as the sunrise. Then you wedded poor Kokua; and the good God knows what is amiss in her—but from that day you have not smiled. Oh!" she cried, "what ails me? I thought I was pretty, and I knew I loved him. What ails me, that I throw this cloud upon my husband?"

"Poor Kokua," said Keawe. He sat down by her side, and sought to take her hand; but that she plucked away. "Poor Kokua," he said again. "My poor child—my pretty. And I had thought all this while to spare you! Well, you shall know all. Then, at least, you will pity poor Keawe; then you will understand how much he loved you in the past—that he dared hell for your possession—and how much he loves you still (the poor condemned one), that he can yet call up a smile when he beholds you."

With that he told her all, even from the beginning.

"You have done this for me?" she cried. "Ah, well, then what do I care!" and she clasped and wept upon him.

"Ah, child!" said Keawe, "and yet, when I consider of the fire of hell, I care a good deal!"

"Never tell me," said she, "no man can be lost because he loved Kokua, and no other fault. I tell you, Keawe, I shall save you with these hands, or perish in your company. What! you loved me and gave your soul, and you think I will not die to save you in return?"

"Ah, my dear, you might die a hundred times, and what difference would that make?" he cried, "except to leave me lonely till the time comes for my damnation?"

"You know nothing," said she. "I was educated in a school in Honolulu; I am no common girl. And I tell you I shall save my lover. What is this you say about a cent? But all the world is not American. In England they have a piece they call a farthing, which is about half a cent. Ah! sorrow!" she cried, "that makes it scarcely better, for the buyer must be lost, and we shall find none so brave as my Keawe! But, then, there is France; they have a small coin there which they call a centime, and these go five to the cent, or thereabout. We could not do better. Come, Keawe, let us go to the French islands; let us go to Tahiti, as fast as ships can bear us. There we have four centimes, three centimes, two centimes, one centime; four possible sales to come and go on; and two of us to push the bargain. Come, my Keawe! kiss me, and banish care. Kokua will defend you."

"Gift of God!" he cried. "I cannot think that God will punish me for desiring aught so good. Be it as you will, then, take me where you please: I put my life and my salvation in your hands."

Early the next day Kokua was about her preparations. She took Keawe's chest that he went with sailoring; and first she put the bottle in a corner, and then packed it with the richest of their clothes and the bravest of the knick-knacks in the house. "For," said she, "we must seem to be rich folks, or who would believe in the bottle?" All the time of her preparation she was as gay as a bird; only when she looked upon Keawe the tears would spring in her eye, and she must run and kiss him. As for Keawe, a weight was off his soul; now that he had his secret shared, and some hope in front of him, he seemed like a new man, his feet went lightly on the earth, and his breath was good to him again. Yet was terror still at his elbow; and ever and again, as the wind blows out a taper, hope died in him, and he saw the flames toss and the red fire burn in hell.

It was given out in the country they were gone pleasuring to the States, which was thought a strange thing, and yet not so strange as the truth, if any could have guessed it. So they went to Honolulu in the *Hall*, and thence in the *Umatilla* to San Francisco with a crowd of Haoles, and at San Francisco took their passage by the mail brigantine, the *Tropic Bird*, for Papeete, the chief place of the French in the south islands. Thither they came, after a pleasant voyage, on a fair day of the trade wind, and saw the reef with the surf breaking and Motuiti with its palms, and the schooner riding withinside, and the white houses of the town low down along the shore among green trees, and overhead the mountains and the clouds of Tahiti, the wise island.

It was judged the most wise to hire a house, which they did accordingly, opposite the British Consul's, to make a great parade of money, and themselves conspicuous with carriages and horses. This it was very easy to do, so long as they had the bottle in their possession; for Kokua was more bold than Keawe, and, whenever she had a mind, called on the imp for twenty or a hundred dollars. At this rate they soon grew to be remarked in the town; and the strangers from Hawaii, their riding and their driving, the fine holokus, and the rich lace of Kokua, became the matter of much talk.

They got on well after the first with the Tahitia language, which is indeed like to the Hawaiian, with a change of certain letters; and as soon as they had any freedom of speech, began to push the bottle. You are to consider it was not an easy subject to introduce; it was not easy to persuade people you are in earnest, when you offer to sell them for four centimes the spring of health and riches inexhaustible. It was necessary besides to explain the dangers of the bottle; and either people disbelieved the whole thing and laughed, or they thought the more of the darker part, became overcast with gravity, and drew away from Keawe and Kokua, as from persons who had dealings with the devil. So far from gaining ground, these two began to find they were avoided in the town; the children ran away from them screaming, a thing intolerable to Kokua; Catholics crossed themselves as they went by; and all persons began with one accord to disengage themselves from their advances.

Depression fell upon their spirits. They would sit at night in their new house, after a day's weariness, and not exchange one word, or the silence would be broken by Kokua bursting suddenly into sobs. Sometimes they would pray together; sometimes they would have the bottle out upon the floor, and sit all evening watching how the shadow hovered in the midst. At such times they would be afraid to go to rest. It was long ere slumber came to them, and, if either dozed off, it would be to wake and find the other silently weeping in the dark, or, perhaps, to wake alone, the other having fled from the house and the neighbourhood of that bottle, to pace under the bananas in the little garden, or to wander on the beach by moonlight.

One night it was so when Kokua awoke. Keawe was gone. She

felt in the bed and his place was cold. Then fear fell upon her, and she sat up in bed. A little moonshine filtered through the shutters. The room was bright, and she could spy that bottle on the floor. Outside it blew high, the great trees of the avenue cried aloud, and the fallen leaves rattled in the verandah. In the midst of this Kokua was aware of another sound; whether of a beast or of a man she could scarce tell, but it was as sad as death, and cut her to the soul. Softly she arose, set the door ajar, and looked forth into the moonlit yard. There, under the bananas, lay Keawe, his mouth in the dust, and as he lay he moaned.

It was Kokua's first thought to run forward and console him; her second potently withheld her. Keawe had borne himself before his wife like a brave man; it became her little in the hour of weakness to intrude upon his shame. With the thought she drew back into the house.

"Heaven," she thought, "how careless have I been—how weak! It is he, not I, that stands in this eternal peril; it was he, not I, that took the curse upon his soul. It is for my sake, and for the love of a creature of so little worth and such poor help, that he now beholds so close to him the flames of hell—ay, and smells the smoke of it, lying without there in the wind and moonlight. Am I so dull of spirit that never till now I have surmised my duty, or have I seen it before and turned aside? But now, at least, I take up my soul in both the hands of my affection; now I say farewell to the white steps of heaven and the waiting faces of my friends. A love for a love, and let mine be equalled with Keawe's! A soul for a soul, and be it mine to perish!"

She was a deft woman with her hands, and was soon apparelled. She took in her hands the change—the precious centimes they kept ever at their side; for this coin is little used, and they had made provision at a government office. When she was forth in the avenue clouds came on the wind, and the moon was blackened. The town slept, and she knew not whither to turn till she heard one coughing in the shadow of the trees.

"Old man," said Kokua, "what do you here abroad in the cold night?"

The old man could scarce express himself for coughing, but she made out that he was old and poor, and a stranger in the island.

"Will you do me a service?" said Kokua. "As one stranger to another, and as an old man to a young woman, will you help a daughter of Hawaii?"

"Ah," said the old man. "So you are the witch from the Eight Islands, and even my old soul you seek to entangle. But I have heard of you, and defy your wickedness."

"Sit down here," said Kokua, "and let me tell you a tale." And she told him the story of Keawe from the beginning to the end.

"And now," said she, "I am his wife, whom he bought with his soul's welfare. And what should I do? If I went to him myself and offered to buy it, he would refuse. But if you go, he will sell it eagerly; I will await you here; you will buy it for four centimes, and I will buy it again for three. And the Lord strengthen a poor girl!"

"If you meant falsely," said the old man, "I think God would strike you dead."

"He would!" cried Kokua. "Be sure He would. I could not be so treacherous—God would not suffer it."

"Give me the four centimes and await me here," said the old man.

Now, when Kokua stood alone in the street, her spirit died. The wind roared in the trees, and it seemed to her the rushing of the flames of hell; the shadows towered in the light of the street lamp, and they seemed to her the snatching hands of evil ones. If she had had the strength, she must have run away, and if she had had the breath, she must have screamed aloud; but, in truth, she could do neither, and stood and trembled in the avenue, like an affrighted child.

Then she saw the old man returning, and he had the bottle in his hand.

"I have done your bidding," said he, "I left your husband weeping like a child; to-night he will sleep easy." And he held the bottle forth.

"Before you give it me," Kokua panted, "take the good with the evil—ask to be delivered from your cough."

"I am an old man," replied the other, "and too near the gate of the grave to take a favour from the devil. But what is this? Why do you not take the bottle? Do you hesitate?"

"Not hesitate!" cried Kokua. "I am only weak. Give me a moment. It is my hand resists, my flesh shrinks back from the accursed thing. One moment only!"

The old man looked upon Kokua kindly. "Poor child!" said he, "you fear; your soul misgives you. Well, let me keep it. I am old, and can never more be happy in this world, and as for the next—"

"Give it me!" gasped Kokua. "There is your money. Do you think I am so base as that? Give me the bottle."

"God bless you, child," said the old man.

Kokua concealed the bottle under her holoku, said farewell to the old man, and walked off along the avenue, she cared not whither. For all roads were now the same to her, and led equally to hell. Sometimes she walked, and sometimes ran; sometimes she screamed out loud in the night, and sometimes lay by the wayside in the dust and wept. All that she had heard of hell came back to her; she saw the flames blaze, and she smelled the smoke, and her flesh withered on the coals.

Near day she came to her mind again, and returned to the house. It was even as the old man said—Keawe slumbered like a child. Kokua stood and gazed upon his face.

"Now, my husband," said she, "it is your turn to sleep. When you wake it will be your turn to sing and laugh. But for poor Kokua, alas! that meant no evil—for poor Kokua no more sleep, no more singing, no more delight, whether in earth or heaven."

With that she lay down in the bed by his side, and her misery was so extreme that she fell in a deep slumber instantly.

Late in the morning her husband woke her and gave her the good news. It seemed he was silly with delight, for he paid no heed to her distress, ill though she dissembled it. The words stuck in her mouth, it mattered not; Keawe did the speaking. She ate not a bite, but who was to observe it? For Keawe cleared the dish. Kokua saw and heard him, like some strange thing in a dream; there were times when she forgot or doubted, and put her hands to her brow; to know herself doomed and hear her husband babble seemed so monstrous.

All the while Keawe was eating and talking, and planning the time of their return, and thanking her for saving him, and fondling her, and calling her the true helper after all. He laughed at the old man that was fool enough to buy that bottle.

"A worthy old man he seemed," Keawe said. "But no one can judge by appearances. For why did the old reprobate require the bottle?"

"My husband," said Kokua humbly, "his purpose may have been good."

Keawe laughed like an angry man.

"Fiddle-de-dee!" cried Keawe. "An old rogue, I tell you; and an old ass to boot. For the bottle was hard enough to sell at four centimes; and at three it will be quite impossible. The margin is not broad enough, the thing begins to smell of scorching—brrr!" said he, and shuddered. "It is true I bought it myself at a cent, when I knew not there were smaller coins. I was a fool for my pains; there will never be found another, and whoever has that bottle now will carry it to the pit."

"O my husband!" said Kokua. "Is it not a terrible thing to save oneself by the eternal ruin of another? It seems to me I could not laugh. I would be humbled. I would be filled with melancholy. I would pray for the poor holder."

Then Keawe, because he felt the truth of what she said, grew the more angry. "Heighty-teighty!" cried he. "You may be filled with melancholy if you please. It is not the mind of a good wife. If you thought at all of me, you would sit shamed."

Thereupon be went out, and Kokua was alone.

What chance had she to sell that bottle at two centimes? None, she perceived. And if she had any, here was her husband hurrying her away to a country where there was nothing lower than a cent. And here—on the morrow of her sacrifice—was her husband leaving her and blaming her.

She would not even try to profit by what time she had, but sat in the house, and now had the bottle out and viewed it with unutterable fear, and now, with loathing, hid it out of sight.

By and by, Keawe came back, and would have her take a drive.

"My husband, I am ill," she said. "I am out of heart. Excuse me, I can take no pleasure."

Then was Keawe more wroth than ever. With her, because he thought she was brooding over the case of the old man; and with himself, because he thought she was right and was ashamed to be so happy.

"This is your truth," cried he, "and this your affection! Your husband is just saved from eternal ruin, which he encountered for the love of you—and you can take no pleasure! Kokua, you have a disloyal heart."

He went forth again furious, and wandered in the town all day. He met friends, and drank with them; they hired a carriage and drove into the country, and there drank again. All the time Keawe was ill at ease, because he was taking this pastime while his wife was sad, and because he knew in his heart that she was more right than he; and the knowledge made him drink the deeper.

Now there was an old brutal Haole drinking with him, one that had been a boatswain of a whaler—a runaway, a digger in gold mines, a convict in prisons. He had a low mind and a foul mouth; he loved to drink and to see others drunken; and he pressed the glass upon Keawe. Soon there was no more money in the company.

"Here, you!" says the boatswain, "you are rich, you have been always saying. You have a bottle or some foolishness."

"Yes," says Keawe, "I am rich; I will go back and get some money from my wife, who keeps it."

"That's a bad idea, mate," said the boatswain. "Never you trust a petticoat with dollars. They're all as false as water; you keep an eye on her."

Now this word stuck in Keawe's mind; for he was muddled with what he had been drinking.

"I should not wonder but she was false, indeed," thought he. "Why else should she be so cast down at my release? But I will show her I am not the man to be fooled. I will catch her in the act."

Accordingly, when they were back in town, Keawe bade the boatswain wait for him at the corner, by the old calaboose, and went forward up the avenue alone to the door of his house. The night had come again; there was a light within, but never a sound; and Keawe crept about the corner, opened the back door softly, and looked in.

There was Kokua on the floor, the lamp at her side; before her was a milk-white bottle, with a round belly and a long neck; and as she viewed it, Kokua wrung her hands.

A long time Keawe stood and looked in the doorway. At first he was struck stupid; and then fear fell upon him that the bargain had been made amiss, and the bottle had come back to him as it came at San Francisco; and at that his knees were loosened, and the fumes of the wine departed from his head like mists off a river in the morning. And then he had another thought; and it was a strange one, that made his cheeks to burn.

"I must make sure of this," thought he.

So he closed the door, and went softly round the corner again, and then came noisily in, as though he were but now returned. And, lo! by the time he opened the front door no bottle was to be seen; and Kokua sat in a chair and started up like one awakened out of sleep.

"I have been drinking all day and making merry," said Keawe. "I have been with good companions, and now I only come back for money, and return to drink and carouse with them again."

Both his face and voice were as stern as judgment, but Kokua was too troubled to observe.

"You do well to use your own, my husband," said she, and her words trembled.

"Oh, I do well in all things," said Keawe, and he went

straight to the chest and took out money. But he looked besides in the corner where they kept the bottle, and there was no bottle there.

At that the chest heaved upon the floor like a sea-billow, and the house span about him like a wreath of smoke, for he saw she was lost now, and there was no escape. "It is what I feared," he thought. "It is she who has bought it."

And then he came to himself a little and rose up; but the sweat streamed on his face as thick as the rain and as cold as the well-water.

"Kokua," said he, "I said to you to-day what ill became me. Now I return to house with my jolly companions," and at that he laughed a little quietly. "I will take more pleasure in the cup if you forgive me."

She clasped his knees in a moment, she kissed his knees with flowing tears.

"Oh," she cried, "I ask but a kind word!"

"Let us never one think hardly of the other," said Keawe, and was gone out of the house.

Now, the money that Keawe had taken was only some of that store of centime pieces they had laid in at their arrival. It was very sure he had no mind to be drinking. His wife had given her soul for him, now he must give his for hers; no other thought was in the world with him.

At the corner, by the old calaboose, there was the boatswain waiting.

"My wife has the bottle," said Keawe, "and, unless you help me to recover it, there can be no more money and no more liquor to-night."

"You do not mean to say you are serious about that bottle?" cried the boatswain.

"There is the lamp," said Keawe. "Do I look as if I was jesting?"

"That is so," said the boatswain. "You look as serious as a ghost."

"Well, then," said Keawe, "here are two centimes; you must go to my wife in the house, and offer her these for the bottle, which (if I am not much mistaken) she will give you instantly. Bring it to me here, and I will buy it back from you for one; for that is the law with this bottle that it must still be sold for a less sum. But whatever you do, never breathe a word to her that you have come from me."

"Mate, I wonder are you making a fool of me?" asked the boatswain.

"It will do you no harm if I am," returned Keawe.

"That is so, mate," said the boatswain.

"And if you doubt me," added Keawe, "you can try. As soon as you are clear of the house, wish to have your pocket full of money, or a bottle of the best rum, or what you please, and you will see the virtue of the thing."

"Very well, Kanaka," says the boatswain. "I will try; but if you are having your fun out of me, I will take my fun out of you with a belaying-pin."

So the whaler-man went off up the avenue; and Keawe stood and waited. It was near the same spot where Kokua had waited the night before; but Keawe was more resolved, and never faltered in his purpose; only his soul was bitter with despair.

It seemed a long time he had to wait before he heard a voice singing in the darkness of the avenue. He knew the voice to be the boatswain's; but it was strange how drunken it appeared upon a sudden.

Next, the man himself came stumbling into the light of the lamp. He had the devil's bottle buttoned to his coat; another bottle was in his hand; and even as he came in view he raised it to his mouth and drank.

"You have it," said Keawe. "I see that."

"Hands off!" cried the boatswain, jumping back. "Take a step near me, and I'll smash your mouth. You thought you could make a cat's-paw of me, did you?"

"What do you mean?" cried Keawe.

"Mean?" cried the boatswain. "This is a pretty good bottle, this is; that's what I mean. How I got it for two centimes I can't make out; but I am sure you sha'nt have it for one."

"You mean you won't sell it?" gasped Keawe.

"No, *sir*," cried the boatswain. "But I'll give you a drink of the rum, if you like."

"I tell you," said Keawe, "the man who has that bottle goes to hell."

"I reckon I'm going anyway," returned the sailor; "and this bottle's the best thing to go with I've struck yet. No, sir!" he cried again, "this is my bottle now, and you can go and fish for another."

"Can this be true?" Keawe cried. "For your own sake, I beseech you, sell it me!"

"I don't value any of your talk," replied the boatswain. "You thought I was a flat, now you see I'm not; and there's an end. If you won't have a swallow of the rum, I'll have one myself. Here's your health, and good-night to you!"

So off he went down the avenue towards town, and there goes the bottle out of the story.

But Keawe ran to Kokua light as the wind; and great was their joy that night; and great, since then, has been the peace of all their days in the Bright House.

THE GREAT GOD PAN

Arthur Machen

(1894)

One could hardly do better than quote H. P. Lovecraft, a master of horror himself and a great connoisseur of the great figures of this tradition, on the special qualities of this story: "No one could begin to describe the cumulative suspense and ultimate horror with which every paragraph abounds . . . the sensitive reader reaches the end with only an appreciative shudder and a tendency to repeat the words of one of the characters: 'It is too incredible, too monstrous; such things can never be in this quiet world.'"

1. The Experiment

"I am glad you came, Clarke; very glad indeed. I was not sure you could spare the time."

"I was able to make arrangements for a few days; things are not very lively just now. But have you no misgivings, Raymond? Is it absolutely safe?"

The two men were slowly pacing the terrace in front of Dr. Raymond's house. The sun still hung above the western mountain line, but it shone with a dull red glow that cast no shadows, and all the air was quiet; a sweet breath came from the great wood on the hillside above, and with it, at intervals, the soft murmuring call of the wild doves. Below, in the long lovely valley, the river wound in and out between the lonely hills, and, as the sun hovered and vanished into the west, a faint mist, pure white, began to rise from the banks. Dr. Raymond turned sharply to his friend.

"Safe? Of course it is. In itself the operation is a perfectly simple one; any surgeon could do it."

"And there is no danger at any other stage?"

"None; absolutely no physical danger whatever, I give you my word. You are always timid, Clarke, always; but you know my history. I have devoted myself to transcendental medicine for the last twenty years. I have heard myself called quack and charlatan and impostor, but all the while I knew I was on the right path. Five years ago I reached the goal, and since then every day has been a preparation for what we shall do tonight."

"I should like to believe it is all true." Clarke knit his brows, and looked doubtfully at Dr. Raymond. "Are you perfectly sure, Raymond, that your theory is not a phantasmagoria—a splendid vision, certainly, but a mere vision after all?"

Dr. Raymond stopped in his walk and turned sharply. He was a middle-aged man, gaunt and thin, of a pale yellow complexion, but as he answered Clarke and faced him, there was a flush on his cheek.

"Look about you, Clarke. You see the mountain, and hill following after hill, as wave on wave, you see the woods and orchards, the fields of ripe corn, and the meadows reaching to the reed beds by the river. You see me standing here beside you, and hear my voice; but I tell you that all these things—yes, from that star that has just shone out in the sky to the solid ground beneath our feet—I say that all these are but dreams and shadows: the shadows that hide the real world from our eyes. There *is* a real world, but it is beyond this glamour and this vision, beyond these 'chases in Arras, dreams in a career,' beyond them all as beyond a veil. I do not know whether any human being has ever lifted that veil; but I do know, Clarke, that you and I shall see it lifted this very night from before another's eyes. You may think all this strange nonsense; it may be strange, but it is true, and the ancients knew what lifting the veil means. They called it seeing the god Pan."

Clarke shivered; the white mist gathering over the river was chilly.

"It is wonderful indeed," he said. "We are standing on the brink of a strange world, Raymond, if what you say is true. I suppose the knife is absolutely necessary?"

"Yes; a slight lesion in the grey matter, that is all; a trifling rearrangement of certain cells, a microscopical alteration that would escape the attention of ninety-nine brain specialists out of a hundred. I don't want to bother you with 'shop,' Clarke; I might give you a mass of technical detail which would sound very imposing, and would leave you as enlightened as you are now. But I suppose you have read, casually, in out-of-the-way corners of your paper, that immense strides have been made recently in the physiology of the brain. I saw a paragraph the other day about Digby's theory, and Browne Faber's discoveries. Theories and discoveries! Where they are standing now, I stood fifteen years ago, and I need not tell you that I have not been standing still for the last fifteen years. It will be enough if I say that five years ago I made the discovery to which I alluded when I said that then I reached the goal. After years of labour, after years of toiling and groping in the dark, after days and nights of disappointment and sometimes of despair, in which I used now and then to tremble and grow cold with the thought that perhaps there were others seeking for what I sought, at last, after so long, a pang of sudden joy thrilled my soul, and I knew the long journey was at an end. By what seemed then and still seems a chance, the suggestion of a moment's idle thought followed up upon familiar lines and paths that I had tracked a hundred times already, the great truth burst upon me, and I saw, mapped out in lines of light, a whole world, a sphere unknown; continents and islands, and great oceans in which no ship has sailed (to my belief) since Man first lifted up his eyes and beheld the sun, and the stars of heaven, and the quiet earth beneath. You will think all this high-flown language, Clarke, but it is hard to be literal. And yet; I do not know whether what I am hinting at cannot be set forth in plain and homely terms. For instance, this world of ours is pretty well girded now with the telegraph wires and cables; thought, with something less than the speed of thought, flashes from sunrise to sunset, from north to south, across the floods and the desert places. Suppose that an electrician of today were suddenly to perceive that he and his friends have merely been playing with pebbles and mistaking them for the foundations of the world; suppose that such a man saw uttermost space lie open before the current, and words of men flash forth to the sun and beyond the sun into the systems beyond, and the voices of articulate-speaking men echo in the waste void that bounds our thought. As analogies go, that is a pretty good analogy of what I have done; you can understand now a little of what I felt as I stood here one evening; it was a summer evening, and the valley looked much as it does now; I stood here, and saw before me the unutterable, the unthinkable gulf that yawns profound between two worlds, the world of matter and the world of spirit; I saw the great empty deep stretch dim before me, and in that instant a bridge of light leapt from the earth to the unknown shore, and the abyss was spanned. You may look in Browne Faber's book, if you like, and you will find that to the present day men of science are unable to account for the presence, or to specify the functions of a certain group of nerve cells in the brain. That group is, as it were, land to let, a mere waste place for fanciful theories. I am not in the position of Browne Faber and the specialists, I am perfectly instructed as to the possible functions of those nerve centres in the scheme of things. With a touch I can bring them into play, with a touch, I say, I can set free the current, with a touch I can complete the communication between this world of sense and—we shall be able to finish the sentence later on. Yes, the knife is necessary; but think what that knife will effect. It will level utterly the solid wall of sense, and probably, for the first time since man was made, a spirit will gaze on a spirit world. Clarke, Mary will see the god Pan!"

"But you remember what you wrote to me? I thought it would be requisite that she—"

He whispered the rest into the doctor's ear.

"Not at all, not at all. That is nonsense, I assure you. Indeed, it is better as it is; I am quite certain of that."

"Consider the matter well, Raymond. It's a great responsibility. Something might go wrong; you would be a miserable man for the rest of your days."

"No, I think not, even if the worst happened. As you know, I rescued Mary from the gutter, and from almost certain starvation, when she was a child; I think her life is mine, to use as I see fit. Come, it is getting late; we had better go in."

Dr. Raymond led the way into the house, through the hall, and down a long dark passage. He took a key from his pocket and opened a heavy door, and motioned Clarke into his laboratory. It had once been a billiard-room, and was lighted by a glass dome in the centre of the ceiling, whence there still shone a sad grey light on the figure of the doctor as he lit a lamp with a heavy shade and placed it on a table in the middle of the room.

Clarke looked about him. Scarcely a foot of wall remained bare; there were shelves all around laden with bottles and phials of all shapes and colours, and at one end stood a little Chippendale book-case. Raymond pointed to this.

"You see that parchment Oswald Crollius? He was one of the first to show me the way, though I don't think he ever found it himself. That is a strange saying of his: 'In every grain of wheat there lies hidden the soul of a star.'"

There was not much of furniture in the laboratory. The table in the centre, a stone slab with a drain in one corner, the two armchairs on which Raymond and Clarke were sitting; that was all, except an odd-looking chair at the furthest end of the room. Clarke looked at it, and raised his eyebrows.

"Yes, that is the chair," said Raymond. "We may as well place it in position." He got up and wheeled the chair to the light, and began raising and lowering it, letting down the seat, setting the back at various angles, and adjusting the foot-rest. It looked comfortable enough, and Clarke passed his hand over the soft green velvet, as the doctor manipulated the levers.

"Now, Clarke, make yourself quite comfortable. I have a couple of hours' work before me; I was obliged to leave certain matters to the last."

Raymond went to the stone slab, and Clarke watched him drearily as he bent over a row of phials and lit the flame under the crucible. The doctor had a small hand-lamp, shaded as the larger one, on a ledge above his apparatus, and Clarke, who sat in the shadows, looked down the great dreary room, wondering at the bizarre effects of brilliant light and undefined darkness contrasting with one another. Soon he became conscious of an odd odour, at first the merest suggestion of odour, in the room; and as it grew more decided he felt surprised that he was not reminded of the chemist's shop or the surgery. Clarke found himself idly endeavouring to analyse the sensation, and half conscious, he began to think of a day, fifteen years ago, that he had spent in roaming through the woods and meadows near his old home. It was a burning day at the beginning of August, the heat had dimmed the outlines of all things and all distances with a faint mist, and people who observed the thermometer spoke of an abnormal register, of a temperature that was almost tropical. Strangely that wonderful hot day of the 'fifties rose up in Clarke's imagination; the sense of dazzling all-pervading sunlight seemed to blot out the shadows and the lights of the laboratory, and he felt again the heated air beating in gusts about his face, saw the shimmer rising from the turf, and heard the myriad murmur of the summer.

"I hope the smell doesn't annoy you, Clarke; there's nothing unwholesome about it. It may make you a bit sleepy, that's all."

Clarke heard the words quite distinctly, and knew that Raymond was speaking to him, but for the life of him he could not rouse himself from his lethargy. He could only think of the lonely walk he had taken fifteen years ago; it was his last look at the fields and woods he had known since he was a child, and now it all stood out in brilliant light, as a picture, before him. Above all there came to his nostrils the scent of summer, the smell of flowers mingled, and the odour of the woods, of cool shaded places, deep in the green depths, drawn forth by the sun's heat; and the scent of the good earth, lying as it were with arms stretched forth, and smiling lips, overpowered all. His fancies made him wander, as he had wandered long ago, from the fields into the wood, tracking a little path between the shining undergrowth of beechtrees; and the trickle of water dropping from the limestone rock sounded as a clear melody in the dream. Thoughts began to go astray and to mingle with other recollections; the beech alley was transformed to a path beneath ilex-trees, and here and there a vine climbed from bough to bough, and sent up waving tendrils and drooped with purple grapes, and the sparse grey-green leaves of a wild olive-tree stood out against the dark shadows of the ilex. Clarke, in the deep folds of dream, was conscious that the path from his father's house had led him into an undiscovered country, and he was wondering at the strangeness of it all, when suddenly, in place of the hum and murmur of the summer, an infinite silence seemed to fall on all things, and the wood was hushed, and for a moment of time he stood face to face there with a presence, that was neither man nor beast, neither the living nor the dead, but all things mingled, the form of all things but devoid of all form. And in that moment, the sacrament of body and soul was dissolved, and a voice seemed to cry, "Let us go hence," and then the darkness of darkness beyond the stars, the darkness of everlasting.

When Clarke woke up with a start he saw Raymond pouring a few drops of some oily fluid into a green phial, which he stoppered tightly.

"You have been dozing," he said: "the journey must have tired you out. It is done now. I am going to fetch Mary; I shall be back in ten minutes."

Clarke lay back in his chair and wondered. It seemed as if he had but passed from one dream into another. He half expected to see the walls of the laboratory melt and disappear, and to awake in London, shuddering at his own sleeping fancies. But at last the door opened, and the doctor returned, and behind him came a girl of about seventeen, dressed all in white. She was so beautiful that Clarke did not wonder at what the doctor had written to him. She was blushing now over face and neck and arms, but Raymond seemed unmoved.

"Mary," he said, "the time has come. You are quite free. Are you willing to trust yourself to me entirely?"

"Yes, dear."

"You hear that, Clarke? You are my witness. Here is the chair, Mary. It is quite easy. Just sit in it and lean back. Are you ready?"

"Yes, dear, quite ready. Give me a kiss before you begin."

The doctor stooped and kissed her mouth, kindly enough. "Now shut your eyes," he said. The girl closed her eyelids, as if she were tired, and longed for sleep, and Raymond held the green phial to her nostrils. Her face grew white, whiter than her dress; she struggled faintly, and then with the feeling of submission strong within her, crossed her arms upon her breast as a little child about to say her prayers. The bright light of the lamp beat full upon her, and Clarke watched changes fleeting over that face as the changes of the hills when the summer clouds float across the sun. And then she lay all white and still, and the doctor turned up one of her eyelids. She was quite unconscious. Raymond pressed hard on one of the levers and the chair instantly sank back. Clarke saw him cutting away a circle, like a tonsure, from her hair, and the lamp moved nearer. Raymond took a small glittering instrument from a little case, and Clarke turned away shuddering. When he looked again the doctor was binding up the wound he had made.

"She will awake in five minutes." Raymond was still perfectly cool. "There is nothing more to be done; we can only wait."

The minutes passed slowly; they could hear a slow, heavy ticking. There was an old clock in the passage. Clarke felt sick and faint; his knees shook beneath him, he could hardly stand.

Suddenly, as they watched, they heard a long-drawn sigh, and suddenly did the colour that had vanished return to the girl's cheeks, and suddenly her eyes opened. Clarke quailed before them. They shone with an awful light, looking far away, and a great wonder fell upon her face, and her hands stretched out as if to touch what was invisible; but in an instant the wonder faded, and gave place to the most awful terror. The muscles of her face were hideously convulsed, she shook from head to foot; the soul seemed struggling and shuddering within the house of flesh. It was a horrible sight, and Clarke rushed forward, as she fell shrieking to the floor.

Three days later Raymond took Clarke to Mary's bedside.

She was lying wide-awake, rolling her head from side to side, and grinning vacantly.

"Yes," said the doctor, still quite cool, "it is a great pity; she is a hopeless idiot. However, it could not be helped; and, after all, she has seen the Great God Pan."

2. Mr. Clarke's Memoirs

Mr. Clarke, the gentleman chosen by Dr. Raymond to witness the strange experiment of the god Pan, was a person in whose character caution and curiosity were oddly mingled; in his sober moments he thought of the unusual and the eccentric with undisguised aversion, and yet, deep in his heart, there was a wide-eyed inquisitiveness with respect to all the more recondite and esoteric elements in the nature of men. The latter tendency had prevailed when he accepted Raymond's invitation, for though his considered judgment had always repudiated the doctor's theories as the wildest nonsense, yet he secretly hugged a belief in fantasy, and would have rejoiced to see that belief confirmed. The horrors that he witnessed in the dreary laboratory were to a certain extent salutary; he was conscious of being involved in an affair not altogether reputable, and for many years afterwards he clung bravely to the commonplace, and rejected all occasions of occult investigation. Indeed, on some homoeopathic principle, he for some time attended the séances of distinguished mediums, hoping that the clumsy tricks of these gentlemen would make him altogether disgusted with mysticism of every kind, but the remedy, though caustic, was not efficacious. Clarke knew that he still pined for the unseen, and little by little, the old passion began to reassert itself, as the face of Mary, shuddering and convulsed with an unknowable terror, faded slowly from his memory. Occupied all day in pursuits both serious and lucrative, the temptation to relax in the evening was too great, especially in the winter months, when the fire cast a warm glow over his snug bachelor apartment, and a bottle of some choice claret stood ready by his elbow. His dinner digested, he would make a brief pretence of reading the evening paper, but the mere catalogue of news soon palled upon him, and Clarke would find himself casting glances of warm desire in the direction of an old Japanese bureau, which stood at a pleasant distance from the hearth. Like a boy before a jam-closet, for a few minutes he would hover indecisive, but lust always prevailed, and Clarke ended by drawing up his chair, lighting a candle, and sitting down before the bureau. Its pigeon-holes and drawers teemed with documents on the most morbid subjects, and in the well reposed a large manuscript volume, in which he had painfully entered the gems of his collection. Clarke had a fine contempt for published literature; the most ghostly story ceased to interest him if it happened to be printed; his sole pleasure was in the reading, compiling, and rearranging what he called his "Memoirs to Prove the Existence of the Devil," and engaged in this pursuit the evening seemed to fly and the night appeared too short.

On one particular evening, an ugly December night, black with fog, and raw with frost, Clarke hurried over his dinner, and scarcely deigned to observe his customary ritual of taking up the paper and laying it down again. He paced two or three times up and down the room, and opened the bureau, stood still a moment, and sat down. He leant back, absorbed in one of those dreams to which he was subject, and at length drew out his book, and opened it at the last entry. There were three or four pages densely covered with Clarke's round, set penmanship, and at the beginning he had written in a somewhat larger hand:

> *Singular Narrative told me by my Friend, Dr. Phillips. He assures me that all the facts related therein are strictly and wholly True, but refuses to give either the Surnames of the Persons concerned, or the Place where these Extraordinary Events occurred.*

Mr. Clarke began to read over the account for the tenth time, glancing now and then at the pencil notes he had made when it was told him by his friend. It was one of his humours to pride himself on a certain literary ability; he thought well of his style, and took pains in arranging the circumstances in dramatic order. He read the following story:

The persons concerned in this statement are Helen V., who, if she is still alive, must now be a woman of twenty-three. Rachel M., since deceased, who was a year younger than the above, and Trevor W., an imbecile, aged eighteen. These persons were at the period of the story inhabitants of a village on the borders of Wales, a place of some importance in the time of the Roman occupation, but now a scattered hamlet, of not more than five hundred souls. It is situated on rising ground, about six miles from the sea, and is sheltered by a large and picturesque forest.

Some eleven years ago, Helen V. came to the village under rather peculiar circumstances. It is understood that she, being an orphan, was adopted in her infancy by a distant relative, who brought her up in his own house till she was twelve years old. Thinking, however, that it would be better for the child to have playmates of her own age, he advertised in several local papers for a good home in a comfortable farmhouse for a girl of twelve, and this advertisement was answered by Mr. R., a well-to-do farmer in the above-mentioned village. His references proving satisfactory, the gentleman sent his adopted daughter to Mr. R., with a letter, in which he stipulated that the girl should have a room to herself, and stated that her guardians need be at no trouble in the matter of education, as she was already sufficiently educated for the position in life which she would occupy. In fact, Mr. R. was given to understand that the girl was to be allowed to find her own occupations, and to spend her time almost as she liked. Mr. R. duly met her at the nearest station, at town some seven miles away from his house, and seems to have remarked nothing extraordinary about the child, except that she was reticent as to her former life and her adopted father. She was, however, of a very different type from the inhabitants of the village; her skin was a pale, clear olive, and her features were strongly marked, and of a somewhat foreign character. She appears to have settled down easily enough into farmhouse life, and became a favourite with the children, who sometimes went with her on her rambles in the forest, for this was her amusement. Mr. R. states that he has known her to go out by herself directly after their early breakfast, and not return till after dusk, and that, feeling uneasy at a young girl being out alone for so many hours, he communicated with her adopted father, who replied in a brief note that Helen must do as she chose. In the winter, when the forest paths are impassable, she spent most of her time in her bedroom, where she slept alone, according to the instructions of her relative. It was on one of these expeditions to the forest that the first of the singular incidents with which this girl is connected occurred, the date being about a year after her arrival at the village. The preceding winter had been remarkably severe, the snow drifting to a great depth, and the frost continuing for an unexampled period, and the summer following was as noteworthy for its extreme heat. On one of the very hottest days in this summer, Helen V. left the farmhouse for one of her long rambles in the forest, taking with her, as usual, some bread and meat for lunch. She was seen by some men in the fields making for the old Roman Road, a green causeway which traverses the highest part of the wood, and they were astonished to observe that the girl had taken off her hat, though the heat of the sun was already almost tropical. As it happened, a labourer, Joseph W. by name, was working in the forest near the Roman Road, and at twelve o'clock his little son, Trevor, brought the man his dinner of bread and cheese. After the meal, the boy, who was about seven years old at the time, left his father at work, and, as he said, went to look for flowers in the wood, and the man, who could hear him shouting with delight over his discoveries, felt no uneasiness. Suddenly, however, he was horrified at hearing the most dreadful screams, evidently the result of great terror, proceeding from the direction in which his son had gone, and he hastily threw down his tools and ran to see what had happened. Tracing his path by the sound, he met the little boy, who was running headlong, and was evidently terribly frightened, and on questioning him the man at last elicited that after picking a posy of flowers he felt tired, and lay down on the grass and fell asleep. He was suddenly awakened, as he stated, by a peculiar noise, a sort of singing he called it, and on peeping through the branches he saw Helen V. playing on the grass with a "strange naked man," whom he seemed unable to describe more fully. He said he felt dreadfully frightened, and ran away crying for his father. Joseph W. proceeded in the direction indicated by his son, and found Helen V. sitting on the grass in the middle of a glade or open space left by charcoal burners. He angrily charged her with frightening his little boy, but she entirely denied the accusation and laughed at the child's story of a "strange man," to which he himself did not attach much credence. Joseph W. came to the conclusion that the boy had woke up with a sudden fright, as children sometimes do, but Trevor persisted in his story, and continued in such evident distress that at last his father took him home, hoping that his mother would be able to soothe him. For many weeks, however, the boy gave his parents much anxiety; he became nervous and strange in his manner, refusing to leave the cottage by himself, and constantly alarming the household by waking in the night with cries of "The man in the wood! Father! Father!"

In course of time, however, the impression seemed to have worn off, and about three months later he accompanied his father to the house of a gentleman in the neighbourhood, for whom Joseph W. occasionally did work. The man was shown into the study, and the little boy was left sitting in the hall, and a few minutes later, while the gentleman was giving W. his instructions, they were both horrified by a piercing shriek and the sound of a fall, and rushing out they found the child lying senseless on the floor, his face contorted with terror. The doctor was immediately summoned, and after some examination he pronounced the child to be suffering from a kind of fit, apparently produced by a sudden shock. The boy was taken to one of the bedrooms, and after some time recovered consciousness, but only to pass into a condition described by the medical man as one of violent hysteria. The doctor exhibited a strong sedative, and in the course of two hours pronounced him fit to walk home, but in passing through the hall the paroxysms of fright returned and with additional violence. The father perceived that the child was pointing at some object and heard the old cry, "The man in the wood," and looking in the direction indicated saw a stone head of grotesque appearance, which had been built into the wall above one of the doors. It seems that the owner of the house had recently made alterations in his premises, and on digging the foundation for some offices, the men had found a curious head, evidently of the Roman period, which had been placed in the hall in the manner described. The head is pronounced by the most experienced archaeologists of the district to be that of a faun or satyr.

From whatever cause arising, this second shock seemed too severe for the boy Trevor, and at the present date he suffers from a weakness of intellect, which gives but little promise of amending. The matter caused a good deal of sensation at the time, and the girl Helen was closely questioned by Mr. R., but to no purpose, she steadfastly denying that she had frightened or in any way molested Trevor.

The second event with which this girl's name is connected took place about six years ago, and is of a still more extraordinary character.

At the beginning of the summer of 1882 Helen contracted a friendship of a peculiarly intimate character with Rachel M., the daughter of a prosperous farmer in the neighbourhood. This girl, who was a year younger than Helen, was considered by most people to be the prettier of the two, though Helen's features had to a great extent softened as she became older. The two girls, who were together on every available opportunity, presented a singular contrast, the one with her clear, olive skin and almost Italian appearance, and the other of the proverbial red and white of our rural districts. It must be stated that the payments made to Mr. R. for the maintenance of Helen were known in the village for their excessive liberality, and the impression was general that she would one day inherit a large sum of money from her relative. The parents of Rachel were therefore not averse from their daughter's friendship with the girl, and even encouraged the intimacy, though they now bitterly regret having done so. Helen still retained her extraordinary fondness for the forest, and on several occasions Rachel accompanied her, the two friends setting out early in the morning, and remaining in the wood till dusk. Once or twice after these excursions Mrs. M. thought her daughter's manner rather peculiar; she seemed languid and dreamy, and as it has been expressed, "different from herself," but these peculiarities seem to have been thought too trifling for remark. One evening, however, after Rachel had come home, her mother heard a noise which sounded like suppressed weeping in the girl's room, and on going in found her lying, half undressed, upon the bed, evidently in the greatest distress. As soon as she saw her mother, she exclaimed, "Ah, Mother, Mother, why did you let me go to the forest with Helen?" Mrs. M. was astonished at so strange a question, and proceeded to make inquiries. Rachel told her a wild story. She said—

Clarke closed the door with a snap, and turned his chair towards the fire. When his friend sat one evening in that very chair, and told his story, Clarke had interrupted him at a point a little subsequent to this, had cut short his words in a paroxysm of horror. "My God!" he had exclaimed, "think, think what you are saying. It is too incrediible, too monstrous; such things can never be in this quiet world, where men and women live and die, and struggle, and conquer, or maybe fail, and fall down under sorrow, and grieve and suffer strange fortunes for many a year; but not this, Phillips, not such things as this. There must be some explanation, some way out of the terror. Why, man, if such a case were possible, our earth would be a nightmare."

But Phillips had told his story to the end, concluding:

"Her flight remains a mystery to this day; she vanished in broad sunlight; they saw her walking in a meadow, and a few moments later she was not there."

Clarke tried to conceive the thing again, as he sat by the fire, and again his mind shuddered and shrank back, appalled before the sight of such awful, unspeakable elements enthroned as it were, and triumphant in human flesh. Before him stretched the long dim vista of the green causeway in the forest, as his friend had described it; he saw the swaying leaves and the quivering shadows on the grass, he saw the sunlight and the flowers, and far away, far in the long distance, the two figures moved towards him. One was Rachel, but the other?

Clarke had tried his best to disbelieve it all, but at the end of the account, as he had written it in his book, he had placed the inscription:

ET DIABOLUS INCARNATES EST. ET HOMO FACTUS EST.

3. The City of Resurrections

"Herbert! Good God! Is it possible?"

"Yes, my name's Herbert. I think I know your face too, but I don't remember your name. My memory is very queer."

"Don't you recollect Villiers of Wadham?"

"So it is, so it is. I beg your pardon, Villiers, I didn't think I was begging of an old college friend. Good-night."

"My dear fellow, this haste is unnecessary. My rooms are close by, but we won't go there just yet. Suppose we walk up Shaftesbury Avenue a little way? But how in heaven's name have you come to this pass, Herbert?"

"It's a long story, Villiers, and a strange one, too, but you can hear it if you like."

"Come on, then. Take my arm, you don't seem very strong."

The ill-assorted pair moved slowly up Rupert Street; the one in dirty, evil-looking rags, and the other attired in the regulation uniform of a man about town, trim, glossy, and eminently well-to-do. Villiers had emerged from his restaurant after an excellent dinner of many courses, assisted by an ingratiating little flask of Chianti, and, in that frame of mind which was with him almost chronic, had delayed a moment by the door, peering round in the dimly lighted street in search of those mysterious incidents and persons with which the streets of London teem in every quarter and at every hour. Villiers prided himself as a practised explorer of such obscure mazes and byways of London life, and in this unprofitable pursuit he displayed an assiduity which was worthy of more serious employment. Thus he stood beside the lamp-post surveying the passers-by with undisguised curiosity, and with that gravity only known to the systematic diner, had just enunciated in his mind the formula: "London has been called the city of encounters; it is more than that, it is the city of resurrections," when these reflections were suddenly interrupted by a piteous whine at his elbow, and a deplorable appeal for alms. He looked around in some irritation, and with a sudden shock found himself confronted with the embodied proof of his somewhat stilted fancies. There, close beside him, his face altered and disfigured by poverty and disgrace, his body barely covered by greasy ill-fitting rags, stood his old friend Charles Herbert, who had matriculated on the same day as himself, with whom he had been merry and wise for twelve revolving terms. Different occupations and varying interests had interrupted the friendship, and it was six years since Villiers had seen Herbert; and now he looked upon this wreck of a man with grief and dismay, mingled with a certain inquisitiveness as to what dreary chain of circumstances had dragged him down to such a doleful pass. Villiers felt together with compassion all the relish of the amateur in mysteries, and congratulated himself on his leisurely speculations outside the restaurant.

They walked on in silence for some time, and more than one passer-by stared in astonishment at the unaccustomed spectacle of a well-dressed man with an unmistakable beggar hanging on to his arm, and observing this, Villiers led the way to an obscure street in Soho. Here he repeated his question.

"How on earth has it happened, Herbert? I always understood you would succeed to an excellent position in Dorsetshire. Did your father disinherit you? Surely not?"

"No, Villiers; I came into all the property at my poor father's death; he died a year after I left Oxford. He was a very good father to me, and I mourned his death sincerely enough. But you know what young men are; a few months later I came up to town and went a good deal into society. Of course I had excellent introductions, and I managed to enjoy myself very much in a harmless sort of way. I played a little, certainly, but never for heavy stakes, and the few bets I made on races brought me in money—only a few pounds, you know, but enough to pay for cigars and such petty pleasures. It was in my second season that the tide turned. Of course you have heard of my marriage?"

"No, I never heard anything about it."

"Yes, I married, Villiers. I met a girl, a girl of the most wonderful and most strange beauty, at the house of some people whom I knew. I cannot tell you her age; I never knew it, but, so far as I can guess, I should think she must have been about nineteen when I made her acquaintance. My friends had come to know her as Florence; she told them she was an orphan, the child of an English father and an Italian mother, and she charmed them as she charmed me. The first time I saw her was at an evening party. I was standing by the door talking to a friend, when suddenly above the hum and babble of conversation I heard a voice which seemed to thrill to my heart. She was singing an Italian song. I was introduced to her that evening, and in three months I married Helen. Villiers, that woman, if I can call her 'woman,' corrupted my soul. The night of the wedding I found myself sitting in her bedroom in the hotel, listening to her talk. She was sitting up in bed, and I listened to her as she spoke in her beautiful voice, spoke of things which even now I would not dare whisper in blackest night, though I stood in the midst of a wilderness. You, Villiers, you may think you know life, and London, and what goes on day and night in this dreadful city; for all I can say you may have heard the talk of the vilest, but I tell you you can have no conception of what I know, not in your most fantastic, hideous dreams can you have imaged forth the faintest shadow of what I have heard—and seen. Yes, seen. I have seen the incredible, such horrors that even I myself sometimes stop in the middle of the street, and ask whether it is possible for a man to hold such things and live. In a year, Villiers, I was a ruined man, in body and soul—in body and soul."

"But your property, Herbert? You had land in Dorset."

"I sold it all; the fields and woods, the dear old house—everything."

"And the money?"

"She took it all from me."

"And then left you?"

"Yes; she disappeared one night. I don't know where she went, but I am sure if I saw her again it would kill me. The rest of my story is of no interest; sordid misery, that is all. You may think, Villiers, that I have exaggerated and talked for effect; but I have not told you half. I could tell you certain things which would convince you, but you would never know a happy day again. You would pass the rest of your life, as I pass mine, a haunted man, a man who has seen hell."

Villiers took the unfortunate man to his rooms, and gave him a meal. Herbert could eat little, and scarcely touched the glass of wine set before him. He sat moody and silent by the fire, and seemed relieved when Villiers sent him away with a small present of money.

"By the way, Herbert," said Villiers, as they parted at the door, "what was your wife's name? You said Helen, I think? Helen what?"

"The name she passed under when I met her was Helen Vaughan, but what her real name was I can't say. I don't think she had a name. No, no, not in that sense. Only human beings have names, Villiers; I can't say any more. Good-bye; yes, I will not fail to call if I see any way in which you can help me. Good-night."

The man went out into the bitter night, and Villiers returned to his fireside. There was something about Herbert which shocked him inexpressibly; not his poor rags nor the marks which poverty had set upon his face, but rather an indefinite terror which hung about him like a mist. He had acknowledged that he himself was not devoid of blame; the woman, he had avowed, had corrupted him body and soul, and Villiers felt that this man, once his friend, had been an actor in scenes evil beyond the power of words. His story needed no confirmation: he himself was the embodied proof of it. Villiers mused curiously over the story he had heard, and wondered whether he had heard both the first and the last of it. "No," he thought, "certainly not the last, probably only the beginning. A case like this is like a nest of Chinese boxes; you open one after another and find a quainter workmanship in every box. Most likely poor Herbert is merely one of the outside boxes; there are stranger ones to follow."

Villiers could not take his mind away from Herbert and his story, which seemed to grow wilder as the night wore on. The fire began to burn low, and the chilly air of the morning crept into the room; Villiers got up with a glance over his shoulder, and shivering slightly, went to bed.

A few days later he saw at his club a gentleman of his acquaintance, named Austin, who was famous for his intimate knowledge of London life, both in its tenebrous and luminous phases. Villiers, still full of his encounter in Soho and its consequences, thought Austin might possibly be able to shed some light on Herbert's history, and so after some casual talk he suddenly put the question:

"Do you happen to know anything of a man named Herbert—Charles Herbert?"

Austin turned round sharply and stared at Viiliers with some astonishment.

"Charles Herbert? Weren't you in town three years ago? No; then you have not heard of the Paul Street case? It caused a good deal of sensation at the time."

"What was the case?"

"Well, a gentleman, a man of very good position, was found dead, stark dead, in the area of a certain house in Paul Street, off Tottenham Court Road. Of course the police did not make the discovery; if you happen to be sitting up all night and have a light in your window, the constable will ring the bell, but if you happen to be lying dead in somebody's area, you will be left alone. In this instance as in many others the alarm was raised by some kind of vagabond; I don't mean a common tramp, or a public-house loafer, but a gentleman, whose business or pleasure, or both, made him a spectator of the London streets at five o'clock in the morning. This individual was, as he said, 'going home,' it did not appear whence or whither, and had occasion to pass through Paul Street between four and five A.M. Something or other caught his eye at Number 20; he said, absurdly enough, that the house had the most unpleasant physiognomy he had ever observed, but, at any rate, he glanced down the area, and was a good deal astonished to see a man lying on the stones, his limbs all huddled together, and his face turned up. Our gentleman thought his face looked peculiarly ghastly, and so set off at a run in search of the nearest policeman. The constable was at first inclined to treat the matter lightly, suspecting common drunkenness; however, he came, and after looking at the man's face, changed his tone, quickly enough. The early bird, who had picked up this fine worm, was sent off for a doctor, and the policeman rang and knocked at the door till a slatternly servant girl came down looking more than half asleep. The constable pointed out the contents of the area to the maid, who screamed loudly enough to wake up the street, but she knew nothing of the man; had never seen him at the house, and so forth. Meanwhile the original discoverer had come back with a medical man, and the next thing was to get into the area. The gate was open, so the whole quartet stumped down the steps. The doctor hardly needed a moment's examination; he said the poor fellow had been dead for several hours, and it was then the case began to get interesting. The dead man had not been robbed, and in one of his pockets were papers identifying him as—well, as a man of good family and means, a favourite in society, and nobody's enemy, so far as could be known. I don't give his name, Villiers, because it has nothing to do with the story, and because it's no good raking up these affairs about the dead when there are no relations living. The next curious point was that the medical men couldn't agree as to how he met his death. There were some slight bruises on his shoulders, but they were so slight that it looked as if he had been pushed roughly out of the kitchen door, and not thrown over the railings from the street or even dragged down the steps. But there were positively no other marks of violence about him, certainly none that would account for his death; and when they came to the autopsy there wasn't a trace of poison of any kind. Of course the police wanted to know all about the people at Number 20, and here again, so I have heard from private sources, one or two other very curious points came out. It appears that the occupants of the house were a Mr. and Mrs. Charles Herbert; he was said to be a landed proprietor, though it struck most people that Paul Street was not exactly the place to look for country gentry. As for Mrs. Herbert, nobody seemed to know who or what she was, and, between ourselves, I fancy the divers after her history found themselves in rather strange waters. Of course they both denied knowing anything about the deceased, and in default of any evidence against them they were discharged. But some very odd things came out about them. Though it was between five and six in the morning when the dead man was removed, a large crowd had collected, and several of the neighbours ran to see what was going on. They were pretty free with their comments, by all accounts, and from these it appeared that Number 20 was in very bad odour in Paul Street. The detectives tried to trace down these rumours to some solid foundation of fact, but could not get hold of anything. People shook their heads and raised their eyebrows and thought the Herberts rather 'queer,' 'would rather not be seen going into their house,' and so on, but there was nothing tangible. The authorities were morally certain that the man met his death in some way or another in the house and was thrown out by the kitchen door, but they couldn't prove it, and the absence of any indications of violence or poisoning left them helpless. An odd case, wasn't it? But curiously enough, there's something more that I haven't told you. I happened to know one of the doctors who was consulted as to the cause of death, and some time after the inquest I met him, and asked him about it. 'Do you really mean to tell me,' I said, 'that you were baffled by the case, that you actually don't know what the man died of?' 'Pardon me,' he replied, 'I know perfectly well what caused death. Blank died of fright, of sheer, awful terror; I never saw features so hideously contorted in the entire course of my practice, and I have seen the faces of a whole host of dead.' The doctor was usually a cool customer enough, and a certain vehemence in his manner struck me, but I couldn't get anything more out of him. I suppose the Treasury didn't see their way to prosecuting the Herberts for frightening a man to death; at any rate, nothing was done, and the case dropped out of men's minds. Do you happen to know anything of Herbert?"

"Well," replied Villiers, "he was an old college friend of mine."

"You don't say so? Have you ever seen his wife?"

"No, I haven't. I have lost sight of Herbert for many years."

"It's queer, isn't it, parting with a man at the college gate or at Paddington, seeing nothing of him for years, and then finding him pop up his head in such an odd place. But I should like to have seen Mrs. Herbert; people said extraordinary things about her."

"What sort of things?"

"Well, I hardly know how to tell you. Everyone who saw her at the police court said she was at once the most beautiful woman and the most repulsive they had ever set eyes on. I have spoken to a man who saw her, and I assure you he positively shuddered as he tried to describe the woman, but he couldn't tell why. She seems to have been a sort of enigma; and I expect if that one dead man could have told tales, he would have told some uncommonly queer ones. And there you are again in another puzzle; what could a respectable country gentleman like Mr. Blank (we'll call him that if you don't mind) want in such a very queer house as Number 20? It's altogether a very odd case, isn't it?"

"It is indeed, Austin; an extraordinary case. I didn't think, when I asked you about my old friend, I should strike on such strange metal. Well, I must be off; good-day."

Villiers went away, thinking of his own conceit of the Chinese boxes; here was quaint workmanship indeed.

4. The Discovery in Paul Street

A few months after Villiers's meeting with Herbert, Mr. Clarke was sitting, as usual, by his after-dinner hearth, resolutely guarding his fancies from wandering in the direction of the bureau. For more than a week he had succeeded in keeping away from the "Memoirs," and he cherished hopes of a complete self-reformation; but, in spite of his endeavours, he could not hush the wonder and the strange curiosity that that last case he had written down had executed within him. He had put the case, or rather the outline of it, conjecturally to a scientific friend, who shook his head, and thought Clarke getting queer, and on this particular evening Clarke was making an effort to rationalise the story, when a sudden knock at this door roused him from his meditations.

"Mr. Villiers to see you, sir."

"Dear me, Villiers, it is very kind of you to look me up; I have not seen you for many months; I should think nearly a year. Come in, come in. And how are you, Villiers? Want any advice about investments?"

"No, thanks. I fancy everything I have in that way is pretty safe. No, Clarke, I have really come to consult you about a rather curious matter that has been brought under my notice of late. I am afraid you will think it all rather absurd when I tell my tale. I sometimes think so myself, and that's just why I made up my mind to come to you, as I know you're a practical man."

Mr. Villiers was ignorant of the "Memoirs to Prove the Existence of the Devil."

"Well, Villiers, I shall be happy to give you my advice, to the best of my ability. What is the nature of the case?"

"It's an extraordinary thing, altogether. You know my ways; I always keep my eyes open in the streets, and in my time I have chanced upon some queer customers, and queer cases too, but this, I think, beats all. I was coming out of a restaurant one nasty winter night about three months ago; I had had a capital dinner and a good bottle of Chianti, and I stood for a moment on the pavement, thinking what a mystery there is about London streets and the companies that pass along them. A bottle of red wine encourages these fancies, Clarke, and I dare say I should have thought a page of small type, but I was cut short by a beggar who had come behind me, and was making the usual appeals. Of course I looked round, and this beggar turned out to be what was left of an old friend of mine, a man named Herbert. I asked him how he had come to such a wretched pass, and he told me. We walked up and down one of those long dark Soho streets, and there I listened to his story. He said he had married a beautiful girl, some years younger than himself, and, as he put it, she had corrupted him body and soul. He wouldn't go into details; he said he dare not, that what he had seen and heard haunted him by night and day, and when I looked in his face I knew he was speaking the truth. There was something about the man that made me shiver. I don't know why, but it was there. I gave him a little money and sent him away, and I assure you that when he was gone I gasped for breath. His presence seemed to chill one's blood."

"Isn't all this just a little fanciful, Villiers? I suppose the poor fellow had made an imprudent marriage, and, in plain English, gone to the bad."

"Well, listen to this." Villiers told Clarke the story he had heard from Austin.

"You see," he concluded, "there can be but little doubt that this Mr. Blank, whoever he was, died of sheer terror; he saw something so awful, so terrible, that it cut short his life. And what he saw, he most certainly saw in that house, which, somehow or other, had got a bad name in the neighbourhood. I had the curiosity to go and look at the place for myself. It's a saddening kind of street; the houses are old enough to be mean and dreary, but not old enough to be quaint. As far as I could see most of them are let in lodgings, furnished and unfurnished, and almost every door has three bells to it. Here and there ground floors have been made into shops of the commonest kind; it's a dismal street in every way. I found Number 20 was to let, and I went to the agent's and got the key. Of course I should have heard nothing of the Herberts in that quarter, but I asked the man, fair and square, how long they had left the house, and whether there had been other tenants in the meanwhile. He looked at me queerly for a minute, and told me the Herberts had left immediately after the unpleasantness, as he called it, and since then the house had been empty."

Mr. Villiers paused for a moment.

"I have always been rather fond of going over empty houses; there's a sort of fascination about the desolate empty rooms, with the nails sticking in the walls, and the dust thick upon the window-sills. But I didn't enjoy going over Number 20, Paul Street. I had hardly put my foot inside the passage before I noticed a queer, heavy feeling about the air of the house. Of course all empty houses are stuffy, and so forth, but this was something quite different; I can't describe it to you, but it seemed to stop the breath. I went into the front room and the back room, and the kitchens downstairs; they were all dirty and dusty enough, as you would expect, but there was something strange about them all. I couldn't define it to you, I only know I felt queer. It was one of the rooms on the first floor, though, that was the worst. It was a largish room, and once on a time the paper must have been cheerful enough, but when I saw it, paint, paper, and everything were most doleful. But the room was full of horror; I felt my teeth grinding as I put my hand on the door, and when I went in, I thought I should have fallen fainting to the floor. However, I pulled myself together, and stood against the end wall, wondering what on earth there could be about the room to make my limbs tremble, and my heart beat as if I were at the hour of death. In one corner there was a pile of newspapers littered about on the floor, and I began looking at them; they were papers of three or four years ago, some of them half torn, and some crumpled as if they had been used for packing. I turned the whole pile over, and among them I found a curious drawing; I will show it you presently. But I couldn't stay in the room; I felt it was overpowering me. I was thankful to come out, safe and sound, into the open air. People stared at me as I walked along the street, and one man said I was drunk. I was staggering about from one side of the pavement to the other, and it was as much as I could do to take the key back to the agent and get home. I was in bed for a week, suffering from what my doctor called nervous shock and exhaustion. One of those days I was reading the evening paper, and happened to notice a paragraph headed: 'Starved to Death.' It was the usual style of thing; a model lodging-house in Marylebone, a door locked for several days, and a dead man in his chair when they broke in. 'The deceased,' said the paragraph, 'was known as Charles Herbert, and is believed to have been once a prosperous country gentleman. His name was familiar to the public three years ago in connection with the mysterious death in Paul Street, Tottenham Court Road, the deceased being the tenant of the house Number 20, in the area of which a gentleman of good position was found dead under circumstances not devoid of suspicion.' A tragic ending, wasn't it? But after all, if what he told me were true, which I am sure it was, the man's life was all a tragedy, and a tragedy of a stranger sort than they put on the boards."

"And that is the story, is it?" said Clarke musingly.

"Yes, that is the story."

"Well, really, Villiers, I scarcely know what to say about it. There are, no doubt, circumstances in the case which seem peculiar, the finding of the dead man in the area of Herbert's house, for instance, and the extraordinary opinion of the physician as to the cause of death; but, after all, it is conceivable that the facts may be explained in a straightforward manner. As to your own sensations, when you went to see the house, I would suggest that they were due to a vivid imagination; you must have been brooding, in a semi-conscious way, over what you had heard. I don't exactly see what more can be said or done in the matter; you evidently think there is a mystery of some kind, but Herbert is dead; where then do you propose to look?"

"I propose to look for the woman; the woman whom he married. *She* is the mystery."

The two men sat silent by the fireside; Clarke secretly congratulating himself on having successfully kept up the character of advocate of the commonplace, and Villiers wrapt in his gloomy fancies.

"I think I will have a cigarette," he said at last, and put his hand in his pocket to feel for the cigarette-case.

"Ah!" he said, starting slightly, "I forgot I had something to show you. You remember my saying that I had found a rather curious sketch among the pile of old newspapers at the house in Paul Street? Here it is."

Villiers drew out a small thin parcel from his pocket. It was covered with brown paper, and secured with string, and the knots were troublesome. In spite of himself Clarke felt inquisitive; he bent forward on his chair as Villiers painfully undid the string, and unfolded the outer covering. Inside was a second wrapping of tissue, and Viiliers took it off and handed the small piece of paper to Clarke without a word.

There was dead silence in the room for five minutes or more; the two men sat so still that they could hear the ticking of the tall old-fashioned clock that stood outside in the hall, and in the mind of one of them the slow monotony of sound woke up a far, far memory. He was looking intently at the small pen-and-ink sketch of the woman's head; it had evidently been drawn with great care, and by a true artist, for the woman's soul looked out of the eyes, and the lips were parted with a strange smile. Clarke gazed still at the face; it brought to his memory one summer evening long ago; he saw again the long lovely valley, the river winding between the hills, the meadows and the cornfields, the dull red sun, and the cold white mist rising from the water. He heard a voice speaking to him across the waves of many years, and saying: "Clarke, Mary will see the God Pan!" and then he was standing in the grim room beside the doctor, listening to the heavy ticking of the clock, waiting and watching, watching the figure lying on the green chair beneath the lamp-light. Mary rose up, and he looked into her eyes, and his heart grew cold within him.

"Who is this woman?" he said at last. His voice was dry and hoarse.

"That is the woman whom Herbert married."

Clarke looked again at the sketch; it was not Mary after all. There certainly was Mary's face, but there was something else, something he had not seen on Mary's features when the white-clad girl entered the laboratory with the doctor, nor at her terrible awakening, nor when she lay grinning on the bed. Whatever it was, the glance that came from those eyes, the smile on the full lips, or the expression of the whole face, Clarke shuddered before it in his inmost soul, and thought, unconsciously, of Dr. Phillips's words, "the most vivid presentment of evil I have ever seen." He turned the paper over mechanically in his hand and glanced at the back.

"Good God! Clarke, what is the matter? You are as white as death."

Villiers had started wildly from his chair, as Clarke fell back with a groan, and let the paper drop from his hands.

"I don't feel very well, Villiers, I am subject to these attacks. Pour me out a little wine; thanks, that will do. I shall feel better in a few minutes."

Villiers picked up the fallen sketch and turned it over as Clarke had done.

"You saw that?" he said. "That's how I identified it as being a portrait of Herbert's wife, or I should say his widow. How do you feel now?"

"Better, thanks, it was only a passing faintness. I don't think I quite catch your meaning. What did you say enabled you to identify the picture?"

"This word—'Helen'—written on the back. Didn't I tell you her name was Helen? Yes; Helen Vaughan."

Clarke groaned; there could be no shadow of doubt.

"Now, don't you agree with me," said Villiers, "that in the story I have told you tonight, and in the part this woman plays in it, there are some very strange points?"

"Yes, Villiers," Clarke muttered, "it is a strange story indeed; a strange story indeed. You must give me time to think it over; I may be able to help you or I may not. Must you be going now?

Well, good-night, Villiers, good-night. Come and see me in the course of a week."

5. The Letter of Advice

"Do you know, Austin," said Villiers, as the two friends were pacing sedately along Piccadilly one pleasant morning in May, "do you know I am convinced that what you told me about Paul Street and the Herberts is a mere episode in an extraordinary history? I may as well confess to you that when I asked you about Herbert a few months ago I had just seen him."

"You had seen him? Where?"

"He begged of me in the street one night. He was in the most pitiable plight, but I recognised the man, and I got him to tell me his history, or at least the outline of it. In brief, it amounted to this—he had been ruined by his wife."

"In what manner?"

"He would not tell me; he would only say that she had destroyed him, body and soul. The man is dead now."

"And what has become of his wife?"

"Ah, that's what I should like to know, and I mean to find her sooner or later. I know a man named Clarke, a dry fellow, in fact a man of business, but shrewd enough. You understand my meaning; not shrewd in the mere business sense of the word, but a man who really knows something about men and life. Well, I laid the case before him, and he was evidently impressed. He said it needed consideration, and asked me to come again in the course of a week. A few days later I received this extraordinary letter."

Austin took the envelope, drew out the letter, and read it curiously. It ran as follows:

> My dear Villiers—I have thought over the matter on which you consulted me the other night, and my advice to you is this. Throw the portrait into the fire, blot out the story from your mind. Never give it another thought, Villiers, or you will be sorry. You will think, no

doubt, that I am in possession of some secret information, and to a certain extent that is the case. But I only know a little; I am like a traveller who has peered over an abyss, and has drawn back in terror. What I know is strange enough and horrible enough, but beyond my knowledge there are depths and horrors more frightful still, more incredible than any tale told of winter nights about the fire. I have resolved, and nothing shall shake that resolve, to explore no whit further, and if you value your happiness you will make the same determination.

Come and see me by all means; but we will talk on more cheerful topics than this.

Austin folded the letter methodically, and returned it to Villiers.

"It is certainly an extraordinary letter," he said, "what does he mean by the portrait?"

"Ah! I forgot to tell you I have been to Paul Street and have made a discovery."

Villiers told his story as he had told it to Clarke, and Austin listened in silence. He seemed puzzled.

"How very curious that you should experience such an unpleasant sensation in that room!" he said at length. "I hardly gather that it was a mere matter of the imagination; a feeling of repulsion, in short."

"No, it was more physical than mental. It was as if I were inhaling at every breath some deadly fume, which seemed to penetrate to every nerve and bone and sinew of my body. I felt racked from head to foot, my eyes began to grow dim; it was like the entrance of death."

"Yes, yes, very strange, certainly. You see, your friend confesses that there is some very black story connected with this woman. Did you notice any particular emotion in him when you were telling your tale?"

"Yes, I did. He became very faint, but he assured me that it was a mere passing attack to which he was subject."

"Did you believe him?"

"I did at the time, but I don't now. He heard what I had to say with a good deal of indifference, till I showed him the portrait. It was then he was seized with the attack of which I spoke. He looked ghastly, I assure you."

"Then he must have seen the woman before. But there might be another explanation; it might have been the name, and not the face, which was familiar to him. What do you think?"

"I couldn't say. To the best of my belief it was after turning the portrait in his hands that he nearly dropped from his chair. The name, you know, was written on the back."

"Quite so. After all, it is impossible to come to any resolution in a case like this. I hate melodrama, and nothing strikes me as more commonplace and tedious than the ordinary ghost story of commerce; but really, Villiers, it looks as if there were something very queer at the bottom of all this."

The two men had, without noticing it, turned up Ashley Street, leading northward from Piccadilly. It was a long street, and rather a gloomy one, but here and there a brighter taste had illuminated the dark houses with flowers, and gay curtains, and a cheerful paint on the doors. Vilhiers glanced up as Austin stopped speaking, and looked at one of these houses; geraniums, red and white, drooped from every sill, and daffodil-coloured curtains were draped back from each window.

"It looks cheerful, doesn't it?" he said.

"Yes, and the inside is still more cheery. One of the pleasantest houses of the season, so I have heard. I haven't been there myself, but I've met several men who have, and they tell me it's uncommonly jovial."

"Whose house is it?"

"A Mrs. Beaumont's."

"And who is she?"

"I couldn't tell you. I have heard she comes from South America, but, after all, who she is is of little consequence. She is a very wealthy woman, there's no doubt of that, and some of the best people have taken her up. I heard she has some wonderful claret, really marvellous wine, which must have cost a fabulous sum. Lord Argentine was telling me about it; he was there last Sunday evening. He assures me he has never tasted such a wine, and Argentine, as you know, is an expert. By the way, that reminds me, she must be an oddish sort of woman, this Mrs. Beaumont. Argentine asked her how old the wine was, and what do you think she said? 'About a thousand years, I believe.' Lord Argentine thought she was chaffing him, you know, but when he laughed she said she was speaking quite seriously, and offered to show him the jar. Of course, he couldn't say anything more after that; but it seems rather antiquated for a beverage, doesn't it? Why, here we are at my rooms. Come in, won't you?"

"Thanks, I think I will. I haven't seen the curiosity-shop for some time."

It was a room furnished richly, yet oddly, where every chair and bookcase and table, and every rug and jar and ornament seemed to be a thing apart, preserving each its own individuality.

"Anything fresh lately?" said Villiers after a while.

"No; I think not; you saw those queer jugs, didn't you? I thought so. I don't think I have come across anything for the last few weeks."

Austin glanced round the room from cupboard to cupboard, from shelf to shelf, in search of some new oddity. His eyes fell at last on an old chest, pleasantly and quaintly carved, which stood in a dark corner of the room.

"Ah," he said, "I was forgetting, I have got something to show you." Austin unlocked the chest, drew out a thick quarto volume, laid it on the table, and resumed the cigar he had put down.

"Did you know Arthur Meyrick the painter, Villiers?"

"A little; I met him two or three times at the house of a friend of mine. What has become of him? I haven't heard his name mentioned for some time."

"He's dead."

"You don't say so! Quite young, wasn't he?"

"Yes; only thirty when he died."

"What did he die of?"

"I don't know. He was an intimate friend of mine, and a thoroughly good fellow. He used to come here and talk to me for hours, and he was one of the best talkers I have met. He could even talk about painting, and that's more than can be said of most painters. About eighteen months ago he was feeling rather overworked, and partly at my suggestion he went off on a sort of roving expedition, with no very definite end or aim about it. I believe New York was to be his first port, but I never heard from him. Three months ago I got this book, with a very civil letter from an English doctor practising in Buenos Aires, stating that he had attended the late Mr. Meyrick during his illness, and that the deceased had expressed an earnest wish that the enclosed packet should be sent to me after his death. That was all."

"And haven't you written for further particulars?"

"I have been thinking of doing so. You would advise me to write to the doctor?"

"Certainly. And what about the book?"

"It was sealed up when I got it. I don't think the doctor had seen it."

"It is something very rare? Meyrick was a collector, perhaps?"

"No, I think not, hardly a collector. Now, what do you think of those Ainu jugs?"

"They are peculiar, but I like them. But aren't you going to show me poor Meyrick's legacy?"

"Yes, yes, to be sure. The fact is, it's rather a peculiar sort of thing, and I haven't shown it to anyone. I wouldn't say anything about it if I were you. There it is."

Villiers took the book, and opened it haphazard.

"It isn't a printed volume then?" he said.

"No. It's a collection of drawings in black and white by my poor friend Meyrick."

Villiers turned to the first page, it was blank; the second bore a brief inscription, which he read:

> Silet per diem universus, nec sine horrore secretus est; lucet nocturnis ignibus, chorus Aegipanum undique

personatur; audiuntur et cantus tibiarum, et tinnitus cymbalorum per oram maritiman.

On the third page was a design which made Villiers start and look up at Austin; he was gazing abstractedly out of the window. Villiers turned page after page, absorbed, in spite of himself, in the frightful Walpurgis-night of evil, strange monstrous evil, that the dead artist had set forth in hard black and white. The figures of fauns and satyrs and Ægipans danced before his eyes, the darkness of the thicket, the dance on the mountain-top, the scenes by lonely shores, in green vineyards, by rocks and desert places, passed before him: a world before which the human soul seemed to shrink back and shudder. Villiers whirled over the remaining pages; he had seen enough, but the picture on the last leaf caught his eye, as he almost closed the book.

"Austin!"

"Well, what is it?"

"Do you know who that is?"

It was a woman's face, alone on the white page.

"Know who it is? No, of course not."

"I do."

"Who is it?"

"It is Mrs. Herbert."

"Are you sure?"

"I am perfectly certain of it. Poor Meyrick! He is one more chapter in her history."

"But what do you think of the designs?"

"They are frightful. Lock the book up again, Austin. If I were you I would burn it; it must be a terrible companion even though it be in a chest."

"Yes, they are singular drawings. But I wonder what connection there could be between Meyrick and Mrs. Herbert, or what link between her and these designs?"

"Ah, who can say? It is possible that the matter may end here, and we shall never know, but in my own opinion this

Helen Vaughan, or Mrs. Herbert, is only the beginning. She will come back to London, Austin; depend upon it, she will come back, and we shall hear more about her then. I don't think it will be very pleasant news."

6. The Suicides

Lord Argentine was a great favourite in London society. At twenty he had been a poor man, decked with the surname of an illustrious family, but forced to earn a livelihood as best he could, and the most speculative of money-lenders would not have entrusted him with fifty pounds on the chance of his ever changing his name for a title, and his poverty for a great fortune. His father had been near enough to the fountain of good things to secure one of the family livings, but the son, even if he had taken orders, would scarcely have obtained so much as this, and moreover felt no vocation for the ecclesiastical estate. Thus he fronted the world with no better armour than the bachelor's gown and the wit of a younger son's grandson, with which equipment he contrived in some way to make a very tolerable fight of it. At twenty-five Mr. Charles Aubernoun saw himself still a man of struggles and of warfare with the world, but out of the seven who stood between him and the high places of his family three only remained. These three, however, were "good lives," but yet not proof against the Zulu assegais and typhoid fever, and so one morning Aubernoun woke up and found himself Lord Argentine, a man of thirty who had faced the difficulties of existence, and had conquered. The situation amused him immensely, and he resolved that riches should be as pleasant to him as poverty had always been. Argentine, after some little consideration, came to the conclusion that dining, regarded as a fine art, was perhaps the most amusing pursuit open to fallen humanity and thus his dinners became famous in London and an invitation to his table a thing covetously desired. After ten years of lordship and dinners Argentine still declined to be jaded, still persisted in enjoying life, and by a kind of infection had become recognised as the cause of joy in others, in short, as the best of company. His sudden and tragical death therefore caused a wide and deep sensation. People could scarce believe it, even though the newspaper was before their eyes, and the cry of "Mysterious Death of a Nobleman" came ringing up from the street. But there stood the brief paragraph: "Lord Argentine was found dead this morning by his valet under distressing circumstances. It is stated that there can be no doubt that his lordship committed suicide, though no motive can be assigned for the act. The deceased nobleman was widely known in society, and much liked for his genial manner and sumptuous hospitality. He is succeeded by," etc., etc.

By slow degrees the details came to light, but the case still remained a mystery. The chief witness at the inquest was the dead nobleman's valet, who said that the night before his death Lord Argentine had dined with a lady of good position, whose name was suppressed in the newspaper reports. At about eleven o'clock Lord Argentine had returned, and informed his man that he should not require his services till the next morning. A little later the valet had occasion to cross the hall and was somewhat astonished to see his master quietly letting himself out at the front door. He had taken off his evening clothes, and was dressed in a Norfolk coat and knicker-bockers, and wore a low brown hat. The valet had no reason to suppose that Lord Argentine had seen him, and though his master rarely kept late hours, thought little of the occurrence till the next morning, when he knocked at the bedroom door at a quarter to nine as usual. He received no answer, and, after knocking two or three times, entered the room, and saw Lord Argentine's body leaning forward at an angle from the bottom of the bed. He found that his master had tied a cord securely to one of the short bedposts, and, after making a running noose and slipping it round his neck, the unfortunate man must have resolutely fallen forward, to die by slow strangulation. He was dressed in the light suit in which the valet had seen him go out, and the doctor who was summoned pronounced that life had been extinct for more than four hours. All papers, letters, and so forth seemed in perfect order, and nothing was discovered which pointed in the most remote way to any scandal either great or small. Here the evidence ended; nothing more could be discovered. Several persons had been present at the dinner-party at which Lord Argentine had assisted, and to all these he seemed in his usual genial spirits. The valet, indeed, said he thought his master appeared a little excited when he came home, but he confessed that the alteration in his manner was very slight, hardly noticeable, indeed. It seemed hopeless to seek for any clue, and the suggestion that Lord Argentine had been suddenly attacked by acute suicidal mania was generally accepted.

It was otherwise, however, when within three weeks, three more gentlemen, one of them a nobleman, and the two others men of good position and ample means, perished miserably in almost precisely the same manner. Lord Swanleigh was found one morning in his dressing-room, hanging from a peg affixed to the wall, and Mr. Collier-Stuart and Mr. Herries had chosen to die as Lord Argentine. There was no explanation in either case; a few bald facts; a living man in the evening, and a dead body with a black swollen face in the morning. The police had been forced to confess themselves powerless to arrest or to explain the sordid murders of Whitechapel; but before the horrible suicides of Piccadilly and Mayfair they were dumbfounded, for not even the mere ferocity which did duty as an explanation of the crimes of the East End, could be of service in the West. Each of these men who had resolved to die a tortured shameful death was rich, prosperous, and to all appearances in love with the world, and not the acutest research could ferret out any shadow of a lurking motive in either case. There was a horror in the air, and men looked at one another's faces when they met, each wondering whether the other was to be the victim of the fifth nameless tragedy. Journalists sought in vain in their scrapbooks for materials whereof to concoct reminiscent articles; and the morning paper was unfolded in many a house with a feeling of awe; no man knew when or where the blow would next light.

A short while after the last of these terrible events, Austin came to see Mr. Villiers. He was curious to know whether Villiers had succeeded in discovering any fresh traces of Mrs. Herbert, either through Clarke or by other sources, and he asked the question soon after he had sat down.

"No," said Viiliers. "I wrote to Clarke, but he remains obdurate, and I have tried other channels, but without any result. I can't find out what became of Helen Vaughan after she left Paul Street, but I think she must have gone abroad. But to tell the truth, Austin, I haven't paid very much attention to the matter for the last few weeks; I knew poor Herries intimately, and his terrible death has been a great shock to me, a great shock."

"I can well believe it," answered Austin gravely; "you know Argentine was a friend of mine. If I remember rightly, we were speaking of him that day you came to my rooms."

"Yes; it was in connection with the house in Ashley Street, Mrs. Beaumont's house. You said something about Argentine's dining there."

"Quite so. Of course you know it was there Argentine dined the night before—before his death."

"No, I haven't heard that."

"Oh yes; the name was kept out of the papers to spare Mrs. Beaumont. Argentine was a great favourite of hers, and it is said she was in a terrible state for some time after."

A curious look came over Villiers's face; he seemed undecided whether to speak or not. Austin began again.

"I never experienced such a feeling of horror as when I read the account of Argentine's death. I didn't understand it at the time, and I don't now. I knew him well, and it completely passes my understanding for what possible cause he—or any of the others for the matter of that—could have resolved in cold blood to die in such an awful manner. You know how men babble away each other's characters in London, you may be sure any buried scandal or hidden skeleton would have been brought to light in such a case as this; but nothing of the sort has taken place. As for the theory of mania, that is very well, of course, for the coroner's jury, but everybody knows that it's all nonsense. Suicidal mania is not smallpox."

Austin relapsed into gloomy silence. Villiers sat silent also, watching his friend. The expression of indecision still fleeted across his face; he seemed as if weighing his thoughts in the balance, and the considerations he was revolving left him still silent. Austin tried to shake off the remembrance of tragedies as hopeless and perplexed as the labyrinth of Daedalus, and began to talk in an indifferent voice of the more pleasant incidents and adventures of the season.

"That Mrs. Beaumont," he said, "of whom we were speaking, is a great success; she has taken London almost by storm. I met her the other night at Fulham's; she is really a remarkable woman."

"You have met Mrs. Beaumont?"

"Yes; she had quite a court around her. She would be called very handsome, I suppose, and yet there is something about her face which I didn't like. The features are exquisite, but the expression is strange. And all the time I was looking at her, and afterwards, when I was going home, I had a curious feeling that that very expression was in some way or other familiar to me."

"You must have seen her in the Row."

"No, I am sure I never set eyes on the woman before; it is that which makes it puzzling. And to the best of my belief I have never seen anybody like her; what I felt was a kind of dim far-off memory, vague but persistent. The only sensation I can compare it to, is that odd feeling one sometimes has in a dream, when fantastic cities and wondrous lands and phantom personages appear familiar and accustomed."

Villiers nodded and glanced aimlessly round the room, possibly in search of something on which to turn the conversation. His eyes fell on an old chest somewhat like that in which the artist's strange legacy lay hid beneath a Gothic scutcheon.

"Have you written to the doctor about poor Meyrick?" he asked.

"Yes; I wrote asking for full particulars as to his illness and death. I don't expect to have an answer for another three weeks or a month. I thought I might as well inquire whether Meyrick knew an Englishwoman named Herbert, and if so, whether the doctor could give me any information about her. But it's very possible that Meyrick fell in with her at New York, or Mexico, or San Francisco; I have no idea as to the extent or direction of his travels."

"Yes, and it's very possible that the woman may have more than one name."

"Exactly. I wish I had thought of asking you to lend me the portrait of her which you possess. I might have enclosed it in my letter to Dr. Matthews."

"So you might; that never occurred to me. We might send it now. Hark! what are those boys calling?"

While the two men had been talking together a confused noise of shouting had been gradually growing louder. The noise rose from the eastward and swelled down Piccadilly, drawing nearer and nearer, a very torrent of sound; surging up streets usually quiet, and making every window a frame for a face, curious or excited. The cries and voices came echoing up the silent street where Villiers lived, growing more distinct as they advanced, and, as Villiers spoke, an answer rang up from the pavement:

THE WEST END HORRORS; ANOTHER AWFUL SUICIDE; FULL DETAILS!

Austin rushed down the stairs and bought a paper and read out the paragraph to Villiers as the uproar in the street rose and fell. The window was open and the air seemed full of noise and terror.

> Another gentleman has fallen a victim to the terrible epidemic of suicide which for the last month has prevailed in the West End. Mr. Sidney Crashaw, of Stoke House, Fulham, and King's Pomeroy, Devon, was found, after a prolonged search, hanging from the branch of a tree in his garden at one o'clock today. The deceased gentleman dined last night at the Canton Club and seemed

> in his usual health and spirits. He left the Club at about ten o'clock, and was seen walking leisurely up St. James's Street a little later. Subsequent to this his movements cannot be traced. On the discovery of the body medical aid was at once summoned, but life had evidently been long extinct. So far as is known, Mr. Crashaw had no trouble or anxiety of any kind. This painful suicide, it will be remembered, is the fifth of the kind in the last month. The authorities at Scotland Yard are unable to suggest any explanation of these terrible occurrences.

Austin put down the paper in mute horror.

"I shall leave London tomorrow," he said, "it is a city of nightmares. How awful this is, Villiers!"

Mr. Villiers was sitting by the window quietly looking out into the street. He had listened to the newspaper report attentively, and the hint of indecision was no longer on his face.

"Wait a moment, Austin," he replied, "I have made up my mind to mention a little matter that occurred last night. It is stated, I think, that Crashaw was last seen alive in St. James's Street shortly after ten?"

"Yes, I think so. I will look again. Yes, you are quite right."

"Quite so. Well, I am in a position to contradict that statement at all events. Crashaw was seen after that; considerably later indeed."

"How do you know?"

"Because I happened to see Crashaw myself at about two o'clock this morning."

"You saw Crashaw? You, Villiers?"

"Yes, I saw him quite distinctly; indeed, there were but a few feet between us."

"Where, in Heaven's name, did you see him?"

"Not far from here. I saw him in Ashley Street. He was just leaving a house."

"Did you notice what house it was?"

"Yes. It was Mrs. Beaumont's."

"Villiers! Think what you are saying; there must be some mistake. How could Crashaw be in Mrs. Beaumont's house at two o'clock in the morning? Surely, surely, you must have been dreaming, Villiers, you were always rather fanciful."

"No; I was wide awake enough. Even if I had been dreaming as you say, what I saw would have roused me effectually."

"What you saw? What did you see? Was there anything strange about Crashaw? But I can't believe it; it is impossible."

"Well, if you like I will tell you what I saw, or if you please, what I think I saw, and you can judge for yourself."

"Very good, Villiers."

The noise and clamour of the street had died away, though now and then the sound of shouting still came from the distance, and the dull, leaden silence seemed like the quiet after an earthquake or a storm. Villiers turned from the window and began speaking.

"I was at a house near Regent's Park last night, and when I came away the fancy took me to walk home instead of taking a hansom. It was a clear pleasant night enough, and after a few minutes I had the streets pretty much to myself. It's a curious thing, Austin, to be alone in London at night, the gas-lamps stretching away in perspective, and the dead silence, and then perhaps the rush and clatter of a hansom on the stones, and the fire starting up under the horse's hoofs. I walked along pretty briskly, for I was feeling a little tired of being out in the night, and as the clocks were striking two I turned down Ashley Street, which, you know, is on my way. It was quieter than ever there, and the lamps were fewer; altogether, it looked as dark and gloomy as a forest in winter. I had done about half the length of the street when I heard a door closed very softly, and naturally I looked up to see who was abroad like myself at such an hour. As it happens, there is a street lamp close to the house in question, and I saw a man standing on the step. He had just shut the door and his face was towards me, and I recognised Crashaw directly. I never knew him to speak to, but I had often seen him, and I am positive that I was not mistaken in my man.

I looked into his face for a moment, and then—I will confess the truth—I set off at a good run, and kept it up till I was within my own door."

"Why?"

"Why? Because it made my blood run cold to see that man's face. I could never have supposed that such an infernal medley of passions could have glared out of any human eyes; I almost fainted as I looked. I knew I had looked into the eyes of a lost soul, Austin; the man's outward form remained, but all hell was within it. Furious lust, and hate that was like fire, and the loss of all hope and horror that seemed to shriek aloud to the night, though his teeth were shut; and the utter blackness of despair. I am sure he did not see me; he saw nothing that you or I can see, but he saw what I hope we never shall. I do not know when he died; I suppose in an hour, perhaps two, but when I passed down Ashley Street and heard the closing door, that man no longer belonged to this world; it was a devil's face I looked upon."

There was an interval of silence in the room when Villiers ceased speaking. The light was failing, and all the tumult of an hour ago was quite hushed. Austin had bent his head at the close of the story, and his hand covered his eyes.

"What can it mean?" he said at length.

"Who knows, Austin, who knows? It's a black business, but I think we had better keep it to ourselves, for the present at any rate. I will see if I cannot learn anything about that house through private channels of information, and if I do light upon anything I will let you know."

7. The Encounter in Soho

Three weeks later Austin received a note from Villiers, asking him to call either that afternoon or the next. He chose the nearer date, and found Villiers sitting as usual by the window, apparently lost in meditation on the drowsy traffic of the street. There was a bamboo table by his side, a fantastic thing, enriched with gilding and queer painted scenes, and on it lay a little pile of papers arranged and cocketed as neatly as anything in Mr. Clarke's office.

"Well, Villiers, have you made any discoveries in the last three weeks?"

"I think so; I have here one or two memoranda which struck me as singular, and there is a statement to which I shall call your attention."

"And these documents relate to Mrs. Beaumont? It was really Crashaw whom you saw that night standing on the doorstep of the house in Ashley Street?"

"As to that matter my belief remains unchanged, but neither my inquiries nor their results have any special relation to Crashaw. But my investigations have had a strange issue. I have found out who Mrs. Beaumont is!"

"Who is she? In what way do you mean?"

"I mean that you and I know her better under another name."

"What name is that?"

"Herbert."

"Herbert!" Austin repeated the word, dazed with astonishment.

"Yes, Mrs. Herbert of Paul Street, Helen Vaughan of earlier adventures unknown to me. You had reason to recognise the expression of her face; when you go home look at the face in Meyrick's book of horrors, and you will know the sources of your recollection."

"And you have proof of this?"

"Yes, the best of proof; I have seen Mrs. Beaumont, or shall we say Mrs. Herbert?"

"Where did you see her?"

"Hardly in a place where you would expect to see a lady who lives in Ashley Street, Piccadilly. I saw her entering a house in one of the meanest and most disreputable streets in Soho. In fact, I had made an appointment, though not with her, and she was precise both to time and place."

"All this seems very wonderful, but I cannot call it incredible.

You must remember, Villiers, that I have seen this woman, in the ordinary adventure of London society, talking and laughing, and sipping her coffee in a commonplace drawing-room with commonplace people. But you know what you are saying?"

"I do; I have not allowed myself to be led by surmises or fancies. It was with no thought of finding Helen Vaughan that I searched for Mrs. Beaumont in the dark waters of the life of London, but such has been the issue."

"You must have been in strange places, Villiers."

"Yes, I have been in very strange places. It would have been useless, you know, to go to Ashley Street, and ask Mrs. Beaumont to give me a short sketch of her previous history. No; assuming, as I had to assume, that her record was not of the cleanest, it would be pretty certain that at some previous time she must have moved in circles not quite so refined as her present ones. If you see mud on the top of a stream, you may be sure that it was once at the bottom. I went to the bottom. I have always been fond of diving into Queer Street for my amusement, and I found my knowledge of that locality and its inhabitants very useful. It is, perhaps, needless to say that my friends had never heard the name of Beaumont, and as I had never seen the lady, and was quite unable to describe her, I had to set to work in an indirect way. The people there know me; I have been able to do some of them a service now and again, so they made no difficulty about giving their information; they were aware I had no communication direct or indirect with Scotland Yard. I had to cast out a good many lines, though, before I got what I wanted, and when I landed the fish I did not for a moment suppose it was my fish. But I listened to what I was told out of a constitutional liking for useless information, and I found myself in possession of a very curious story, though, as I imagined, not the story I was looking for. It was to this effect. Some five or six years ago, a woman named Raymond suddenly made her appearance in the neighbourhood to which I am referring. She was described to me as being quite young, probably not more than seventeen or eighteen, very handsome, and looking as if she came from the country. I should be wrong in saying that she found her level in going to this particular quarter, or associating with these people, for from what I was told, I should think the worst den in London far too good for her. The person from whom I got my information, as you may suppose, no great Puritan, shuddered and grew sick in telling me of the nameless infamies which were laid to her charge. After living there for a year, or perhaps a little more, she disappeared as suddenly as she came, and they saw nothing of her till about the time of the Paul Street case. At first she came to her old haunts only occasionally, then more frequently, and finally took up her abode there as before, and remained for six or eight months. It's of no use my going into details as to the life that woman led; if you want particulars you can look at Meyrick's legacy. Those designs were not drawn from his imagination. She again disappeared, and the people of the place saw nothing of her till a few months ago. My informant told me that she had taken some rooms in a house which he pointed out, and these rooms she was in the habit of visiting two or three times a week and always at ten in the morning. I was led to expect that one of these visits would be paid on a certain day about a week ago, and I accordingly managed to be on the look-out in company with my cicerone at a quarter to ten, and the hour and the lady came with equal punctuality. My friend and I were standing under an archway, a little way back from the street, but she saw us, and gave me a glance that I shall be long in forgetting. That look was quite enough for me; I knew Miss Raymond to be Mrs. Herbert; as for Mrs. Beaumont she had quite gone out of my head. She went into the house, and I watched it till four o'clock, when she came out, and then I followed her. It was a long chase, and I had to be very careful to keep a long way in the background, and yet not lose sight of the woman. She took me down to the Strand, and then to Westminster, and then up St. James's Street, and along Piccadilly. I felt queerish when I saw her turn up Ashley Street; the thought that Mrs. Herbert was Mrs. Beaumont came into my mind, but it seemed too improbable to be true. I waited at the corner, keeping my eye on her all the time, and I took particular care to note the house at which she stopped. It was the house with the gay curtains, the house of flowers, the house out of which Crashaw came the night he hanged himself in his garden. I was just going away with my discovery, when I saw an empty carriage come round and draw up in front of the house, and I came to the conclusion that Mrs. Herbert was going out for a drive, and I was right. I took a hansom and followed the carriage into the Park. There, as it happened, I met a man I know, and we stood talking together a little distance from the carriage-way, to which I had my back. We had not been there for ten minutes when my friend took off his hat, and I glanced round and saw the lady I had been following all day. "Who is that?" I said, and his answer was, "Mrs. Beaumont; lives in Ashley Street." Of course there could be no doubt after that. I don't know whether she saw me, but I don't think she did. I went home at once, and, in consideration, I thought that I had a sufficiently good case with which to go to Clarke."

"Why to Clarke?"

"Because I am sure that Clarke is in possession of facts about this woman, facts of which I know nothing."

"Well, what then?"

Mr. Villiers leaned back in his chair and looked reflectively at Austin for a moment before he answered:

"My idea was that Clarke and I should call on Mrs. Beaumont."

"You would never go into such a house as that? No, no, Villiers, you cannot do it. Besides, consider; what result . . ."

"I will tell you soon. But I was going to say that my information does not end here; it has been completed in an extraordinary manner.

"Look at this neat little packet of manuscript; it is paginated, you see, and I have indulged in the civil coquetry of a ribbon of red tape. It has almost a legal air, hasn't it? Run your eye over it, Austin. It is an account of the entertainment Mrs. Beaumont provided for her choicer guests. The man who wrote this escaped with his life, but I do not think he will live many years. The doctors tell him he must have sustained some severe shock to the nerves."

Austin took the manuscript, but never read it. Opening the neat pages at haphazard his eye was caught by a word and a phrase that followed it; and, sick at heart, with white lips and a cold sweat pouring like water from his temples, he flung the paper down.

"Take it away, Villiers, never speak of this again. Are you made of stone, man? Why, the dread and horror of death itself, the thoughts of the man who stands in the keen morning air on the black platform, bound, the bell tolling in his ears, and waits for the harsh rattle of the bolt, are as nothing compared to this. I will not read it; I should never sleep again."

"Very good. I can fancy what you saw. Yes; it is horrible enough; but after all, it is an old story, an old mystery played in our day, and in dim London streets instead of amidst the vineyards and the olive gardens. We know what happened to those who chanced to meet the Great God Pan, and those who are wise know that all symbols are symbols of something, not of nothing. It was, indeed, an exquisite symbol beneath which men long ago veiled their knowledge of the most awful, most secret forces which lie at the heart of all things; forces before which the souls of men must wither and die and blacken, as their bodies blacken under the electric current. Such forces cannot be named, cannot be spoken, cannot be imagined except under a veil and a symbol, a symbol to the most of us appearing a quaint, poetic fancy, to some a foolish tale. But you and I, at all events, have known something of the terror that may dwell in the secret place of life, manifested under human flesh; that which is without form taking to itself a form. Oh, Austin, how can it be? How is it that the very sunlight does not turn to blackness before this thing, the hard earth melt and boil beneath such a burden?"

Villiers was pacing up and down the room, and the beads of sweat stood out on his forehead. Austin sat silent for a while, but Villiers saw him make a sign upon his breast.

"I say again, Villiers, you will surely never enter such a house as that? You would never pass out alive."

"Yes, Austin, I shall go out alive—I, and Clarke with me."

"What do you mean? You cannot, you would not dare . . ."

"Wait a moment. The air was very pleasant and fresh this morning; there was a breeze blowing, even through this dull street, and I thought I would take a walk. Piccadilly stretched before me a clear, bright vista, and the sun flashed on the carriages and on the quivering leaves in the park. It was a joyous morning, and men and women looked at the sky and smiled as they went about their work or their pleasure, and the wind blew as blithely as upon the meadows and the scented gorse. But somehow or other I got out of the bustle and the gaiety, and found myself walking slowly along a quiet, dull street, where there seemed to be no sunshine and no air, and where the few foot-passengers loitered as they walked, and hung indecisively about corners and archways. I walked along, hardly knowing where I was going or what I did there, but feeling impelled, as one sometimes is, to explore still further, with a vague idea of reaching some unknown goal. Thus I forged up the street, noting the small traffic in the milk-shop, and wondering at the incongruous medley of penny pipes, black tobacco, sweets, newspapers, and comic songs which here and there jostled one another in the short compass of a single window. I think it was a cold shudder that suddenly passed through me that first told me that I had found what I wanted. I looked up from the pavement and stopped before a dusty shop, above which the lettering had faded, where the red bricks of two hundred years ago had grimed to black; where the windows had gathered to themselves the fog and the dirt of winters innumerable. I saw what I required; but I think it was five minutes before I had steadied myself and could walk in and ask for it in a cool voice and with a calm face. I think there must even then have been a tremor in my words, for the old man who came out from his back parlour, and fumbled slowly among his goods, looked oddly at me as he tied the parcel. I paid what he asked, and stood leaning by the counter, with a strange reluctance to take up my goods and go. I asked about the business, and learnt that trade was bad and the profits cut down sadly; but then the street was not what it was before traffic had been diverted, but that was done forty years ago, 'just before my father died,' he said. I got away at last, and walked along sharply; it was a dismal street indeed, and I was glad to return to the bustle and the noise. Would you like to see my purchase?"

Austin said nothing, but nodded his head slightly; he still looked white and sick. Villiers pulled out a drawer in the bamboo table, and showed Austin a long coil of cord, hard and new; and at one end was a running noose.

"It is the best hempen cord," said Villiers, "just as it used to be made for the old trade, the man told me. Not an inch of jute from end to end."

Austin set his teeth hard, and stared at Villiers, growing whiter as he looked.

"You would not do it," he murmured at last. "You would not have blood on your hands. My God!" he exclaimed, with sudden vehemence, "you cannot mean this, Villiers, that you will make yourself a hangman?"

"No. I shall offer a choice, and leave Helen Vaughan alone with this cord in a locked room for fifteen minutes. If when we go in it is not done, I shall call the nearest policeman. That is all."

"I must go now. I cannot stay here any longer; I cannot bear this. Good-night."

"Good-night, Austin."

The door shut, but in a moment it was opened again, and Austin stood, white and ghastly, in the entrance.

"I was forgetting," he said, "that I too have something to tell. I have received a letter from Dr. Harding of Buenos Aires. He says that he attended Meyrick for three weeks before his death."

"And does he say what carried him off in the prime of life? It was not fever?"

"No, it was not fever. According to the doctor, it was an utter collapse of the whole system, probably caused by some severe shock. But he states that the patient would tell him nothing, and that he was consequently at some disadvantage in treating the case."

"Is there anything more?"

"Yes. Dr. Harding ends his letter by saying: 'I think this is all the information I can give you about your poor friend. He had not been long in Buenos Aires, and knew scarcely anyone, with the exception of a person who did not bear the best of characters, and has since left—a Mrs. Vaughan.'"

8. The Fragments

Among the papers of the well-known physician, Dr. Robert Matheson, of Ashley Street, Piccadilly, who died suddenly, of apoplectic seizure, at the beginning of 1892, a leaf of manuscript paper was found, covered with pencil jottings. These notes were in Latin, much abbreviated, and had evidently been made in great haste. The MS. was only deciphered with great difficulty, and some words have up to the present time evaded all the efforts of the experts employed. The date, "XXV Jul. 1888," is written on the right-hand corner of the MS. The following is a translation of Dr. Matheson's manuscript.

> Whether science would benefit by these brief notes if they could be published, I do not know, but rather doubt. But certainly I shall never take the responsibility of publishing or divulging one word of what is here written, not only on account of my oath freely given to those two persons who were present, but also because the details are too abominable. It is probably that, upon mature consideration, and after weighing the good and

evil, I shall one day destroy this paper, or at least leave it under seal to my friend D., trusting in his discretion, to use it or to burn it, as he may think fit.

As was befitting, I did all that my knowledge suggested to make sure that I was suffering under no delusion. At first astounded, I could hardly think, but in a minute's time I was sure that my pulse was steady and regular, and that I was in my real and true senses. I then fixed my eyes quietly on what was before me.

Though horror and revolting nausea rose up within me, and an odour of corruption choked my breath, I remained firm. I was then privileged or accursed, I dare not say which, to see that which was on the bed, lying there black like ink, transformed before my eyes. The skin, and the flesh, and the muscles, and the bones, and the firm structure of the human body that I had thought to be unchangeable, and permanent as adamant, began to melt and dissolve.

I knew that the body may be separated into its elements by external agencies, but I should have refused to believe what I saw. For here there was some internal force, of which I knew nothing, that caused dissolution and change.

Here too was all the work by which man had been made repeated before my eyes. I saw the form waver from sex to sex, dividing itself from itself, and then again reunited. Then I saw the body descend to the beasts whence it ascended, and that which was on the heights go down to the depths, even to the abyss of all being. The principle of life, which makes organism, always remained, while the outward form changed.

The light within the room had turned to blackness, not the darkness of night, in which objects are seen dimly, for I could see clearly and without difficulty. But it was the negation of light; objects were presented to my eyes, if I may say so, without any medium, in such a manner that if there had been a prism in the room I should have seen no colours represented in it.

I watched, and at last I saw nothing but a substance as jelly. Then the ladder was ascended again . . . [here the MS. is illegible] . . . for one instant I saw a Form, shaped in dimness before me, which I will not farther describe. But the symbol of this form may be seen in ancient sculptures, and in paintings which survived beneath the lava, too foul to be spoken of . . . as a horrible and unspeakable shape, neither man nor beast, was changed into human form, there came finally death.

I who saw all this, not without great horror and loathing of soul, here write my name, declaring all that I have set on this paper to be true.

Robert Matheson, Med. Dr.

. . . Such, Raymond, is the story of what I know and what I have seen. The burden of it was too heavy for me to bear alone, and yet I could tell it to none but you. Villiers, who was with me at the last, knows nothing of that awful secret of the wood, of how what we both saw die, lay upon the smooth, sweet turf amidst the summer flowers, half in sun and half in shadow, and holding the girl Rachel's hand, called and summoned those companions, and shaped in solid form, upon the earth we tread on, the horror which we can but hint at, which we can only name under a figure. I would not tell Villiers of this, nor of that resemblance, which struck me as with a blow upon my heart, when I saw the portrait, which filled the cup of terror at the end. What this can mean I dare not guess. I know that what I saw perish was not Mary, and yet in the last agony Mary's eyes looked into mine. Whether there be anyone who can show the last link in this chain of awful mystery, I do not know, but if there be anyone who can do this, you, Raymond, are the man. And if you know the secret, it rests with you to tell it or not, as you please.

I am writing this letter to you immediately on my getting

back to town. I have been in the country for the last few days; perhaps you may be able to guess in what part. While the horror and wonder of London was at its height—"Mrs. Beaumont," as I have told you, was well known in society—I wrote to my friend Dr. Phillips, giving some brief outline, or rather hint, of what had happened, and asking him to tell me the name of the village where the events he had related to me occurred. He gave me the name, as he said with the less hesitation, because Rachel's father and mother were dead, and the rest of the family had gone to a relative in the state of Washington six months before. The parents, he said, had undoubtedly died of grief and horror caused by the terrible death of their daughter, and by what had gone before that death. On the evening of the day on which I received Phillips's letter I was at Caermaen, and standing beneath the mouldering Roman walls, white with the winters of seventeen hundred years. I looked over the meadow where once had stood the older temple of the "God of the Deeps," and saw a house gleaming in the sunlight. It was the house where Helen had lived. I stayed at Caermaen for several days. The people of the place, I found, knew little and had guessed less. Those whom I spoke to on the matter seemed surprised that an antiquarian (as I professed myself to be) should trouble about a village tragedy, of which they gave a very commonplace version, and, as you may imagine, I told nothing of what I knew. Most of my time was spent in the great wood that rises just above the village and climbs the hillside, and goes down to the river in the valley; such another long lovely valley, Raymond, as that on which we looked one summer night, walking to and fro before your house. For many an hour I strayed through the maze of the forest, turning now to right and now to left, pacing slowly down long alleys of undergrowth, shadowy and chill, even under the midday sun, and halting beneath great oaks; lying on the short turf of a clearing where the faint sweet scent of wild roses came to me on the wind and mixed with the heavy perfume of the elder, whose mingled odour is like the odour of the room of the dead, a vapour of incense and corruption. I stood at the edges of the wood, gazing at all the pomp and procession of the foxgloves towering amidst the bracken and shining red in the broad sunshine, and beyond them into deep thickets of close undergrowth where springs boil up from the rock and nourish the waterweeds, dank and evil. But in all my wanderings I avoided one part of the wood; it was not till yesterday that I climbed to the summit of the hill, and stood upon the ancient Roman road that threads the highest ridge of the wood. Here they had walked, Helen and Rachel, along this quiet causeway, upon the pavement of green turf, shut in on either side by high banks of red earth, and tall hedges of shining beech, and here I followed in their steps, looking out, now and again, through partings in the boughs, and seeing on one side the sweep of the wood stretching far to right and left, and sinking into the broad level, and beyond, the yellow sea, and the land over the sea. On the other side was the valley and the river and hill following hill as wave on wave, and wood and meadow, and cornfield, and white houses gleaming, and a great wall of mountain, and far blue peaks in the north. And so at last I came to the place. The track went up a gentle slope, and widened out into an open space with a wall of thick undergrowth around it, and then, narrowing again, passed on into the distance and the faint blue mist of summer heat. And into this pleasant summer glade Rachel passed a girl, and left it, who shall say what? I did not stay long there.

In a small town near Caermaen there is a museum, containing for the most part Roman remains which had been found in the neighbourhood at various times. On the day after my arrival at Caermaen I walked over to the town in question, and took the opportunity of inspecting the museum. After I had seen most of the sculptured stones, the coffins, rings, coins, and fragments of tessellated pavement which the place contains, I was shown a small square pillar of white stone, which had been recently discovered in the wood of which I have been speaking, and, as I found on inquiry, in that open space where the Roman road broadens out. On one side of the pillar was an inscription, of which I took a note. Some of the letters have been defaced, but I do not think there can be any doubt as to those which I supply. The inscription is as follows:

DEVOMNODENTI
FLAVIVSSENILISPOSSVIT
PROPTERNVPTIAS
QUASVIDITSVBVMBRA

"To the great god Nodens (the god of the Great Deep or Abyss) Flavius Senilis has erected this pillar on account of the marriage which he saw beneath the shade."

The custodian of the museum informed me that local antiquaries were much puzzled, not by the inscription, or by any difficulty in translating it, but as to the circumstance or rite to which allusion is made.

. . . And now, my dear Clarke, as to what you tell me about Helen Vaughn, whom you say you saw die under circumstances of the utmost and almost incredible horror. I was interested in your account, but a good deal, nay all, of what you told me I knew already. I can understand the strange likeness you remarked both in the portrait and in the actual face; you have seen Helen's mother. You remember that still summer night so many years ago, when I talked to you of the world beyond the shadows, and of the god Pan. You remember Mary. She was the mother of Helen Vaughan, who was born nine months after that night.

Mary never recovered her reason. She lay, as you saw her, all the while upon her bed, and a few days after the child was born she died. I fancy that just at the last she knew me; I was standing by the bed, and the old look came into her eyes for a second, and then she shuddered and groaned and died. It was an ill work I did that night when you were present; I broke open the door of the house of life without knowing or caring what might pass forth or enter in. I recollect your telling me at the time, sharply enough, and rightly enough too, in one sense, that I had ruined the reason of a human being by a foolish experiment, based on an absurd theory. You did well to blame me, but my theory was not all absurdity. What I said Mary would see, she saw, but I forgot that no human eyes could look on such a vision with impunity. And I forgot, as I have just said, that when the house of life is thus thrown open, there may enter in that for which we have no name, and human flesh may become the veil of a horror one dare not express. I played with energies which I did not understand, and you have seen the ending of it. Helen Vaughan did well to bind the cord about her neck and die, though the death was horrible. The blackened face, the hideous form upon the bed, changing and melting before your eyes from woman to man, from man to beast, and from beast to worse than beast, all the strange horror that you witnessed, surprises me but little. What you say the doctor whom you sent for saw and shuddered at I noticed long ago; I knew what I had done the moment the child was born, and when it was scarcely five years old I surprised it, not once or twice but several times with a playmate, you may guess of what kind. It was for me a constant, an incarnate horror, and after a few years I felt I could bear it no longer, and I sent Helen Vaughan away. You know now what frightened the boy in the wood. The rest of the strange story, and all else that you tell me, as discovered by your friend, I have contrived to learn from time to time, almost to the last chapter. And now Helen is with her companions . . .

DRACULA'S GUEST

Bram Stoker

(1897)

"Dracula's Guest" was cut from the original manuscript of the classic novel by its publisher because of the length of the original. It was published as a short story in 1914, two years after the author's death.

When we started for our drive the sun was shining brightly on Munich, and the air was full of the joyousness of early summer. Just as we were about to depart, Herr Delbrück (the maître d'hôtel of the Quatre Saisons, where I was staying) came down, bareheaded, to the carriage and, after wishing me a pleasant drive, said to the coachman, still holding his hand on the handle of the carriage door:

"Remember you are back by nightfall. The sky looks bright but there is a shiver in the north wind that says there may be a sudden storm. But I am sure you will not be late." Here he smiled, and added, "For you know what night it is."

Johann answered with an emphatic, "Ja, mein Herr," and, touching his hat, drove off quickly. When we had cleared the town, I said, after signalling to him to stop:

"Tell me, Johann, what is tonight?"

He crossed himself, as he answered laconically: "Walpurgis Nacht." Then he took out his watch, a great, old-fashioned German silver thing as big as a turnip, and looked at it, with his eyebrows gathered together and a little impatient shrug of his shoulders. I realised that this was his way of respectfully protesting against the unnecessary delay, and sank back in the carriage, merely motioning him to proceed. He started off rapidly, as if to make up for lost time. Every now and then the horses seemed to throw up their heads and sniffed the air suspiciously. On such occasions I often looked round in alarm. The road was pretty bleak, for we were traversing a sort of high, wind-swept plateau. As we drove, I saw a road that looked but little used, and which seemed to dip through a little, winding valley. It looked so inviting that, even at the risk of offending him, I called Johann to stop—and when he had pulled up, I told him I would like to drive down that road. He made all sorts of excuses, and frequently crossed himself as he spoke. This somewhat piqued my curiosity, so I asked him various questions. He answered fencingly, and repeatedly looked at his watch in protest. Finally I said:

"Well, Johann, I want to go down this road. I shall not ask you to come unless you like; but tell me why you do not like to go, that is all I ask." For answer he seemed to throw himself off the box, so quickly did he reach the ground. Then he stretched out his hands appealingly to me, and implored me not to go. There was just enough of English mixed with the German for me to understand the drift of his talk. He seemed always just about to tell me something—the very idea of which evidently frightened him; but each time he pulled himself up, saying, as he crossed himself: "Walpurgis Nacht!"

I tried to argue with him, but it was difficult to argue with a man who did not know one's language. The advantage certainly rested with him, for although he began to speak in English, of a very crude and broken kind, he always got excited and broke into his native tongue—and every time he did so, he looked at his watch. Then the horses became restless and sniffed the air. At this he grew very pale, and, looking around in a frightened way, he suddenly jumped forward, took them by the bridles and led them on some twenty feet. I followed, and asked why he had done this. For answer he crossed himself, pointed to the spot we had left and drew his carriage in the direction of the other road, indicating a cross, and said, first in German, then in English: "Buried him—him what killed themselves."

I remembered the old custom of burying suicides at crossroads: "Ah! I see, a suicide. How interesting!" But for the life of me I could not make out why the horses were frightened.

Whilst we were talking, we heard a sort of sound between a yelp and a bark. It was far away; but the horses got very restless, and it took Johann all this time to quiet them. He was pale, and said, "It sounds like a wolf—but yet there are no wolves here now."

"No?" I said, questioning him; "isn't it long since the wolves were so near the city?"

"Long, long," he answered, "in the spring and summer; but with the snow the wolves have been here not so 1ong."

Whilst he was petting the horses and trying to quiet them, dark clouds drifted rapidly across the sky. The sunshine passed away, and a breath of cold wind seemed to drift past us. It was only a breath, however, and more in the nature of a warning than a fact, for the sun came out brightly again. Johann looked under his lifted hand at the horizon and said:

"The storm of snow he comes before long time." Then he looked at his watch again, and, straightway holding his reins firmly—for the horses were still pawing the ground restlessly and shaking their heads—he climbed to his box as though the time had come for proceeding on our journey.

I felt a little obstinate and did not at once get into the carriage.

"Tell me," I said, "about this place where the road leads," and I pointed down.

Again he crossed himself and mumbled a prayer, before he answered, "It is unholy."

"What is unholy?" I enquired.

"The village."

"Then there is a village?"

"No, no. No one lives there hundreds of years."

My curiosity was piqued. "But you said there was a village."

"There was."

"Where is it now?"

Whereupon he burst out into a long story in German and English, so mixed up that I could not quite understand exactly what he said, but roughly I gathered that long ago, hundreds of years, men had died there and been buried in their graves; and sounds were heard under the clay, and when the graves were opened, men and women were found rosy with life, and their mouths red with blood. And so, in haste to save their lives (aye, and their souls!—and here he crossed himself) those who were left fled away to other places, where the living lived, and the dead were dead and not—not something. He was evidently afraid to speak the last words. As he proceeded with his narration, he grew more and more excited. It seemed as if his imagination had got hold of him, and he ended in a perfect paroxysm of fear—white-faced, perspiring, trembling and looking round him, as if expecting that sonic dreadful presence would manifest itself there in the bright sunshine on the open plain. Finally, in an agony of desperation, he cried:

"Walpurgis Nacht!" and pointed to the carriage for me to get in. All my English blood rose at this, and, standing back, I said:

"You are afraid, Johann—you are afraid. Go home; I shall return alone; the walk will do me good." The carriage door was open. I took from the seat my walking-stick—which I always carry on my holiday excursions—and closed the door, pointing back to Munich, and said, "Go home, Johann—Walpurgis Nacht doesn't concern Englishmen."

The horses were now more restive than ever, and Johann was trying to hold them in, while excitedly imploring me not to do anything so foolish. I pitied the poor fellow, he was deeply in earnest; but all the same I could not help laughing. His English was quite gone now. In his anxiety he had forgotten that his only means of making me understand was to talk my language, so he jabbered away in his native German. It began to be a little tedious. After giving the direction, "Home!" I turned to go down the cross-road into the valley.

With a despairing gesture, Johann turned his horses towards Munich. I leaned on my stick and looked after him. He went slowly along the road for a while: then there came over the crest of the hill a man tall and thin. I could see so much in the distance. When he drew near the horses, they began to jump and kick about, then to scream with terror. Johann could not hold them in; they bolted down the road, running away madly. I watched them out of sight, then looked for the stranger, but I found that he, too, was gone.

With a light heart I turned down the side road through the deepening valley to which Johann had objected. There was not the slightest reason, that I could see, for his objection; and I daresay I tramped for a couple of hours without thinking of time or distance, and certainly without seeing a person or a house. So far as the place was concerned, it was desolation itself. But I did not notice this particularly till, on turning a bend in the road, I came upon a scattered fringe of wood; then I recognised that I had been impressed unconsciously by the desolation of the region through which I had passed.

I sat down to rest myself, and began to look around. It struck me that it was considerably colder than it had been at the commencement of my walk—a sort of sighing sound seemed to be around me, with, now and then, high overhead, a sort of muffled roar. Looking upwards I noticed that great thick clouds were drifting rapidly across the sky from North to South at a great height. There were signs of coming storm in some lofty stratum of the air. I was a little chilly, and, thinking that it was the sitting still after the exercise of walking, I resumed my journey.

The ground I passed over was now much more picturesque. There were no striking objects that the eye might single out; but in all there was a charm of beauty. I took little heed of time and it was only when the deepening twilight forced itself upon me that I began to think of how I should find my way home. The brightness of the day had gone. The air was cold, and the drifting of clouds high overhead was more marked. They were accompanied by a sort of far-away rushing sound, through which seemed to come at intervals that mysterious cry which the driver had said came from a wolf. For a while I hesitated. I had said I would see the deserted village, so on I went, and presently came on a wide stretch of open country, shut in by hills all around. Their sides were covered with trees which spread down to the plain, dotting, in clumps, the gentler slopes and hollows which showed here and there. I followed with my eye the winding of the road, and saw that it curved close to one of the densest of these clumps and was lost behind it.

As I looked there came a cold shiver in the air, and the snow began to fall. I thought of the miles and miles of bleak country I had passed, and then hurried on to seek the shelter of the wood in front. Darker and darker grew the sky, and faster and heavier fell the snow, till the earth before and around me was a glistening white carpet the further edge of which was lost in misty vagueness. The road was here but crude, and when on the level its boundaries were not so marked as when it passed through the cuttings; and in a little while I found that I must have strayed from it, for I missed underfoot the hard surface, and my feet sank deeper in the grass and moss. Then the wind grew stronger and blew with ever increasing force, till I was fain to run before it. The air became icy-cold, and in spite of my exercise I began to suffer. The snow was now falling so thickly and whirling around me in such rapid eddies that I could hardly keep my eyes open. Every now and then the heavens were torn asunder by vivid lightning, and in the flashes I could see ahead of me a great mass of trees, chiefly yew and cypress all heavily coated with snow.

I was soon amongst the shelter of the trees, and there, in comparative silence, I could hear the rush of the wind high overhead. Presently the blackness of the storm had become merged in the darkness of the night. By-and-by the storm seemed to be passing away: it now only came in fierce puffs or blasts. At such moments the weird sound of the wolf appeared to be echoed by many similar sounds around me.

Now and again, through the black mass of drifting cloud, came a straggling ray of moonlight, which lit up the expanse, and showed me that I was at the edge of a dense mass of cypress and yew trees. As the snow had ceased to fall, I walked out from the shelter and began to investigate more closely. It appeared to me that, amongst so many old foundations as I had passed, there might be still standing a house in which, though in ruins,

I could find some sort of shelter for a while. As I skirted the edge of the copse, I found that a low wall encircled it, and following this I presently found an opening. Here the cypresses formed an alley leading up to a square mass of some kind of building. Just as I caught sight of this, however, the drifting clouds obscured the moon, and I passed up the path in darkness. The wind must have grown colder, for I felt myself shiver as I walked; but there was hope of shelter, and I groped my way blindly on.

I stopped, for there was a sudden stillness. The storm had passed; and, perhaps in sympathy with nature's silence, my heart seemed to cease to beat. But this was only momentarily; for suddenly the moonlight broke through the clouds, showing me that I was in a graveyard, and that the square object before me was a great massive tomb of marble, as white as the snow that lay on and all around it. With the moonlight there came a fierce sigh of the storm, which appeared to resume its course with a long, low howl, as of many dogs or wolves. I was awed and shocked, and felt the cold perceptibly grow upon me till it seemed to grip me by the heart. Then while the flood of moonlight still fell on the marble tomb, the storm gave further evidence of renewing, as though it was returning on its track. Impelled by some sort of fascination, I approached the sepulchre to see what it was, and why such a thing stood alone in such a place. I walked around it, and read, over the Doric door, in German:

COUNTESS DOLINGEN OF GRATZ
IN STYRIA
SOUGHT AND FOUND DEATH
1801

On the top of the tomb, seemingly driven through the solid marble—for the structure was composed of a few vast blocks of stone—was a great iron spike or stake. On going to the back I saw, graven in Great Russian letters:

The dead travel fast.

There was something so weird and uncanny about the whole thing that it gave me a turn and made me feel quite faint. I began to wish, for the first time, that I had taken Johann's advice. Here a thought struck me, which came under almost mysterious circumstances and with a terrible shock. This was Walpurgis Night!

Walpurgis Night, when, according to the belief of millions of people, the devil was abroad—when the graves were opened and the dead came forth and walked. When all evil things of earth and air and water held revel. This very place the driver had specially shunned. This was the depopulated village of centuries ago. This was where the suicide lay; and this was the place where I was alone—unmanned, shivering with cold in a shroud of snow with a wild storm gathering again upon me! It took all my philosophy, all the religion I had been taught, all my courage, not to collapse in a paroxysm of fright.

And now a perfect tornado burst upon me. The ground shook as though thousands of horses thundered across it; and this time the storm bore on its icy wings, not snow, but great hailstones which drove with such violence that they might have come from the throngs of Balearic slingers—hailstones that beat down leaf and branch and made the shelter of the cypresses of no more avail than though their stems were standing-corn. At the first I had rushed to the nearest tree; but I was soon fain to leave it and seek the only spot that seemed to afford refuge, the deep Doric doorway of the marble tomb. There, crouching against the massive bronze door, I gained a certain amount of protection from the beating of the hailstones, for now they only drove against me as they ricocheted from the ground and the side of the marble.

As I leaned against the door, it moved slightly and opened inwards. The shelter of even a tomb was welcome in that pitiless tempest, and I was about to enter it when there came a flash of forked-lightning that lit up the whole expanse of the heavens. In the instant, as I am a living man, I saw, as my eyes were turned into the darkness of the tomb, a beautiful woman, with rounded cheeks and red lips, seemingly sleeping on a bier. As the thunder broke overhead, I was grasped as by the hand of a giant and hurled out into the storm. The whole thing was so sudden that, before I could realise the shock, moral as well as physical, I found the hailstones beating me down. At the same time I had a strange, dominating feeling that I was not alone. I looked towards the tomb. Just then there came another blinding flash, which seemed to strike the iron stake that surmounted the tomb and to pour through to the earth, blasting and crumbling the marble, as in a burst of flame. The dead woman rose for a moment of agony, while she was lapped in the flame, and her bitter scream of pain was drowned in the thundercrash. The last thing I heard was this mingling of dreadful sound, as again I was seized in the giant-grasp and dragged away, while the hailstones beat on me, and the air around seemed reverberant with the howling of wolves. The last sight that I remembered was a vague, white, moving mass, as if all the graves around me had sent out the phantoms of their sheeted-dead, and that they were closing in on me through the white cloudiness of the driving hail.

Gradually there came a sort of vague beginning of consciousness; then a sense of weariness that was dreadful. For a time I remembered nothing; but slowly my senses returned. My feet seemed positively racked with pain, yet I could not move them. They seemed to be numbed. There was an icy feeling at the back of my neck and all down my spine, and my ears, like my feet, were dead, yet in torment; but there was in my breast a sense of warmth which was, by comparison, delicious. It was as a nightmare—a physical nightmare, if one may use such an expression; for some heavy weight on my chest made it difficult for me to breathe.

This period of semi-lethargy seemed to remain a long time, and as it faded away I must have slept or swooned. Then came a sort of loathing, like the first stage of sea-sickness, and a wild desire to be free from something—I knew not what. A vast stillness enveloped me, as though all the world were asleep or dead—only broken by the low panting as of some animal close to me. I felt a warm rasping at my throat, then came a consciousness of the awful truth, which chilled me to the heart and sent the blood surging up through my brain. Some great animal was lying on me and now licking my throat. I feared to stir, for some instinct of prudence bade me lie still; but the brute seemed to realise that there was now some change in me, for it raised its head. Through my eye-lashes I saw above me the two great flaming eyes of a gigantic wolf. Its sharp white teeth gleamed in the gaping red mouth, and I could feel its hot breath fierce and acrid upon me.

For another spell of time I remembered no more. Then I became conscious of a low growl, followed by a yelp, renewed again and again. Then, seemingly very far away, I heard a "Holloa! holloa!" as of many voices calling in unison. Cautiously I raised my head and looked in the direction whence the sound came; but the cemetery blocked my view. The wolf still continued to yelp in a strange way, and a red glare began to move round the grove of cypresses, as though following the sound. As the voices drew closer, the wolf yelped faster and louder, I feared to make either sound or motion. Nearer came the red glow, over the white pall which stretched into the darkness around me. Then all at once from beyond the trees there came at a trot a troop of horsemen bearing torches. The wolf rose from my breast and made for the cemetery. I saw one of the horsemen (soldiers by their caps and their military cloaks) raise his carbine and take aim. A companion knocked up his arm, and I heard the ball whizz over my head. He had evidently taken my body for that of the wolf. Another sighted the animal as it slunk away, and a shot followed. Then, at a gallop, the troop rode forward—some towards me, others following the wolf as it disappeared amongst the snow-clad cypresses.

As they drew nearer I tried to move, but was powerless, although I could see and hear all that went on around me. Two or three of the soldiers jumped from their horses and knelt beside me. One of them raised my head, and placed his hand over my heart.

"Good news, comrades!" he cried. "His heart still beats!"

Then some brandy was poured down my throat; it put vigour into me, and I was able to open my eyes fully and look around. Lights and shadows were moving among the trees, and I heard men call to one another. They drew together, uttering frightening exclamations; and the lights flashed as the others came pouring out of the cemetery pell-mell, like men possessed. When the further ones came close to us, those who were around me asked them eagerly:

"Well, have you found him?"

The reply rang out hurriedly:

"No! no! Come away quick—quick! This is no place to stay, and on this of all nights!"

"What was it?" was the question, asked in all manner of keys. The answer came variously and all indefinitely as though the men were moved by some common impulse to speak, yet were restrained by some common fear from giving their thoughts.

"It—it—indeed!" gibbered one, whose wits had plainly given out for the moment.

"A wolf—and yet not a wolf!" another put in shudderingly.

"No use trying for him without the sacred bullet," a third remarked in a more ordinary manner.

"Serve us right for coming out on this night! Truly we have earned our thousand marks!" were the ejaculations of a fourth.

"There was blood on the broken marble," another said after a pause—"the lightning never brought that there. And for him—is he safe? Look at his throat! See, comrades, the wolf has been lying on him and keeping his blood warm."

The officer looked at my throat and replied:

"He is all right; the skin is not pierced. What does it all mean? We should never have found him but for the yelping of the wolf."

"What became of it?" asked the man who was holding up my head, and who seemed the least panic-stricken of the party, for his hands were steady and without tremor. On his sleeve was the chevron of a petty officer.

"It went to its home," answered the man, whose long face

was pallid, and who actually shook with terror as he glanced around fearfully. "There are graves enough there in which it may lie. Come, comrades—come quickly! Let us leave this cursed spot."

The officer raised me to a sitting posture, as he uttered a word of command; then several men placed me upon a horse. He sprang to the saddle behind me, took me in his arms, gave the word to advance; and, turning our faces away from the cypresses, we rode away in swift, military order.

As yet my tongue refused its office, and I was perforce silent. I must have fallen asleep; for the next thing I remembered was finding myself standing up, supported by a soldier on each side of me. It was almost broad daylight, and to the north a red streak of sunlight was reflected, like a path of blood, over the waste of snow. The officer was telling the men to say nothing of what they had seen, except that they found an English stranger, guarded by a large dog.

"Dog! that was no dog," cut in the man who had exhibited such fear. "I think I know a wolf when I see one."

The young officer answered calmly: "I said a dog."

"Dog!" reiterated the other ironically. It was evident that his courage was rising with the sun; and, pointing to me, he said, "Look at his throat. Is that the work of a dog, master?"

Instinctively I raised my hand to my throat, and as I touched it I cried out in pain. The men crowded round to look, some stooping down from their saddles; and again there came the calm voice of the young officer.

"A dog, as I said. If aught else were said we should only be laughed at?"

I was then mounted behind a trooper, and we rode on into the suburbs of Munich. Here we came across a stray carriage, into which I was lifted, and it was driven off to the Quatre Saisons—the young officer accompanying me, whilst a trooper followed with his horse, and the others rode off to their barracks.

When we arrived, Herr Delbrück rushed so quickly down the steps to meet me, that it was apparent he had been watching within. Taking me by both hands he solicitously led me in. The officer saluted me and was turning to withdraw, when I recognised his purpose, and insisted that he should come to my rooms. Over a glass of wine I warmly thanked him and his brave comrades for saving me. He replied simply that he was more than glad, and that Herr Delbrück had at the first taken steps to make all the searching party pleased; at which ambiguous utterance the maître d'hôtel smiled, while the officer pleaded duty and withdrew.

"But Herr Delbrück," I enquired, "how and why was it that the soldiers searched for me?"

He shrugged his shoulders, as if in depreciation of his own deed, as he replied:

"I was so fortunate as to obtain leave from the commander of the regiment in which I served, to ask for volunteers."

"But how did you know that I was lost?" I asked.

"The driver came hither with the remains of his carriage, which had been upset when the horses ran away."

"But surely you would not send a search-party of soldiers merely on this account."

"Oh, no!" he answered; "but even before the coachman arrived, I had this telegram from the Boyar whose guest you are," and he took from his pocket a telegram which he handed to me, and I read:

> *Bistritz.*
>
> Be careful of my guest—his safety is most precious to me. Should aught happen to him, or if he be missed, spare nothing to find him and ensure his safety. He is English and therefore adventurous. There are often dangers from snow and wolves and night. Lose not a moment if you suspect harm to him. I answer your zeal with my fortune.—*Dracula.*

As I held the telegram in my hand, the room seemed to whirl around me; and, if the attentive maître d'hôtel had not

THE MONKEY'S PAW

W. W. Jacobs

(1902)

The domestic tranquility of the opening of this version of the three-wishes legend seems to intensify the horror of its ghastly conclusion. The result is a simple, chilling tale that has the potency of an ancient myth.

I

Without, the night was cold and wet, but in the small parlour of Laburnum Villa the blinds were drawn and the fire burned brightly. Father and son were at chess; the former, who possessed ideas about the game involving radical changes, putting his king into such sharp and unnecessary perils that it even provoked comment from the white-haired old lady knitting placidly by the fire.

"Hark at the wind," said Mr. White, who, having seen a fatal mistake after it was too late, was amiably desirous of preventing his son from seeing it.

"I'm listening," said the latter, grimly surveying the board as he stretched out his hand. "Check."

"I should hardly think that he'd come to-night," said his father, with his hand poised over the board.

"Mate," replied the son.

"That's the worst of living so far out," bawled Mr. White, with sudden and unlooked-for violence; "of all the beastly, slushy, out-of-the-way places to live in, this is the worst. Path's a bog, and the road's a torrent. I don't know what people are thinking about. I suppose because only two houses in the road are let, they think it doesn't matter."

"Never mind, dear," said his wife soothingly; "perhaps you'll win the next one."

Mr. White looked up sharply, just in time to intercept a

knowing glance between mother and son. The words died away on his lips, and he hid a guilty grin in his thin gray beard.

"There he is," said Herbert White, as the gate banged to loudly and heavy footsteps came toward the door.

The old man rose with hospitable haste, and opening the door, was heard condoling with the new arrival. The new arrival also condoled with himself, so that Mrs. White said, "Tut tut!" and coughed gently as her husband entered the room, followed by a tall, burly man, beady of eye and rubicund of visage.

"Sergeant-Major Morris," he said, introducing him.

The sergeant-major shook hands, and taking the proffered seat by the fire, watched contentedly while his host got out whisky and tumblers and stood a small copper kettle on the fire.

At the third glass his eyes got brighter, and he began to talk, the little family circle regarding with eager interest this visitor from distant parts, as he squared his broad shoulders in the chair, and spoke of wild scenes and doughty deeds; of wars and plagues, and strange peoples.

"Twenty-one years of it," said Mr. White, nodding at his wife and son. "When he went away he was a slip of a youth in the warehouse. Now look at him."

"He don't look to have taken much harm," said Mrs. White politely.

"I'd like to go to India myself," said the old man, "just to look around a bit, you know."

"Better where you are," said the sergeant-major, shaking his head. He put down the empty glass, and sighing softly, shook it again.

"I should like to see those old temples and fakirs and jugglers," said the old man. "What was that you started telling me the other day about a monkey's paw or something, Morris?"

"Nothing," said the soldier hastily. "Leastways nothing worth hearing."

"Monkey's paw?" said Mrs. White curiously.

"Well, it's just a bit of what you might call magic, perhaps," said the sergeant-major off-handedly.

His three listeners leaned forward eagerly. The visitor absent-mindedly put his empty glass to his lips and then set it down again. His host filled it for him.

"To look at," said the sergeant-major, fumbling in his pocket, "it's just an ordinary little paw, dried to a mummy."

He took something out of his pocket and proffered it. Mrs. White drew back with a grimace, but her son, taking it, examined it curiously.

"And what is there special about it?" inquired Mr. White as he took it from his son, and having examined it, placed it upon the table.

"It had a spell put on it by an old fakir," said the sergeant-major, "a very holy man. He wanted to show that fate ruled people's lives, and that those who interfered with it did so to their sorrow. He put a spell on it so that three separate men could each have three wishes from it."

His manner was so impressive that his hearers were conscious that their light laughter jarred somewhat.

"Well, why don't you have three, sir?" said Herbert White cleverly.

The soldier regarded him in the way that middle age is wont to regard presumptuous youth. "I have," he said quietly, and his blotchy face whitened.

"And did you really have the three wishes granted?" asked Mrs. White.

"I did," said the sergeant-major, and his glass tapped against his strong teeth.

"And has anybody else wished?" persisted the old lady.

"The first man had his three wishes. Yes," was the reply; "I don't know what the first two were, but the third was for death. That's how I got the paw."

His tones were so grave that a hush fell upon the group.

"If you've had your three wishes, it's no good to you now then, Morris," said the old man at last. "What do you keep it for?"

The soldier shook his head. "Fancy, I suppose," he said slowly. "I did have some idea of selling it, but I don't think I will. It has caused enough mischief already. Besides, people won't buy. They think it's a fairy tale, some of them; and those who do think anything of it want to try it first and pay me afterward."

"If you could have another three wishes," said the old man, eyeing him keenly, "would you have them?"

"I don't know," said the other. "I don't know."

He took the paw, and dangling it between his forefinger and thumb, suddenly threw it upon the fire. White, with a slight cry, stooped down and snatched it off.

"Better let it burn," said the soldier solemnly.

"If you don't want it, Morris," said the other, "give it to me."

"I won't," said his friend doggedly. "I threw it on the fire. If you keep it, don't blame me for what happens. Pitch it on the fire again like a sensible man."

The other shook his head and examined his new possession closely. "How do you do it?" he inquired.

"Hold it up in your right hand and wish aloud," said the sergeant-major, "but I warn you of the consequences."

"Sounds like the *Arabian Nights*," said Mrs. White, as she rose and began to set the supper. "Don't you think you might wish for four pairs of hands for me?"

Her husband drew the talisman from his pocket, and then all three burst into laughter as the sergeant-major, with a look of alarm on his face, caught him by the arm.

"If you must wish," he said gruffly, "wish for something sensible."

Mr. White dropped it back in his pocket, and placing chairs, motioned his friend to the table. In the business of supper the talisman was partly forgotten, and afterward the three sat listening in an enthralled fashion to a second installment of the soldier's adventures in India.

"If the tale about the monkey's paw is not more truthful than those he has been telling us," said Herbert, as the door closed behind their guest, just in time to catch the last train, "we shan't make much out of it."

"Did you give him anything for it, father?" inquired Mrs. White, regarding her husband closely.

"A trifle," said he, colouring slightly. "He didn't want it, but I made him take it. And he pressed me again to throw it away."

"Likely," said Herbert, with pretended horror. "Why, we're going to be rich, and famous, and happy. Wish to be an emperor, father, to begin with; then you can't be henpecked."

He darted round the table, pursued by the maligned Mrs. White armed with an antimacassar.

Mr. White took the paw from his pocket and eyed it dubiously. "I don't know what to wish for, and that's a fact," he said slowly. "It seems to me I've got all I want."

"If you only cleared the house, you'd be quite happy, wouldn't you!" said Herbert, with his hand on his shoulder. "Well, wish for two hundred pounds, then; that'll just do it."

His father, smiling shamefacedly at his own credulity, held up the talisman, as his son, with a solemn face, somewhat marred by a wink at his mother, sat down at the piano and struck a few impressive chords.

"I wish for two hundred pounds," said the old man distinctly.

A fine crash from the piano greeted the words, interrupted by a shuddering cry from the old man. His wife and son ran toward him.

"It moved," he cried, with a glance of disgust at the object as it lay on the floor. "As I wished, it twisted in my hand like a snake."

"Well, I don't see the money," said his son, as he picked it up and placed it on the table, "and I bet I never shall."

"It must have been your fancy, father," said his wife, regarding him anxiously.

He shook his head. "Never mind, though; there's no harm done, but it gave me a shock all the same."

They sat down by the fire again while the two men finished their pipes. Outside, the wind was higher than ever, and the old man started nervously at the sound of a door banging upstairs. A silence unusual and depressing settled upon all three, which lasted until the old couple rose to retire for the night.

"I expect you'll find the cash tied up in a big bag in the middle of your bed," said Herbert, as he bade them good night, "and something horrible squatting up on top of the wardrobe watching you pocket your ill-gotten gains."

He sat alone in the darkness, gazing at the dying fire, and seeing faces in it. The last face was so horrible and so simian that he gazed at it with amazement. It got so vivid that, with a little uneasy laugh, he felt on the table for a glass containing a little water to throw over it. His hand grasped the monkey's paw, and with a little shiver he wiped his hand on his coat and went up to bed.

II

In the brightness of the wintery sun next morning as it streamed over the breakfast table he laughed at his fears. There was an air of prosaic wholesomeness about the room which it had lacked on the previous night, and the dirty, shrivelled little paw was pitched on the side-board with a carelessness which betokened no great belief in its virtues.

"I suppose all old soldiers are the same," said Mrs. White. "The idea of our listening to such nonsense! How could wishes be granted in these days? And if they could, how could two hundred pounds hurt you, father?"

"Might drop on his head from the sky," said the frivolous Herbert.

"Morris said the things happened so naturally," said his father, "that you might if you so wished attribute it to coincidence."

"Well, don't break into the money before I come back," said Herbert as he rose from the table. "I'm afraid it'll turn you into a mean, avaricious man, and we will have to disown you."

His mother laughed, and following him to the door, watched him down the road; and returning to the breakfast table, was very happy at the expense of her husband's credulity. All of which did not prevent her from scurrying to the door at the postman's knock, nor prevent her from referring somewhat shortly to retired sergeant-majors of bibulous habits when she found that the post brought a tailor's bill.

"Herbert will have some more of his funny remarks, I expect, when he comes home," she said, as they sat at dinner.

"I dare say," said Mr. White, pouring himself out some beer; "but for all that, the thing moved in my hand; that I'll swear to."

"You thought it did," said the old lady soothingly.

"I say it did," replied the other. "There was no thought about it; I had just—What's the matter?"

His wife made no reply. She was watching the mysterious movements of a man outside, who, peering in an undecided fashion at the house, appeared to be trying to make up his mind to enter. In mental connection with the two hundred pounds, she noticed that the stranger was well dressed, and wore a silk hat of glossy newness. Three times he paused at the gate, and then walked on again. The fourth time he stood with his hand upon it, and then with a sudden resolution flung it open and walked up the path. Mrs. White at the same moment placed her hands behind her, and hurriedly unfastening the strings on her apron, put that useful article of apparel beneath the cushion of her chair.

She brought the stranger, who seemed ill at ease, into the room. He gazed at her furtively, and listened in a preoccupied fashion as the old lady apologized for the appearance of the room, and her husband's coat, a garment he usually reserved for the garden. She then waited as patiently as her sex would permit, for him to broach his business, but he was at first strangely silent.

"I was asked to call," he said at last, and stooped and picked a piece of cotton from his trousers. "I come from Maw and Meggins."

The old lady started. "Is anything the matter?" she asked breathlessly. "Has anything happened to Herbert? What is it? What is it?"

Her husband interposed. "There, there, mother," he said hastily. "Sit down, and don't jump to conclusions. You've not brought bad news, I'm sure, sir;" and he eyed the other wistfully.

"I'm sorry—" began the visitor.

"Is he hurt?" demanded the mother wildly.

The visitor bowed in assent. "Badly hurt," he said quietly, "but he is not in any pain."

"Oh, thank God!" said the old woman, clasping her hands. "Thank God for that! Thank—"

She broke off suddenly as the sinister meaning of the assurance dawned upon her, and she saw the awful confirmation of her fears in the other's averted face. She caught her breath, and turning to her slower-witted husband, laid her trembling old hand upon his. There was a long silence.

"He was caught in the machinery," said the visitor at length in a low voice.

"Caught in the machinery," repeated Mr. White, in a dazed fashion, "yes."

He sat staring blankly out at the window, and taking his wife's hand between his own, pressed it as he had been wont to do in their old courting days nearly forty years before.

"He was the only one left to us," he said, turning gently to the visitor. "It is hard."

The other coughed, and rising, walked slowly to the window.

"The firm wished me to convey their sincere sympathy with you in your great loss," he said, without looking round. "I beg that you will understand I am only their servant and merely obeying orders."

There was no reply; the old woman's face was white, her eyes staring, and her breath inaudible; on the husband's face was a look such as his friend the sergeant might have carried into his first action.

"I was to say that Maw and Meggins disclaim all responsibility," continued the other. "They admit no liability at all, but in consideration of your son's services, they wish to present you with a certain sum as compensation."

Mr. White dropped his wife's hand, and rising to his feet, gazed with a look of horror at his visitor. His dry lips shaped the words, "How much?"

"Two hundred pounds," was the answer.

Unconscious of his wife's shriek, the old man smiled faintly, put out his hands like a sightless man, and dropped, a senseless heap, to the floor.

III

In the huge new cemetery, some two miles distant, the old people buried their dead, and came back to the house steeped in shadow and silence. It was all over so quickly that at first they could hardly realise it, and remained in a state of expectation as though of something else to happen—something else which was to lighten this load, too heavy for old hearts to bear.

But the days passed, and expectation gave place to resignation—the hopeless resignation of the old, sometimes miscalled apathy. Sometimes they hardly exchanged a word, for now they had nothing to talk about, and their days were long to weariness.

It was about a week after, that the old man, waking suddenly in the night, stretched out his hand and found himself alone. The room was in darkness, and the sound of subdued weeping came from the window. He raised himself in bed and listened.

"Come back," he said tenderly. "You will be cold."

"It is colder for my son," said the old woman, and wept afresh.

The sound of her sobs died away on his ears. The bed was warm, and his eyes heavy with sleep. He dozed fitfully, and then slept until a sudden wild cry from his wife awoke him with a start.

"*The paw!*" she cried wildly. "The monkey's paw!"

He started up in alarm. "Where? Where is it? What's the matter?"

She came stumbling across the room toward him. "I want it," she said quietly. "You've not destroyed it?"

"It's in the parlour, on the bracket," he replied, marvelling. "Why?"

She cried and laughed together, and bending over, kissed his cheek.

"I only just thought of it," she said hysterically. "Why didn't I think of it before? Why didn't *you* think of it?"

"Think of what?" he questioned.

"The other two wishes," she replied rapidly. "We've only had one."

"Was not that enough?" he demanded fiercely.

"No," she cried triumphantly; "we'll have one more. Go down and get it quickly, and wish our boy alive again."

The man sat up in bed and flung the bedclothes from his quaking limbs. "Good God, you are mad!" he cried, aghast.

"Get it," she panted; "get it quickly, and wish—Oh, my boy, my boy!"

Her husband struck a match and lit the candle. "Get back to bed," he said unsteadily. "You don't know what you are saying."

"We had the first wish granted," said the old woman feverishly; "why not the second?"

"A coincidence," stammered the old man.

"Go and get it and wish," cried his wife, quivering with excitement.

The old man turned and regarded her, and his voice shook. "He has been dead ten days, and besides he—I would not tell you else, but—I could only recognize him by his clothing. If he was too terrible for you to see then, how now?"

"Bring him back," cried the old woman, and dragged him toward the door. "Do you think I fear the child I have nursed?"

He went down in the darkness, and felt his way to the parlour, and then to the mantelpiece. The talisman was in its place, and a horrible fear that the unspoken wish might bring his mutilated son before him ere he could escape from the room seized upon him, and he caught his breath as he found that he had lost the direction of the door. His brow cold with sweat, he felt his way round the table, and groped along the wall until he found himself in the small passage with the unwholesome thing in his hand.

Even his wife's face seemed changed as he entered the room. It was white and expectant, and to his fears seemed to have an unnatural look upon it. He was afraid of her.

"*Wish!*" she cried, in a strong voice.

"It is foolish and wicked," he faltered.

"*Wish!*" repeated his wife.

He raised his hand. "I wish my son alive again."

The talisman fell to the floor, and he regarded it fearfully. Then he sank trembling into a chair as the old woman, with burning eyes, walked to the window and raised the blind.

He sat until he was chilled with the cold, glancing occasionally at the figure of the old woman peering through the window. The candle-end, which had burned below the rim of the china candlestick, was throwing pulsating shadows on the ceiling and walls, until, with a flicker larger than the rest it expired. The old man, with an unspeakable sense of relief at the failure of the talisman, crept back to his bed, and a minute or two afterward the old woman came silently and apathetically beside him.

Neither spoke, but lay silently listening to the ticking of the clock. A stair creaked, and a squeaky mouse scurried noisily through the wall. The darkness was oppressive, and after lying for some time screwing up his courage, he took the box of matches, and striking one, went downstairs for a candle.

At the foot of the stairs the match went out, and he paused to strike another; and at the same moment a knock, so quiet and stealthy as to be scarcely audible, sounded on the front door.

The matches fell from his hand and spilled in the passage. He stood motionless, his breath suspended until the knock was repeated. Then he turned and fled swiftly back to his room, and closed the door behind him. A third knock sounded through the house.

"*What's that*?" cried the old woman, starting up.

"A rat," said the old man in shaking tones—"a rat. It passed me on the stairs."

His wife sat up in bed listening. A loud knock resounded through the house.

"It's Herbert!" she screamed. "It's Herbert!"

She ran to the door, but her husband was before her, and catching her by the arm, held her tightly.

"What are you going to do?" he whispered hoarsely.

"It's my boy; it's Herbert!" she cried, struggling mechanically.

"I forgot it was two miles away. What are you holding me for? Let go. I must open the door."

"For God's sake don't let it in," cried the old man, trembling.

"You're afraid of your own son," she cried, struggling. "Let me go. I'm coming, Herbert; I'm coming."

There was another knock, and another. The old woman with a sudden wrench broke free and ran from the room. Her husband followed to the landing, and called after her appealingly as she hurried downstairs. He heard the chain rattle back and the bottom bolt drawn slowly and stiffly from the socket. Then the old woman's voice strained and panting.

"The bolt," she cried loudly. "Come down. I can't reach it."

But her husband was on his hands and knees groping wildly on the floor in search of the paw. If he could only find it before the thing outside got in. A perfect fusillade of knocks reverberated through the house, and he heard the scraping of a chair as his wife put it down in the passage against the door. He heard the creaking of the bolt as it came slowly back, and at the same moment he found the monkey's paw, and frantically breathed his third and last wish.

The knocking ceased suddenly, although the echoes of it were still in the house. He heard the chair drawn back, and the door opened. A cold wind rushed up the staircase, and a long loud wail of disappointment and misery from his wife gave him courage to run down to her side, and then to the gate beyond. The street lamp flickering opposite shone on a quiet and deserted road.

OH, WHISTLE AND I'LL COME TO YOU, MY LAD

M. R. James

(1904)

That a story could be at once humorous and eerie may seem paradoxical, but this one achieves this feat. The very sensible Professor Parkins would seem to be the last person to be shaken by the supernatural, which makes the events of the narrative that much more enjoyable.

"I suppose you will be getting away pretty soon, now Fall term is over, Professor," said a person not in the story to the Professor of Ontography, soon after they had sat down next to each other at a feast in the hospitable hall of St James's College.

The Professor was young, neat, and precise in speech. "Yes," he said; "my friends have been making me take up golf this term, and I mean to go to the East Coast—in point of fact to Burnstow (I dare say you know it)—for a week or ten days, to improve my game. I hope to get off tomorrow."

"Oh, Parkins," said his neighbour on the other side, "if you are going to Burnstow, I wish you would look at the site of the Templars' preceptory, and let me know if you think it would be any good to have a dig there in the summer."

It was, as you might suppose, a person of antiquarian pursuits who said this, but, since he merely appears in this prologue, there is no need to give his entitlements.

"Certainly," said Parkins, the Professor: "if you will describe to me whereabouts the site is, I will do my best to give you an idea of the lie of the land when I get back; or I could write to you about it, if you would tell me where you are likely to be."

"Don't trouble to do that, thanks. It's only that I'm thinking of taking my family in that direction in the Long, and it occurred to me that, as very few of the English preceptories have ever been properly planned, I might have an opportunity of doing something useful on offdays."

The Professor rather sniffed at the idea that planning out a preceptory could be described as useful. His neighbour continued:

"The site—I doubt if there is anything showing above ground—must be down quite close to the beach now. The sea has encroached tremendously, as you know, all along that bit of coast. I should think, from the map, that it must be about three-quarters of a mile from the Globe Inn, at the north end of the town. Where are you going to stay?"

"Well, at the Globe Inn, as a matter of fact," said Parkins; "I have engaged a room there. I couldn't get in anywhere else; most of the lodging-houses are shut up in winter, it seems; and, as it is, they tell me that the only room of any size I can have is really a double-bedded one, and that they haven't a corner in which to store the other bed, and so on. But I must have a fairly large room, for I am taking some books down, and mean to do a bit of work; and though I don't quite fancy having an empty bed—not to speak of two—in what I may call for the time being my study, I suppose I can manage to rough it for the short time I shall be there."

"Do you call having an extra bed in your room roughing it, Parkins?" said a bluff person opposite. "Look here, I shall come down and occupy it for a bit; it'll be company for you."

The Professor quivered, but managed to laugh in a courteous manner.

"By all means, Rogers; there's nothing I should like better. But I'm afraid you would find it rather dull; you don't play golf, do you?"

"No, thank Heaven!" said rude Mr. Rogers.

"Well, you see, when I'm not writing I shall most likely be out on the links, and that, as I say, would be rather dull for you, I'm afraid."

"Oh, I don't know! There's certain to be somebody I know in the place; but, of course, if you don't want me, speak the word, Parkins; I shan't be offended. Truth, as you always tell us, is never offensive."

Parkins was, indeed, scrupulously polite and strictly truthful. It is to be feared that Mr. Rogers sometimes practised upon his knowledge of these characteristics. In Parkins's breast there was a conflict now raging, which for a moment or two did not allow him to answer. That interval being over, he said:

"Well, if you want the exact truth, Rogers, I was considering whether the room I speak of would really be large enough to accommodate us both comfortably; and also whether (mind, I shouldn't have said this if you hadn't pressed me) you would not constitute something in the nature of a hindrance to my work." Rogers laughed loudly.

"Well done, Parkins!" he said. "It's all right. I promise not to interrupt your work; don't you disturb yourself about that. No, I won't come if you don't want me; but I thought I should do so nicely to keep the ghosts off." Here he might have been seen to wink and to nudge his next neighbour. Parkins might also have been seen to become pink. "I beg pardon, Parkins," Rogers continued; "I oughtn't to have said that. I forgot you didn't like levity on these topics."

"Well," Parkins said, "as you have mentioned the matter, I freely own that I do not like careless talk about what you call ghosts. A man in my position," he went on, raising his voice a little, "cannot, I find, be too careful about appearing to sanction the current beliefs on such subjects. As you know, Rogers, or as you ought to know; for I think I have never concealed my views—"

"No, you certainly have not, old man," put in Rogers sotto voce.

"—I hold that any semblance, any appearance of concession to the view that such things might exist is equivalent to a renunciation of all that I hold most sacred. But I'm afraid I have not succeeded in securing your attention."

"Your undivided attention, was what Dr. Blimber actually

said," Rogers interrupted, with every appearance of an earnest desire for accuracy. "But I beg your pardon, Parkins; I'm stopping you."

"No, not at all," said Parkins. "I don't remember Blimber; perhaps he was before my time. But I needn't go on. I'm sure you know what I mean."

"Yes, yes," said Rogers, rather hastily—"just so. We'll go into it fully at Burnstow, or somewhere."

In repeating the above dialogue I have tried to give the impression which it made on me, that Parkins was something of an old woman—rather hen-like, perhaps, in his little ways; totally destitute, alas! of the sense of humour, but at the same time dauntless and sincere in his convictions, and a man deserving of the greatest respect. Whether or not the reader has gathered so much, that was the character which Parkins had.

On the following day Parkins did, as he had hoped, succeed in getting away from his college, and in arriving at Burnstow. He was made welcome at the Globe Inn, was safely installed in the large double-bedded room of which we have heard, and was able before retiring to rest to arrange his materials for work in apple-pie order upon a commodious table which occupied the outer end of the room, and was surrounded on three sides by windows looking out seaward; that is to say, the central window looked straight out to sea, and those on the left and right commanded prospects along the shore to the north and south respectively. On the south you saw the village of Burnstow. On the north no houses were to be seen, but only the beach and the low cliff backing it. Immediately in front was a strip—not considerable—of rough grass, dotted with old anchors, capstans, and so forth; then a broad path; then the beach. Whatever may have been the original distance between the Globe Inn and the sea, not more than sixty yards now separated them.

The rest of the population of the inn was, of course, a golfing one, and included few elements that call for a special description. The most conspicuous figure was, perhaps, that of an ancient militaire, secretary of a London club, and possessed of a voice of incredible strength, and of views of a pronouncedly Protestant type. These were apt to find utterance after his attendance upon the ministrations of the Vicar, an estimable man with inclinations towards a picturesque ritual, which he gallantly kept down as far as he could out of deference to East Anglian tradition.

Professor Parkins, one of whose principal characteristics was pluck, spent the greater part of the day following his arrival at Burnstow in what he had called improving his game, in company with this Colonel Wilson: and during the afternoon—whether the process of improvement were to blame or not, I am not sure—the Colonel's demeanour assumed a colouring so lurid that even Parkins jibbed at the thought of walking home with him from the links. He determined, after a short and furtive look at that bristling moustache and those incarnadined features, that it would be wiser to allow the influences of tea and tobacco to do what they could with the Colonel before the dinner-hour should render a meeting inevitable.

"I might walk home tonight along the beach," he reflected, "yes, and take a look—there will be light enough for that—at the ruins of which Disney was talking. I don't exactly know where they are, by the way; but I expect I can hardly help stumbling on them." This he accomplished, I may say, in the most literal sense, for in picking his way from the links to the shingle beach his foot caught, partly in a gorse-root and partly in a biggish stone, and over he went. When he got up and surveyed his surroundings, he found himself in a patch of somewhat broken ground covered with small depressions and mounds. These latter, when he came to examine them, proved to be simply masses of flints embedded in mortar and grown over with turf. He must, he quite rightly concluded, be on the site of the preceptory he had promised to look at. It seemed not unlikely to reward the spade of the explorer; enough of the foundations was probably left at no great depth to throw a good deal of light on the general plan. He remembered vaguely that the Templars, to whom this site had belonged, were in the habit of building round churches, and he thought a particular series of the humps or mounds near him did appear to be arranged in something of a circular form. Few people can resist the temptation to try a little amateur research in a department quite outside their own, if only for the satisfaction of showing how successful they would have been had they only taken it up seriously. Our Professor, however, if he felt something of this mean desire, was also truly anxious to oblige Mr. Disney. So he paced with care the circular area he had noticed, and wrote down its rough dimensions in his pocket-book. Then he proceeded to examine an oblong eminence which lay east of the centre of the circle, and seemed to his thinking likely to be the base of a platform or altar. At one end of it, the northern, a patch of the turf was gone—removed by some boy or other creature ferae naturae. It might, he thought, be as well to probe the soil here for evidences of masonry, and he took out his knife and began scraping away the earth. And now followed another little discovery: a portion of soil fell inward as he scraped, and disclosed a small cavity. He lighted one match after another to help him to see of what nature the hole was, but the wind was too strong for them all. By tapping and scratching the sides with his knife, however, he was able to make out that it must be an artificial hole in masonry. It was rectangular, and the sides, top, and bottom, if not actually plastered, were smooth and regular. Of course it was empty. No! As he withdrew the knife he heard a metallic clink, and when he introduced his hand it met with a cylindrical object lying on the floor of the hole. Naturally enough, he picked it up, and when he brought it into the light, now fast fading, he could see that it, too, was of man's making—a metal tube about four inches long, and evidently of some considerable age.

By the time Parkins had made sure that there was nothing else in this odd receptacle, it was too late and too dark for him to think of undertaking any further search. What he had done had proved so unexpectedly interesting that he determined to sacrifice a little more of the daylight on the morrow to archaeology. The object which he now had safe in his pocket was bound to be of some slight value at least, he felt sure.

Bleak and solemn was the view on which he took a last look before starting homeward. A faint yellow light in the west showed the links, on which a few figures moving towards the club-house were still visible, the squat martello tower, the lights of Aldsey village, the pale ribbon of sands intersected at intervals by black wooden groynes, the dim and murmuring sea. The wind was bitter from the north, but was at his back when he set out for the Globe. He quickly rattled and clashed through the shingle and gained the sand, upon which, but for the groynes which had to be got over every few yards, the going was both good and quiet. One last look behind, to measure the distance he had made since leaving the ruined Templars' church, showed him a prospect of company on his walk, in the shape of a rather indistinct personage, who seemed to be making great efforts to catch up with him, but made little, if any, progress. I mean that there was an appearance of running about his movements, but that the distance between him and Parkins did not seem materially to lessen. So, at least, Parkins thought, and decided that he almost certainly did not know him, and that it would be absurd to wait until he came up. For all that, company, he began to think, would really be very welcome on that lonely shore, if only you could choose your companion. In his unenlightened days he had read of meetings in such places which even now would hardly bear thinking of. He went on thinking of them, however, until he reached home, and particularly of one which catches most people's fancy at some time of their childhood. "Now I saw in my dream that Christian had gone but a very little way when he saw a foul fiend coming over the field to meet him." "What should I do now," he thought, "if I looked back and caught sight of a black figure sharply defined against the yellow sky, and saw that it had horns and wings? I wonder whether I should stand or run for it. Luckily, the gentleman behind is not of that kind, and he seems to be about as far off now as when I saw him first. Well, at this rate he won't get his dinner as soon as I shall; and, dear me! it's within a quarter of an hour of the time now. I must run!"

Parkins had, in fact, very little time for dressing. When he met the Colonel at dinner, peace—or as much of her as that gentleman could manage—reigned once more in the military bosom; nor was she put to flight in the hours of bridge that followed dinner, for Parkins was a more than respectable player. When, therefore, he retired towards twelve o'clock, he felt that he had spent his evening in quite a satisfactory way, and that, even for so long as a fortnight or three weeks, life at the Globe would be supportable under similar conditions—"especially," thought he, "if I go on improving my game."

As he went along the passages he met the boots of the Globe, who stopped and said: "Beg your pardon, sir, but as I was a-brushing your coat just now there was somethink fell out of the pocket. I put it on your chest of drawers, sir, in your room, sir—a piece of a pipe or somethink of that, sir. Thank you, sir. You'll find it on your chest of drawers, sir—yes, sir. Good night, sir."

The speech served to remind Parkins of his little discovery of that afternoon. It was with some considerable curiosity that he turned it over by the light of his candles. It was of bronze, he now saw, and was shaped very much after the manner of the modern dog-whistle; in fact it was—yes, certainly it was—actually no more nor less than a whistle. He put it to his lips, but it was quite full of a fine, caked-up sand or earth, which would not yield to knocking, but must be loosened with a knife. Tidy as ever in his habits, Parkins cleared out the earth onto a piece of paper, and took the latter to the window to empty it out. The night was clear and bright, as he saw when he had opened the casement, and he stopped for an instant to look at the sea and note a belated wanderer stationed on the shore in front of the inn. Then he shut the window, a little surprised at the late hours people kept at Burnstow, and took his whistle to the light again. Why, surely there were marks on it, and not merely marks, but letters! A very little rubbing rendered the deeply-cut inscription quite legible, but the Professor had to confess, after some earnest thought, that the meaning of it was as obscure to him as the writing on the wall to Belshazzar. There were legends both on the front and on the back of the whistle. The one read thus:

FLA
FUR BIS
FLE

The other:

QUIS EST ISTE QUI VENIT

"I ought to be able to make it out," he thought; "but I suppose I am a little rusty in my Latin. When I come to think of it, I don't believe I even know the word for a whistle. The long one does seem simple enough. It ought to mean, 'Who is this who is coming?' Well, the best way to find out is evidently to whistle for him."

He blew tentatively and stopped suddenly, startled and yet pleased at the note he had elicited. It had a quality of infinite distance in it, and, soft as it was, he somehow felt it must be audible for miles round. It was a sound, too, that seemed to have the power (which many scents possess) of forming pictures in the brain. He saw quite clearly for a moment a vision of a wide, dark expanse at night, with a fresh wind blowing and in the midst a lonely figure—how employed, he could not tell. Perhaps he would have seen more had not the picture been broken by the sudden surge of a gust of wind against his casement, so sudden that it made him look up, just in time to see the white glint of a sea-bird's wing somewhere outside the dark panes.

The sound of the whistle had so fascinated him that he could not help trying it once more, this time more boldly. The note was little, if at all, louder than before, and repetition broke the illusion—no picture followed, as he had half hoped it might. "But what is this? Goodness! what force the wind can get up in a few minutes! What a tremendous gust! There! I knew that window-fastening was no use! Ah! I thought so—both candles out. It's enough to tear the room to pieces."

The first thing was to get the window shut. While you might count twenty Parkins was struggling with the small casement, and felt almost as if he were pushing back a sturdy burglar, so strong was the pressure. It slackened all at once, and the window banged to and latched itself. Now to relight the candles and see what damage, if any, had been done. No, nothing seemed amiss; no glass even was broken in the casement. But the noise had evidently roused at least one member of the household: the Colonel was to be heard slumping in his stockinged feet on the floor above, and growling.

Quickly as it had risen, the wind did not fall at once. On it went, moaning and rushing past the house, at times rising to a cry so desolate that, as Parkins disinterestedly said, it might have made fanciful people feel quite uncomfortable; even the unimaginative, he thought after a quarter of an hour, might be happier without it.

Whether it was the wind, or the excitement of golf, or of the researches in the preceptory that kept Parkins awake, he was not sure. Awake he remained, in any case, long enough to fancy (as I am afraid I often do myself under such conditions) that he was the victim of all manner of fatal disorders: he would lie counting the beats of his heart, convinced that it was going to stop work every moment, and would entertain grave suspicions of his lungs, brain, liver, etc.—suspicions which he was sure would be dispelled by the return of daylight, but which until then refused to be put aside. He found a little vicarious comfort in the idea that someone else was in the same boat. A near neighbour (in the darkness it was not easy to tell his direction) was tossing and rustling in his bed, too.

The next stage was that Parkins shut his eyes and determined to give sleep every chance. Here again overexcitement asserted itself in another form—that of making pictures. Experto crede, pictures do come to the closed eyes of one trying to sleep, and are often so little to his taste that he must open his eyes and disperse them.

Parkins's experience on this occasion was a very distressing one. He found that the picture which presented itself to him was continuous. When he opened his eyes, of course, it went;

but when he shut them once more it framed itself afresh, and acted itself out again, neither quicker nor slower than before. What he saw was this: A long stretch of shore—shingle edged by sand, and intersected at short intervals with black groynes running down to the water—a scene, in fact, so like that of his afternoon's walk that, in the absence of any landmark, it could not be distinguished therefrom. The light was obscure, conveying an impression of gathering storm, late winter evening, and slight cold rain. On this bleak stage at first no actor was visible. Then, in the distance, a bobbing black object appeared; a moment more, and it was a man running, jumping, clambering over the groynes, and every few seconds looking eagerly back. The nearer he came the more obvious it was that he was not only anxious, but even terribly frightened, though his face was not to be distinguished. He was, moreover, almost at the end of his strength. On he came; each successive obstacle seemed to cause him more difficulty than the last. "Will he get over this next one?" thought Parkins; "it seems a little higher than the others." Yes; half-climbing, half-throwing himself, he did get over, and fell all in a heap on the other side (the side nearest to the spectator). There, as if really unable to get up again, he remained crouching under the groyne, looking up in an attitude of painful anxiety.

So far no cause whatever for the fear of the runner had been shown; but now there began to be seen, far up the shore, a little flicker of something light-coloured moving to and fro with great swiftness and irregularity. Rapidly growing larger, it, too, declared itself as a figure in pale, fluttering draperies, ill-defined. There was something about its motion which made Parkins very unwilling to see it at close quarters. It would stop, raise arms, bow itself toward the sand, then run stooping across the beach to the water-edge and back again; and then, rising upright, once more continue its course forward at a speed that was startling and terrifying. The moment came when the pursuer was hovering about from left to right only a few yards beyond the groyne where the runner lay in hiding. After two or three ineffectual castings hither and thither it came to a stop, stood upright, with arms raised high, and then darted straight forward towards the groyne.

It was at this point that Parkins always failed in his resolution to keep his eyes shut. With many misgivings as to incipient failure of eyesight, over-worked brain, excessive smoking, and so on, he finally resigned himself to light his candle, get out a book, and pass the night waking, rather than be tormented by this persistent panorama, which he saw clearly enough could only be a morbid reflection of his walk and his thoughts on that very day.

The scraping of match on box and the glare of light must have startled some creatures of the night—rats or what not—which he heard scurry across the floor from the side of his bed with much rustling. Dear, dear! the match is out! Fool that it is! But the second one burnt better, and a candle and book were duly procured, over which Parkins pored till sleep of a wholesome kind came upon him, and that in no long space. For about the first time in his orderly and prudent life he forgot to blow out the candle, and when he was called next morning at eight there was still a flicker in the socket and a sad mess of guttered grease on the top of the little table.

After breakfast he was in his room, putting the finishing touches to his golfing costume—fortune had again allotted the Colonel to him for a partner—when one of the maids came in.

"Oh, if you please," she said, "would you like any extra blankets on your bed, sir?"

"Ah! thank you," said Parkins. "Yes, I think I should like one. It seems likely to turn rather colder."

In a very short time the maid was back with the blanket.

"Which bed should I put it on, sir?" she asked.

"What? Why, that one—the one I slept in last night," he said, pointing to it.

"Oh, yes! I beg your pardon, sir, but you seemed to have tried both of 'em; leastways, we had to make 'em both up this morning."

"Really? How very absurd!" said Parkins. "I certainly never

touched the other, except to lay some things on it. Did it actually seem to have been slept in?"

"Oh, yes, sir!" said the maid. "Why, all the things was crumpled and throwed about all ways, if you'll excuse me, sir—quite as if anyone 'adn't passed but a very poor night, sir."

"Dear me," said Parkins. "Well, I may have disordered it more than I thought when I unpacked my things. I'm very sorry to have given you the extra trouble, I'm sure. I expect a friend of mine soon, by the way—a gentleman from Cambridge—to come and occupy it for a night or two. That will be all right, I suppose, won't it?"

"Oh yes, to be sure, sir. Thank you, sir. It's no trouble, I'm sure," said the maid, and departed to giggle with her colleagues.

Parkins set forth, with a stern determination to improve his game.

I am glad to be able to report that he succeeded so far in this enterprise that the Colonel, who had been rather repining at the prospect of a second day's play in his company, became quite chatty as the morning advanced; and his voice boomed out over the flats, as certain also of our own minor poets have said, "like some great bourdon in a minster tower."

"Extraordinary wind, that, we had last night," he said. "In my old home we should have said someone had been whistling for it."

"Should you, indeed!" said Parkins, "Is there a superstition of that kind still current in your part of the country?"

"I don't know about superstition," said the Colonel. "They believe in it all over Denmark and Norway, as well as on the Yorkshire coast; and my experience is, mind you, that there's generally something at the bottom of what these country-folk hold to, and have held to for generations. But it's your drive" (or whatever it might have been: the golfing reader will have to imagine appropriate digressions at the proper intervals).

When conversation was resumed, Parkins said, with a slight hesitancy:

"Apropos of what you were saying just now, Colonel, I think

I ought to tell you that my own views on such subjects are very strong. I am, in fact, a convinced disbeliever in what is called the 'supernatural.'"

"What!" said the Colonel, "do you mean to tell me you don't believe in second-sight, or ghosts, or anything of that kind?"

"In nothing whatever of that kind," returned Parkins firmly.

"Well," said the Colonel, "but it appears to me at that rate, sir, that you must be little better than a Sadducee."

Parkins was on the point of answering that, in his opinion, the Sadducees were the most sensible persons he had ever read of in the Old Testament; but, feeling some doubt as to whether much mention of them was to be found in that work, he preferred to laugh the accusation off.

"Perhaps I am," he said; "but—Here, give me my cleek, boy!—Excuse me one moment. Colonel." A short interval. "Now, as to whistling for the wind, let me give you my theory about it. The laws which govern winds are really not at all perfectly known—to fisher-folk and such, of course, not known at all. A man or woman of eccentric habits, perhaps, or a stranger, is seen repeatedly on the beach at some unusual hour, and is heard whistling. Soon afterwards a violent wind rises; a man who could read the sky perfectly or who possessed a barometer could have foretold that it would. The simple people of a fishing-village have no barometers, and only a few rough rules for prophesying weather. What more natural than that the eccentric personage I postulated should be regarded as having raised the wind, or that he or she should clutch eagerly at the reputation of being able to do so? Now, take last night's wind: as it happens, I myself was whistling. I blew a whistle twice, and the wind seemed to come absolutely in answer to my call. If anyone had seen me—"

The audience had been a little restive under this harangue, and Parkins had, I fear, fallen somewhat into the tone of a lecturer; but at the last sentence the Colonel stopped.

"Whistling, were you?" he said. "And what sort of whistle did you use? Play this stroke first." Interval.

"About that whistle you were asking, Colonel. It's rather a

curious one. I have it in my—No; I see I've left in it my room. As a matter of fact, I found it yesterday."

And then Parkins narrated the manner of his discovery of the whistle, upon hearing which the Colonel grunted, and opined that, in Parkins's place, he should himself be careful about using a thing that had belonged to a set of Papists, of whom, speaking generally, it might be affirmed that you never knew what they might not have been up to. From this topic he diverged to the enormities of the Vicar, who had given notice on the previous Sunday that Friday would be the Feast of St. Thomas the Apostle, and that there would be service at eleven o'clock in the church. This and other similar proceedings constituted in the Colonel's view a strong presumption that the Vicar was a concealed Papist, if not a Jesuit; and Parkins, who could not very readily follow the Colonel in this region, did not disagree with him. In fact, they got on so well together in the morning that there was no talk on either side of their separating after lunch.

Both continued to play well during the afternoon, or, at least, well enough to make them forget everything else until the light began to fail them. Not until then did Parkins remember that he had meant to do some more investigating at the preceptory; but it was of no great importance, he reflected. One day was as good as another; he might as well go home with the Colonel.

As they turned the corner of the house, the Colonel was almost knocked down by a boy who rushed into him at the very top of his speed, and then, instead of running away, remained hanging on to him and panting. The first words of the warrior were naturally those of reproof and objurgation, but he very quickly discerned that the boy was almost speechless with fright. Inquiries were useless at first. When the boy got his breath he began to howl, and still clung to the Colonel's legs. He was at last detached, but continued to howl.

"What in the world is the matter with you? What have you been up to? What have you seen?" said the two men.

"Ow, I seen it wive at me out of the winder," wailed the boy, "and I don't like it."

"What window?" said the irritated Colonel. "Come, pull yourself together, my boy."

"The front winder it was, at the 'otel," said the boy.

At this point Parkins was in favour of sending the boy home, but the Colonel refused; he wanted to get to the bottom of it, he said; it was most dangerous to give a boy such a fright as this one had had, and if it turned out that people had been playing jokes, they should suffer for it in some way. And by a series of questions he made out this story. The boy had been playing about on the grass in front of the Globe with some others; then they had gone home to their teas, and he was just going, when he happened to look up at the front winder and see it a wiving at him. It seemed to be a figure of some sort, in white as far as he knew—couldn't see its face; but it wived at him, and it warn't a right thing—not to say not a right person. Was there a light in the room? No, he didn't think to look if there was a light. Which was the window? Was it the top one or the second one? The seckind one it was—the big winder what got two little 'uns at the sides.

"Very well, my boy," said the Colonel, after a few more questions. "You run away home now. I expect it was some person trying to give you a start. Another time, like a brave English boy, you just throw a stone—well, no, not that exactly, but you go and speak to the waiter, or to Mr. Simpson, the landlord, and—yes—and say that I advised you to do so."

The boy's face expressed some of the doubt he felt as to the likelihood of Mr. Simpson's lending a favourable ear to his complaint, but the Colonel did not appear to perceive this, and went on:

"And here's a sixpence—no, I see it's a shilling—and you be off home, and don't think any more about it."

The youth hurried off with agitated thanks, and the Colonel and Parkins went round to the front of the Globe and reconnoitred. There was only one window answering to the description they had been hearing.

"Well, that's curious," said Parkins; "it's evidently my window the lad was talking about. Will you come up for a moment,

Colonel Wilson? We ought to be able to see if anyone has been taking liberties in my room."

They were soon in the passage, and Parkins made as if to open the door. Then he stopped and felt in his pockets.

"This is more serious than I thought," was his next remark. "I remember now that before I started this morning I locked the door. It is locked now, and, what is more, here is the key." And he held it up. "Now," he went on, "if the servants are in the habit of going into one's room during the day when one is away, I can only say that—well, that I don't approve of it at all." Conscious of a somewhat weak climax, he busied himself in opening the door (which was indeed locked) and in lighting candles. "No," he said, "nothing seems disturbed."

"Except your bed," put in the Colonel.

"Excuse me, that isn't my bed," said Parkins. "I don't use that one. But it does look as if someone has been playing tricks with it."

It certainly did: The clothes were bundled up and twisted together in a most tortuous confusion. Parkins pondered. "That must be it," he said at last: "I disordered the clothes last night in unpacking, and they haven't made it since. Perhaps they came in to make it, and that boy saw them through the window; and then they were called away and locked the door after them. Yes, I think that must be it."

"Well, ring and ask," said the Colonel, and this appealed to Parkins as practical.

The maid appeared, and, to make a long story short, deposed that she had made the bed in the morning when the gentleman was in the room, and hadn't been there since. No, she hadn't no other key. Mr. Simpson he kep' the keys; he'd be able to tell the gentleman if anyone had been up.

This was a puzzle. Investigation showed that nothing of value had been taken, and Parkins remembered the disposition of the small objects on tables and so forth well enough to be pretty sure that no pranks had been played with them. Mr. and Mrs. Simpson furthermore agreed that neither of them had given the duplicate key of the room to any person whatever during the day. Nor could Parkins, fair-minded man as he was, detect anything in the demeanour of master, mistress, or maid that indicated guilt. He was much more inclined to think that the boy had been imposing on the Colonel.

The latter was unwontedly silent and pensive at dinner and throughout the evening. When he bade good night to Parkins, he murmured in a gruff undertone: "You know where I am if you want me during the night."

"Why, yes, thank you, Colonel Wilson, I think I do; but there isn't much prospect of my disturbing you, I hope. By the way," he added, "did I show you that old whistle I spoke of? I think not. Well, here it is."

The Colonel turned it over gingerly in the light of the candle.

"Can you make anything of the inscription?" asked Parkins, as he took it back.

"No, not in this light. What do you mean to do with it?"

"Oh, well, when I get back to Cambridge I shall submit it to some of the archaeologists there, and see what they think of it; and very likely, if they consider it worth having, I may present it to one of the museums."

"M!" said the Colonel. "Well, you may be right. All I know is that, if it were mine, I should chuck it straight into the sea. It's no use talking, I'm well aware, but I expect that with you it's a case of live and learn. I hope so. I'm sure, and I wish you a good night."

He turned away, leaving Parkins in act to speak at the bottom of the stair, and soon each was in his own bedroom.

By some unfortunate accident, there were neither blinds nor curtains to the windows of the Professor's room. The previous night he had thought little of this, but tonight there seemed every prospect of a bright moon rising to shine directly on his bed, and probably wake him later on. When he noticed this he was a good deal annoyed, but, with an ingenuity which I can only envy, he succeeded in rigging up, with the help of a railway-rug, some safety-pins, and a stick and umbrella, a screen which, if it only held together, would completely keep the moonlight off his bed.

And shortly afterwards he was comfortably in that bed. When he had read a somewhat solid work long enough to produce a decided wish for sleep, he cast a drowsy glance round the room, blew out the candle, and fell back upon the pillow.

He must have slept soundly for an hour or more, when a sudden clatter shook him up in a most unwelcome manner. In a moment he realised what had happened: His carefully-constructed screen had given way, and a very bright frosty moon was shining directly on his face. This was highly annoying. Could he possibly get up and reconstruct the screen? Or could he manage to sleep if he did not?

For some minutes he lay and pondered over the possibilities; then he turned over sharply, and with all his eyes open lay breathlessly listening. There had been a movement, he was sure, in the empty bed on the opposite side of the room. Tomorrow he would have it moved, for there must be rats or something playing about in it. It was quiet now. No! The commotion began again. There was a rustling and shaking: surely more than any rat could cause.

I can figure to myself something of the Professor's bewilderment and horror, for I have in a dream thirty years back seen the same thing happen; but the reader will hardly, perhaps, imagine how dreadful it was to him to see a figure suddenly sit up in what he had known was an empty bed. He was out of his own bed in one bound, and made a dash towards the window, where lay his only weapon, the stick with which he had propped his screen. This was, as it turned out, the worst thing he could have done, because the personage in the empty bed, with a sudden smooth motion, slipped from the bed and took up a position, with outspread arms, between the two beds, and in front of the door. Parkins watched it in a horrid perplexity. Somehow, the idea of getting past it and escaping through the door was intolerable to him; he could not have borne—he didn't know why—to touch it; and as for its touching him, he would sooner dash himself through the window than have that happen. It stood for the moment in a band of dark shadow, and he had not seen what its face was like. Now it began to move, in a stooping posture, and all at once the spectator realised, with some horror and some relief, that it must be blind, for it seemed to feel about it with its muffled arms in a groping and random fashion. Turning half away from him, it became suddenly conscious of the bed he had just left, and darted towards it, and bent over and felt the pillows in a way which made Parkins shudder as he had never in his life thought it possible. In a very few moments it seemed to know that the bed was empty, and then, moving forward into the area of light and facing the window, it showed for the first time what manner of thing it was.

Parkins, who very much dislikes being questioned about it, did once describe something of it in my hearing, and I gathered that what he chiefly remembers about it is a horrible, an intensely horrible, face of crumbled linen. What expression he read upon it he could not or would not tell, but that the fear of it went nigh to maddening him is certain.

But he was not at leisure to watch it for long. With formidable quickness it moved into the middle of the room, and, as it groped and waved, one corner of its draperies swept across Parkins's face. He could not—though he knew how perilous a sound was—he could not keep back a cry of disgust, and this gave the searcher an instant clue. It leapt towards him upon the instant, and the next moment he was half-way through the window backwards, uttering cry upon cry at the utmost pitch of his voice, and the linen face was thrust close into his own. At this, almost the last possible second, deliverance came, as you will have guessed: The Colonel burst the door open, and was just in time to see the dreadful group at the window. When he reached the figures only one was left. Parkins sank forward into the room in a faint, and before him on the floor lay a tumbled heap of bedclothes.

Colonel Wilson asked no questions, but busied himself in keeping everyone else out of the room and in getting Parkins back to his bed; and himself, wrapped in a rug, occupied the other bed for the rest of the night. Early on the next day Rogers arrived, more welcome than he would have been a day before, and the three of them held a very long consultation in the Professor's room. At the end of it the Colonel left the hotel door carrying a small object between his finger and thumb, which he cast as far into the sea as a very brawny arm could send it. Later on the smoke of a burning ascended from the back premises of the Globe.

Exactly what explanation was patched up for the staff and visitors at the hotel I must confess I do not recollect. The Professor was somehow cleared of the ready suspicion of delirium tremens, and the hotel of the reputation of a troubled house.

There is not much question as to what would have happened to Parkins if the Colonel had not intervened when he did. He would either have fallen out of the window or else lost his wits. But it is not so evident what more the creature that came in answer to the whistle could have done than frighten. There seemed to be absolutely nothing material about it save the bedclothes of which it had made itself a body. The Colonel, who remembered a not very dissimilar occurrence in India, was of opinion that if Parkins had closed with it it could really have done very little, and that its one power was that of frightening. The whole thing, he said, served to confirm his opinion of the Church of Rome.

There is really nothing more to tell, but, as you may imagine, the Professor's views on certain points are less clear cut than they used to be. His nerves, too, have suffered: He cannot even now see a surplice hanging on a door quite unmoved, and the spectacle of a scarecrow in a field late on a winter afternoon has cost him more than one sleepless night.

THE COUNTRY OF THE BLIND

H. G. Wells

(1904)

Although Wells is best known today for his early science fiction, he was an active social thinker, and many of his works have philosophical themes that enrich the experience of reading them. This story reorients the perspective of the old saying that "in the country of the blind the one-eyed man is king," in a narrative that is both plausible and ultimately chilling.

Three hundred miles and more from Chimborazo, one hundred from the snows of Cotopaxi, in the wildest wastes of Ecuador's Andes, there lies that mysterious mountain valley, cut off from all the world of men, the Country of the Blind. Long years ago that valley lay so far open to the world that men might come at last through frightful gorges and over an icy pass into its equable meadows, and thither indeed men came, a family or so of Peruvian half-breeds fleeing from the lust and tyranny of an evil Spanish ruler. Then came the stupendous outbreak of Mindobamba, when it was night in Quito for seventeen days, and the water was boiling at Yaguachi and all the fish floating dying even as far as Guayaquil; everywhere along the Pacific slopes there were land-slips and swift thawings and sudden floods, and one whole side of the old Arauca crest slipped and came down in thunder, and cut off the Country of the Blind for ever from the exploring feet of men. But one of these early settlers had chanced to be on the hither side of the gorges when the world had so terribly shaken itself, and he perforce had to forget his wife and his child and all the friends and possessions he had left up there, and start life over again in the lower world. He started it again but ill, blindness overtook him, and he died of punishment in the mines; but the story he told begot a legend that lingers along the length of the Cordilleras of the Andes to this day.

He told of his reason for venturing back from that fastness, into which he had first been carried lashed to a llama, beside a vast bale of gear, when he was a child. The valley, he said, had in it all that the heart of man could desire—sweet water, pasture, an even climate, slopes of rich brown soil with tangles of a shrub that bore an excellent fruit, and on one side great hanging forests of pine that held the avalanches high. Far overhead, on three sides, vast cliffs of grey-green rock were capped by cliffs of ice; but the glacier stream came not to them, but flowed away by the farther slopes, and only now and then huge ice masses fell on the valley side. In this valley it neither rained nor snowed, but the abundant springs gave a rich green pasture, that irrigation would spread over all the valley space. The settlers did well indeed there. Their beasts did well and multiplied, and but one thing marred their happiness. Yet it was enough to mar it greatly. A strange disease had come upon them and had made all the children born to them there—and, indeed, several older children also—blind. It was to seek some charm or antidote against this plague of blindness that he had with fatigue and danger and difficulty returned down the gorge. In those days, in such cases, men did not think of germs and infections, but of sins, and it seemed to him that the reason of this affliction must be in the negligence of these priestless immigrants to set up a shrine so soon as they entered the valley. He wanted a shrine—a handsome, cheap, effectual shrine—to be erected in the valley; he wanted relics and such-like potent things of faith, blessed objects and mysterious medals and prayers. In his wallet he had a bar of native silver for which he would not account; he insisted there was none in the valley with something of the insistence of an inexpert liar. They had all clubbed their money and ornaments together, having little need for such treasure up there, he said, to buy them holy help against their ill. I figure this dim-eyed young mountaineer, sunburnt, gaunt, and anxious, hat brim clutched feverishly, a man all unused to the ways of the lower world, telling this story to some keen-eyed, attentive priest before the great convulsion; I can picture him presently seeking to return with pious and infallible remedies against that trouble, and the infinite dismay with which he must have faced the tumbled vastness where the gorge had once come out. But the rest of his story of mischances is lost to me, save that I know of his evil death after several years. Poor stray from that remoteness! The stream that had once made the gorge now bursts from the mouth of a rocky cave, and the legend his poor, ill-told story set going developed into the legend of a race of blind men somewhere "over there" one may still hear to-day.

And amidst the little population of that now isolated and forgotten valley the disease ran its course. The old became groping, the young saw but dimly, and the children that were born to them never saw at all. But life was very easy in that snow-rimmed basin, lost to all the world, with neither thorns nor briers, with no evil insects nor any beasts save the gentle breed of llamas they had lugged and thrust and followed up the beds of the shrunken rivers in the gorges up which they had come. The seeing had become purblind so gradually that they scarcely noticed their loss. They guided the sightless youngsters hither and thither until they knew the whole valley marvellously, and when at last sight died out among them the race lived on. They had even time to adapt themselves to the blind control of fire, which they made carefully in stoves of stone. They were a simple strain of people at the first, unlettered, only slightly touched with the Spanish civilisation, but with something of a tradition of the arts of old Peru and of its lost philosophy. Generation followed generation. They forgot many things; they devised many things. Their tradition of the greater world they came from became mythical in colour and uncertain. In all things save sight they were strong and able, and presently chance sent one who had an original mind and who could talk and persuade among them, and then afterwards another. These two passed, leaving their effects, and the little community grew in numbers and in understanding, and met and settled social and economic problems that arose. Generation followed generation. Generation followed generation. There came a time when a child was born who was fifteen generations from that ancestor who went out of the valley with a bar of silver to seek God's aid, and who never returned. Thereabout it chanced that a man came into this community from the outer world. And this is the story of that man.

He was a mountaineer from the country near Quito, a man who had been down to the sea and had seen the world, a reader of books in an original way, an acute and enterprising man, and he was taken on by a party of Englishmen who had come out to Ecuador to climb mountains, to replace one of their three Swiss guides who had fallen ill. He climbed here and he climbed there, and then came the attempt on Parascotopetl, the Matterhorn of the Andes, in which he was lost to the outer world. The story of that accident has been written a dozen times. Pointer's narrative is the best. He tells how the little party worked their difficult and almost vertical way up to the very foot of the last and greatest precipice, and how they built a night shelter amidst the snow upon a little shelf of rock, and, with a touch of real dramatic power, how presently they found Nunez had gone from them. They shouted, and there was no reply; shouted and whistled, and for the rest of that night they slept no more.

As the morning broke they saw the traces of his fall. It seems impossible he could have uttered a sound. He had slipped eastward towards the unknown side of the mountain; far below he had struck a steep slope of snow, and ploughed his way down it in the midst of a snow avalanche. His track went straight to the edge of a frightful precipice, and beyond that everything was hidden. Far, far below, and hazy with distance, they could see trees rising out of a narrow, shut-in valley—the lost Country of the Blind. But they did not know it was the lost Country of the Blind, nor distinguish it in any way from any other narrow streak of upland valley. Unnerved by this disaster, they abandoned their attempt in the afternoon, and Pointer was called away to the war before he could make another attack. To this day Parascotopetl lifts an unconquered crest, and Pointer's shelter crumbles unvisited amidst the snows.

And the man who fell survived.

At the end of the slope he fell a thousand feet, and came down in the midst of a cloud of snow upon a snow-slope even steeper than the one above. Down this he was whirled, stunned and insensible, but without a bone broken in his body; and then at last came to gentler slopes, and at last rolled out and lay still, buried amidst a softening heap of the white masses that had accompanied and saved him. He came to himself with a dim fancy that he was ill in bed; then realized his position with a mountaineer's intelligence and worked himself loose and, after a rest or so, out until he saw the stars. He rested flat upon his chest for a space, wondering where he was and what had happened to him. He explored his limbs, and discovered that several of his buttons were gone and his coat turned over his head. His knife had gone from his pocket and his hat was lost, though he had tied it under his chin. He recalled that he had been looking for loose stones to raise his piece of the shelter wall. His ice-axe had disappeared.

He decided he must have fallen, and looked up to see, exaggerated by the ghastly light of the rising moon, the tremendous flight he had taken. For a while he lay, gazing blankly at the vast, pale cliff towering above, rising moment by moment out of a subsiding tide of darkness. Its phantasmal, mysterious beauty held him for a space, and then he was seized with a paroxysm of sobbing laughter . . .

After a great interval of time he became aware that he was near the lower edge of the snow. Below, down what was now a moon-lit and practicable slope, he saw the dark and broken appearance of rock-strewn turf. He struggled to his feet, aching in every joint and limb, got down painfully from the heaped loose snow about him, went downward until he was on the turf, and there dropped rather than lay beside a boulder, drank deep from the flask in his inner pocket, and instantly fell asleep . . .

He was awakened by the singing of birds in the trees far below.

He sat up and perceived he was on a little alp at the foot of a vast precipice that sloped only a little in the gully down which he and his snow had come. Over against him another wall of rock reared itself against the sky. The gorge between these precipices ran east and west and was full of the morning sunlight, which lit to the westward the mass of fallen mountain that closed the descending gorge. Below him it seemed there was a precipice equally steep, but behind the snow in the gully he found a sort of chimney-cleft dripping with snow-water, down which a desperate man might venture. He found it easier than it seemed, and came at last to another desolate alp, and then after a rock climb of no particular difficulty, to a steep slope of trees. He took his bearings and turned his face up the gorge, for he saw it opened out above upon green meadows, among which he now glimpsed quite distinctly a cluster of stone huts of unfamiliar fashion. At times his progress was like clambering along the face of a wall, and after a time the rising sun ceased to strike along the gorge, the voices of the singing birds died away, and the air grew cold and dark about him. But the distant valley with its houses was all the brighter for that. He came presently to talus, and among the rocks he noted—for he was an observant man—an unfamiliar fern that seemed to clutch out of the crevices with intense green hands. He picked a frond or so and gnawed its stalk, and found it helpful.

About midday he came at last out of the throat of the gorge into the plain and the sunlight. He was stiff and weary; he sat down in the shadow of a rock, filled up his flask with water from a spring and drank it down, and remained for a time, resting before he went on to the houses.

They were very strange to his eyes, and indeed the whole aspect of that valley became, as he regarded it, queerer and more unfamiliar. The greater part of its surface was lush green meadow, starred with many beautiful flowers, irrigated with extraordinary care, and bearing evidence of systematic cropping piece by piece. High up and ringing the valley about was a wall, and what appeared to be a circumferential water channel, from which the little trickles of water that fed the meadow plants came, and on the higher slopes above this flocks of llamas cropped the scanty herbage. Sheds, apparently shelters or feeding-places for the llamas, stood against the boundary wall here and there. The irrigation streams ran together into a main channel down the centre of the valley, and this was enclosed on either side by a wall breast high. This gave a singularly urban quality to this secluded place, a quality that was greatly enhanced by the fact that a number of paths paved with black and white stones, and each with a curious little kerb at the side, ran hither and thither in an orderly manner. The houses of the central village were quite unlike the casual and higgledy-piggledy agglomeration of the mountain villages he knew; they stood in a continuous row on either side of a central street of astonishing cleanness, here and there their parti-coloured facade was pierced by a door, and not a solitary window broke their even frontage. They were parti-coloured with extraordinary irregularity, smeared with a sort of plaster that was sometimes grey, sometimes drab, sometimes slate-coloured or dark brown; and it was the sight of this wild plastering first brought the word "blind" into the thoughts of the explorer. "The good man who did that," he thought, "must have been as blind as a bat."

He descended a steep place, and so came to the wall and channel that ran about the valley, near where the latter spouted out its surplus contents into the deeps of the gorge in a thin and wavering thread of cascade. He could now see a number of men and women resting on piled heaps of grass, as if taking a siesta, in the remoter part of the meadow, and nearer the village a number of recumbent children, and then nearer at hand three men carrying pails on yokes along a little path that ran from the encircling wall towards the houses. These latter were clad in garments of llama cloth and boots and belts of leather, and they wore caps of cloth with back and ear flaps. They followed one another in single file, walking slowly and yawning as they walked, like men who have been up all night. There was something so reassuringly prosperous and respectable in their bearing that after a moment's hesitation Nunez stood forward as conspicuously as possible upon his rock, and gave vent to a mighty shout that echoed round the valley.

The three men stopped, and moved their heads as though they were looking about them. They turned their faces this way and that, and Nunez gesticulated with freedom. But they did not appear to see him for all his gestures, and after a time, directing themselves towards the mountains far away to the right, they shouted as if in answer. Nunez bawled again, and then once more, and as he gestured ineffectually the word "blind" came up to the top of his thoughts. "The fools must be blind," he said.

When at last, after much shouting and wrath, Nunez crossed the stream by a little bridge, came through a gate in the wall, and approached them, he was sure that they were blind. He was sure that this was the Country of the Blind of which the legends told. Conviction had sprung upon him, and a sense of great and rather enviable adventure. The three stood side by side, not looking at him, but with their ears directed towards him, judging him by his unfamiliar steps.

They stood close together like men a little afraid, and he could see their eyelids closed and sunken, as though the very balls beneath had shrunk away. There was an expression near awe on their faces.

"A man," one said, in hardly recognisable Spanish. "A man it is—a man or a spirit—coming down from the rocks."

But Nunez advanced with the confident steps of a youth who enters upon life. All the old stories of the lost valley and the Country of the Blind had come back to his mind, and through his thoughts ran this old proverb, as if it were a refrain:—

"In the Country of the Blind the One-Eyed Man is King."

"In the Country of the Blind the One-Eyed Man is King."

And very civilly he gave them greeting. He talked to them and used his eyes.

"Where does he come from, brother Pedro?" asked one.

"Down out of the rocks."

"Over the mountains I come," said Nunez, "out of the country beyond there—where men can see. From near Bogota—where there are a hundred thousands of people, and where the city passes out of sight."

"Sight?" muttered Pedro. "Sight?"

"He comes," said the second blind man, "out of the rocks."

The cloth of their coats, Nunez saw was curious fashioned, each with a different sort of stitching.

They startled him by a simultaneous movement towards him, each with a hand outstretched. He stepped back from the advance of these spread fingers.

"Come hither," said the third blind man, following his motion and clutching him neatly.

And they held Nunez and felt him over, saying no word further until they had done so.

"Carefully," he cried, with a finger in his eye, and found they thought that organ, with its fluttering lids, a queer thing in him. They went over it again.

"A strange creature, Correa," said the one called Pedro. "Feel the coarseness of his hair. Like a llama's hair."

"Rough he is as the rocks that begot him," said Correa, investigating Nunez's unshaven chin with a soft and slightly moist hand. "Perhaps he will grow finer."

Nunez struggled a little under their examination, but they gripped him firm.

"Carefully," he said again.

"He speaks," said the third man. "Certainly he is a man."

"Ugh!" said Pedro, at the roughness of his coat.

"And you have come into the world?" asked Pedro.

"*Out* of the world. Over mountains and glaciers; right over above there, half-way to the sun. Out of the great, big world that goes down, twelve days' journey to the sea."

They scarcely seemed to heed him. "Our fathers have told us men may be made by the forces of Nature," said Correa. "It is the warmth of things, and moisture, and rottenness—rottenness."

"Let us lead him to the elders," said Pedro.

"Shout first," said Correa, "lest the children be afraid. This is a marvellous occasion."

So they shouted, and Pedro went first and took Nunez by the hand to lead him to the houses.

He drew his hand away. "I can see," he said.

"See?" said Correa.

"Yes; see," said Nunez, turning towards him, and stumbled against Pedro's pail.

"His senses are still imperfect," said the third blind man. "He stumbles, and talks unmeaning words. Lead him by the hand."

"As you will," said Nunez, and was led along laughing.

It seemed they knew nothing of sight.

Well, all in good time he would teach them.

He heard people shouting, and saw a number of figures gathering together in the middle roadway of the village.

He found it tax his nerve and patience more than he had anticipated, that first encounter with the population of the Country of the Blind. The place seemed larger as he drew near to it, and the smeared plasterings queerer, and a crowd of children and men and women (the women and girls he was pleased to note had, some of them, quite sweet faces, for all that their eyes were shut and sunken) came about him, holding on to him, touching him with soft, sensitive hands, smelling at him, and listening at every word he spoke. Some of the maidens and children, however, kept aloof as if afraid, and indeed his voice seemed coarse and rude beside their softer notes. They mobbed him. His three guides kept close to him with an effect of proprietorship, and said again and again, "A wild man out of the rocks."

"Bogota," he said. "Bogota. Over the mountain crests."

"A wild man—using wild words," said Pedro. "Did you hear that—*Bogota*? His mind has hardly formed yet. He has only the beginnings of speech."

A little boy nipped his hand. "Bogota!" he said mockingly.

"Aye! A city to your village. I come from the great world—where men have eyes and see."

"His name's Bogota," they said.

"He stumbled," said Correa—"stumbled twice as we came hither."

"Bring him in to the elders."

And they thrust him suddenly through a doorway into a room as black as pitch, save at the end there faintly glowed a fire. The crowd closed in behind him and shut out all but the faintest glimmer of day, and before he could arrest himself he had fallen headlong over the feet of a seated man. His arm, outflung, struck the face of someone else as he went down; he felt the soft impact of features and heard a cry of anger, and for a moment he struggled against a number of hands that clutched him. It was a one-sided fight. An inkling of the situation came to him and he lay quiet.

"I fell down," he said; "I couldn't see in this pitchy darkness."

There was a pause as if the unseen persons about him tried to understand his words. Then the voice of Correa said: "He is but newly formed. He stumbles as he walks and mingles words that mean nothing with his speech."

Others also said things about him that he heard or understood imperfectly.

"May I sit up?" he asked, in a pause. "I will not struggle against you again."

They consulted and let him rise.

The voice of an older man began to question him, and Nunez found himself trying to explain the great world out of which he had fallen, and the sky and mountains and such-like marvels, to these elders who sat in darkness in the Country of the Blind. And they would believe and understand nothing whatever that he told them, a thing quite outside his expectation. They would not even understand many of his words. For fourteen generations these people had been blind and cut off from all the seeing world; the names for all the things of sight had faded and changed; the story of the outer world was faded and changed to a child's story; and they had ceased to concern themselves with anything beyond the rocky slopes above their circling wall. Blind men of genius had arisen among them and questioned the shreds of belief and tradition they had brought with them from their seeing days, and had dismissed all these things as idle fancies and replaced them with new and saner explanations. Much of their imagination had shrivelled with their eyes, and they had made for themselves new imaginations with their ever more sensitive ears and finger-tips. Slowly Nunez realised this: that his expectation of wonder and reverence at his origin and his gifts was not to be borne out; and after his poor attempt to explain sight to them had been set aside as the confused version of a new-made being describing the marvels of his incoherent sensations, he subsided, a little dashed, into listening to their instruction. And the eldest of the blind men explained to him life and philosophy and religion, how that the world (meaning their valley) had been first an empty hollow in the rocks, and then had come first inanimate things without the gift of touch, and llamas and a few other creatures that had little sense, and then men, and at last angels, whom one could hear singing and making fluttering sounds, but whom no one could touch at all, which puzzled Nunez greatly until he thought of the birds.

He went on to tell Nunez how this time had been divided into the warm and the cold, which are the blind equivalents of day and night, and how it was good to sleep in the warm and work during the cold, so that now, but for his advent, the whole town of the blind would have been asleep. He said Nunez must have been specially created to learn and serve the wisdom they had acquired, and that for all his mental incoherency and stumbling behaviour he must have courage and do his best to learn, and at that all the people in the door-way murmured encouragingly. He said the night—for the blind call their day night—was now far gone, and it behooved everyone to go back to sleep. He asked Nunez if he knew how to sleep, and Nunez said he did, but that before sleep he wanted food. They brought him food, llama's milk in a bowl and rough salted bread, and led him into a lonely place to eat out of their hearing, and afterwards to slumber until the chill of the mountain evening roused them to begin their day again. But Nunez slumbered not at all.

Instead, he sat up in the place where they had left him, resting his limbs and turning the unanticipated circumstances of his arrival over and over in his mind.

Every now and then he laughed, sometimes with amusement and sometimes with indignation.

"Unformed mind!" he said. "Got no senses yet! They little know they've been insulting their Heaven-sent King and master. . . .

"I see I must bring them to reason.

"Let me think.

"Let me think."

He was still thinking when the sun set.

Nunez had an eye for all beautiful things, and it seemed to him that the glow upon the snow-fields and glaciers that rose about the valley on every side was the most beautiful thing he had ever seen. His eyes went from that inaccessible glory to the village and irrigated fields, fast sinking into the twilight, and suddenly a wave of emotion took him, and he thanked God from the bottom of his heart that the power of sight had been given him.

He heard a voice calling to him from out of the village.

"Yaho there, Bogota! Come hither!"

At that he stood up, smiling. He would show these people once and for all what sight would do for a man. They would seek him, but not find him.

"You move not, Bogota," said the voice.

He laughed noiselessly and made two stealthy steps aside from the path.

"Trample not on the grass, Bogota; that is not allowed."

Nunez had scarcely heard the sound he made himself. He stopped, amazed.

The owner of the voice came running up the piebald path towards him.

He stepped back into the pathway. "Here I am," he said.

"Why did you not come when I called you?" said the blind man. "Must you be led like a child? Cannot you hear the path as you walk?"

Nunez laughed. "I can see it," he said.

"There is no such word as *see,*" said the blind man, after a pause. "Cease this folly and follow the sound of my feet."

Nunez followed, a little annoyed.

"My time will come," he said.

"You'll learn," the blind man answered. "There is much to learn in the world."

"Has no one told you, 'In the Country of the Blind the One-Eyed Man is King?'"

"What is blind?" asked the blind man, carelessly, over his shoulder.

Four days passed and the fifth found the King of the Blind still incognito, as a clumsy and useless stranger among his subjects.

It was, he found, much more difficult to proclaim himself than he had supposed, and in the meantime, while he meditated his coup d'etat, he did what he was told and learnt the manners and customs of the Country of the Blind. He found working and going about at night a particularly irksome thing, and he decided that that should be the first thing he would change.

They led a simple, laborious life, these people, with all the elements of virtue and happiness as these things can be understood by men. They toiled, but not oppressively; they had food and clothing sufficient for their needs; they had days and seasons of rest; they made much of music and singing, and there was love among them and little children. It was marvellous with what confidence and precision they went about their ordered world. Everything, you see, had been made to fit their needs; each of the radiating paths of the valley area had a constant angle to the others, and was distinguished by a special notch upon its kerbing; all obstacles and irregularities of path or meadow had long since been cleared away; all their methods and procedure arose naturally from their special needs. Their senses had become marvellously acute; they could hear and judge the slightest gesture of a man a dozen paces away—could hear the very beating of his heart. Intonation had long replaced expression with them, and touches gesture, and their work with hoe and spade and fork was as free and confident as garden work can be. Their sense of smell was extraordinarily fine; they could distinguish individual differences as readily as a dog can, and they went about the tending of llamas, who lived among the rocks above and came to the wall for food and shelter, with ease and confidence. It was only when at last Nunez sought to assert himself that he found how easy and confident their movements could be.

He rebelled only after he had tried persuasion.

He tried at first on several occasions to tell them of sight. "Look you here, you people," he said. "There are things you do not understand in me."

Once or twice one or two of them attended to him; they sat with faces downcast and ears turned intelligently towards him, and he did his best to tell them what it was to see. Among his hearers was a girl, with eyelids less red and sunken than the others, so that one could almost fancy she was hiding eyes, whom especially he hoped to persuade. He spoke of the beauties of sight, of watching the mountains, of the sky and the sunrise, and they heard him with amused incredulity that presently became condemnatory. They told him there were indeed no mountains at all, but that the end of the rocks where the llamas grazed was indeed the end of the world; thence sprang a cavernous roof of the universe, from which the dew and the avalanches fell; and when he maintained stoutly the world had neither end nor roof such as they supposed, they said his thoughts were wicked. So far as he could describe sky and clouds and stars to them it seemed to them a hideous void, a terrible blankness in the place of the smooth roof to things in which they believed—it was an article of faith with them that the cavern roof was exquisitely smooth to the touch. He saw that in some manner he shocked them, and gave up that aspect of the matter altogether, and tried to show them the practical value of sight. One morning he saw Pedro in the path called Seventeen and coming towards the central houses, but still too far off for hearing or scent, and he told them as much. "In a little while," he prophesied, "Pedro will be here." An old man remarked that Pedro had no business on path

Seventeen, and then, as if in confirmation, that individual as he drew near turned and went transversely into path Ten, and so back with nimble paces towards the outer wall. They mocked Nunez when Pedro did not arrive, and afterwards, when he asked Pedro questions to clear his character, Pedro denied and outfaced him, and was afterwards hostile to him.

Then he induced them to let him go a long way up the sloping meadows towards the wall with one complaisant individual, and to him he promised to describe all that happened among the houses. He noted certain goings and comings, but the things that really seemed to signify to these people happened inside of or behind the windowless houses—the only things they took note of to test him by—and of those he could see or tell nothing; and it was after the failure of this attempt, and the ridicule they could not repress, that he resorted to force. He thought of seizing a spade and suddenly smiting one or two of them to earth, and so in fair combat showing the advantage of eyes. He went so far with that resolution as to seize his spade, and then he discovered a new thing about himself, and that was that it was impossible for him to hit a blind man in cold blood.

He hesitated, and found them all aware that he had snatched up the spade. They stood all alert, with their heads on one side, and bent ears towards him for what he would do next.

"Put that spade down," said one, and he felt a sort of helpless horror. He came near obedience.

Then he had thrust one backwards against a house wall, and fled past him and out of the village.

He went athwart one of their meadows, leaving a track of trampled grass behind his feet, and presently sat down by the side of one of their ways. He felt something of the buoyancy that comes to all men in the beginning of a fight, but more perplexity. He began to realise that you cannot even fight happily with creatures who stand upon a different mental basis to yourself. Far away he saw a number of men carrying spades and sticks come out of the street of houses and advance in a spreading line along the several paths towards him. They advanced slowly, speaking frequently to one another, and ever and again the whole cordon would halt and sniff the air and listen.

The first time they did this Nunez laughed. But afterwards he did not laugh.

One struck his trail in the meadow grass and came stooping and feeling his way along it.

For five minutes he watched the slow extension of the cordon, and then his vague disposition to do something forthwith became frantic. He stood up, went a pace or so towards the circumferential wall, turned, and went back a little way. There they all stood in a crescent, still and listening.

He also stood still, gripping his spade very tightly in both hands. Should he charge them?

The pulse in his ears ran into the rhythm of "In the Country of the Blind the One-Eyed Man is King."

Should he charge them?

He looked back at the high and unclimbable wall behind—unclimbable because of its smooth plastering, but withal pierced with many little doors and at the approaching line of seekers. Behind these others were now coming out of the street of houses.

Should he charge them?

"Bogota!" called one. "Bogota! where are you?"

He gripped his spade still tighter and advanced down the meadows towards the place of habitations, and directly he moved they converged upon him. "I'll hit them if they touch me," he swore; "by Heaven, I will. I'll hit." He called aloud, "Look here, I'm going to do what I like in this valley! Do you hear? I'm going to do what I like and go where I like."

They were moving in upon him quickly, groping, yet moving rapidly. It was like playing blind man's buff with everyone blindfolded except one. "Get hold of him!" cried one. He found himself in the arc of a loose curve of pursuers. He felt suddenly he must be active and resolute.

"You don't understand," he cried, in a voice that was meant to be great and resolute, and which broke. "You are blind and I can see. Leave me alone!"

"Bogota! Put down that spade and come off the grass!"

The last order, grotesque in its urban familiarity, produced a gust of anger. "I'll hurt you," he said, sobbing with emotion. "By Heaven, I'll hurt you! Leave me alone!"

He began to run—not knowing clearly where to run. He ran from the nearest blind man, because it was a horror to hit him. He stopped, and then made a dash to escape from their closing ranks. He made for where a gap was wide, and the men on either side, with a quick perception of the approach of his paces, rushed in on one another. He sprang forward, and then saw he must be caught, and *swish*! the spade had struck. He felt the soft thud of hand and arm, and the man was down with a yell of pain, and he was through.

Through! And then he was close to the street of houses again, and blind men, whirling spades and stakes, were running with a reasoned swiftness hither and thither.

He heard steps behind him just in time, and found a tall man rushing forward and swiping at the sound of him. He lost his nerve, hurled his spade a yard wide of this antagonist, and whirled about and fled, fairly yelling as he dodged another.

He was panic-stricken. He ran furiously to and fro, dodging when there was no need to dodge, and, in his anxiety to see on every side of him at once, stumbling. For a moment he was down and they heard his fall. Far away in the circumferential wall a little doorway looked like Heaven, and he set off in a wild rush for it. He did not even look round at his pursuers until it was gained, and he had stumbled across the bridge, clambered a little way among the rocks, to the surprise and dismay of a young llama, who went leaping out of sight, and lay down sobbing for breath.

And so his coup d'etat came to an end.

He stayed outside the wall of the valley of the blind for two nights and days without food or shelter, and meditated upon the Unexpected. During these meditations he repeated very frequently and always with a profounder note of derision the exploded proverb: "In the Country of the Blind the One-Eyed Man is King." He thought chiefly of ways of fighting and conquering these people, and it grew clear that for him no practicable way was possible. He had no weapons, and now it would be hard to get one.

The canker of civilisation had got to him even in Bogota, and he could not find it in himself to go down and assassinate a blind man. Of course, if he did that, he might then dictate terms on the threat of assassinating them all. But—Sooner or later he must sleep! . . .

He tried also to find food among the pine trees, to be comfortable under pine boughs while the frost fell at night, and—with less confidence—to catch a llama by artifice in order to try to kill it—perhaps by hammering it with a stone—and so finally, perhaps, to eat some of it. But the llamas had a doubt of him and regarded him with distrustful brown eyes and spat when he drew near. Fear came on him the second day and fits of shivering. Finally he crawled down to the wall of the Country of the Blind and tried to make his terms. He crawled along by the stream, shouting, until two blind men came out to the gate and talked to him.

"I was mad," he said. "But I was only newly made."

They said that was better.

He told them he was wiser now, and repented of all he had done.

Then he wept without intention, for he was very weak and ill now, and they took that as a favourable sign.

They asked him if he still thought he could "*see*."

"No," he said. "That was folly. The word means nothing. Less than nothing!"

They asked him what was overhead.

"About ten times ten the height of a man there is a roof above the world—of rock—and very, very smooth. So smooth—so beautifully smooth . . ." He burst again into hysterical tears. "Before you ask me any more, give me some food or I shall die!"

He expected dire punishments, but these blind people were capable of toleration. They regarded his rebellion as but one more proof of his general idiocy and inferiority, and after they had whipped him they appointed him to do the simplest and heaviest work they had for anyone to do, and he, seeing no other way of living, did submissively what he was told.

He was ill for some days and they nursed him kindly. That refined his submission. But they insisted on his lying in the dark, and that was a great misery. And blind philosophers came and talked to him of the wicked levity of his mind, and reproved him so impressively for his doubts about the lid of rock that covered their cosmic casserole that he almost doubted whether indeed he was not the victim of hallucination in not seeing it overhead.

So Nunez became a citizen of the Country of the Blind, and these people ceased to be a generalised people and became individualities to him, and familiar to him, while the world beyond the mountains became more and more remote and unreal. There was Yacob, his master, a kindly man when not annoyed; there was Pedro, Yacob's nephew; and there was Medina-sarote, who was the youngest daughter of Yacob. She was little esteemed in the world of the blind, because she had a clear-cut face and lacked that satisfying, glossy smoothness that is the blind man's ideal of feminine beauty, but Nunez thought her beautiful at first, and presently the most beautiful thing in the whole creation. Her closed eyelids were not sunken and red after the common way of the valley, but lay as though they might open again at any moment; and she had long eyelashes, which were considered a grave disfigurement. And her voice was weak and did not satisfy the acute hearing of the valley swains. So that she had no lover.

There came a time when Nunez thought that, could he win her, he would be resigned to live in the valley for all the rest of his days.

He watched her; he sought opportunities of doing her little services and presently he found that she observed him. Once at a rest-day gathering they sat side by side in the dim starlight, and the music was sweet. His hand came upon hers and he dared to clasp it. Then very tenderly she returned his pressure. And one day, as they were at their meal in the darkness, he felt her hand very softly seeking him, and as it chanced the fire leapt then, and he saw the tenderness of her face.

He sought to speak to her.

He went to her one day when she was sitting in the summer moonlight spinning. The light made her a thing of silver and mystery. He sat down at her feet and told her he loved her, and told her how beautiful she seemed to him. He had a lover's voice, he spoke with a tender reverence that came near to awe, and she had never before been touched by adoration. She made him no definite answer, but it was clear his words pleased her.

After that he talked to her whenever he could take an opportunity. The valley became the world for him, and the world beyond the mountains where men lived by day seemed no more than a fairy tale he would some day pour into her ears. Very tentatively and timidly he spoke to her of sight.

Sight seemed to her the most poetical of fancies, and she listened to his description of the stars and the mountains and her own sweet white-lit beauty as though it was a guilty indulgence. She did not believe, she could only half understand, but she was mysteriously delighted, and it seemed to him that she completely understood.

His love lost its awe and took courage. Presently he was for demanding her of Yacob and the elders in marriage, but she became fearful and delayed. And it was one of her elder sisters who first told Yacob that Medina-sarote and Nunez were in love.

There was from the first very great opposition to the marriage of Nunez and Medina-sarote; not so much because they valued her as because they held him as a being apart, an idiot, incompetent thing below the permissible level of a man. Her sisters opposed it bitterly as bringing discredit on them all; and old Yacob, though he had formed a sort of liking for his clumsy, obedient serf, shook his head and said the thing could not be. The young men were all angry at the idea of corrupting the race, and one went so far as to revile and strike Nunez. He struck back. Then for the first time he found an advantage in seeing, even by twilight, and after that fight was over no one was disposed to raise a hand against him. But they still found his marriage impossible.

Old Yacob had a tenderness for his last little daughter, and was grieved to have her weep upon his shoulder.

"You see, my dear, he's an idiot. He has delusions; he can't do anything right."

"I know," wept Medina-sarote. "But he's better than he was. He's getting better. And he's strong, dear father, and kind—stronger and kinder than any other man in the world. And he loves me—and, father, I love him."

Old Yacob was greatly distressed to find her inconsolable, and, besides—what made it more distressing—he liked Nunez for many things. So he went and sat in the windowless council-chamber with the other elders and watched the trend of the talk, and said, at the proper time, "He's better than he was. Very likely, some day, we shall find him as sane as ourselves."

Then afterwards one of the elders, who thought deeply, had an idea. He was a great doctor among these people, their medicine-man, and he had a very philosophical and inventive mind, and the idea of curing Nunez of his peculiarities appealed to him. One day when Yacob was present he returned to the topic of Nunez. "I have examined Nunez," he said, "and the case is clearer to me. I think very probably he might be cured."

"This is what I have always hoped," said old Yacob.

"His brain is affected," said the blind doctor.

The elders murmured assent.

"Now, *what* affects it?"

"Ah!" said old Yacob.

"This," said the doctor, answering his own question. "Those queer things that are called the eyes, and which exist to make an agreeable depression in the face, are diseased, in the case of Nunez, in such a way as to affect his brain. They are greatly distended, he has eyelashes, and his eyelids move, and consequently his brain is in a state of constant irritation and distraction."

"Yes?" said old Yacob. "Yes?"

"And I think I may say with reasonable certainty that, in order to cure him complete, all that we need to do is a simple and easy surgical operation—namely, to remove these irritant bodies."

"And then he will be sane?"

"Then he will be perfectly sane, and a quite admirable citizen."

"Thank Heaven for science!" said old Yacob, and went forth at once to tell Nunez of his happy hopes.

But Nunez's manner of receiving the good news struck him as being cold and disappointing.

"One might think," he said, "from the tone you take that you did not care for my daughter."

It was Medina-sarote who persuaded Nunez to face the blind surgeons.

"*You* do not want me," he said, "to lose my gift of sight?"

She shook her head.

"My world is sight."

Her head drooped lower.

"There are the beautiful things, the beautiful little things—the flowers, the lichens amidst the rocks, the light and softness on a piece of fur, the far sky with its drifting dawn of clouds, the sunsets and the stars. And there is *you*. For you alone it is good to have sight, to see your sweet, serene face, your kindly lips, your dear, beautiful hands folded together . . . It is these eyes of mine you won, these eyes that hold me to you, that these idiots seek. Instead, I must touch you, hear you, and never see you again. I must come under that roof of rock and stone and darkness, that horrible roof under which your imaginations stoop . . . *no; you* would not have me do that?"

A disagreeable doubt had arisen in him. He stopped and left the thing a question.

"I wish," she said, "sometimes—" She paused.

"Yes?" he said, a little apprehensively.

"I wish sometimes—you would not talk like that."

"Like what?"

"I know it's pretty—it's your imagination. I love it, but *now*—"

He felt cold. "*Now*?" he said, faintly.

She sat quite still.

"You mean—you think—I should be better, better perhaps—"

He was realising things very swiftly. He felt anger perhaps, anger at the dull course of fate, but also sympathy for her lack of understanding—a sympathy near akin to pity.

"Dear," he said, and he could see by her whiteness how tensely her spirit pressed against the things she could not say. He put his arms about her, he kissed her ear, and they sat for a time in silence.

"If I were to consent to this?" he said at last, in a voice that was very gentle.

She flung her arms about him, weeping wildly. "Oh, if you would," she sobbed, "if only you would!"

For a week before the operation that was to raise him from his servitude and inferiority to the level of a blind citizen Nunez knew nothing of sleep, and all through the warm, sunlit hours, while the others slumbered happily, he sat brooding or wandered aimlessly, trying to bring his mind to bear on his dilemma. He had given his answer, he had given his consent, and still he was not sure. And at last work-time was over, the sun rose in splendour over the golden crests, and his last day of vision began for him. He had a few minutes with Medina-sarote before she went apart to sleep.

"To-morrow," he said, "I shall see no more."

"Dear heart!" she answered, and pressed his hands with all her strength.

"They will hurt you but little," she said; "and you are going through this pain, you are going through it, dear lover, for *me* . . . Dear, if a woman's heart and life can do it, I will repay you. My dearest one, my dearest with the tender voice, I will repay."

He was drenched in pity for himself and her.

He held her in his arms, and pressed his lips to hers and looked on her sweet face for the last time. "Good-bye!" he whispered to that dear sight, "good-bye!"

And then in silence he turned away from her.

She could hear his slow retreating footsteps, and something in the rhythm of them threw her into a passion of weeping.

He walked away.

He had fully meant to go to a lonely place where the meadows were beautiful with white narcissus, and there remain until the hour of his sacrifice should come, but as he walked he lifted up his eyes and saw the morning, the morning like an angel in golden armour, marching down the steeps. . . .

It seemed to him that before this splendour he and this blind world in the valley, and his love and all, were no more than a pit of sin.

He did not turn aside as he had meant to do, but went on and passed through the wall of the circumference and out upon the rocks, and his eyes were always upon the sunlit ice and snow.

He saw their infinite beauty, and his imagination soared over them to the things beyond he was now to resign for ever!

He thought of that great free world that he was parted from, the world that was his own, and he had a vision of those further slopes, distance beyond distance, with Bogota, a place of multitudinous stirring beauty, a glory by day, a luminous mystery by night, a place of palaces and fountains and statues and white houses, lying beautifully in the middle distance. He thought how for a day or so one might come down through passes drawing ever nearer and nearer to its busy streets and ways. He thought of the river journey, day by day, from great Bogota to the still vaster world beyond, through towns and villages, forest and desert places, the rushing river day by day, until its banks receded, and the big steamers came splashing by and one had reached the sea—the limitless sea, with its thousand islands, its thousands of islands, and its ships seen dimly far away in their incessant journeyings round and about that greater world. And there, unpent by mountains, one saw the sky—the sky, not such a disc as one saw it here, but an arch of immeasurable blue, a deep of deeps in which the circling stars were floating. . . .

His eyes began to scrutinise the great curtain of the mountains with a keener inquiry.

For example; if one went so, up that gully and to that chimney there, then one might come out high among those stunted pines that ran round in a sort of shelf and rose still higher and higher as it passed above the gorge. And then? That talus might be managed. Thence perhaps a climb might be found to take him up to the precipice that came below the snow; and if that chimney failed, then another farther to the east might serve his purpose better. And then? Then one would be out upon the amber-lit snow there, and half-way up to the crest of those beautiful desolations. And suppose one had good fortune!

He glanced back at the village, then turned right round and regarded it with folded arms.

He thought of Medina-sarote, and she had become small and remote.

He turned again towards the mountain wall down which the day had come to him.

Then very circumspectly he began his climb.

When sunset came he was not longer climbing, but he was far and high. His clothes were torn, his limbs were blood-stained, he was bruised in many places, but he lay as if he were at his ease, and there was a smile on his face.

From where he rested the valley seemed as if it were in a pit and nearly a mile below. Already it was dim with haze and shadow, though the mountain summits around him were things of light and fire. The mountain summits around him were things of light and fire, and the little things in the rocks near at hand were drenched with light and beauty, a vein of green mineral piercing the grey, a flash of small crystal here and there, a minute, minutely-beautiful orange lichen close beside his face. There were deep, mysterious shadows in the gorge, blue deepening into purple, and purple into a luminous darkness, and overhead was the illimitable vastness of the sky. But he heeded these things no longer, but lay quite still there, smiling as if he were content now merely to have escaped from the valley of the Blind, in which he had thought to be King. And the glow of the sunset passed, and the night came, and still he lay there, under the cold, clear stars.

THE WILLOWS

Algernon Blackwood

(1907)

This tale, which describes how two young adventurers encounter another dimension impinging upon our own, was reckoned by Lovecraft to be not only "foremost of all" Blackwood's tales but the best "weird tale" of all time.

After leaving Vienna, and long before you come to Buda-Pesth, the Danube enters a region of singular loneliness and desolation, where its waters spread away on all sides regardless of a main channel, and the country becomes a swamp for miles upon miles, covered by a vast sea of low willow bushes. On the big maps this deserted area is painted in a fluffy blue, growing fainter in colour as it leaves the banks, and across it may be seen in large straggling letters the word *Sümpfe*, meaning marshes.

In high flood this great acreage of sand, shingle-beds, and willow-grown islands is almost topped by the water, but in normal seasons the bushes bend and rustle in the free winds, showing their silver leaves to the sunshine in an ever-moving plain of bewildering beauty. These willows never attain to the dignity of trees; they have no rigid trunks; they remain humble bushes, with rounded tops and soft outline, swaying on slender stems that answer to the least pressure of the wind; supple as grasses, and so continually shifting that they somehow give the impression that the entire plain is moving and *alive*. For the wind sends waves rising and falling over the whole surface, waves of leaves instead of waves of water, green swells like the sea, too, until the branches turn and lift, and then silvery white as their under-side turns to the sun.

Happy to slip beyond the control of the stern banks, the

Danube here wanders about at will among the intricate network of channels intersecting the islands everywhere with broad avenues down which the waters pour with a shouting sound; making whirlpools, eddies, and foaming rapids; tearing at the sandy banks; carrying away masses of shore and willow-clumps; and forming new islands innumerable which shift daily in size and shape and possess at best an impermanent life, since the flood-time obliterates their very existence.

Properly speaking, this fascinating part of the river's life begins soon after leaving Pressburg, and we, in our Canadian canoe, with gipsy tent and frying-pan on board, reached it on the crest of a rising flood about mid-July. That very same morning, when the sky was reddening before sunrise, we had slipped swiftly through still-sleeping Vienna, leaving it a couple of hours later a mere patch of smoke against the blue hills of the Wienerwald on the horizon; we had breakfasted below Fischerarmend under a grove of birch trees roaring in the wind; and had then swept on the tearing current past Orth, Hamburg, Petronell (the old Roman Carnuntum of Marcus Aurelius), and so under the frowning heights of Theben on a spur of the Carpathians, where the March steals in quietly from the left and the frontier is crossed between Austria and Hungary.

Racing along at twelve kilometres an hour soon took us well into Hungary, and the muddy waters—sure sign of flood—sent us aground on many a shingle-bed, and twisted us like a cork in many a sudden belching whirlpool before the towers of Pressburg (Hungarian, Poszóny) showed against the sky; and then the canoe, leaping like a spirited horse, flew at top speed under the grey walls, negotiated safely the sunken chain of the Fliegende Brücke ferry, turned the corner sharply to the left, and plunged on yellow foam into the wilderness of islands, sand-banks, and swampland beyond—the land of the willows.

The change came suddenly, as when a series of bioscope pictures snaps down on the streets of a town and shifts without warning into the scenery of lake and forest. We entered the land of desolation on wings, and in less than half an hour there was neither boat nor fishing-hut nor red roof, nor any single sign of human habitation and civilisation within sight. The sense of remoteness from the world of human kind, the utter isolation, the fascination of this singular world of willows, winds, and waters, instantly laid its spell upon us both, so that we allowed laughingly to one another that we ought by rights to have held some special kind of passport to admit us, and that we had, somewhat audaciously, come without asking leave into a separate little kingdom of wonder and magic—a kingdom that was reserved for the use of others who had a right to it, with everywhere unwritten warnings to trespassers for those who had the imagination to discover them.

Though still early in the afternoon, the ceaseless buffetings of a most tempestuous wind made us feel weary, and we at once began casting about for a suitable camping-ground for the night. But the bewildering character of the islands made landing difficult; the swirling flood carried us in-shore and then swept us out again; the willow branches tore our hands as we seized them to stop the canoe, and we pulled many a yard of sandy bank into the water before at length we shot with a great sideways blow from the wind into a backwater and managed to beach the bows in a cloud of spray. Then we lay panting and laughing after our exertions on hot yellow sand, sheltered from the wind, and in the full blaze of a scorching sun, a cloudless blue sky above, and an immense army of dancing, shouting willow bushes, closing in from all sides, shining with spray and clapping their thousand little hands as though to applaud the success of our efforts.

"What a river!" I said to my companion, thinking of all the way we had travelled from the source in the Black Forest, and how he had often been obliged to wade and push in the upper shallows at the beginning of June.

"Won't stand much nonsense now, will it?" he said, pulling the canoe a little farther into safety up the sand, and then composing himself for a nap.

I lay by his side, happy and peaceful in the bath of the elements—water, wind, sand, and the great fire of the sun—thinking of the long journey that lay behind us, and of the great stretch before us to the Black Sea, and how lucky I was to have such a delightful and charming travelling companion as my friend, the Swede.

We had made many similar journeys together, but the Danube, more than any other river I knew, impressed us from the very beginning with its *aliveness*. From its tiny bubbling entry into the world among the pinewood gardens of Donaueschingen, until this moment when it began to play the great river-game of losing itself among the deserted swamps, unobserved, unrestrained, it had seemed to us like following the growth of some living creature. Sleepy at first, but later developing violent desires as it became conscious of its deep soul, it rolled, like some huge fluid being, through all the countries we had passed, holding our little craft on its mighty shoulders, playing roughly with us sometimes, yet always friendly and well-meaning, till at length we had come inevitably to regard it as a Great Personage.

How, indeed, could it be otherwise, since it told us so much of its secret life? At night we heard it singing to the moon as we lay in our tent, uttering that odd sibilant note peculiar to itself and said to be caused by the rapid tearing of the pebbles along its bed, so great is its hurrying speed. We knew, too, the voice of its gurgling whirlpools, suddenly bubbling up on a surface previously quite calm; the roar of its shallows and swift rapids; its constant steady thundering below all mere surface sounds; and that ceaseless tearing of its icy waters at the banks. How it stood up and shouted when the rains fell flat upon its face! And how its laughter roared out when the wind blew upstream and tried to stop its growing speed! We knew all its sounds and voices, its tumblings and foamings, its unnecessary splashing against the bridges; that self-conscious chatter when there were hills to look on; the affected dignity of its speech when it passed through the little towns, far too important to laugh; and all these faint, sweet whisperings when the sun caught it fairly in some slow curve and poured down upon it till the steam rose.

It was full of tricks, too, in its early life before the great world knew it. There were places in the upper reaches among the Swabian forests, when yet the first whispers of its destiny had not reached it, where it elected to disappear through holes in the ground, to appear again on the other side of the porous limestone hills and start a new river with another name; leaving, too, so little water in its own bed that we had to climb out and wade and push the canoe through miles of shallows.

And a chief pleasure, in those early days of its irresponsible youth, was to lie low, like Brer Fox, just before the little turbulent tributaries came to join it from the Alps, and to refuse to acknowledge them when in, but to run for miles side by side, the dividing line well marked, the very levels different, the Danube utterly declining to recognise the newcomer. Below Passau, however, it gave up this particular trick, for there the Inn comes in with a thundering power impossible to ignore, and so pushes and incommodes the parent river that there is hardly room for them in the long twisting gorge that follows, and the Danube is shoved this way and that against the cliffs, and forced to hurry itself with great waves and much dashing to and fro in order to get through in time. And during the fight our canoe slipped down from its shoulder to its breast, and had the time of its life among the struggling waves. But the Inn taught the old river a lesson, and after Passau it no longer pretended to ignore new arrivals.

This was many days back, of course, and since then we had come to know other aspects of the great creature, and across the Bavarian wheat plain of Straubing she wandered so slowly under the blazing June sun that we could well imagine only the surface inches were water, while below there moved, concealed as by a silken mantle, a whole army of Undines, passing silently and unseen down to the sea, and very leisurely too, lest they be discovered.

Much, too, we forgave her because of her friendliness to the birds and animals that haunted the shores. Cormorants lined the banks in lonely places in rows like short black palings; grey crows crowded the shingle-beds; storks stood fishing in the vistas of shallower water that opened up between the islands, and hawks, swans, and marsh birds of all sorts filled the air with glinting wings and singing, petulant cries. It was impossible to feel annoyed with the river's vagaries after seeing a deer leap with a splash into the water at sunrise and swim past the bows of the canoe; and often we saw fawns peering at us from the underbrush, or looked straight into the brown eyes of a stag as we charged full tilt round a corner and entered another reach of the river. Foxes, too, everywhere haunted the banks, tripping daintily among the driftwood and disappearing so suddenly that it was impossible to see how they managed it.

But now, after leaving Pressburg, everything changed a little, and the Danube became more serious. It ceased trifling. It was halfway to the Black Sea, within scenting distance almost of other, stranger countries where no tricks would be permitted or understood. It became suddenly grown-up, and claimed our respect and even our awe. It broke out into three arms, for one thing, that only met again a hundred kilometres farther down, and for a canoe there were no indications which one was intended to be followed.

"If you take a side channel," said the Hungarian officer we met in the Pressburg shop while buying provisions, "you may find yourselves, when the flood subsides, forty miles from anywhere, high and dry, and you may easily starve. There are no people, no farms, no fishermen. I warn you not to continue. The river, too, is still rising, and this wind will increase."

The rising river did not alarm us in the least, but the matter of being left high and dry by a sudden subsidence of the waters might be serious, and we had consequently laid in an extra stock of provisions. For the rest, the officer's prophecy held true, and the wind, blowing down a perfectly clear sky, increased steadily till it reached the dignity of a westerly gale.

It was earlier than usual when we camped, for the sun was a good hour or two from the horizon, and leaving my friend still asleep on the hot sand, I wandered about in desultory examination of our hotel. The island, I found, was less than an acre in extent, a mere sandy bank standing some two or three feet above the level of the river. The far end, pointing into the sunset, was covered with flying spray which the tremendous wind drove off the crests of the broken waves. It was triangular in shape, with the apex up stream.

I stood there for several minutes, watching the impetuous crimson flood bearing down with a shouting roar, dashing in waves against the bank as though to sweep it bodily away, and then swirling by in two foaming streams on either side. The ground seemed to shake with the shock and rush, while the furious movement of the willow bushes as the wind poured over them increased the curious illusion that the island itself actually moved. Above, for a mile or two, I could see the great river descending upon me: it was like looking up the slope of a sliding hill, white with foam, and leaping up everywhere to show itself to the sun.

The rest of the island was too thickly grown with willows to make walking pleasant, but I made the tour, nevertheless. From the lower end the light, of course, changed, and the river looked dark and angry. Only the backs of the flying waves were visible, streaked with foam, and pushed forcibly by the great puffs of wind that fell upon them from behind. For a short mile it was visible, pouring in and out among the islands, and then disappearing with a huge sweep into the willows, which closed about it like a herd of monstrous antediluvian creatures crowding down to drink. They made me think of gigantic sponge-like growths that sucked the river up into themselves. They caused it to vanish from sight. They herded there together in such overpowering numbers.

Altogether it was an impressive scene, with its utter loneliness, its bizarre suggestion; and as I gazed, long and curiously, a singular emotion began to stir somewhere in the depths of me. Midway in my delight of the wild beauty, there crept, unbidden and unexplained, a curious feeling of disquietude, almost of alarm.

A rising river, perhaps, always suggests something of the ominous: many of the little islands I saw before me would probably have been swept away by the morning; this resistless, thundering flood of water touched the sense of awe. Yet I was aware that my uneasiness lay deeper far than the emotions of awe and wonder. It was not that I felt. Nor had it directly to do with the power of the driving wind—this shouting hurricane that might almost carry up a few acres of willows into the air and scatter them like so much chaff over the landscape. The wind was simply enjoying itself, for nothing rose out of the flat landscape to stop it, and I was conscious of sharing its great game with a kind of pleasurable excitement. Yet this novel emotion had nothing to do with the wind. Indeed, so vague was the sense of distress I experienced, that it was impossible to trace it to its source and deal with it accordingly, though I was aware somehow that it had to do with my realisation of our utter insignificance before this unrestrained power of the elements about me. The huge-grown river had I something to do with it too—a vague, unpleasant idea that we had somehow trifled with these great elemental forces in whose power we lay helpless every hour of the day and night. For here, indeed, they were gigantically at play together, and the sight appealed to the imagination.

But my emotion, so far as I could understand it, seemed to attach itself more particularly to the willow bushes, to these acres and acres of willows, crowding, so thickly growing there, swarming everywhere the eye could reach, pressing upon the river as though to suffocate it, standing in dense array mile after mile beneath the sky, watching, waiting, listening. And, apart quite from the elements, the willows connected themselves subtly with my malaise, attacking the mind insidiously somehow by reason of their vast numbers, and contriving in some way or other to represent to the imagination a new and mighty power, a power, moreover, not altogether friendly to us.

Great revelations of nature, of course, never fail to impress in one way or another, and I was no stranger to moods of the kind. Mountains overawe and oceans terrify, while the mystery of great forests exercises a spell peculiarly its own. But all these, at one point or another, somewhere link on intimately with human life and human experience. They stir comprehensible, even if alarming, emotions. They tend on the whole to exalt.

With this multitude of willows, however, it was something far different, I felt. Some essence emanated from them that besieged the heart. A sense of awe awakened, true, but of awe touched somewhere by a vague terror. Their serried ranks, growing everywhere darker about me as the shadows deepened, moving furiously yet softly in the wind, woke in me the curious and unwelcome suggestion that we had trespassed here upon the borders of an alien world, a world where we were intruders, a world where we were not wanted or invited to remain—where we ran grave risks perhaps!

The feeling, however, though it refused to yield its meaning entirely to analysis, did not at the time trouble me by passing into menace. Yet it never left me quite, even during the very practical business of putting up the tent in a hurricane of wind and building a fire for the stew-pot. It remained, just enough to bother and perplex, and to rob a most delightful camping-ground of a good portion of its charm. To my companion, however, I said nothing, for he was a man I considered devoid of imagination. In the first place, I could never have explained to him what I meant, and in the second, he would have laughed stupidly at me if I had.

There was a slight depression in the centre of the island, and here we pitched the tent. The surrounding willows broke the wind a bit.

"A poor camp," observed the imperturbable Swede when at last the tent stood upright; "no stones and precious little firewood. I'm for moving on early to-morrow—eh? This sand won't hold anything."

But the experience of a collapsing tent at midnight had taught us many devices, and we made the cosy gipsy house as safe as possible, and then set about collecting a store of wood to last till bed-time. Willow bushes drop no branches, and driftwood was our only source of supply. We hunted the shores pretty thoroughly. Everywhere the banks were crumbling as the rising flood tore at them and carried away great portions with a splash and a gurgle.

"The island's much smaller than when we landed," said the accurate Swede. "It won't last long at this rate. We'd better drag the canoe close to the tent, and be ready to start at a moment's notice. *I* shall sleep in my clothes."

He was a little distance off, climbing along the bank, and I heard his rather jolly laugh as he spoke.

"By Jove!" I heard him call, a moment later, and turned to see what had caused his exclamation. But for the moment he was hidden by the willows, and I could not find him.

"What in the world's this?" I heard him cry again, and this time his voice had become serious.

I ran up quickly and joined him on the bank. He was looking over the river, pointing at something in the water.

"Good heavens, it's a man's body!" he cried excitedly. "Look!"

A black thing, turning over and over in the foaming waves, swept rapidly past. It kept disappearing and coming up to the surface again. It was about twenty feet from the shore, and just as it was opposite to where we stood it lurched round and looked straight at us. We saw its eyes reflecting the sunset, and gleaming an odd yellow as the body turned over. Then it gave a swift, gulping plunge, and dived out of sight in a flash.

"An otter, by gad!" we exclaimed in the same breath, laughing.

It *was* an otter, alive, and out on the hunt; yet it had looked exactly like the body of a drowned man turning helplessly in the current. Far below it came to the surface once again, and we saw its black skin, wet and shining in the sunlight.

Then, too, just as we turned back, our arms full of driftwood, another thing happened to recall us to the river bank. This time it really was a man, and what was more, a man in a boat. Now a small boat on the Danube was an unusual sight at any time, but here in this deserted region, and at flood time, it was so unexpected as to constitute a real event. We stood and stared.

Whether it was due to the slanting sunlight, or the refraction from the wonderfully illumined water, I cannot say, but, whatever the cause, I found it difficult to focus my sight properly upon the flying apparition. It seemed, however, to be a man standing upright in a sort of flat-bottomed boat, steering with a long oar, and being carried down the opposite shore at a tremendous pace. He apparently was looking across in our direction, but the distance was too great and the light too uncertain for us to make out very plainly what he was about. It seemed to me that he was gesticulating and making signs at us. His voice came across the water to us shouting something furiously, but the wind drowned it so that no single word was audible. There was something curious about the whole appearance—man, boat, signs, voice—that made an impression on me out of all proportion to its cause.

"He's crossing himself!" I cried. "Look, he's making the sign of the Cross!"

"I believe you're right," the Swede said, shading his eyes with his hand and watching the man out of sight. He seemed to be gone in a moment, melting away down there into the sea of willows where the sun caught them in the bend of the river and turned them into a great crimson wall of beauty. Mist, too, had begun to rise, so that the air was hazy.

"But what in the world is he doing at nightfall on this flooded river?" I said, half to myself. "Where is he going at such a time, and what did he mean by his signs and shouting? D'you think he wished to warn us about something?"

"He saw our smoke, and thought we were spirits probably," laughed my companion. "These Hungarians believe in all sorts of rubbish: you remember the shopwoman at Pressburg warning us that no one ever landed here because it belonged to some sort of beings outside man's world! I suppose they believe in fairies and elementals, possibly demons too. That peasant in the boat saw people on the islands for the first time in his life," he added, after a slight pause, "and it scared him, that's all."

The Swede's tone of voice was not convincing, and his manner lacked something that was usually there. I noted the change instantly while he talked, though without being able to label it precisely.

"If they had enough imagination," I laughed loudly—I remember trying to make as much *noise* as I could—"they might well people a place like this with the old gods of antiquity. The Romans must have haunted all this region more or less with their shrines and sacred groves and elemental deities."

The subject dropped and we returned to our stew-pot, for my friend was not given to imaginative conversation as a rule. Moreover, just then I remember feeling distinctly glad that he was not imaginative; his stolid, practical nature suddenly seemed to me welcome and comforting. It was an admirable temperament, I felt: he could steer down rapids like a red Indian, shoot dangerous bridges and whirlpools better than any white man I ever saw in a canoe. He was a grand fellow for an adventurous trip, a tower of strength when untoward things happened. I looked at his strong face and light curly hair as he staggered along under his pile of driftwood (twice the size of mine!), and I experienced a feeling of relief. Yes, I was distinctly glad just then that the Swede was—what he was, and that he never made remarks that suggested more than they said.

"The river's still rising, though," he added, as if following out some thoughts of his own, and dropping his load with a gasp. "This island will be under water in two days if it goes on."

"I wish the *wind* would go down," I said. "I don't care a fig for the river."

The flood, indeed, had no terrors for us; we could get off at ten minutes' notice, and the more water the better we liked it. It meant an increasing current and the obliteration of the treacherous shingle-beds that so often threatened to tear the bottom out of our canoe.

Contrary to our expectations, the wind did not go down with the sun. It seemed to increase with the darkness; howling overhead and shaking the willows round us like straws. Curious sounds accompanied it sometimes, like the explosion of heavy guns, and it fell upon the water and the island in great flat blows of immense power. It made me think of the sounds a planet must make, could we only hear it, driving along through space.

But the sky kept wholly clear of clouds, and soon after supper the full moon rose up in the east and covered the river and the plain of shouting willows with a light like the day.

We lay on the sandy patch beside the fire, smoking, listening to the noises of the night round us, and talking happily of the journey we had already made, and of our plans ahead. The map lay spread in the door of the tent, but the high wind made it hard to study, and presently we lowered the curtain and extinguished the lantern. The firelight was enough to smoke and see each other's faces by, and the sparks flew about overhead like fireworks. A few yards beyond, the river gurgled and hissed, and from time to time a heavy splash announced the falling away of further portions of the bank.

Our talk, I noticed, had to do with the far-away scenes and incidents of our first camps in the Black Forest, or of other subjects altogether remote from the present setting, for neither of us spoke of the actual moment more than was necessary—almost as though we had agreed tacitly to avoid discussion of the camp and its incidents. Neither the otter nor the boatman, for instance, received the honour of a single mention, though ordinarily these would have furnished discussion for the greater part of the evening. They were, of course, distinct events in such a place.

The scarcity of wood made it a business to keep the fire going, for the wind, that drove the smoke in our faces wherever we sat, helped at the same time to make a forced draught. We took it in turn to make foraging expeditions into the darkness, and the quantity the Swede brought back always made me feel that he took an absurdly long time finding it; for the fact was I did not care much about being left alone, and yet it always seemed to be my turn to grub about among the bushes or scramble along the slippery banks in the moonlight. The long day's battle with wind and water—such wind and such water!—had tired us both, and an early bed was the obvious programme. Yet neither of us made the move for the tent. We lay there, tending the fire, talking in desultory fashion, peering about us into the dense willow bushes, and listening to the thunder of wind and river. The loneliness of the place had entered our very bones, and silence seemed natural, for after a bit the sound of our voices became a trifle unreal and forced; whispering would have been the fitting mode of communication, I felt, and the human voice, always rather absurd amid the roar of the elements, now carried with it something almost illegitimate. It was like talking out loud in church, or in some place where it was not lawful, perhaps not quite *safe*, to be overheard.

The eeriness of this lonely island, set among a million willows, swept by a hurricane, and surrounded by hurrying deep waters, touched us both, I fancy. Untrodden by man, almost unknown to man, it lay there beneath the moon, remote from human influence, on the frontier of another world, an alien world, a world tenanted by willows only and the souls of willows. And we, in our rashness, had dared to invade it, even to make use of it! Something more than the power of its mystery stirred in me as I lay on the sand, feet to fire, and peered up through the leaves at the stars. For the last time I rose to get firewood.

"When this has burnt up," I said firmly, "I shall turn in," and my companion watched me lazily as I moved off into the surrounding shadows.

For an unimaginative man I thought he seemed unusually receptive that night, unusually open to suggestion of things other than sensory. He too was touched by the beauty and loneliness of the place. I was not altogether pleased, I remember, to recognise this slight change in him, and instead of immediately collecting sticks, I made my way to the far point of the island where the moonlight on plain and river could be seen to better advantage. The desire to be alone had come suddenly upon me; my former dread returned in force; there was a vague feeling in me I wished to face and probe to the bottom.

When I reached the point of sand jutting out among the waves, the spell of the place descended upon me with a positive shock. No mere "scenery" could have produced such an effect. There was something more here, something to alarm.

I gazed across the waste of wild waters; I watched the whispering willows; I heard the ceaseless beating of the tireless wind; and, one and all, each in its own way, stirred in me this sensation of a strange distress. But the *willows* especially: for ever they went on chattering and talking among themselves, laughing a little, shrilly crying out, sometimes sighing—but what it was they made so much to-do about belonged to the secret life of the great plain they inhabited. And it was utterly alien to the world I knew, or to that of the wild yet kindly elements. They made me think of a host of beings from another plane of life, another evolution altogether, perhaps, all discussing a mystery known only to themselves. I watched them moving busily together, oddly shaking their big bushy heads, twirling their myriad leaves even when there was no wind. They moved of their own will as though alive, and they touched, by some incalculable method, my own keen sense of the *horrible*.

There they stood in the moonlight, like a vast army surrounding our camp, shaking their innumerable silver spears defiantly, formed all ready for an attack.

The psychology of places, for some imaginations at least, is very vivid; for the wanderer, especially, camps have their "note" either of welcome or rejection. At first it may not always be apparent, because the busy preparations of tent and cooking prevent, but with the first pause—after supper usually—it comes and announces itself. And the note of this willow-camp now became unmistakably plain to me: we were interlopers, trespassers; we were not welcomed. The sense of unfamiliarity grew upon me as I stood there watching. We touched the frontier of a region where our presence was resented. For a night's lodging we might perhaps be tolerated; but for a prolonged and inquisitive stay—No! by all the gods of the trees and the wilderness, no! We were the first human influences upon this island, and we were not wanted. *The willows were against us.*

Strange thoughts like these, bizarre fancies, borne I know not whence, found lodgment in my mind as I stood listening. What, I thought, if, after all, these crouching willows proved to be alive; if suddenly they should rise up, like a swarm of living creatures, marshalled by the gods whose territory we had invaded, sweep towards us off the vast swamps, booming overhead in the night—and then *settle down!* As I looked it was so easy to imagine they actually moved, crept nearer, retreated a little, huddled together in masses, hostile, waiting for the great wind that should finally start them a-running. I could have sworn their aspect changed a little, and their ranks deepened and pressed more closely together.

The melancholy shrill cry of a night-bird sounded overhead, and suddenly I nearly lost my balance as the piece of bank I stood upon fell with a great splash into the river, undermined by the flood. I stepped back just in time, and went on hunting for firewood again, half laughing at the odd fancies that crowded so thickly into my mind and cast their spell upon me. I recalled the Swede's remark about moving on next day, and I was just thinking that I fully agreed with him, when I turned with a start and saw the subject of my thoughts standing immediately in front of me. He was quite close. The roar of the elements had covered his approach.

"You've been gone so long," he shouted above the wind, "I thought something must have happened to you."

But there was that in his tone, and a certain look in his face as well, that conveyed to me more than his actual words, and in a flash I understood the real reason for his coming. It was because the spell of the place had entered his soul too, and he did not like being alone.

"River still rising," he cried, pointing to the flood in the moonlight, "and the wind's simply awful."

He always said the same things, but it was the cry for companionship that gave the real importance to his words.

"Lucky," I cried back, "our tent's in the hollow. I think it'll hold all right." I added something about the difficulty of finding wood, in order to explain my absence, but the wind caught my words and flung them across the river, so that he did not hear, but just looked at me through the branches, nodding his head.

"Lucky if we get away without disaster!" he shouted, or words to that effect; and I remember feeling half angry with him for putting the thought into words, for it was exactly what I felt myself. There was disaster impending somewhere, and the sense of presentiment lay unpleasantly upon me.

We went back to the fire and made a final blaze, poking it up with our feet. We took a last look round. But for the wind the heat would have been unpleasant. I put this thought into words, and I remember my friend's reply struck me oddly: that he would rather have the heat, the ordinary July weather, than this "diabolical wind."

Everything was snug for the night; the canoe lying turned over beside the tent, with both yellow paddles beneath her; the provision sack hanging from a willow-stem, and the washed-up dishes removed to a safe distance from the fire, all ready for the morning meal.

We smothered the embers of the fire with sand, and then turned in. The flap of the tent door was up, and I saw the branches and the stars and the white moonlight. The shaking willows and the heavy buffetings of the wind against our taut little house were the last things I remembered as sleep came down and covered all with its soft and delicious forgetfulness.

Suddenly I found myself lying awake, peering from my sandy mattress through the door of the tent. I looked at my watch pinned against the canvas, and saw by the bright moonlight that it was past twelve o'clock—the threshold of a new day—and I had therefore slept a couple of hours. The Swede was asleep still beside me; the wind howled as before; something plucked at my heart and made me feel afraid. There was a sense of disturbance in my immediate neighbourhood.

I sat up quickly and looked out. The trees were swaying violently to and fro as the gusts smote them, but our little bit of green canvas lay snugly safe in the hollow, for the wind passed over it without meeting enough resistance to make it vicious. The feeling of disquietude did not pass, however, and I crawled quietly out of the tent to see if our belongings were safe. I moved carefully so as not to waken my companion. A curious excitement was on me.

I was half-way out, kneeling on all fours, when my eye first took in that the tops of the bushes opposite, with their moving tracery of leaves, made shapes against the sky. I sat back on my haunches and stared. It was incredible, surely, but there, opposite and slightly above me, were shapes of some indeterminate sort among the willows, and as the branches swayed in the wind they seemed to group themselves about these shapes, forming a series of monstrous outlines that shifted rapidly beneath the moon. Close, about fifty feet in front of me, I saw these things.

My first instinct was to waken my companion, that he too might see them, but something made me hesitate—the sudden realisation, probably, that I should not welcome corroboration; and meanwhile I crouched there staring in amazement with smarting eyes. I was wide awake. I remember saying to myself that I was *not* dreaming.

They first became properly visible, these huge figures, just within the tops of the bushes—immense, bronze-coloured, moving, and wholly independent of the swaying of the branches. I saw them plainly and noted, now I came to examine them more calmly, that they were very much larger than human, and indeed that something in their appearance proclaimed them to be *not human* at all. Certainly they were not merely the moving tracery of the branches against the moonlight. They shifted independently. They rose upwards in a continuous stream from earth to sky, vanishing utterly as soon as they reached the dark of the sky. They were interlaced one with another, making a great column, and I saw their limbs and huge bodies melting in and out of each other, forming this serpentine line that bent and swayed and twisted spirally with the contortions of the wind-tossed trees. They were nude, fluid shapes, passing up the bushes, *within* the leaves almost—rising up in a living column into the heavens. Their faces I never could see. Unceasingly they poured upwards, swaying in great bending curves, with a hue of dull bronze upon their skins.

I stared, trying to force every atom of vision from my eyes. For a long time I thought they *must* every moment disappear and resolve themselves into the movements of the branches and prove to be an optical illusion. I searched everywhere for a proof of reality, when all the while I understood quite well that the standard of reality had changed. For the longer I looked the more certain I became that these figures were real and living, though perhaps not according to the standards that the camera and the biologist would insist upon.

Far from feeling fear, I was possessed with a sense of awe and wonder such as I have never known. I seemed to be gazing at the personified elemental forces of this haunted and primeval region. Our intrusion had stirred the powers of the place into activity. It was we who were the cause of the disturbance, and my brain filled to bursting with stories and legends of the spirits and deities of places that have been acknowledged and worshipped by men in all ages of the world's history. But, before I could arrive at any possible explanation, something impelled me to go farther out, and I crept forward on to the sand and stood upright. I felt the ground still warm under my bare feet; the wind tore at my hair and face; and the sound of the river burst upon my ears with a sudden roar. These things, I knew, were real, and proved that my senses were acting normally. Yet the figures still rose from earth to heaven, silent, majestically, in a great spiral of grace and strength that overwhelmed me at length with a genuine deep emotion of worship. I felt that I must fall down and worship—absolutely worship.

Perhaps in another minute I might have done so, when a gust of wind swept against me with such force that it blew me sideways, and I nearly stumbled and fell. It seemed to shake the dream violently out of me. At least it gave me another point of view somehow. The figures still remained, still ascended into heaven from the heart of the night, but my reason at last began to assert itself. It must be a subjective experience, I argued—none the less real for that, but still subjective. The moonlight and the branches combined to work out these pictures upon the mirror of my imagination, and for some reason I projected them outwards and made them appear objective. I knew this must be the case, of course. I was the subject of a vivid and interesting hallucination. I took courage, and began to move forward across the open patches of sand. By Jove, though, was it all hallucination? Was it merely subjective? Did not my reason argue in the old futile way from the little standard of the known?

I only know that great column of figures ascended darkly into the sky for what seemed a very long period of time, and with a very complete measure of reality as most men are accustomed to gauge reality. Then suddenly they were gone!

And, once they were gone and the immediate wonder of their great presence had passed, fear came down upon me with a cold rush. The esoteric meaning of this lonely and haunted region suddenly flamed up within me, and I began to tremble dreadfully. I took a quick look round—a look of horror that came near to panic—calculating vainly ways of escape; and then, realising how helpless I was to achieve anything really effective, I crept back silently into the tent and lay down again upon my sandy mattress, first lowering the door-curtain to shut out the sight of the willows in the moonlight, and then burying my head as deeply as possible beneath the blankets to deaden the sound of the terrifying wind.

As though further to convince me that I had not been dreaming, I remember that it was a long time before I fell again into a troubled and restless sleep; and even then only the upper crust of me slept, and underneath there was something that never quite lost consciousness, but lay alert and on the watch.

But this second time I jumped up with a genuine start of terror. It was neither the wind nor the river that woke me, but the slow approach of something that caused the sleeping portion of me to grow smaller and smaller till at last it vanished altogether, and I found myself sitting bolt upright—listening.

Outside there was a sound of multitudinous little patterings. They had been coming, I was aware, for a long time, and in my sleep they had first become audible. I sat there nervously wide awake as though I had not slept at all. It seemed to me that my breathing came with difficulty, and that there was a great weight upon the surface of my body. In spite of the hot night, I felt clammy with cold and shivered. Something surely was pressing steadily against the sides of the tent and weighing down upon it from above. Was it the body of the wind? Was this the pattering rain, the dripping of the leaves? The spray blown from the river by the wind and gathering in big drops? I thought quickly of a dozen things.

Then suddenly the explanation leaped into my mind: a bough from the poplar, the only large tree on the island, had fallen with the wind. Still half caught by the other branches, it would fall with the next gust and crush us, and meanwhile its leaves brushed and tapped upon the tight canvas surface of the tent. I raised the loose flap and rushed out, calling to the Swede to follow.

But when I got out and stood upright I saw that the tent was free. There was no hanging bough; there was no rain or spray; nothing approached.

A cold, grey light filtered down through the bushes and lay on the faintly gleaming sand. Stars still crowded the sky directly overhead, and the wind howled magnificently, but the fire no longer gave out any glow, and I saw the east reddening in streaks through the trees. Several hours must have passed since I stood there before watching the ascending figures, and the memory of it now came back to me horribly, like an evil dream. Oh, how tired it made me feel, that ceaseless raging wind! Yet, though the deep lassitude of a sleepless night was on me, my nerves were tingling with the activity of an equally tireless apprehension, and all idea of repose was out of the question. The river I saw had risen further. Its thunder filled the air, and a fine spray made itself felt through my thin sleeping shirt.

Yet nowhere did I discover the slightest evidences of anything to cause alarm. This deep, prolonged disturbance in my heart remained wholly unaccounted for.

My companion had not stirred when I called him, and there was no need to waken him now. I looked about me carefully, noting everything: the turned-over canoe; the yellow paddles—two of them, I'm certain; the provision sack and the extra lantern hanging together from the tree; and, crowding everywhere about me, enveloping all, the willows, those endless, shaking willows. A bird uttered its morning cry, and a string of duck passed with whirring flight overhead in the twilight. The sand whirled, dry and stinging, about my bare feet in the wind.

I walked round the tent and then went out a little way into the bush, so that I could see across the river to the farther landscape, and the same profound yet indefinable emotion of distress seized upon me again as I saw the interminable sea of bushes stretching to the horizon, looking ghostly and unreal in the wan light of dawn. I walked softly here and there, still puzzling over that odd sound of infinite pattering, and of that pressure upon the tent that had wakened me. It *must* have been the wind, I reflected—the wind beating upon the loose, hot sand, driving the dry particles smartly against the taut canvas—the wind dropping heavily upon our fragile roof.

Yet all the time my nervousness and malaise increased appreciably.

I crossed over to the farther shore and noted how the coastline had altered in the night, and what masses of sand the river had torn away. I dipped my hands and feet into the cool torrent, and bathed my forehead. Already there was a glow of sunrise in the sky and the exquisite freshness of coming day. On my way back I passed purposely beneath the very bushes where I had seen the column of figures rising into the air, and midway among the clumps I suddenly found myself overtaken by a sense of vast terror. From the shadows a large figure went swiftly by. Someone passed me, as sure as ever man did . . .

It was a great staggering blow from the wind that helped me forward again, and once out in the more open space, the sense of terror diminished strangely. The winds were about and walking, I remember saying to myself; for the winds often move like great presences under the trees. And altogether the fear that hovered about me was such an unknown and immense kind of fear, so unlike anything I had ever felt before, that it woke a sense of awe and wonder in me that did much to counteract its worst effects; and when I reached a high point in the middle of the island from which I could see the wide stretch of river, crimson in the sunrise, the whole magical beauty of it all was so overpowering that a sort of wild yearning woke in me and almost brought a cry up into the throat.

But this cry found no expression, for as my eyes wandered from the plain beyond to the island round me and noted our little tent half hidden among the willows, a dreadful discovery leaped out at me, compared to which my terror of the walking winds seemed as nothing at all.

For a change, I thought, had somehow come about in the arrangement of the landscape. It was not that my point of vantage gave me a different view, but that an alteration had apparently been effected in the relation of the tent to the willows, and of the willows to the tent. Surely the bushes now crowded much closer—unnecessarily, unpleasantly close. *They had moved nearer.*

Creeping with silent feet over the shifting sands, drawing imperceptibly nearer by soft, unhurried movements, the willows had come closer during the night. But had the wind moved them, or had they moved of themselves? I recalled the sound of infinite small patterings and the pressure upon the tent and upon my own heart that caused me to wake in terror. I swayed for a moment in the wind like a tree, finding it hard to keep my upright position on the sandy hillock. There was a suggestion here of personal agency, of deliberate intention, of aggressive hostility, and it terrified me into a sort of rigidity.

Then the reaction followed quickly. The idea was so bizarre, so absurd, that I felt inclined to laugh. But the laughter came no more readily than the cry, for the knowledge that my mind was so receptive to such dangerous imaginings brought the additional terror that it was through our minds and not through our physical bodies that the attack would come, and was coming.

The wind buffeted me about, and, very quickly it seemed, the sun came up over the horizon, for it was after four o'clock, and I must have stood on that little pinnacle of sand longer than I knew, afraid to come down to close quarters with the willows. I returned quietly, creepily, to the tent, first taking another exhaustive look round and—yes, I confess it—making a few measurements. I paced out on the warm sand the distances between the willows and the tent, making a note of the shortest distance particularly.

I crawled stealthily into my blankets. My companion, to all appearances, still slept soundly, and I was glad that this was so. Provided my experiences were not corroborated, I could find strength somehow to deny them, perhaps. With the daylight I could persuade myself that it was all a subjective hallucination, a fantasy of the night, a projection of the excited imagination.

Nothing further came to disturb me, and I fell asleep almost at once, utterly exhausted, yet still in dread of hearing again that weird sound of multitudinous pattering, or of feeling the pressure upon my heart that had made it difficult to breathe.

The sun was high in the heavens when my companion woke me from a heavy sleep and announced that the porridge was cooked and there was just time to bathe. The grateful smell of frizzling bacon entered the tent door.

"River still rising," he said, "and several islands out in mid-stream have disappeared altogether. Our own island's much smaller."

"Any wood left?" I asked sleepily.

"The wood and the island will finish to-morrow in a dead heat," he laughed, "but there's enough to last us till then."

I plunged in from the point of the island, which had indeed altered a lot in size and shape during the night, and was swept down in a moment to the landing-place opposite the tent. The water was icy, and the banks flew by like the country from an express train. Bathing under such conditions was an exhilarating operation, and the terror of the night seemed cleansed out of me by a process of evaporation in the brain. The sun was blazing hot; not a cloud showed itself anywhere; the wind, however, had not abated one little jot.

Quite suddenly then the implied meaning of the Swede's words flashed across me, showing that he no longer wished to leave post-haste, and had changed his mind. "Enough to last till to-morrow"—he assumed we should stay on the island another night. It struck me as odd. The night before he was so positive the other way. How had the change come about?

Great crumblings of the banks occurred at breakfast, with heavy splashings and clouds of spray which the wind brought into our frying-pan, and my fellow-traveller talked incessantly about the difficulty the Vienna-Pesth steamers must have to find the channel in flood. But the state of his mind interested and impressed me far more than the state of the river or the difficulties of the steamers. He had changed somehow since the evening before. His manner was different—a trifle excited, a trifle shy, with a sort of suspicion about his voice and gestures. I hardly know how to describe it now in cold blood, but at the time I remember being quite certain of one thing—that he had become frightened.

He ate very little breakfast, and for once omitted to smoke his pipe. He had the map spread open beside him, and kept studying its markings.

"We'd better get off sharp in an hour," I said presently, feeling for an opening that must bring him indirectly to a partial confession at any rate. And his answer puzzled me uncomfortably: "Rather! If they'll let us."

"Who'll let us? The elements?" I asked quickly, with affected indifference.

"The powers of this awful place, whoever they are," he replied, keeping his eyes on the map. "The gods are here, if they are anywhere at all in the world."

"The elements are always the true immortals," I replied, laughing as naturally as I could manage, yet knowing quite well that my face reflected my true feelings when he looked up gravely at me and spoke across the smoke:

"We shall be fortunate if we get away without further disaster."

This was exactly what I had dreaded, and I screwed myself up to the point of the direct question. It was like agreeing to allow the dentist to extract the tooth; it *had* to come anyhow in the long run, and the rest was all pretence.

"Further disaster! Why, what's happened?"

"For one thing—the steering paddle's gone," he said quietly.

"The steering paddle gone!" I repeated, greatly excited, for this was our rudder, and the Danube in flood without a rudder was suicide. "But what—"

"And there's a tear in the bottom of the canoe," he added, with a genuine little tremor in his voice.

I continued staring at him, able only to repeat the words in his face somewhat foolishly. There, in the heat of the sun, and on this burning sand, I was aware of a freezing atmosphere descending round us. I got up to follow him, for he merely nodded his head gravely and led the way towards the tent a few yards on the other side of the fireplace. The canoe still lay there as I had last seen her in the night, ribs uppermost, the paddles, or rather, *the* paddle, on the sand beside her.

"There's only one," he said, stooping to pick it up. "And here's the rent in the base-board."

It was on the tip of my tongue to tell him that I had clearly noticed *two* paddles a few hours before, but a second impulse made me think better of it, and I said nothing. I approached to see.

There was a long, finely-made tear in the bottom of the canoe where a little slither of wood had been neatly taken clean out; it looked as if the tooth of a sharp rock or snag had eaten down her length, and investigation showed that the hole went through. Had we launched out in her without observing it we must inevitably have foundered. At first the water would have made the wood swell so as to close the hole, but once out in mid-stream the water must have poured in, and the canoe, never more than two inches above the surface, would have filled and sunk very rapidly.

"There, you see an attempt to prepare a victim for the sacrifice," I heard him saying, more to himself than to me, "two victims rather," he added as he bent over and ran his fingers along the slit.

I began to whistle—a thing I always do unconsciously when utterly nonplussed—and purposely paid no attention to his words. I was determined to consider them foolish.

"It wasn't there last night," he said presently, straightening up from his examination and looking anywhere but at me.

"We must have scratched her in landing, of course," I stopped whistling to say. "The stones are very sharp—"

I stopped abruptly, for at that moment he turned round and met my eye squarely. I knew just as well as he did how impossible my explanation was. There were no stones, to begin with.

"And then there's this to explain too," he added quietly, handing me the paddle and pointing to the blade.

A new and curious emotion spread freezingly over me as I took and examined it. The blade was scraped down all over, beautifully scraped, as though someone had sandpapered it with care, making it so thin that the first vigorous stroke must have snapped it off at the elbow.

"One of us walked in his sleep and did this thing," I said feebly, "or—or it has been filed by the constant stream of sand particles blown against it by the wind, perhaps."

"Ah," said the Swede, turning away, laughing a little, "you can explain everything!"

"The same wind that caught the steering paddle and flung it so near the bank that it fell in with the next lump that crumbled," I called out after him, absolutely determined to find an explanation for everything he showed me.

"I see," he shouted back, turning his head to look at me before disappearing among the willow bushes.

Once alone with these perplexing evidences of personal agency, I think my first thought took the form of "One of us must have done this thing, and it certainly was not I." But my second thought decided how impossible it was to suppose, under all the circumstances, that either of us had done it. That my companion, the trusted friend of a dozen similar expeditions, could have knowingly had a hand in it, was a suggestion not to be entertained for a moment. Equally absurd seemed the explanation that this imperturbable and densely practical nature had suddenly become insane and was busied with insane purposes.

Yet the fact remained that what disturbed me most, and kept my fear actively alive even in this blaze of sunshine and wild beauty, was the clear certainty that some curious alteration had come about in his *mind*—that he was nervous, timid, suspicious, aware of goings on he did not speak about, watching a series of secret and hitherto unmentionable events—waiting, in a word, for a climax that he expected, and, I thought, expected very soon. This grew up in my mind intuitively—I hardly knew how.

I made a hurried examination of the tent and its surroundings, but the measurements of the night remained the same. There were deep hollows formed in the sand I now noticed for the first time, basin-shaped and of various depths and sizes, varying from that of a tea-cup to a large bowl. The wind, no doubt, was responsible for these miniature craters, just as it was for lifting the paddle and tossing it towards the water. The rent in the canoe was the only thing that seemed quite inexplicable; and, after all, it *was* conceivable that a sharp point had caught it when we landed. The examination I made of the shore did not assist this theory, but all the same I clung to it with that diminishing portion of my intelligence which I called my "reason." An explanation of some kind was an absolute necessity, just as some working explanation of the universe is necessary—however absurd—to the happiness of every individual who seeks to do his duty in the world and face the problems of life. The simile seemed to me at the time an exact parallel.

I at once set the pitch melting, and presently the Swede joined me at the work, though under the best conditions in the world the canoe could not be safe for travelling till the following day. I drew his attention casually to the hollows in the sand.

"Yes," he said, "I know. They're all over the island. But *you* can explain them, no doubt!"

"Wind, of course," I answered without hesitation. "Have you never watched those little whirlwinds in the street that twist and twirl everything into a circle? This sand's loose enough to yield, that's all."

He made no reply, and we worked on in silence for a bit. I watched him surreptitiously all the time, and I had an idea he was watching me. He seemed, too, to be always listening attentively to something I could not hear, or perhaps for something that he expected to hear, for he kept turning about and staring into the bushes, and up into the sky, and out across the water where it was visible through the openings among the willows. Sometimes he even put his hand to his ear and held it there for several minutes. He said nothing to me, however, about it, and I asked no questions. And meanwhile, as he mended that torn canoe with the skill and address of a red Indian, I was glad to notice his absorption in the work, for there was a vague dread in my heart that he would speak of the changed aspect of the willows. And, if he had noticed *that,* my imagination could no longer be held a sufficient explanation of it.

At length, after a long pause, he began to talk.

"Queer thing," he added in a hurried sort of voice, as though he wanted to say something and get it over. "Queer thing, I mean, about that otter last night."

I had expected something so totally different that he caught me with surprise, and I looked up sharply.

"Shows how lonely this place is. Otters are awfully shy things—"

"I don't mean that, of course," he interrupted. "I mean—do you think—did you think it really *was* an otter?"

"What else, in the name of Heaven, what else?"

"You know, I saw it before you did, and at first it seemed—so *much* bigger than an otter."

"The sunset as you looked up-stream magnified it, or something," I replied.

He looked at me absently a moment, as though his mind we busy with other thoughts.

"It had such extraordinary yellow eyes," he went on half to himself.

"That was the sun too," I laughed, a trifle boisterously. "I suppose you'll wonder next if that fellow in the boat—"

I suddenly decided not to finish the sentence. He was in the act again of listening, turning his head to the wind, and something in the expression of his face made me halt. The subject dropped, and we went on with our caulking. Apparently he had not noticed my unfinished sentence. Five minutes, later, however, he looked at me across the canoe, the smoking pitch in his hand, his face grave.

"I *did* rather wonder, if you want to know," he said slowly, "what that thing in the boat was. I remember thinking at the time it was not a man. The whole business seemed to rise quite suddenly out of the water."

I laughed again boisterously in his face, but this time there was impatience, and a strain of anger too, in my feeling.

"Look here now," I cried, "this place is quite queer enough without going out of our way to imagine things! That boat was an ordinary boat, and the man in it was an ordinary man, and they were both going down-stream as fast as they could lick. And that otter was an otter, so don't let's play the fool about it!"

He looked steadily at me with the same grave expression. He was not in the least annoyed. I took courage from his silence.

"And, for Heaven's sake," I went on, "don't keep pretending you hear things, because it only gives me the jumps, and there's nothing to hear but the river and this cursed old thundering wind."

"You *fool!*" he answered in a low, shocked voice, "you utter fool. That's just the way all victims talk. As if you didn't understand just as well as I do!" he sneered with scorn in his voice, and a sort of resignation. "The best thing you can do is to keep quiet and try to hold your mind as firm as possible. This feeble attempt at self-deception only makes the truth harder when you're forced to meet it."

My little effort was over, and I found nothing more to say, for I knew quite well his words were true, and that *I* was the fool, not *he*. Up to a certain stage in the adventure he kept ahead of me easily, and I think I felt annoyed to be out of it, to be thus proved less psychic, less sensitive than himself to these extraordinary happenings, and half ignorant all the time of what was going on under my very nose. *He knew* from the very beginning, apparently. But at the moment I wholly missed the point of his words about the necessity of there being a victim, and that we ourselves were destined to satisfy the want. I dropped all pretence thenceforward, but thenceforward likewise my fear increased steadily to the climax.

"But you're quite right about one thing," he added, before the subject passed, "and that is that we're wiser not to talk about it, or even to think about it, because what one *thinks* finds expression in words, and what one says, happens."

That afternoon, while the canoe dried and hardened, we spent trying to fish, testing the leak, collecting wood, and watching the enormous flood of rising water. Masses of driftwood swept near our shores sometimes, and we fished for them with long willow branches. The island grew perceptibly smaller as the banks were torn away with great gulps and splashes. The weather kept brilliantly fine till about four o'clock, and then for the first time for three days the wind showed signs of abating. Clouds began to gather in the south-west, spreading thence slowly over the sky.

This lessening of the wind came as a great relief, for the incessant roaring, banging, and thundering had irritated our nerves. Yet the silence that came about five o'clock with its sudden cessation was in a manner quite as oppressive. The booming of the river had everything in its own way then: it filled the air with deep murmurs, more musical than the wind noises, but infinitely more monotonous. The wind held many notes, rising, falling, always beating out some sort of great elemental tune; whereas the river's song lay between three notes at most—dull pedal notes, that held a lugubrious quality foreign to the wind, and somehow seemed to me, in my then nervous state, to sound wonderfully well the music of doom.

It was extraordinary, too, how the withdrawal suddenly of bright sunlight took everything out of the landscape that made for cheerfulness; and since this particular landscape had already managed to convey the suggestion of something sinister, the change of course was all the more unwelcome and noticeable. For me, I know, the darkening outlook became distinctly more alarming, and I found myself more than once calculating how soon after sunset the full moon would get up in the east, and whether the gathering clouds would greatly interfere with her lighting of the little island.

With this general hush of the wind—though it still indulged in occasional brief gusts—the river seemed to me to grow blacker, the willows to stand more densely together. The latter, too, kept up a sort of independent movement of their own, rustling among themselves when no wind stirred, and shaking oddly from the roots upwards. When common objects in this way become charged with the suggestion of horror, they stimulate the imagination far more than things of unusual appearance; and these bushes, crowding huddled about us, assumed for me in the darkness a bizarre *grotesquerie* of appearance that lent to them somehow the aspect of purposeful and living creatures. Their very ordinariness, I felt, masked what was malignant and hostile to us. The forces of the region drew nearer with the coming of night. They were focusing upon our island, and more particularly upon ourselves. For thus, somehow, in the terms of the imagination, did my really indescribable sensations in this extraordinary place present themselves.

I had slept a good deal in the early afternoon, and had thus recovered somewhat from the exhaustion of a disturbed night, but this only served apparently to render me more susceptible than before to the obsessing spell of the haunting. I fought against it, laughing at my feelings as absurd and childish, with very obvious physiological explanations, yet, in spite of every effort, they gained in strength upon me so that I dreaded the night as a child lost in a forest must dread the approach of darkness.

The canoe we had carefully covered with a waterproof sheet during the day, and the one remaining paddle had been securely tied by the Swede to the base of a tree, lest the wind should rob us of that too. From five o'clock onwards I busied myself with the stew-pot and preparations for dinner, it being my turn to cook that night. We had potatoes, onions, bits of bacon fat to add flavour, and a general thick residue from former stews at the bottom of the pot; with black bread broken up into it the result was most excellent, and it was followed by a stew of plums with sugar and a brew of strong tea with dried milk. A good pile of wood lay close at hand, and the absence of wind made my duties easy. My companion sat lazily watching me, dividing his attentions between cleaning his pipe and giving useless advice—an admitted privilege of the off-duty man. He had been very quiet all the afternoon, engaged in re-caulking the canoe, strengthening the tent ropes, and fishing for driftwood while I slept. No more talk about undesirable things had passed between us, and I think his only remarks had to do with the gradual destruction of the island, which he declared was now fully a third smaller than when we first landed.

The pot had just begun to bubble when I heard his voice calling to me from the bank, where he had wandered away without my noticing. I ran up.

"Come and listen," he said, "and see what you make of it." He held his hand cupwise to his ear, as so often before.

"*Now* do you hear anything?" he asked, watching me curiously.

We stood there, listening attentively together. At first I heard only the deep note of the water and the hissings rising from its turbulent surface. The willows, for once, were motionless and silent. Then a sound began to reach my ears faintly, a peculiar sound—something like the humming of a distant gong. It seemed to come across to us in the darkness from the waste of swamps and willows opposite. It was repeated at regular intervals, but it was certainly neither the sound of a bell nor the hooting of a distant steamer. I can liken it to nothing so much as to the sound of an immense gong, suspended far up in the sky, repeating incessantly its muffled metallic note, soft and musical, as it was repeatedly struck. My heart quickened as I listened.

"I've heard it all day," said my companion. "While you slept this afternoon it came all round the island. I hunted it down, but could never get near enough to see—to localise it correctly. Sometimes it was overhead, and sometimes it seemed under the water. Once or twice, too, I could have sworn it was not outside at all, but *within myself*—you know—the way a sound in the fourth dimension is supposed to come."

I was too much puzzled to pay much attention to his words. I listened carefully, striving to associate it with any known familiar sound I could think of, but without success. It changed in the direction, too, coming nearer, and then sinking utterly away into remote distance. I cannot say that it was ominous in quality, because to me it seemed distinctly musical, yet I must admit it set going a distressing feeling that made me wish I had never heard it.

"The wind blowing in those sand-funnels," I said, determined to find an explanation, "or the bushes rubbing together after the storm perhaps."

"It comes off the whole swamp," my friend answered. "It comes from everywhere at once." He ignored my explanations. "It comes from the willow bushes somehow—"

"But now the wind has dropped," I objected. "The willows can hardly make a noise by themselves, can they?"

His answer frightened me, first because I had dreaded it, and secondly, because I knew intuitively it was true.

"It is *because* the wind has dropped we now hear it. It was drowned before. It is the cry, I believe, of the—"

I dashed back to my fire, warned by a sound of bubbling that the stew was in danger, but determined at the same time to escape further conversation. I was resolute, if possible, to avoid the exchanging of views. I dreaded, too, that he would begin about the gods, or the elemental forces, or something else disquieting, and I wanted to keep myself well in hand for what might happen later. There was another night to be faced before we escaped from this distressing place, and there was no knowing yet what it might bring forth.

"Come and cut up bread for the pot," I called to him, vigorously stirring the appetising mixture. That stew-pot held sanity for us both, and the thought made me laugh.

He came over slowly and took the provision sack from the tree, fumbling in its mysterious depths, and then emptying the entire contents upon the ground-sheet at his feet.

"Hurry up!" I cried; "it's boiling."

The Swede burst out into a roar of laughter that startled me. It was forced laughter, not artificial exactly, but mirthless.

"There's nothing here!" he shouted, holding his sides.

"Bread, I mean."

"It's gone. There is no bread. They've taken it!"

I dropped the long spoon and ran up. Everything the sack had contained lay upon the ground-sheet, but there was no loaf.

The whole dead weight of my growing fear fell upon me and shook me. Then I burst out laughing too. It was the only thing to do: and the sound of my laughter also made me understand his. The strain of psychical pressure caused it—this explosion of unnatural laughter in both of us; it was an effort of repressed forces to seek relief; it was a temporary safety-valve. And with both of us it ceased quite suddenly.

"How criminally stupid of me!" I cried, still determined to be consistent and find an explanation. "I clean forgot to buy a loaf at Pressburg. That chattering woman put everything out of my head, and I must have left it lying on the counter or—"

"The oatmeal, too, is much less than it was this morning," the Swede interrupted.

Why in the world need he draw attention to it? I thought angrily.

"There's enough for to-morrow," I said, stirring vigorously, "and we can get lots more at Komorn or Gran. In twenty-four hours we shall be miles from here."

"I hope so—to God," he muttered, putting the things back into the sack, "unless we're claimed first as victims for the sacrifice," he added with a foolish laugh. He dragged the sack into the tent, for safety's sake, I suppose, and I heard him mumbling on to himself, but so indistinctly that it seemed quite natural for me to ignore his words.

Our meal was beyond question a gloomy one, and we ate it almost in silence, avoiding one another's eyes, and keeping the fire bright. Then we washed up and prepared for the night, and, once smoking, our minds unoccupied with any definite duties, the apprehension I had felt all day long became more and more acute. It was not then active fear, I think, but the very vagueness of its origin distressed me far more than if I had been able to ticket and face it squarely. The curious sound I have likened to the note of a gong became now almost incessant, and filled the stillness of the night with a faint, continuous ringing rather than a series of distinct notes. At one time it was behind and at another time in front of us. Sometimes I fancied it came from the bushes on our left, and then again from the clumps on our right. More often it hovered directly overhead like the whirring of wings. It was really everywhere at once, behind, in front, at our sides and over our heads, completely surrounding us. The sound really defies description. But nothing within my knowledge is like that ceaseless muffled humming rising off the deserted world of swamps and willows.

We sat smoking in comparative silence, the strain growing every minute greater. The worst feature of the situation seemed to me that we did not know what to expect, and could therefore make no sort of preparation by way of defence. We could anticipate nothing. My explanations made in the sunshine, moreover, now came to haunt me with their foolish and wholly unsatisfactory nature, and it was more and more clear to us that some kind of plain talk with my companion was inevitable, whether I liked it or not. After all, we had to spend the night together, and to sleep in the same tent side by side. I saw that I could not get along much longer without the support of his mind, and for that, of course, plain talk was imperative. As long as possible, however, I postponed this little climax, and tried to ignore or laugh at the occasional sentences he flung into the emptiness.

Some of these sentences, moreover, were confoundedly disquieting to me, coming as they did to corroborate much that I felt myself: corroboration, too—which made it so much more convincing—from a totally different point of view. He composed such curious sentences, and hurled them at me in such an inconsequential sort of way, as though his main line of thought was secret to himself, and these fragments were bits he found it impossible to digest. He got rid of them by uttering them. Speech relieved him. It was like being sick.

"There are things about us, I'm sure, that make for disorder, disintegration, destruction, *our* destruction," he said once, while the fire blazed between us. "We've strayed out of a safe line somewhere."

And another time, when the gong sounds had come nearer, ringing much louder than before, and directly over our heads, he said as though talking to himself:

"I don't think a gramophone would show any record of that. The sound doesn't come to me by the ears at all. The vibrations reach me in another manner altogether, and seem to be within me, which is precisely how a fourth dimensional sound might be supposed to make itself heard."

I purposely made no reply to this, but I sat up a little closer to the fire and peered about me into the darkness. The clouds were massed all over the sky, and no trace of moonlight came through. Very still, too, everything was, so that the river and the frogs had things all their own way.

"It has that about it," he went on, "which is utterly out of common experience. It is *unknown*. Only one thing describes it really: it is a non-human sound; I mean a sound outside humanity."

Having rid himself of this indigestible morsel, he lay quiet for a time; but he had so admirably expressed my own feeling that it was a relief to have the thought out, and to have confined it by the limitation of words from dangerous wandering to and fro in the mind.

The solitude of that Danube camping-place, can I ever forget it? The feeling of being utterly alone on an empty planet! My thoughts ran incessantly upon cities and the haunts of men. I would have given my soul, as the saying is, for the "feel" of those Bavarian villages we had passed through by the score; for the normal, human common-places: peasants drinking beer, tables beneath the trees, hot sunshine, and a ruined castle on the rocks behind the red-roofed church. Even the tourists would have been welcome.

Yet what I felt of dread was no ordinary ghostly fear. It was infinitely greater, stranger, and seemed to arise from some dim ancestral sense of terror more profoundly disturbing than anything I had known or dreamed of. We had "strayed," as the Swede put it, into some region or some set of conditions where the risks were great, yet unintelligible to us; where the frontiers of some unknown world lay close about us. It was a spot held by the dwellers in some outer space, a sort of peep-hole whence they could spy upon the earth, themselves unseen, a point where the veil between had worn a little thin. As the final result of too long a sojourn here, we should be carried over the border and deprived of what we called "our lives," yet by mental, not physical, processes. In that sense, as he said, we should be the victims of our adventure—a sacrifice.

It took us in different fashion, each according to the measure of his sensitiveness and powers of resistance. I translated it vaguely into a personification of the mightily disturbed elements, investing them with the horror of a deliberate and malefic purpose, resentful of our audacious intrusion into their breeding-place; whereas my friend threw it into the unoriginal form at first of a trespass on some ancient shrine, some place where the old gods still held sway, where the emotional forces of former worshippers still clung, and the ancestral portion of him yielded to the old pagan spell.

At any rate, here was a place unpolluted by men, kept clean by the winds from coarsening human influences, a place where spiritual agencies were within reach and aggressive. Never, before or since, have I been so attacked by indescribable suggestions of a "beyond region," of another scheme of life, another revolution not parallel to the human. And in the end our minds would succumb under the weight of the awful spell, and we should be drawn across the frontier into *their* world.

Small things testified to the amazing influence of the place, and now in the silence round the fire they allowed themselves to be noted by the mind. The very atmosphere had proved itself a magnifying medium to distort every indication: the otter rolling in the current, the hurrying boatman making signs, the shifting willows, one and all had been robbed of its natural character, and revealed in something of its other aspect—as it existed across the border in that other region. And this changed aspect I felt was new not merely to me, but to the race. The whole experience whose verge we touched was unknown to humanity at all. It was a new order of experience, and in the true sense of the word *unearthly*.

"It's the deliberate, calculating purpose that reduces one's courage to zero," the Swede said suddenly, as if he had been actually following my thoughts. "Otherwise imagination might count for muck But the paddle, the canoe, the lessening food—"

"Haven't I explained all that once?" I interrupted viciously.

"You have," he answered dryly; "you have indeed."

He made other remarks too, as usual, about what he called the "plain determination to provide a victim"; but, having now arranged my thoughts better, I recognised that this was simply the cry of his frightened soul against the knowledge that he was being attacked in a vital part, and that he would be somehow taken or destroyed. The situation called for a courage and calmness of reasoning that neither of us could compass, and I have never before been so clearly conscious of two persons in me—the one that explained everything, and the other that laughed at such foolish explanations, yet was horribly afraid.

Meanwhile, in the pitchy night the fire died down and the wood pile grew small. Neither of us moved to replenish the stock, and the darkness consequently came up very close to our faces. A few feet beyond the circle of firelight it was inky black. Occasionally a stray puff of wind set the willows shivering about us, but apart from this not very welcome sound a deep and depressing silence reigned, broken only by the gurgling of the river and the humming in the air overhead.

We both missed, I think, the shouting company of the winds.

At length, at a moment when a stray puff prolonged itself as though the wind were about to rise again, I reached the point for me of saturation, the point where it was absolutely necessary to find relief in plain speech, or else to betray myself by some hysterical extravagance that must have been far worse in its effect upon both of us. I kicked the fire into a blaze, and turned to my companion abruptly. He looked up with a start.

"I can't disguise it any longer," I said; "I don't like this place, and the darkness, and the noises, and the awful feelings I get. There's something here that beats me utterly. I'm in a blue funk, and that's the plain truth. If the other shore was—different, I swear I'd be inclined to swim for it!"

The Swede's face turned very white beneath the deep tan of sun and wind. He stared straight at me and answered quietly, but his voice betrayed his huge excitement by its unnatural calmness. For the moment, at any rate, he was the strong man of the two. He was more phlegmatic, for one thing.

"It's not a physical condition we can escape from by running away," he replied, in the tone of a doctor diagnosing some grave disease; "we must sit tight and wait. There are forces close here that could kill a herd of elephants in a second as easily as you or I could squash a fly. Our only chance is to keep perfectly still. Our insignificance perhaps may save us."

I put a dozen questions into my expression of face, but found no words. It was precisely like listening to an accurate description of a disease whose symptoms had puzzled me.

"I mean that so far, although aware of our disturbing presence, they have not *found* us—not 'located' us, as the Americans say," he went on. "They're blundering about like men hunting for a leak of gas. The paddle and canoe and provisions prove that. I think they *feel* us, but cannot actually see us. We must keep our minds quiet—it's our minds they feel. We must control our thoughts, or it's all up with us."

"Death, you mean?" I stammered, icy with the horror of his suggestion.

"Worse—by far," he said. "Death, according to one's belief, means either annihilation or release from the limitations of the senses, but it involves no change of character. *You* don't suddenly alter just because the body's gone. But this means a radical alteration, a complete change, a horrible loss of oneself by substitution—far worse than death, and not even annihilation. We happen to have camped in a spot where their region touches ours, where the veil between has worn thin"—horrors! he was using my very own phrase, my actual words—"so that they are aware of our being in their neighbourhood."

"But *who* are aware?" I asked.

I forgot the shaking of the willows in the windless calm, the humming overhead, everything except that I was waiting for an answer that I dreaded more than I can possibly explain.

He lowered his voice at once to reply, leaning forward a little over the fire, an indefinable change in his face that made me avoid his eyes and look down upon the ground.

"All my life," he said, "I have been strangely, vividly conscious of another region—not far removed from our own world in one sense, yet wholly different in kind—where great things go on unceasingly, where immense and terrible personalities hurry by, intent on vast purposes compared to which earthly affairs, the rise and fall of nations, the destinies of empires, the fate of armies and continents, are all as dust in the balance; vast purposes, I mean, that deal directly with the soul, and not indirectly with mere expressions of the soul—"

"I suggest just now—" I began, seeking to stop him, feeling

as though I was face to face with a madman. But he instantly overbore me with his torrent that *had* to come.

"You think," he said, "it is the spirits of the elements, and I thought perhaps it was the old gods. But I tell you now it is—*neither*. These would be comprehensible entities, for they have relations with men, depending upon them for worship or sacrifice, whereas these beings who are now about us have absolutely nothing to do with mankind, and it is mere chance that their space happens just at this spot to touch our own."

The mere conception, which his words somehow made so convincing, as I listened to them there in the dark stillness of that lonely island, set me shaking a little all over. I found it impossible to control my movements.

"And what do you propose?" I began again.

"A sacrifice, a victim, might save us by distracting them until we could get away," he went on, "just as the wolves stop to devour the dogs and give the sleigh another start. But—I see no chance of any other victim now."

I stared blankly at him. The gleam in his eyes was dreadful. Presently he continued.

"It's the willows, of course. The willows *mask* the others, but the others are feeling about for us. If we let our minds betray our fear, we're lost, lost utterly." He looked at me with an expression so calm, so determined, so sincere, that I no longer had any doubts as to his sanity. He was as sane as any man ever was. "If we can hold out through the night," he added, "we may get off in the daylight unnoticed, or rather, *undiscovered*."

"But you really think a sacrifice would—"

That gong-like humming came down very close over our heads as I spoke, but it was my friend's scared face that really stopped my mouth.

"Hush!" he whispered, holding up his hand. "Do not mention them more than you can help. Do not refer to them *by name*. To name is to reveal: it is the inevitable clue, and our only hope lies in ignoring them, in order that they may ignore us."

"Even in thought?" He was extraordinarily agitated.

"Especially in thought. Our thoughts make spirals in their world. We must keep them *out of our minds* at all costs if possible."

I raked the fire together to prevent the darkness having everything its own way. I never longed for the sun as I longed for it then in the awful blackness of that summer night.

"Were you awake all last night?" he went on suddenly.

"I slept badly a little after dawn," I replied evasively, trying to follow his instructions, which I knew instinctively were true, "but the wind, of course—"

"I know. But the wind won't account for all the noises."

"Then you heard it too?"

"The multiplying countless little footsteps I heard," he said, adding, after a moment's hesitation, "and that other sound—"

"You mean above the tent, and the pressing down upon us of something tremendous, gigantic?"

He nodded significantly.

"It was like the beginning of a sort of inner suffocation." I said.

"Partly, yes. It seemed to me that the weight of the atmosphere had been altered—had increased enormously, so that we should be crushed."

"And *that,*" I went on, determined to have it all out, pointing upwards where the gong-like note hummed ceaselessly, rising and falling like wind. "What do you make of that?"

"It's *their* sound," he whispered gravely. "It's the sound of their world, the humming in their region. The division here is so thin that it leaks through somehow. But, if you listen carefully, you'll find it's not above so much as around us. It's in the willows. It's the willows themselves humming, because here the willows have been made symbols of the forces that are against us."

I could not follow exactly what he meant by this, yet the thought and idea in my mind were beyond question the thought and idea in his. I realised what he realised, only with less power of analysis than his. It was on the tip of my tongue to tell him at last about my hallucination of the ascending figures and the moving bushes, when he suddenly thrust his face again close into mine across the firelight and began to speak in a very earnest whisper. He amazed me by his calmness and pluck, his apparent control of the situation. This man I had for years deemed unimaginative, stolid!

"Now listen," he said. "The only thing for us to do is to go on as though nothing had happened, follow our usual habits, go to bed, and so forth; pretend we feel nothing and notice nothing. It is a question wholly of the mind, and the less we think about them the better our chance of escape. Above all, don't *think*, for what you think happens!"

"All right," I managed to reply, simply breathless with his words and the strangeness of it all; "all right, I'll try, but tell me one thing more first. Tell me what you make of those hollows in the ground all about us, those sand-funnels?"

"No!" he cried, forgetting to whisper in his excitement. "I dare not, simply dare not, put the thought into words. If you have not guessed I am glad. Don't try to. *They* have put it into my mind; try your hardest to prevent their putting it into yours."

He sank his voice again to a whisper before he finished, and I did not press him to explain. There was already just about as much horror in me as I could hold. The conversation came to an end, and we smoked our pipes busily in silence.

Then something happened, something unimportant apparently, as the way is when the nerves are in a very great state of tension, and this small thing for a brief space gave me an entirely different point of view. I chanced to look down at my sand-shoe—the sort we used for the canoe—and something to do with the hole at the toe suddenly recalled to me the London shop where I had bought them, the difficulty the man had in fitting me, and other details of the uninteresting but practical operation. At once, in its train, followed a wholesome view of the modern sceptical world I was accustomed to move in at home. I thought of roast beef and ale, motor-cars, policemen, brass bands, and a dozen other things that proclaimed the soul of ordinariness or utility. The effect was immediate and astonishing even to myself. Psychologically, I suppose, it was simply a sudden and violent reaction after the strain of living in an atmosphere of things that to the normal consciousness must seem impossible and incredible. But, whatever the cause, it momentarily lifted the spell from my heart, and left me for the short space of a minute feeling free and utterly unafraid. I looked up at my friend opposite.

"You damned old pagan!" I cried, laughing aloud in his face. "You imaginative idiot! You superstitious idolator! You—"

I stopped in the middle, seized anew by the old horror. I tried to smother the sound of my voice as something sacrilegious. The Swede, of course, heard it too—the strange cry overhead in the darkness—and that sudden drop in the air as though something had come nearer.

He had turned ashen white under the tan. He stood bolt upright in front of the fire, stiff as a rod, staring at me.

"After that," he said in a sort of helpless, frantic way, "we must go! We can't stay now; we must strike camp this very instant and go on—down the river."

He was talking, I saw, quite wildly, his words dictated by abject terror—the terror he had resisted so long, but which had caught him at last.

"In the dark?" I exclaimed, shaking with fear after my hysterical outburst, but still realising our position better than he did. "Sheer madness! The river's in flood, and we've only got a single paddle. Besides, we only go deeper into their country! There's nothing ahead for fifty miles but willows, willows, willows!"

He sat down again in a state of semi-collapse. The positions, by one of those kaleidoscopic changes nature loves, were suddenly reversed, and the control of our forces passed over into my hands. His mind at last had reached the point where it was beginning to weaken.

"What on earth possessed you to do such a thing?" he whispered with the awe of genuine terror in his voice and face.

I crossed round to his side of the fire. I took both his hands in mine, kneeling down beside him and looking straight into his frightened eyes.

"We'll make one more blaze," I said firmly, "and then turn in for the night. At sunrise we'll be off full speed for Komorn. Now, pull yourself together a bit, and remember your own advice about *not thinking fear!*"

He said no more, and I saw that he would agree and obey. In some measure, too, it was a sort of relief to get up and make an excursion into the darkness for more wood. We kept close together, almost touching, groping among the bushes and along the bank. The humming overhead never ceased, but seemed to me to grow louder as we increased our distance from the fire. It was shivery work!

We were grubbing away in the middle of a thickish clump of willows where some driftwood from a former flood had caught high among the branches, when my body was seized in a grip that made me half drop upon the sand. It was the Swede. He had fallen against me, and was clutching me for support. I heard his breath coming and going in short gasps.

"Look! By my soul!" he whispered, and for the first time in my experience I knew what it was to hear tears of terror in a human voice. He was pointing to the fire, some fifty feet away. I followed the direction of his finger, and I swear my heart missed a beat.

There, in front of the dim glow, *something was moving.*

I saw it through a veil that hung before my eyes like the gauze drop-curtain used at the back of a theatre—hazily a little. It was neither a human figure nor an animal. To me it gave the strange impression of being as large as several animals grouped together, like horses, two or three, moving slowly. The Swede, too, got a similar result, though expressing it differently, for he thought it was shaped and sized like a clump of willow bushes, rounded at the top, and moving all over upon its surface—"coiling upon itself like smoke," he said afterwards.

"I watched it settle downwards through the bushes," he sobbed at me. "Look, by God! It's coming this way! Oh, oh!"—he gave a kind of whistling cry. *"They've found us."*

I gave one terrified glance, which just enabled me to see that the shadowy form was swinging towards us through the bushes, and then I collapsed backwards with a crash into the branches. These failed, of course, to support my weight, so that with the Swede on the top of me we fell in a struggling heap upon the sand. I really hardly knew what was happening. I was conscious only of a sort of enveloping sensation of icy fear that plucked the nerves out of their fleshly covering, twisted them this way and that, and replaced them quivering. My eyes were tightly shut; something in my throat choked me; a feeling that my consciousness was expanding, extending out into space, swiftly gave way to another feeling that I was losing it altogether, and about to die.

An acute spasm of pain passed through me, and I was aware that the Swede had hold of me in such a way that he hurt me abominably. It was the way he caught at me in failing.

But it was the pain, he declared afterwards, that saved me: it caused me to *forget them* and think of something else at the very instant when they were about to find me. It concealed my mind from them at the moment of discovery, yet just in time to evade their terrible seizing of me. He himself, he says, actually swooned at the same moment, and that was what saved him.

I only know that at a later date, how long or short is impossible to say, I found myself scrambling up out of the slippery network of willow branches, and saw my companion standing in front of me holding out a hand to assist me. I stared at him in a dazed way, rubbing the arm he had twisted for me. Nothing came to me to say, somehow.

"I lost consciousness for a moment or two," I heard him say. "That's what saved me. It made me stop thinking about them."

"You nearly broke my arm in two," I said, uttering my only connected thought at the moment. A numbness came over me.

"That's what saved *you!*" he replied. "Between us, we've managed to set them off on a false tack somewhere. The humming has ceased. It's gone—for the moment at any rate!"

A wave of hysterical laughter seized me again, and this time spread to my friend too—great healing gusts of shaking laughter that brought a tremendous sense of relief in their train. We made our way back to the fire and put the wood on so that it blazed at once. Then we saw that the tent had fallen over and lay in a tangled heap upon the ground.

We picked it up, and during the process tripped more than once and caught our feet in sand.

"It's those sand-funnels," exclaimed the Swede, when the tent was up again and the firelight lit up the ground for several yards about us. "And look at the size of them!"

All round the tent and about the fireplace where we had seen the moving shadows there were deep funnel-shaped hollows in the sand, exactly similar to the ones we had already found over the island, only far bigger and deeper, beautifully formed, and wide enough in some instances to admit the whole of my foot and leg.

Neither of us said a word. We both knew that sleep was the safest thing we could do, and to bed we went accordingly without further delay, having first thrown sand on the fire and taken the provision sack and the paddle inside the tent with us. The canoe, too, we propped in such a way at the end of the tent that our feet touched it, and the least motion would disturb and wake us.

In case of emergency, too, we again went to bed in our clothes, ready for a sudden start.

It was my firm intention to lie awake all night and watch, but the exhaustion of nerves and body decreed otherwise, and sleep after a while came over me with a welcome blanket of oblivion. The fact that my companion also slept quickened its approach. At first he fidgeted and constantly sat up, asking me if I "heard this" or "heard that." He tossed about on his cork mattress, and said the tent was moving and the river had risen over the point of the island, but each time I went out to look I returned with the report that all was well, and finally he grew calmer and lay still. Then at length his breathing became regular and I heard unmistakable sounds of snoring—the first and only time in my life when snoring has been a welcome and calming influence.

This, I remember, was the last thought in my mind before dozing off.

A difficulty in breathing woke me, and I found the blanket over my face. But something else besides the blanket was pressing upon me, and my first thought was that my companion had rolled off his mattress on to my own in his sleep. I called to him and sat up, and at the same moment it came to me that the tent was *surrounded*. That sound of multitudinous soft pattering was again audible outside, filling the night with horror.

I called again to him, louder than before. He did not answer, but I missed the sound of his snoring and also noticed that the flap of the tent door was down. This was the unpardonable sin. I crawled out in the darkness to hook it back securely, and it was then for the first time I realised positively that the Swede was not there. He had gone.

I dashed out in a mad run, seized by a dreadful agitation, and the moment I was out I plunged into a sort of torrent of humming that surrounded me completely and came out of every quarter of the heavens at once. It was that same familiar humming—gone mad! A swarm of great invisible bees might have been about me in the air. The sound seemed to thicken the very atmosphere, and I felt that my lungs worked with difficulty.

But my friend was in danger, and I could not hesitate.

The dawn was just about to break, and a faint whitish light spread upwards over the clouds from a thin strip of clear horizon. No wind stirred. I could just make out the bushes and river beyond, and the pale sandy patches. In my excitement I ran frantically to and fro about the island, calling him by name, shouting at the top of my voice the first words that came into my head. But the willows smothered my voice, and the humming muffled it, so that the sound only travelled a few feet round me. I plunged among the bushes, tripping headlong, tumbling over roots, and scraping my face as I tore this way and that among the preventing branches.

Then, quite unexpectedly, I came out upon the island's point and saw a dark figure outlined between the water and the sky.

It was the Swede. And already he had one foot in the river! A moment more and he would have taken the plunge.

I threw myself upon him, flinging my arms about his waist and dragging him shorewards with all my strength. Of course he struggled furiously, making a noise all the time just like that cursed humming, and using the most outlandish phrases in his anger about "going *inside* to Them," and "taking the way of the water and the wind," and God only knows what more besides, that I tried in vain to recall afterwards, but which turned me sick with horror and amazement as I listened. But in the end I managed to get him into the comparative safety of the tent, and flung him breathless and cursing upon the mattress where I held him until the fit had passed.

I think the suddenness with which it all went and he grew calm, coinciding as it did with the equally abrupt cessation of the humming and pattering outside—I think this was almost the strangest part of the whole business perhaps. For he just opened his eyes and turned his tired face up to me so that the dawn threw a pale light upon it through the doorway, and said, for all the world just like a frightened child:

"My life, old man—it's my life I owe you. But it's all over now anyhow. They've found a victim in our place!"

Then he dropped back upon his blankets and went to sleep literally under my eyes. He simply collapsed, and began to snore again as healthily as though nothing had happened and he had never tried to offer his own life as a sacrifice by drowning. And when the sunlight woke him three hours later—hours of ceaseless vigil for me—it became so clear to me that he remembered absolutely nothing of what he had attempted to do, that I deemed it wise to hold my peace and ask no dangerous questions.

He woke naturally and easily, as I have said, when the sun was already high in a windless hot sky, and he at once got up and set about the preparation of the fire for breakfast. I followed him anxiously at bathing, but he did not attempt to plunge in, merely dipping his head and making some remark about the extra coldness of the water.

"River's falling at last," he said, "and I'm glad of it."

"The humming has stopped too," I said.

He looked up at me quietly with his normal expression. Evidently he remembered everything except his own attempt at suicide.

"Everything has stopped," he said, "because—"

He hesitated. But I knew some reference to that remark he had made just before he fainted was in his mind, and I was determined to know it.

"Because 'They've found another victim'?" I said, forcing a little laugh.

"Exactly," he answered, "exactly! I feel as positive of it as though—as though—I feel quite safe again, I mean," he finished.

He began to look curiously about him. The sunlight lay in hot patches on the sand. There was no wind. The willows were motionless. He slowly rose to his feet.

"Come," he said; "I think if we look, we shall find it."

He started off on a run, and I followed him. He kept to the banks, poking with a stick among the sandy bays and caves and little backwaters, myself always close on his heels.

"Ah!" he exclaimed presently, "ah!"

The tone of his voice somehow brought back to me a vivid sense of the horror of the last twenty-four hours, and I hurried up to join him. He was pointing with his stick at a large black object that lay half in the water and half on the sand. It appeared to be caught by some twisted willow roots so that the river could not sweep it away. A few hours before the spot must have been under water.

"See," he said quietly, "the victim that made our escape possible!"

And when I peered across his shoulder I saw that his stick rested on the body of a man. He turned it over. It was the corpse of a peasant, and the face was hidden in the sand. Clearly the man had been drowned but a few hours before, and his body must have been swept down upon our island somewhere about the hour of the dawn—*at the very time the fit had passed.*

"We must give it a decent burial, you know."

"I suppose so," I replied. I shuddered a little in spite of myself, for there was something about the appearance of that poor drowned man that turned me cold.

The Swede glanced up sharply at me, an undecipherable expression on his face, and began clambering down the bank. I followed him more leisurely. The current, I noticed, had torn away much of the clothing from the body, so that the neck and part of the chest lay bare.

Half-way down the bank my companion suddenly stopped and held up his hand in warning; but either my foot slipped, or I had gained too much momentum to bring myself quickly to a halt, for I bumped into him and sent him forward with a sort of leap to save himself. We tumbled together on to the hard sand so that our feet splashed into the water. And, before anything could be done, we had collided a little heavily against the corpse.

The Swede uttered a sharp cry. And I sprang back as if I had been shot.

At the moment we touched the body there rose from its surface the loud sound of humming—the sound of several hummings—which passed with a vast commotion as of winged things in the air about us and disappeared upwards into the sky, growing fainter and fainter till they finally ceased in the distance. It was exactly as though we had disturbed some living yet invisible creatures at work.

My companion clutched me, and I think I clutched him, but before either of us had time properly to recover from the unexpected shock, we saw that a movement of the current was turning the corpse round so that it became released from the grip of the willow roots. A moment later it had turned completely over, the dead face uppermost, staring at the sky. It lay on the edge of the main stream. In another moment it would be swept away.

The Swede started to save it, shouting again something I did not catch about a "proper burial"—and then abruptly dropped upon his knees on the sand and covered his eyes with his hands. I was beside him in an instant.

I saw what he had seen.

For just as the body swung round to the current the face and the exposed chest turned full towards us, and showed plainly how the skin and flesh were indented with small hollows, beautifully formed, and exactly similar in shape and kind to the sand-funnels that we had found all over the island.

"Their mark!" I heard my companion mutter under his breath. "Their awful mark!"

And when I turned my eyes again from his ghastly face to the river, the current had done its work, and the body had been swept away into mid-stream and was already beyond our reach and almost out of sight, turning over and over on the waves like an otter.

THE BECKONING FAIR ONE

Oliver Onions

(1911)

Paul Oleron, a writer, rents an out-of-the-way London apartment at a very reasonable price, a secluded place where he can finish the novel he's promised his publisher. But the apartment is apparently not as empty as it seems, and as Paul's life begins to change almost imperceptibly, he finds himself humming a strange old tune, a song called "The Beckoning Fair One" . . .

I

The three or four "To Let" boards had stood within the low paling as long as the inhabitants of the little triangular "Square" could remember, and if they had ever been vertical it was a very long time ago. They now overhung the palings each at its own angle, and resembled nothing so much as a row of wooden choppers, ever in the act of falling upon some passer-by, yet never cutting off a tenant for the old house from the stream of his fellows. Not that there was ever any great "stream" through the square; the stream passed a furlong and more away, beyond the intricacy of tenements and alleys and byways that had sprung up since the old house had been built, hemming it in completely; and probably the house itself was only suffered to stand pending the falling-in of a lease or two, when doubtless a clearance would be made of the whole neighbourhood.

It was of bloomy old red brick, and built into its walls were the crowns and clasped hands and other insignia of insurance companies long since defunct. The children of the secluded square had swung upon the low gate at the end of the entrance-alley until little more than the solid top bar of it remained, and the alley itself ran past boarded basement windows on which tramps had chalked their cryptic marks. The path was washed and worn uneven by the spilling of water from the eaves of the encroaching next house, and cats and dogs had made the approach their own. The chances of a tenant did not seem such as to warrant the keeping of the "To Let" boards in a state of legibility and repair, and as a matter of fact they were not so kept.

For six months Oleron had passed the old place twice a day or oftener, on his way from his lodgings to the room, ten minutes' walk away, he had taken to work in; and for six months no hatchet-like notice-board had fallen across his path. This might have been due to the fact that he usually took the other side of the square. But he chanced one morning to take the side that ran past the broken gate and the rain-worn entrance alley, and to pause before one of the inclined boards. The board bore, besides the agent's name, the announcement, written apparently about the time of Oleron's own early youth, that the key was to be had at Number Six.

Now Oleron was already paying, for his separate bedroom and workroom, more than an author who, without private means, habitually disregards his public, can afford; and he was paying in addition a small rent for the storage of the greater part of his grandmother's furniture. Moreover, it invariably happened that the book he wished to read in bed was at his working-quarters half a mile or more away, while the note or letter he had sudden need of during the day was as likely as not to be in the pocket of another coat hanging behind his bedroom door. And there were other inconveniences in having a divided domicile. Therefore Oleron, brought suddenly up by the hatchet-like notice-board, looked first down through some scanty privet-bushes at the boarded basement windows, then up at the blank and grimy windows of the first floor, and so up to the second floor and the flat stone coping of the leads. He stood for a minute thumbing his lean and shaven jaw; then, with another glance at the board, he walked slowly across the square to Number Six.

He knocked, and waited for two or three minutes, but,

although the door stood open, received no answer. He was knocking again when a long-nosed man in shirt-sleeves appeared.

"I was arsking a blessing on our food," he said in severe explanation.

Oleron asked if he might have the key of the old house; and the long-nosed man withdrew again.

Oleron waited for another five minutes on the step; then the man, appearing again and masticating some of the food of which he had spoken, announced that the key was lost.

"But you won't want it," he said. "The entrance door isn't closed, and a push'll open any of the others. I'm a agent for it, if you're thinking of taking it—"

Oleron recrossed the square, descended the two steps at the broken gate, passed along the alley, and turned in at the old wide doorway. To the right, immediately within the door, steps descended to the roomy cellars, and the staircase before him had a carved rail, and was broad and handsome and filthy. Oleron ascended it, avoiding contact with the rail and wall, and stopped at the first landing. A door facing him had been boarded up, but he pushed at that on his right hand, and an insecure bolt or staple yielded. He entered the empty first floor.

He spent a quarter of an hour in the place, and then came out again. Without mounting higher, he descended and recrossed the square to the house of the man who had lost the key.

"Can you tell me how much the rent is?" he asked.

The man mentioned a figure, the comparative lowness of which seemed accounted for by the character of the neighbourhood and the abominable state of unrepair of the place.

"Would it be possible to rent a single floor?"

The long-nosed man did not know; they might. . . .

"Who are they?"

The man gave Oleron the name of a firm of lawyers in Lincoln's Inn.

"You might mention my name—Barrett," he added.

Pressure of work prevented Oleron from going down to Lincoln's Inn that afternoon, but he went on the morrow, and was instantly offered the whole house as a purchase for fifty pounds down, the remainder of the purchase-money to remain on mortgage. It took him half an hour to disabuse the lawyer's mind of the idea that he wished anything more of the place than to rent a single floor of it. This made certain hums and haws of a difference, and the lawyer was by no means certain that it lay within his power to do as Oleron suggested; but it was finally extracted from him that, provided the notice-boards were allowed to remain up, and that, provided it was agreed that in the event of the whole house letting, the arrangement should terminate automatically without further notice, something might be done. That the old place should suddenly let over his head seemed to Oleron the slightest of risks to take, and he promised a decision within a week. On the morrow he visited the house again, went through it from top to bottom, and then went home to his lodgings to take a bath.

He was immensely taken with that portion of the house he had already determined should be his own. Scraped clean and repainted, and with that old furniture of Oleron's grandmother's, it ought to be entirely charming. He went to the storage warehouse to refresh his memory of his half-forgotten belongings, and to take measurements; and thence he went to a decorator's. He was very busy with his regular work, and could have wished that the notice-board had caught his attention either a few months earlier or else later in the year; but the quickest way would be to suspend work entirely until after his removal. . . .

A fortnight later his first floor was painted throughout in a tender, elder-flower white, the paint was dry, and Oleron was in the middle of his installation. He was animated, delighted; and he rubbed his hands as he polished and made disposals of his grandmother's effects—the tall lattice-paned china cupboard with its Derby and Mason and Spode, the large folding Sheraton table, the long, low bookshelves (he had had two of them "copied"), the chairs, the Sheffield candlesticks, the riveted rose-bowls. These things he set against his newly painted elder-white walls—walls of wood panelled in the happiest proportions, and moulded and coffered to the low-seated window-recesses in a mood of gaiety and rest that the builders of rooms no longer know. The ceilings were lofty, and faintly painted with an old pattern of stars; even the tapering mouldings of his iron fireplace were as delicately designed as jewellery; and Oleron walked about rubbing his hands, frequently stopping for the mere pleasure of the glimpses from white room to white room. . . .

"Charming, charming!" he said to himself. "I wonder what Elsie Bengough will think of this!"

He bought a bolt and a Yale lock for his door, and shut off his quarters from the rest of the house. If he now wanted to read in bed, his book could be had for stepping into the next room. All the time, he thought how exceedingly lucky he was to get the place. He put up a hat-rack in the little square hall, and hung up his hats and caps and coats; and passers through the small triangular square late at night, looking up over the little serried row of wooden "To Let" hatchets, could see the light within Oleron's red blinds, or else the sudden darkening of one blind and the illumination of another, as Oleron, candlestick in hand, passed from room to room, making final settlings of his furniture, or preparing to resume the work that his removal had interrupted.

II

As far as the chief business of his life—his writing—was concerned, Paul Oleron treated the world a good deal better than he was treated by it; but he seldom took the trouble to strike a balance, or to compute how far, at forty-four years of age, he was behind his points on the handicap. To have done so wouldn't have altered matters, and it might have depressed Olerom. He had chosen his path, and was committed to it beyond possibility of withdrawal. Perhaps he had chosen it in the days when he had been easily swayed by something a little disinterested, a little generous, a little noble; and had he ever thought of questioning himself he would still have held to it that a life without nobility and generosity and disinterestedness was no life for him. Only quite recently, and rarely, had he even vaguely suspected that there was more in it than this; but it was no good anticipating the day when, he supposed, he would reach that maximum point of his powers beyond which he must inevitably decline, and be left face to face with the question whether it would not have profited him better to have ruled his life by less exigent ideals.

In the meantime, his removal into the old house with the insurance marks built into its brick merely interrupted *Romilly Bishop* at the fifteenth chapter.

As this tall man with the lean, ascetic face moved about his new abode, arranging, changing, altering, hardly yet into his working-stride again, he gave the impression of almost spinster-like precision and nicety. For twenty years past, in a score of lodgings, garrets, flats, and rooms furnished and unfurnished, he had been accustomed to do many things for himself, and he had discovered that it saves time and temper to be methodical. He had arranged with the wife of the long-nosed Barrett, a stout Welsh woman with a falsetto voice, the Merionethshire accent of which long residence in London had not perceptibly modified, to come across the square each morning to prepare his breakfast, and also to "turn the place out" on Saturday mornings; and for the rest, he even welcomed a little housework as a relaxation from the strain of writing.

His kitchen, together with the adjoining strip of an apartment into which a modern bath had been fitted, overlooked the alley at the side of the house; and at one end of it was a large closet with a door, and a square sliding hatch in the upper part of the door. This had been a powder-closet, and through the hatch the elaborately dressed head had been thrust to receive the click and puff of the powder-pistol. Oleron puzzled a little over this closet; then, as its use occurred to him, he smiled faintly, a little moved, he knew not by what . . . He would have to put it to a very different purpose from its original one; it would probably have to serve as his larder. . . . It was in this closet that he made a discovery. The back of it was shelved, and, rummaging on an upper shelf that ran deeply into the wall, Oleron found a couple of mushroom-shaped old wooden wig-stands. He did not know how they had come to be there. Doubtless the painters had turned them up somewhere or other, and had put them there. But his five rooms, as a whole, were short of cupboard and closet-room; and it was only by the exercise of some ingenuity that he was able to find places for the bestowal of his household linen, his boxes, and his seldom-used but not-to-be-destroyed accumulation of papers.

It was in early spring that Oleron entered on his tenancy, and he was anxious to have *Romilly* ready for publication in the coming autumn. Nevertheless, he did not intend to force its production. Should it demand longer in the doing, so much the worse; he realised its importance, its crucial importance, in his artistic development, and it must have its own length and time. In the workroom he had recently left he had been making excellent progress; *Romilly* had begun, as the saying is, to speak and act of herself; and he did not doubt she would continue to do so the moment the distraction of his removal was over. This distraction was almost over; he told himself it was time he pulled himself together again; and on a March morning he went out, returned again with two great bunches of yellow daffodils, placed one bunch on his mantel-piece between the Sheffield sticks and the other on the table before him, and took out the half-completed manuscript of *Romilly Bishop*.

But before beginning work he went to a small rosewood cabinet and took from a drawer his cheque-book and passbook. He totted them up, and his monk-like face grew thoughtful. His installation had cost him more than he had intended it should, and his balance was rather less than fifty pounds, with no immediate prospect of more.

"Hm! I'd forgotten rugs and chintz curtains and so forth mounted up so," said Oleron. "But it would have been a pity to spoil the place for the want of ten pounds or so . . . Well, *Romilly* simply *must* be out for the autumn, that's all. So here goes—"

He drew his papers towards him.

But he worked badly; or, rather, he did not work at all. The square outside had its own noises, frequent and new, and Oleron could only hope that he would speedily become accustomed to these. First came hawkers, with their carts and cries; at midday the children, returning from school, trooped into the square and swung on Oleron's gate; and when the children had departed again for afternoon school, an itinerant musician with a mandoline posted himself beneath Oleron's window and began to strum. This was a not unpleasant distraction, and Oleron, pushing up his window, threw the man a penny. Then he returned to his table again. . . .

But it was no good. He came to himself, at long intervals, to find that he had been looking about his room and wondering how it had formerly been furnished—whether a settee in buttercup or petunia satin had stood under the farther window, whether from the centre moulding of the light lofty ceiling had depended a glimmering crystal chandelier, or where the tambour-frame or the picquet-table had stood. . . . No, it was no good; he had far better be frankly doing nothing than getting fruitlessly tired; and he decided that he would take a walk, but, chancing to sit down for a moment, dozed in his chair instead.

"This won't do," he yawned when he awoke at half-past four in the afternoon; "I must do better than this tomorrow—"

And he felt so deliciously lazy that for some minutes he even contemplated the breach of an appointment he had for the evening.

The next morning he sat down to work without even permitting himself to answer one of his three letters—two of them tradesmen's accounts, the third a note from Miss Bengough, forwarded from his old address. It was a jolly day of white and blue, with a gay noisy wind and a subtle turn in the colour of growing things; and over and over again, once or twice a minute, his room became suddenly light and then subdued again, as the shining white clouds rolled north-eastwards over the square. The soft fitful illumination was reflected in the polished surface of the table and even in the footworn old floor; and the morning noises had begun again.

Oleron made a pattern of dots on the paper before him, and then broke off to move the jar of daffodils exactly opposite the centre of a creamy panel. Then he wrote a sentence that ran continuously for a couple of lines, after which it broke off into notes and jottings. For a time he succeeded in persuading himself that in making these memoranda he was really working; then he rose and began to pace his room. As he did so, he was struck by an idea. It was that the place might possibly be a little better for more positive colour. It was, perhaps, a thought *too* pale—mild and sweet as a kind old face, but a little devitalised, even wan. . . . Yes, decidedly it would bear a robuster note—more and richer flowers, and possibly some warm and gay stuff for cushions for the window-seats. . . .

"Of course, I really can't afford it," he muttered, as he went for a two-foot and began to measure the width of the window recesses. . . .

In stooping to measure a recess, his attitude suddenly changed to one of interest and attention. Presently he rose again, rubbing his hands with gentle glee.

"Oho, oho!" he said. "These look to me very much like window-boxes, nailed up. We must look into this! Yes, those are boxes, or I'm . . . oho, this is an adventure!"

On that wall of his sitting-room there were two windows (the third was in another corner), and, beyond the open bedroom door, on the same wall, was another. The seats of all had been painted, repainted, and painted again; and Oleron's investigating finger had barely detected the old nailheads beneath the paint. Under the ledge over which he stooped an old keyhole also had been puttied up. Oleron took out his penknife.

He worked carefully for five minutes, and then went into the kitchen for a hammer and chisel. Driving the chisel cautiously under the seat, he started the whole lid slightly. Again using the penknife, he cut along the hinged edge and outward along the ends; and then he fetched a wedge and a wooden mallet.

"Now for our little mystery—" he said.

The sound of the mallet on the wedge seemed, in that sweet and pale apartment, somehow a little brutal—nay, even shocking. The panelling rang and rattled and vibrated to the blows like a sounding-board. The whole house seemed to echo; from the roomy cellarage to the garrets above a flock of echoes seemed to awake; and the sound got a little on Oleron's nerves. All at once he paused, fetched a duster, and muffled the mallet. . . . When the edge was sufficiently raised he put his fingers under it and lifted. The paint flaked and starred a little; the rusty old nails squeaked and grunted; and the lid came up, laying open the box beneath. Oleron looked into it. Save for a couple of inches of scurf and mould and old cobwebs it was empty.

"No treasure there," said Oleron, a little amused that he should have fancied there might have been. "*Romilly* will still have to be out by the autumn. Let's have a look at the others."

He turned to the second window.

The raising of the two remaining seats occupied him until well into the afternoon. That of the bedroom, like the first, was empty; but from the second seat of his sitting-room he drew out something yielding and folded and furred over an inch thick with dust. He carried the object into the kitchen, and having swept it over a bucket, took a duster to it.

It was some sort of a large bag, of an ancient frieze-like material, and when unfolded it occupied the greater part of the small kitchen floor. In shape it was an irregular, a very irregular, triangle, and it had a couple of wide flaps, with the remains of straps and buckles. The patch that had been uppermost in the folding was of a faded yellowish brown; but the rest of it was of shades of crimson that varied according to the exposure of the parts of it.

"Now whatever can that have been?" Oleron mused as he stood surveying it. . . . "I give it up. Whatever it is, it's settled my work for to-day, I'm afraid—"

He folded the object up carelessly and thrust it into a corner of the kitchen; then, taking pans and brushes and an old knife, he returned to the sitting-room and began to scrape and to wash and to line with paper his newly discovered receptacles. When he had finished, he put his spare boots and books and papers into them; and he closed the lids again, amused with his little adventure, but also a little anxious for the hour to come when he should settle fairly down to his work again.

III

It piqued Oleron a little that his friend, Miss Bengough, should dismiss with a glance the place he himself had found so singularly winning. Indeed she scarcely lifted her eyes to it. But then she had always been more or less like that—a little indifferent to the graces of life, careless of appearances, and perhaps a shade more herself when she ate biscuits from a paper bag than when she dined with greater observance of the convenances. She was an unattached journalist of thirty-four, large, showy, fair as butter, pink as a dog-rose, reminding one of a florist's picked specimen bloom, and given to sudden and ample movements and moist and explosive utterances. She "pulled a better living out of the pool" (as she expressed it) than Oleron did; and by cunningly disguised puffs of drapers and haberdashers she "pulled" also the greater part of her very varied wardrobe. She left small whirlwinds of air behind her when she moved, in which her veils and scarves fluttered and spun.

Oleron heard the flurry of her skirts on his staircase and her single loud knock at his door when he had been a month in his new abode. Her garments brought in the outer air, and she flung a bundle of ladies' journals down on a chair.

"Don't knock off for me," she said across a mouthful of large-headed hatpins as she removed her hat and veil. "I didn't know whether you were straight yet, so I've brought some sandwiches for lunch. You've got coffee, I suppose?—No, don't get up—I'll find the kitchen—"

"Oh, that's all right, I'll clear these things away. To tell the truth, I'm rather glad to be interrupted," said Oleron.

He gathered his work together and put it away. She was already in the kitchen; he heard the running of water into the kettle. He joined her, and ten minutes later followed her back to the sitting-room with the coffee and sandwiches on a tray. They sat down, with the tray on a small table between them.

"Well, what do you think of the new place?" Oleron asked as she poured out coffee.

"Hm! . . . Anybody'd think you were going to get married, Paul."

He laughed.

"Oh no. But it's an improvement on some of them, isn't it?"

"Is it? I suppose it is; I don't know. I liked the last place, in spite of the black ceiling and no watertap. How's *Romilly*?"

Oleron thumbed his chin.

"Hm! I'm rather ashamed to tell you. The fact is, I've not got on very well with it. But it will be all right on the night, as you used to say."

"Stuck?"

"Rather stuck."

"Got any of it you care to read to me? . . ."

Oleron had long been in the habit of reading portions of his work to Miss Bengough occasionally. Her comments were always quick and practical, sometimes directly useful, sometimes indirectly suggestive. She, in return for his confidence, always kept all mention of her own work sedulously from him. His, she said, was "real work"; hers merely filled space, not always even grammatically.

"I'm afraid there isn't," Oleron replied, still meditatively dry-shaving his chin. Then he added, with a little burst of candour, "The fact is, Elsie, I've not written—not actually written—very much more of it—*any* more of it, in fact. But, of course, that doesn't mean I haven't progressed. I've progressed, in one sense, rather alarmingly. I'm now thinking of reconstructing the whole thing."

Miss Bengough gave a gasp. "Reconstructing!"

"Making Romilly herself a different type of woman. Somehow, I've begun to feel that I'm not getting the most out of her. As she stands, I've certainly lost interest in her to some extent."

"But—but—" Miss Bengough protested, "you had her so real, so *living*, Paul!"

Oleron smiled faintly. He had been quite prepared for Miss

Bengough's disapproval. He wasn't surprised that she liked Romilly as she at present existed; she would. Whether she realised it or not, there was much of herself in his fictitious creation. Naturally Romilly would seem "real," "living," to her. . . .

"But are you really serious, Paul?" Miss Bengough asked presently, with a round-eyed stare.

"Quite serious."

"You're really going to scrap those fifteen chapters?"

"I didn't exactly say that."

"That fine, rich love-scene?"

"I should only do it reluctantly, and for the sake of something I thought better."

"And that beautiful, *beautiful* description of Romilly on the shore?"

"It wouldn't necessarily be wasted," he said a little uneasily.

But Miss Bengough made a large and windy gesture, and then let him have it.

"Really, you are *too* trying!" she broke out. "I do wish sometimes you'd remember you're human, and live in a world! You know I'd be the *last* to wish you to lower your standard one inch, but it wouldn't be lowering it to bring it within human comprehension. Oh, you're sometimes altogether too godlike! . . . Why, it would be a wicked, criminal waste of your powers to destroy those fifteen chapters! Look at it reasonably, now. You've been working for nearly twenty years; you've now got what you've been working for almost within your grasp; your affairs are at a most critical stage (oh, don't tell me; I know you're about at the end of your money); and here you are, deliberately proposing to withdraw a thing that will probably make your name, and to substitute for it something that ten to one nobody on earth will ever want to read—and small blame to them! Really, you try my patience!"

Oleron had shaken his head slowly as she had talked. It was an old story between them. The noisy, able, practical journalist was an admirable friend—up to a certain point; beyond that . . . well, each of us knows that point beyond which we stand alone. Elsie Bengough sometimes said that had she had one-tenth part of

Oleron's genius there were few things she could not have done—thus making that genius a quantitatively divisible thing, a sort of ingredient, to be added to or to subtracted from in the admixture of his work. That it was a qualitative thing, essential, indivisible, informing, passed her comprehension. Their spirits parted company at that point. Oleron knew it. She did not appear to know it.

"Yes, yes, yes," he said a little wearily, by-and-by, "practically you're quite right, entirely right, and I haven't a word to say. If I could only turn *Romilly* over to you you'd make an enormous success of her. But that can't be, and I, for my part, am seriously doubting whether she's worth my while. You know what that means."

"What does it mean?" she demanded bluntly.

"Well," he said, smiling wanly, "what *does* it mean when you're convinced a thing isn't worth doing? You simply don't do it."

Miss Bengough's eyes swept the ceiling for assistance against this impossible man.

"What utter rubbish!" she broke out at last. "Why, when I saw you last you were simply oozing *Romilly*; you were turning her off at the rate of four chapters a week; if you hadn't moved you'd have had her three-parts done by now. What on earth possessed you to move right in the middle of your most important work?"

Oleron tried to put her off with a recital of inconveniences, but she wouldn't have it. Perhaps in her heart she partly suspected the reason. He was simply mortally weary of the narrow circumstances of his life. He had had twenty years of it—twenty years of garrets and roof-chambers and dingy flats and shabby lodgings, and he was tired of dinginess and shabbiness. The reward was as far off as ever—or if it was not, he no longer cared as once he would have cared to put out his hand and take it. It is all very well to tell a man who is at the point of exhaustion that only another effort is required of him; if he cannot make it he is as far off as ever. . . .

"Anyway," Oleron summed up, "I'm happier here than I've been for a long time. That's some sort of a justification."

"And doing no work," said Miss Bengough pointedly.

At that a trifling petulance that had been gathering in Oleron came to a head.

"And why should I do nothing but work?" he demanded. "How much happier am I for it? I don't say I don't love my work—when it's done; but I hate doing it. Sometimes it's an intolerable burden that I simply long to be rid of. Once in many weeks it has a moment, one moment, of glow and thrill for me; I remember the days when it was all glow and thrill; and now I'm forty-four, and it's becoming drudgery. Nobody wants it; I'm ceasing to want it myself; and if any ordinary sensible man were to ask me whether I didn't think I was a fool to go on, I think I should agree that I was."

Miss Bengough's comely pink face was serious.

"But you knew all that, many, many years ago, Paul—and still you chose it," she said in a low voice.

"Well, and how should I have known?" he demanded. "I didn't know. I was told so. My heart, if you like, told me so, and I thought I knew. Youth always thinks it knows; then one day it discovers that it is nearly fifty—"

"Forty-four, Paul—"

"—forty-four, then—and it finds that the glamour isn't in front, but behind. Yes, I knew and chose, if *that's* knowing and choosing . . . but it's a costly choice we're called on to make when we're young!"

Miss Bengough's eyes were on the floor. Without moving them she said, "You're not regretting it, Paul?"

"Am I not?" he took her up. "Upon my word, I've lately thought I am! What *do* I get in return for it all?"

"You know what you get," she replied.

He might have known from her tone what else he could have had for the holding up of a finger—herself. She knew, but could not tell him, that he could have done no better thing for himself. Had he, any time these ten years, asked her to marry him, she would have replied quietly, "Very well; when?" He had never thought of it. . . .

"Yours is the real work," she continued quietly. "Without

you we jackals couldn't exist. You and a few like you hold everything upon your shoulders."

For a minute there was a silence. Then it occurred to Oleron that this was common vulgar grumbling. It was not his habit. Suddenly he rose and began to stack cups and plates on the tray.

"Sorry you catch me like this, Elsie," he said, with a little laugh. . . . "No, I'll take them out; then we'll go for a walk, if you like. . . .

He carried out the tray, and then began to show Miss Bengough round his flat. She made few comments. In the kitchen she asked what an old faded square of reddish frieze was, that Mrs. Barrett used as a cushion for her wooden chair.

"That? I should be glad if you could tell *me* what it is," Oleron replied as he unfolded the bag and related the story of its finding in the window-seat.

"I think I know what it is," said Miss Bengough. "It's been used to wrap up a harp before putting it into its case."

"By Jove, that's probably just what it was," said Oleron. "I could make neither head nor tail of it. . . ."

They finished the tour of the flat, and returned to the sitting-room.

"And who lives in the rest of the house?" Miss Bengough asked.

"I dare say a tramp sleeps in the cellar occasionally. Nobody else."

"Hm! . . . Well, I'll tell you what I think about it, if you like."

"I should like."

"You'll never work here."

"Oh?" said Oleron quickly. "Why not?"

"You'll never finish *Romilly* here. Why, I don't know, but you won't. I know it. You'll have to leave before you get on with that book."

He mused for a moment, and then said:

"Isn't that a little—prejudiced, Elsie?"

"Perfectly ridiculous. As an argument it hasn't a leg to stand on. But there it is," she replied, her mouth once more full of the large-headed hat pins.

Oleron was reaching down his hat and coat. He laughed.

"I can only hope you're entirely wrong," he said, "for I shall be in a serious mess if *Romilly* isn't out in the autumn."

IV

As Oleron sat by his fire that evening, pondering Miss Bengough's prognostication that difficulties awaited him in his work, he came to the conclusion that it would have been far better had she kept her beliefs to herself. No man does a thing better for having his confidence damped at the outset, and to speak of difficulties is in a sense to make them. Speech itself becomes a deterrent act, to which other discouragements accrete until the very event of which warning is given is as likely as not to come to pass. He heartily confounded her. An influence hostile to the completion of *Romilly* had been born.

And in some illogical, dogmatic way women seem to have, she had attached this antagonistic influence to his new abode. Was ever anything so absurd! "You'll never finish *Romilly* here." . . . Why not? Was this her idea of the luxury that saps the springs of action and brings a man down to indolence and dropping out of the race? The place was well enough—it was entirely charming, for that matter—but it was not so demoralising as all that! No; Elsie had missed the mark that time. . . .

He moved his chair to look round the room that smiled, positively smiled, in the firelight. He too smiled, as if pity was to be entertained for a maligned apartment. Even that slight lack of robust colour he had remarked was not noticeable in the soft glow. The drawn chintz curtains—they had a flowered and trellised pattern, with baskets and oaten pipes—fell in long quiet folds to the window-seats; the rows of bindings in old book cases took the light richly; the last trace of sallowness had gone with the daylight; and, if the truth must be told, it had been Elsie herself who had seemed a little out of the picture.

That reflection struck him a little, and presently he returned to it. Yes, the room had, quite accidentally, done Miss Bengough a disservice that afternoon. It had, in some subtle but unmistakable way, placed her, marked a contrast of qualities. Assuming for the sake of argument the slightly ridiculous proposition that the room in which Oleron sat *was* characterised by a certain sparsity and lack of vigour; so much the worse for Miss Bengough; she certainly erred on the side of redundancy and general muchness. And if one must contrast abstract qualities, Oleron inclined to the austere in taste. . . .

Yes, here Oleron had made a distinct discovery; he wondered he had not made it before. He pictured Miss Bengough again as she had appeared that afternoon—large, showy, moistly pink, with that quality of the prize bloom exuding, as it were from her; and instantly she suffered in his thought. He even recognised now that he had noticed something odd at the time, and that unconsciously his attitude, even while she had been there, had been one of criticism. The mechanism of her was a little obvious; her melting humidity was the result of analysable processes; and behind her there had seemed to lurk some dim shape emblematic of mortality. He had never, during the ten years of their intimacy, dreamed for a moment of asking her to marry him; none the less, he now felt for the first time a thankfulness that he had not done so. . . .

Then, suddenly and swiftly, his face flamed that he should be thinking thus of his friend. What! Elsie Bengough, with whom he had spent weeks and weeks of afternoons—she, the good chum, on whose help he would have counted had all the rest of the world failed him—she, whose loyalty to him would not, he knew, swerve as long as there was breath in her—Elsie to be even in thought dissected thus! He was an ingrate and a cad. . . .

Had she been there in that moment he would have abased himself before her.

For ten minutes and more he sat, still gazing into the fire, with that humiliating red fading slowly from his cheeks. All was still within and without, save for a tiny musical tinkling that came from his kitchen—the dripping of water from an imperfectly turned-off tap into the vessel beneath it. Mechanically he began to beat with his fingers to the faintly heard falling of the drops; the tiny regular movement seemed to hasten that shameful withdrawal from his face. He grew cool once more; and when he resumed his meditation he was all unconscious that he took it up again at the same point. . . .

It was not only her florid superfluity of build that he had approached in the attitude of criticism; he was conscious also of the wide differences between her mind and his own. He felt no thankfulness that up to a certain point their natures had ever run companionably side by side; he was now full of questions beyond that point. Their intellects diverged; there was no denying it; and, looking back, he was inclined to doubt whether there had been any real coincidence. True, he had read his writings to her and she had appeared to speak comprehendingly and to the point; but what can a man do who, having assumed that another sees as he does, is suddenly brought up sharp by something that falsifies and discredits all that has gone before? He doubted all now. . . . It did for a moment occur to him that the man who demands of a friend more than can be given to him is in danger of losing that friend, but he put the thought aside.

Again he ceased to think, and again moved his finger to the distant dripping of the tap. . . .

And now (he resumed by-and-by), if these things were true of Elsie Bengough, they were also true of the creation of which she was the prototype—Romilly Bishop. And since he could say of Romilly what for very shame he could not say of Elsie, he gave his thoughts rein. He did so in that smiling, fire-lighted room, to the accompaniment of the faintly heard tap.

There was no longer any doubt about it; he hated the central character of his novel. Even as he had described her physically she overpowered the senses; she was coarse-fibred, over-coloured, rank. It became true the moment he formulated his thought; Gulliver had described the Brobdingnagian maids-of-honour thus: and mentally and spiritually she corresponded—was unsensitive, limited, common. The model (he closed his eyes for a moment)—

the model stuck out through fifteen vulgar and blatant chapters to such a pitch that, without seeing the reason, he had been unable to begin the sixteenth. He marvelled that it had only just dawned upon him.

And *this* was to have been his Beatrice, his vision! As Elsie she was to have gone into the furnace of his art, and she was to have come out the Woman all men desire! Her thoughts were to have been culled from his own finest, her form from his dearest dreams, and her setting wherever he could find one fit for her worth. He had brooded long before making the attempt; then one day he had felt her stir within him as a mother feels a quickening, and he had begun to write; and so he had added chapter to chapter. . . .

And those fifteen sodden chapters were what he had produced!

Again he sat, softly moving his finger. . . .

Then he bestirred himself.

She must go, all fifteen chapters of her. That was settled. For what was to take her place his mind was a blank; but one thing at a time; a man is not excused from taking the wrong course because the right one is not immediately revealed to him. Better would come if it was to come; in the meantime—

He rose, fetched the fifteen chapters, and read them over before he should drop them into the fire.

But instead of putting them into the fire he let them fall from his hand. He became conscious of the dripping of the tap again. It had a tinkling gamut of four or five notes, on which it rang irregular changes, and it was foolishly sweet and dulcimer-like. In his mind Oleron could see the gathering of each drop, its little tremble on the lip of the tap, and the tiny percussion of its fall "Plink—plunk," minimised almost to inaudibility. Following the lowest note there seemed to be a brief phrase, irregularly repeated; and presently Oleron found himself waiting for the recurrence of this phrase. It was quite pretty. . . .

But it did not conduce to wakefulness, and Oleron dozed over his fire.

When he awoke again the fire had burned low and the flames of the candles were licking the rims of the Sheffield sticks. Sluggishly he rose, yawned, went his nightly round of door-locks, and window-fastenings, and passed into his bedroom. Soon, he slept soundly.

But a curious little sequel followed on the morrow. Mrs. Barrett usually tapped, not at his door, but at the wooden wall beyond which lay Oleron's bed; and then Oleron rose, put on his dressing-gown, and admitted her. He was not conscious that as he did so that morning he hummed an air; but Mrs. Barrett lingered with her hand on the door-knob and her face a little averted and smiling.

"De-ar me!" her soft falsetto rose. "But that will be a very o-ald tune, Mr. Oleron! I will not have heard it this for-ty years!"

"What tune?" Oleron asked.

"The tune, indeed, that you was humming, sir."

Oleron had his thumb in the flap of a letter. It remained there.

"*I* was humming? . . . Sing it, Mrs. Barrett."

Mrs. Barrett prut-prutted.

"I have no voice for singing, Mr. Oleron; it was Ann Pugh was the singer of our family; but the tune will be very o-ald, and it is called 'The Beckoning Fair One.'"

"Try to sing it," said Oleron, his thumb still in the envelope; and Mrs. Barrett, with much dimpling and confusion, hummed the air.

"They do say it was sung to a harp, Mr. Oleron, and it will be very o-ald," she concluded.

"And *I* was singing that?"

"Indeed you was. I would not be likely to tell you lies."

With a "Very well—let me have breakfast," Oleron opened his letter; but the trifling circumstance struck him as more odd than he would have admitted to himself. The phrase he had hummed had been that which he had associated with the falling from the tap on the evening before.

V

Even more curious than that the commonplace dripping of an ordinary water-tap should have tallied so closely with an actually existing air was another result it had, namely, that it awakened, or seemed to awaken, in Oleron an abnormal sensitiveness to other noises of the old house. It has been remarked that silence obtains its fullest and most impressive quality when it is broken by some minute sound; and, truth to tell, the place was never still. Perhaps the mildness of the spring air operated on its torpid old timbers; perhaps Oleron's fires caused it to stretch its old anatomy; and certainly a whole world of insect life bored and burrowed in its baulks and joists. At any rate Oleron had only to sit quiet in his chair and to wait for a minute or two in order to become aware of such a change in the auditory scale as comes upon a man who, conceiving the mid-summer woods to be motionless and still, all at once finds his ear sharpened to the crepitation of a myriad insects.

And he smiled to think of man's arbitrary distinction between that which has life and that which has not. Here, quite apart from such recognisable sounds as the scampering of mice, the falling of plaster behind his panelling, and the popping of purses or coffins from his fire, was a whole house talking to him had he but known its language. Beams settled with a tired sigh into their old mortices; creatures ticked in the walls; joints cracked, boards complained; with no palpable stirring of the air window-sashes changed their positions with a soft knock in their frames. And whether the place had life in this sense or not, it had at all events a winsome personality. It needed but an hour of musing for Oleron to conceive the idea that, as his own body stood in friendly relation to his soul, so, by an extension and an attenuation, his habitation might fantastically be supposed to stand in some relation to himself. He even amused himself with the far-fetched fancy that he might so identify himself with the place that some future tenant, taking possession, might regard it as in a sense haunted. It would be rather a joke if he, a perfectly harmless author, with nothing on his mind worse than a novel he had discovered he must begin again, should turn out to be laying the foundation of a future ghost! . . .

In proportion, however, as he felt this growing attachment to the fabric of his abode, Elsie Bengough, from being merely unattracted, began to show a dislike of the place that was more and more marked. And she did not scruple to speak of her aversion.

"It doesn't belong to to-day at all, and for you especially it's bad," she said with decision. "You're only too ready to let go your hold on actual things and to slip into apathy; *you* ought to be in a place with concrete floors and a patent gas-meter and a tradesman's lift. And it would do you all the good in the world if you had a job that made you scramble and rub elbows with your fellow-men. Now, if I could get you a job, for, say, two or three days a week, one that would allow you heaps of time for your proper work—would you take it?"

Somehow, Oleron resented a little being diagnosed like this. He thanked Miss Bengough, but without a smile.

"Thank you, but I don't think so. After all each of us has his own life to live," he could not refrain from adding.

"His own life to live! . . . How long is it since you were out, Paul?"

"About two hours."

"I don't mean to buy stamps or to post a letter. How long is it since you had anything like a stretch?"

"Oh, some little time perhaps. I don't know."

"Since I was here last?"

"I haven't been out much."

"And has *Romilly* progressed much better for your being cooped up?"

"I think she has. I'm laying the foundations of her. I shall begin the actual writing presently."

It seemed as if Miss Bengough had forgotten their tussle about the first *Romilly*. She frowned, turned half away, and then quickly turned again.

"Ah! . . . So you've still got that ridiculous idea in your head?"

"If you mean," said Oleron slowly, "that I've discarded the

old *Romilly*, and am at work on a new one, you're right. I have still got that idea in my head."

Something uncordial in his tone struck her; but she was a fighter. His own absurd sensitiveness hardened her. She gave a "Pshaw!" of impatience.

"Where is the old one?" she demanded abruptly.

"Why?" asked Oleron.

"I want to see it. I want to show some of it to you. I want, if you're not wool-gathering entirely, to bring you back to your senses."

This time it was he who turned his back. But when he turned round again he spoke more gently.

"It's no good, Elsie. I'm responsible for the way I go, and you must allow me to go it—even if it should seem wrong to you. Believe me, I am giving thought to it. . . . The manuscript? I was on the point of burning it, but I didn't. It's in that window-seat, if you must see it."

Miss Bengough crossed quickly to the window-seat, and lifted the lid. Suddenly she gave a little exclamation, and put the back of her hand to her mouth. She spoke over her shoulder:

"You ought to knock those nails in, Paul," she said.

He strode to her side.

"What? What is it? What's the matter?" he asked. "I did knock them in—or, rather, pulled them out."

"You left enough to scratch with," she replied, showing her hand. From the upper wrist to the knuckle of the little finger a welling red wound showed.

"Good—Gracious!" Oleron ejaculated. . . . "Here, come to the bathroom and bathe it quickly—"

He hurried her to the bathroom, turned on warm water, and bathed and cleansed the bad gash. Then, still holding the hand, he turned cold water on it, uttering broken phrases of astonishment and concern.

"Good Lord, how did that happen! As far as I knew I'd . . . is this water too cold? Does that hurt? I can't imagine how on earth . . . there; that'll do—"

"No—one moment longer—I can bear it," she murmured, her eyes closed. . . .

Presently he led her back to the sitting-room and bound the hand in one of his handkerchiefs; but his face did not lose its expression of perplexity. He had spent half a day in opening and making serviceable the three window-boxes, and he could not conceive how he had come to leave an inch and a half of rusty nail standing in the wood. He himself had opened the lids of each of them a dozen times and had not noticed any nail; but there it was. . . .

"It shall come out now, at all events," he muttered, as he went for a pair of pincers. And he made no mistake about it that time.

Elsie Bengough had sunk into a chair, and her face was rather white; but in her hand was the manuscript of *Romilly*. She had not finished with *Romilly* yet. Presently she returned to the charge.

"Oh, Paul, it will be the greatest mistake you ever, *ever* made if you do not publish this!" she said.

He hung his head, genuinely distressed. He couldn't get that incident of the nail out of his head, and *Romilly* occupied a second place in his thoughts for the moment. But still she insisted; and when presently he spoke it was almost as if he asked her pardon for something.

"What can I say, Elsie? I can only hope that when you see the new version, you'll see how right I am. And if in spite of all you *don't* like her, well . . ." He made a hopeless gesture. "Don't you see that I *must* be guided by my own lights?"

She was silent.

"Come, Elsie," he said gently. "We've got along well so far; don't let us split on this."

The last words had hardly passed his lips before he regretted them. She had been nursing her injured hand, with her eyes once more closed; but her lips and lids quivered simultaneously. Her voice shook as she spoke.

"I can't help saying it, Paul, but you are so greatly changed."

"Hush, Elsie," he murmured soothingly; "you've had a shock; rest for a while. How could I change?"

"I don't know, but you are. You've not been yourself ever since you came here. I wish you'd never seen the place. It's stopped your work, it's making you into a person I hardly know, and it's made me horribly anxious about you. . . . Oh, how my hand is beginning to throb!"

"Poor child!" he murmured. "Will you let me take you to a doctor and have it properly dressed?"

"No—I shall be all right presently—I'll keep it raised—"

She put her elbow on the back of her chair, and the bandaged hand rested lightly on his shoulder.

At that touch an entirely new anxiety stirred suddenly within him. Hundreds of times previously, on their jaunts and excursions, she had slipped her hand within his arm as she might have slipped it into the arm of a brother, and he had accepted the little affectionate gesture as a brother might have accepted it. But now, for the first time, there rushed into his mind a hundred startling questions. Her eyes were still closed, and her head had fallen pathetically back; and there was a lost and ineffable smile on her parted lips. The truth broke in upon him. Good God! . . . And he had never divined it!

And stranger than all was that, now that he did see that she was lost in love of him, there came to him, not sorrow and humility and abasement, but something else that he struggled in vain against—something entirely strange and new, that, had he analysed it, he would have found to be petulance and irritation and resentment and ungentleness. The sudden selfish prompting mastered him before he was aware. He all but gave it words. What was she doing there at all? Why was she not getting on with her own work? Why was she here interfering with his? Who had given her this guardianship over him that lately she had put forward so assertively?—"Changed?" It was she, not himself, who had changed. . . .

But by the time she had opened her eyes again he had overcome his resentment sufficiently to speak gently, albeit with reserve.

"I wish you would let me take you to a doctor."

She rose.

"No, thank you, Paul," she said. "I'll go now. If I need a dressing I'll get one; take the other hand, please. Good-bye—"

He did not attempt to detain her. He walked with her to the foot of the stairs. Halfway along the narrow alley she turned.

"It would be a long way to come if you happened not to be in," she said; "I'll send you a postcard the next time."

At the gate she turned again.

"Leave here, Paul," she said, with a mournful look. "Everything's wrong with this house."

Then she was gone.

Oleron returned to his room. He crossed straight to the window-box. He opened the lid and stood long looking at it. Then he closed it again and turned away.

"That's rather frightening," he muttered. "It's simply not possible that I should not have removed that nail. . . ."

VI

Oleron knew very well what Elsie had meant when she had said that her next visit would be preceded by a postcard. She, too, had realised that at last, at last he knew—knew, and didn't want her. It gave him a miserable, pitiful pang, therefore, when she came again within a week, knocking at the door unannounced. She spoke from the landing; she did not intend to stay, she said; and he had to press her before she would so much as enter.

Her excuse for calling was that she had heard of an inquiry for short stories that he might be wise to follow up. He thanked her. Then, her business over, she seemed anxious to get away again. Oleron did not seek to detain her; even he saw through the pretext of the stories; and he accompanied her down the stairs.

But Elsie Bengough had no luck whatever in that house. A second accident befell her. Half-way down the staircase there was the sharp sound of splintering wood, and she checked a loud cry. Oleron knew the woodwork to be old, but he himself had ascended and descended frequently enough without mishap. . . .

Elsie had put her foot through one of the stairs.

He sprang to her side in alarm.

"Oh, I say! My poor girl!"

She laughed hysterically.

"It's my weight—I know I'm getting fat—"

"Keep still—let me clear these splinters away," he muttered between his teeth.

She continued to laugh and sob that it was her weight—she was getting fat—

He thrust downwards at the broken boards. The extrication was no easy matter, and her torn boot showed him how badly the foot and ankle within it must be abraded.

"Good God—good God!" he muttered over and over again.

"I shall be too heavy for anything soon," she sobbed and laughed.

But she refused to reascend and to examine her hurt.

"No, let me go quickly—let me go quickly," she repeated.

"But it's a frightful gash!"

"No—not so bad—let me get away quickly—I'm—I'm not wanted."

At her words, that she was not wanted, his head dropped as if she had given him a buffet.

"Elsie!" he choked, brokenly and shocked.

But she too made a quick gesture, as if she put something violently aside.

"Oh, Paul, not *that*—not *you*—of course I do mean that too in a sense—oh, you know what I mean! . . . But if the other can't be, spare me this now! I—I wouldn't have come, but—but oh, I did, I *did* try to keep away!"

It was intolerable, heartbreaking; but what could he do—what could he say? He did not love her. . . .

"Let me go—I'm not wanted—let me take away what's left of me—"

"Dear Elsie—you are very dear to me—"

But again she made the gesture, as of putting something violently aside.

"No, not that—not anything less—don't offer me anything less—leave me a little pride—"

"Let me get my hat and coat—let me take you to a doctor," he muttered.

But she refused. She refused even the support of his arm. She gave another unsteady laugh.

"I'm sorry I broke your stairs, Paul. . . . You will go and see about the short stories, won't you?"

He groaned.

"Then if you won't see a doctor, will you go across the square and let Mrs. Barrett look at you? Look, there's Barrett passing now—"

The long-nosed Barrett was looking curiously down the alley, but as Oleron was about to call him he made off without a word. Elsie seemed anxious for nothing so much as to be clear of the place, and finally promised to go straight to a doctor, but insisted on going alone.

"Good-bye," she said.

And Oleron watched her until she was past the hatchet-like "To Let" boards, as if he feared that even they might fall upon her and maim her.

That night Oleron did not dine. He had far too much on his mind. He walked from room to room of his flat, as if he could have walked away from Elsie Bengough's haunting cry that still rang in his ears. "I'm not wanted—don't offer me anything less—let me take away what's left of me—"

Oh, if he could only have persuaded himself that he loved her!

He walked until twilight fell, then, without lighting candles, he stirred up the fire and flung himself into a chair.

Poor, poor Elsie! . . .

But even while his heart ached for her, it was out of the question. If only he had known! If only he had used common observation! But those walks, those sisterly takings of the arm—what a fool he had been! . . . Well, it was too late now. It was she, not he, who must now act—act by keeping away. He would help her all he could. He himself would not sit in her presence. If she came, he would hurry her out again as fast as he could. . . . Poor, poor Elsie!

His room grew dark; the fire burned dead; and he continued to sit, wincing from time to time as a fresh tortured phrase rang again in his ears.

Then suddenly, he knew not why, he found himself anxious for her in a new sense—uneasy about her personal safety. A horrible fancy that even then she might be looking over an embankment down into dark water, that she might even now be glancing up at the hook on the door, took him. Women had been known to do those things. . . . Then there would be an inquest, and he himself would be called upon to identify her, and would be asked how she had come by an ill-healed wound on the hand and a bad abrasion of the ankle. Barrett would say that he had seen her leaving his house. . . .

Then he recognised that his thoughts were morbid. By an effort of will he put them aside, and sat for a while listening to the faint creakings and tickings and rappings within his panelling. . . .

If only he could have married her! . . . But he couldn't. Her face had risen before him again as he had seen it on the stairs, drawn with pain and ugly and swollen with tears. Ugly—yes, positively blubbered; if tears were women's weapons, as they were said to be, such tears were weapons turning against themselves . . . suicide again. . . .

Then all at once he found himself attentively considering her two accidents.

Extraordinary they had been, both of them. He *could not* have left that old nail standing in the wood; why, he had fetched tools specially from the kitchen; and he was convinced that that step that had broken beneath her weight had been as sound as the others. It was inexplicable. If these things could happen, anything could happen. There was not a beam nor a jamb in the place that might not fall without warning, not a plank that might not crash inwards, not a nail that might not become a dagger. The whole place was full of life even now; as he sat there in the dark he heard its crowds of noises as if the house had been one great microphone. . . .

Only half conscious that he did so, he had been sitting for some time identifying these noises, attributing to each crack or creak or knock its material cause; but there was one noise which, again not fully conscious of the omission, he had not sought to account for. It had last come some minutes ago; it came again now—a sort of soft sweeping rustle that seemed to hold an almost inaudible minute crackling. For half a minute or so it had Oleron's attention; then his heavy thoughts were of Elsie Bengough again.

He was nearer to loving her in that moment than he had ever been. He thought how to some men their loved ones were but the dearer for those poor mortal blemishes that tell us we are but sojourners on earth, with a common fate not far distant that makes it hardly worth while to do anything but love for the time remaining. Strangling sobs, blearing tears, bodies buffeted by sickness, hearts and mind callous and hard with the rubs of the world—how little love there would be were these things a barrier to love! In that sense he did love Elsie Bengough. What her happiness had never moved in him her sorrow almost awoke. . . .

Suddenly his meditation went. His ear had once more become conscious of that soft and repeated noise—the long sweep with the almost inaudible crackle in it. Again and again it came, with a curious insistence and urgency. It quickened a little as he became increasingly attentive . . . it seemed to Oleron that it grew louder. . . .

All at once he started bolt upright in his chair, tense and listening. The silky rustle came again; he was trying to attach it to something. . . .

The next moment he had leapt to his feet, unnerved and terrified. His chair hung poised for a moment, and then went over, setting the fire-irons clattering as it fell. There was only one noise in the world like that which had caused him to spring thus to his feet. . . .

The next time it came Oleron felt behind him at the empty air with his hand, and backed slowly until he found himself against the wall.

"God in Heaven!" The ejaculation broke from Oleron's lips. The sound had ceased.

The next moment he had given a high cry.

"What is it? What's there? *Who's* there?"

A sound of scuttling caused his knees to bend under him for a moment; but that, he knew, was a mouse. That was not something that his stomach turned sick and his mind reeled to entertain. That other sound, the like of which was not in the world, had now entirely ceased; and again he called. . . .

He called and continued to call; and then another terror, a terror of the sound of his own voice, seized him. He did not dare to call again. His shaking hand went to his pocket for a match, but found none. He thought there might be matches on the mantel-piece—

He worked his way to the mantel-piece round a little recess, without for a moment leaving the wall. Then his hand encountered the mantel-piece, and groped along it. A box of matches fell to the hearth. He could just see them in the firelight, but his hand could not pick them up until he had cornered them inside the fender.

Then he rose and struck a light.

The room was as usual. He struck a second match. A candle stood on the table. He lighted it, and the flame sank for a moment and then burned up clear. Again he looked round.

There was nothing.

There was nothing; but there had been something, and might still be something. Formerly, Oleron had smiled at the fantastic thought that, by a merging and interplay of identities between himself and his beautiful room, he might be preparing a ghost for the future; it had not occurred to him *that there might have been a similar merging and coalescence in the past.* Yet with this staggering impossibility he was now face to face. Something did persist in the house; it had a tenant other than himself; and that tenant, whatsoever or whosoever, had appalled Oleron's soul by producing the sound of a woman brushing her hair.

VII

Without quite knowing how he came to be there Oleron found himself striding over the loose board he had temporarily placed on the step broken by Miss Bengough. He was hatless, and descending the stairs. Not until later did there return to him a hazy memory that he had left the candle burning on the table, had opened the door no wider than was necessary to allow the passage of his body, and had sidled out, closing the door softly behind him. At the foot of the stairs another shock awaited him. Something dashed with a flurry up from the disused cellars and disappeared out of the door. It was only a cat, but Oleron gave a childish sob.

He passed out of the gate, and stood for a moment under the "To Let" boards, plucking foolishly at his lip and looking up at the glimmer of light behind one of his red blinds. Then, still looking over his shoulder, he moved stumblingly up the square. There was a small public-house round the corner; Oleron had never entered it; but he entered it now, and put down a shilling that missed the counter by inches.

"B—b—bran—brandy," he said, and then stooped to look for the shilling.

He had the little sawdusted bar to himself; what company there was—carters and labourers and the small tradesmen of the neighbourhood—was gathered in the farther compartment, beyond the space where the white-haired landlady moved among her taps and bottles. Oleron sat down on a hardwood settee with a perforated seat, drank half his brandy, and then, thinking he might as well drink it as spill it, finished it.

Then he fell to wondering which of the men whose voices he heard across the public-house would undertake the removal of his effects on the morrow.

In the meantime he ordered more brandy.

For he did not intend to go back to that room where he had left the candle burning. Oh no! He couldn't have faced even the entry and the staircase with the broken step—certainly not that pith-white, fascinating room. He would go back for the present to his old arrangement, of work-room and separate sleeping-quarters; he would go to his old landlady at once—presently—when he had finished his brandy—and see if she could put him up for the night. His glass was empty now. . . .

He rose, had it refilled, and sat down again.

And if anybody asked his reason for removing again? Oh, he had reason enough—reason enough! Nails that put themselves back into wood again and gashed people's hands, steps that broke when you trod on them, and women who came into a man's place and brushed their hair in the dark, were reasons enough! He was querulous and injured about it all. He had taken the place for himself, not for invisible women to brush their hair in; that lawyer fellow in Lincoln's Inn should be told so, too, before many hours were out; it was outrageous, letting people in for agreements like that!

A cut-glass partition divided the compartment where Oleron sat from the space where the white-haired landlady moved; but it stopped seven or eight inches above the level of the counter. There was no partition at the further bar. Presently Oleron, raising his eyes, saw that faces were watching him through the aperture. The faces disappeared when he looked at them.

He moved to a corner where he could not be seen from the other bar; but this brought him into line with the white-haired landlady.

She knew him by sight—had doubtless seen him passing and repassing; and presently she made a remark on the weather. Oleron did not know what he replied, but it sufficed to call forth the further remark that the winter had been a bad one for influenza, but that the spring weather seemed to be coming at last. . . . Even this slight contact with the commonplace steadied Oleron a little; an idle, nascent wonder whether the landlady brushed her hair every night, and, if so, whether it gave out those little electric cracklings, was shut down with a snap; and Oleron was better. . . .

With his next glass of brandy he was all for going back to his flat. Not go back? Indeed, he would go back! They should very soon see whether he was to be turned out of his place like that! He began to wonder why he was doing the rather unusual thing he was doing at that moment, unusual for him—sitting hatless, drinking brandy, in a public-house. Suppose he were to tell the white-haired landlady all about it—to tell her that a caller had scratched her hand on a nail, had later had the bad luck to put her foot through a rotten stair, and that he himself, in an old house full of squeaks and creaks and whispers, had heard a minute noise and had bolted from it in fright—what would she think of him? That he was mad, of course. . . . Pshaw! The real truth of the matter was that he hadn't been doing enough work to occupy him. He had been dreaming his days away, filling his head with a lot of moonshine about a new *Romilly* (as if the old one was not good enough), and now he was surprised that the devil should enter an empty head!

Yes, he would go back. He would take a walk in the air first—he hadn't walked enough lately—and then he would take himself in hand, settle the hash of that sixteenth chapter of *Romilly* (fancy, he had actually been fool enough to think of destroying fifteen chapters!) and thenceforward he would remember that he had obligations to his fellow men and work to do in the world. There was the matter in a nutshell.

He finished his brandy and went out.

He had walked for some time before any other bearing of the matter than that on himself occurred to him. At first, the fresh air had increased the heady effect of the brandy he had drunk; but afterwards his mind grew clearer than it had been since morning. And the clearer it grew, the less final did his boastful self-assurances become, and the firmer his conviction that, when all explanations had been made, there remained something that could not be explained. His hysteria of an hour before had passed; he grew steadily calmer; but the disquieting conviction remained. A deep fear took possession of him. It was a fear for Elsie.

For something in his place was inimical to her safety. Of themselves, her two accidents might not have persuaded him of this; but she herself had said it. *"I'm not wanted here. . . ."* And she had declared that there was something wrong with the place. She had seen it before he had. Well and good. One thing stood out clearly: namely, that if this was so, she must be kept away for quite another reason than that which had so confounded and humiliated Oleron. Luckily she had expressed her intention of staying away; she must be held to that intention. He must see to it.

And he must see to it all the more that he now saw his first example, never to set foot in the place again, was absurd. People did not do that kind of thing. With Elsie made secure, he could not with any respect to himself suffer himself to be turned out by a shadow, nor even by a danger merely because it was a danger. He had to live somewhere, and he would live there. He must return.

He mastered the faint chill of fear that came with the decision, and turned in his walk abruptly. Should fear grow on him again he would, perhaps, take one more glass of brandy. . . .

But by the time he reached the short street that led to the square he was too late for more brandy. The little public-house was still lighted, but closed, and one or two men were standing talking on the kerb. Oleron noticed that a sudden silence fell on them as he passed, and he noticed further that the long-nosed Barrett, whom he passed a little lower down, did not return his good-night. He turned in at the broken gate, hesitated merely an instant in the alley, and then mounted his stairs again.

Only an inch of candle remained in the Sheffield stick, and Oleron did not light another one. Deliberately he forced himself to take it up and to make the tour of his five rooms before retiring. It was as he returned from the kitchen across his little hail that he noticed that a letter lay on the floor. He carried it into his sitting-room, and glanced at the envelope before opening it.

It was unstamped, and had been put into the door by hand. Its handwriting was clumsy, and it ran from beginning to end without comma or period. Oleron read the first line, turned to the signature, and then finished the letter.

It was from the man Barrett, and it informed Oleron that he, Barrett, would be obliged if Mr. Oleron would make other arrangements for the preparing of his breakfasts and the cleaning-out of his place. The sting lay in the tail, that is to say, the post-script. This consisted of a text of Scripture. It embodied an allusion that could only be to Elsie Bengough. . . .

A seldom-seen frown had cut deeply into Oleron's brow. So! That was it! Very well; they would see about that on the morrow. . . . For the rest, this seemed merely another reason why Elsie should keep away. . . .

Then his suppressed rage broke out. . . .

The foul-minded lot! The devil himself could not have given a leer at anything that had ever passed between Paul Oleron and Elsie Bengough, yet this nosing rascal must be prying and talking! . . .

Oleron crumpled the paper up, held it in the candle flame, and then ground the ashes under his heel.

One useful purpose, however, the letter had served: it had created in Oleron a wrathful blaze that effectually banished pale shadows. Nevertheless, one other puzzling circumstance was to close the day. As he undressed, he chanced to glance at his bed. The coverlets bore an impress as if somebody had lain on them. Oleron could not remember that he himself had lain down during the day—off-hand, he would have said that certainly he had not; but after all he could not be positive. His indignation for Elsie, acting possibly with the residue of the brandy in him, excluded all other considerations; and he put out his candle, lay down, and passed immediately into a deep and dreamless sleep, which, in the absence of Mrs. Barrett's morning call, lasted almost once round the clock.

VIII

To the man who pays heed to that voice within him which warns him that twilight and danger are settling over his soul, terror is apt to appear an absolute thing, against which his heart must be safe-guarded in a twink unless there is to take place an alteration in the whole range and scale of his nature. Mercifully, he has never far to look for safeguards. Of the immediate and small and common and momentary things of life, of usages and observances and modes and conventions, he builds up fortifications against the powers of darkness. He is even content that, not terror only, but joy also, should for working purposes be placed in the category of the absolute things; and the last treason he will commit will be that breaking down of terms and limits that strikes, not at one man, but at the welfare of the souls of all.

In his own person, Oleron began to commit this treason. He began to commit it by admitting the inexplicable and horrible to an increasing familiarity. He did it insensibly, unconsciously, by a neglect of the things that he now regarded it as an impertinence in Elsie Bengough to have prescribed. Two months before, the words "a haunted house," applied to his lovely bemusing dwelling, would have chilled his marrow; now, his scale of sensation becoming depressed, he could ask "Haunted by what?" and remain unconscious that horror, when it can be proved to be relative, by so much loses its proper quality. He was setting aside the landmarks. Mists and confusion had begun to enwrap him.

And he was conscious of nothing so much as of a voracious inquisitiveness. He wanted *to know*. He was resolved to know. Nothing but the knowledge would satisfy him; and craftily he cast about for means whereby he might attain it.

He might have spared his craft. The matter was the easiest imaginable. As in time past he had known, in his writing, moments when his thoughts had seemed to rise of themselves and to embody themselves in words not to be altered afterwards, so now the question he put himself seemed to be answered even in the moment of their asking. There was exhilaration in the swift, easy processes. He had known no such joy in his own power since the days when his writing had been a daily freshness and a delight to him. It was almost as if the course he must pursue was being dictated to him.

And the first thing he must do, of course, was to define the problem. He defined it in terms of mathematics. Granted that he had not the place to himself; granted that the old house had inexpressibly caught and engaged his spirit; granted that, by virtue of the common denominator of the place, this unknown co-tenant stood in some relation to himself: what next? Clearly, the nature of the other numerator must be ascertained.

And how? Ordinarily this would not have seemed simple, but to Oleron it was now pellucidly clear. The key, *of course*, lay in his half-written novel—or rather, in both *Romilly*s, the old and the proposed new one.

A little while before Oleron would have thought himself mad to have embraced such an opinion; now he accepted the dizzying hypothesis without a quiver.

He began to examine the first and second *Romilly*s.

From the moment of his doing so the thing advanced by leaps and bounds. Swiftly he reviewed the history of the *Romilly* of the fifteen chapters. He remembered clearly now that he had found her insufficient on the very first morning on which he had sat down to work in his new place. Other instances of his aversion leaped up to confirm his obscure investigation. There had come the night when he had hardly forborne to throw the whole thing into the fire; and the next morning he had begun the planning of the new *Romilly*. It had been on that morning that Mrs. Barrett, overhearing him humming a brief phrase that the dripping of a tap the night before had suggested, had informed him that he was singing some air he had never in his life heard before, called "The Beckoning Fair One." . . .

The Beckoning Fair One! . . .

With scarcely a pause in thought he continued:

The first *Romilly* having been definitely thrown over, the second had instantly fastened herself upon him, clamouring for birth in his brain. He even fancied now, looking back, that there had been something like passion, hate almost, in the supplanting, and that more than once a stray thought given to his discarded creation had—(it was astonishing how credible Oleron found the almost unthinkable idea)—had offended the supplanter.

Yet that a malignancy almost homicidal should be extended to his fiction's poor mortal prototype. . . .

In spite of his inuring to a scale in which the horrible was now a thing to be fingered and turned this way and that, a "Good God!" broke from Oleron.

This intrusion of the first *Romilly*'s prototype into his thought again was a factor that for the moment brought his inquiry into the nature of his problem to a termination; the mere thought of Elsie was fatal to anything abstract. For another thing, he could not yet think of that letter of Barrett's, nor of a little scene that had followed it, without a mounting of colour and a quick contraction of the brow. For, wisely or not, he had had that argument out at once. Striding across the square on the following morning, he had bearded Barrett on his own doorstep. Coming back again a few minutes later, he had been strongly of opinion that he had only made matters worse. The man had been vagueness itself. He had not been able to be either challenged or brow-beaten into anything more definite than a muttered farrago in which the words "Certain things . . . Mrs. Barrett . . . respectable house . . . if the cap fits . . . proceedings that shall be nameless," had been constantly repeated.

"Not that I make any charge—" he had concluded.

"Charge!" Oleron had cried.

"I 'ave my idears of things, as I don't doubt you 'ave yours—"

"Ideas—mine!" Oleron had cried wrathfully, immediately dropping his voice as heads had appeared at windows of the square. "Look you here, my man; you've an unwholesome mind, which probably you can't help, but a tongue which you can help, and shall! If there is a breath of this repeated . . ."

"I'll not be talked to on my own doorstep like this by anybody. . . ." Barrett had blustered. . . .

"You shall, and I'm doing it . . ."

"Don't you forget there's a Gawd above all, Who 'as said . . ."

"You're a low scandalmonger! . . ."

And so forth, continuing badly what was already badly begun. Oleron had returned wrathfully to his own house, and thenceforward, looking out of his windows, had seen Barrett's face at odd times, lifting blinds or peering round curtains, as if he sought to put himself in possession of Heaven knew what evidence, in case it should be required of him.

The unfortunate occurrence made certain minor differences in Oleron's domestic arrangements. Barrett's tongue, he gathered, had already been busy; he was looked at askance by the dwellers of the square; and he judged it better, until he should be able to obtain other help, to make his purchases of provisions a little farther afield rather than at the small shops of the immediate neighbourhood. For the rest, housekeeping was no new thing to him, and he would resume his old bachelor habits. . . .

Besides, he was deep in certain rather abstruse investigations, in which it was better that he should not be disturbed.

He was looking out of his window one midday rather tired, not very well, and glad that it was not very likely he would have to stir out of doors, when he saw Elsie Bengough crossing the square towards his house. The weather had broken; it was a raw and gusty day; and she had to force her way against the wind that set her ample skirts bellying about her opulent figure and her veil spinning and streaming behind her.

Oleron acted swiftly and instinctively. Seizing his hat, he sprang to the door and descended the stairs at a run. A sort of panic had seized him. She must be prevented from setting foot in the place. As he ran along the alley he was conscious that his eyes went up to the eaves as if something drew them. He did not know that a slate might not accidentally fall. . . .

He met her at the gate, and spoke with curious volubleness.

"This is really too bad, Elsie! Just as I'm urgently called away! I'm afraid it can't be helped though, and that you'll have to think me an inhospitable beast." He poured it out just as it came into his head.

She asked if he was going to town.

"Yes, yes—to town," he replied. "I've got to call on—on Chambers. You know Chambers, don't you? No, I remember you don't; a big man you once saw me with. . . . I ought to have gone yesterday, and"—this he felt to be a brilliant effort—"and he's going out of town this afternoon. To Brighton. I had a letter from him this morning."

He took her arm and led her up the square. She had to remind him that his way to town lay in the other direction.

"Of course—how stupid of me!" he said, with a little loud laugh. "I'm so used to going the other way with you—of course; it's the other way to the bus. Will you come along with me? I am so awfully sorry it's happened like this. . . ."

They took the street to the bus terminus.

This time Elsie bore no signs of having gone through interior struggles. If she detected anything unusual in his manner she made no comment, and he, seeing her calm, began to talk less recklessly through silences. By the time they reached the bus terminus, nobody, seeing the pallid-faced man without an overcoat and the large ample-skirted girl at his side, would have supposed that one of them was ready to sink on his knees for thankfulness that he had, as he believed, saved the other from a wildly unthinkable danger.

They mounted to the top of the bus, Oleron protesting that he should not miss his overcoat, and that he found the day, if anything, rather oppressively hot. They sat down on a front seat.

Now that this meeting was forced upon him, he had something else to say that would make demands upon his tact. It had been on his mind for some time, and was, indeed, peculiarly difficult to put. He revolved it for some minutes, and then, remembering the success of his story of a sudden call to town, cut the knot of his difficulty with another lie.

"I'm thinking of going away for a little while, Elsie," he said.

She merely said, "Oh?"

"Somewhere for a change. I need a change. I think I shall go to-morrow, or the day after. Yes, to-morrow, I think."

"Yes," she replied.

"I don't quite know how long I shall be," he continued. "I shall have to let you know when I am back."

"Yes, let me know," she replied in an even tone.

The tone was, for her, suspiciously even. He was a little uneasy.

"You don't ask me where I'm going," he said, with a little cumbrous effort to rally her.

She was looking straight before her, past the bus-driver.

"I know," she said.

He was startled. "How, you know?"

"You're not going anywhere," she replied.

He found not a word to say. It was a minute or so before she continued, in the same controlled voice she had employed from the start.

"You're not going anywhere. You weren't going out this morning. You only came out because I appeared; don't behave as if we were strangers, Paul."

A flush of pink had mounted to his cheeks. He noticed that the wind had given her the pink of early rhubarb. Still he found nothing to say.

"Of course, you ought to go away," she continued. "I don't know whether you look at yourself often in the glass, but you're rather noticeable. Several people have turned to look at you this morning. So, of course, you ought to go away. But you won't, and I know why."

He shivered, coughed a little, and then broke silence.

"Then if you know, there's no use in continuing this discussion," he said curtly.

"Not for me, perhaps, but there is for you," she replied. "Shall I tell you what I know?"

"No," he said in a voice slightly raised.

"No?" she asked, her round eyes earnestly on him.

"No."

Again he was getting out of patience with her; again he was conscious of the strain. Her devotion and fidelity and love plagued him; she was only humiliating both herself and him. It would have been bad enough had he ever, by word or deed, given her cause for thus fastening herself on him . . . but there; that was the worst of that kind of life for a woman. Women such as she, business women, in and out of offices all the time, always, whether they realised it or not, made comradeship a cover for something else. They accepted the unconventional status, came and went freely, as men did, were honestly taken by men at their own valuation—and then it turned out to be the other thing after all, and they went and fell in love. No wonder there was gossip in shops and squares and public-houses! In a sense the gossipers were in the right of it. Independent, yet not efficient; with some of womanhood's graces forgone, and yet with all the woman's hunger and need; half sophisticated, yet not wise; Oleron was tired of it all. . . .

And it was time he told her so.

"I suppose," he said tremblingly, looking down between his knees, "I suppose the real trouble is in the life women who earn their own living are obliged to lead."

He could not tell in what sense she took the lame generality; she merely replied, "I suppose so."

"It can't be helped," he continued, "but you do sacrifice a good deal."

She agreed: a good deal; and then she added after a moment, "What, for instance?"

"You may or may not be gradually attaining a new status, but you're in a false position to-day."

It was very likely, she said; she hadn't thought of it much in that light—

"And," he continued desperately, "you're bound to suffer. Your most innocent acts are misunderstood; motives you never dreamed of are attributed to you; and in the end it comes to"—he hesitated a moment and then took the plunge—"to the sidelong look and the leer."

She took his meaning with perfect ease. She merely shivered a little as she pronounced the name.

"Barrett?"

His silence told her the rest.

Anything further that was to be said must come from her. It came as the bus stopped at a stage and fresh passengers mounted the stairs.

"You'd better get down here and go back, Paul," she said. "I understand perfectly—perfectly. It isn't Barrett. You'd be able to deal with Barrett. It's merely convenient for you to say it's Barrett. I know what it is . . . but you said I wasn't to tell you that. Very well. But before you go let me tell you why I came up this morning."

In a dull tone he asked her why. Again she looked straight before her as she replied:

"I came to force your hand. Things couldn't go on as they have been going, you know; and now that's all over."

"All over," he repeated stupidly.

"All over. I want you now to consider yourself, as far as I'm concerned, perfectly free. I make only one reservation."

He hardly had the spirit to ask her what that was.

"If *I* merely need *you*," she said, "please don't give that a thought; that's nothing; I shan't come near for that. But," she dropped her voice, "if *you're* in need of me, Paul—I shall know if you are, *and you will be*—then I shall come at no matter what cost. You understand that?"

He could only groan.

"So that's understood," she concluded. "And I think that's all. Now go back. I should advise you to walk back, for you're shivering—good-bye—"

She gave him a cold hand, and he descended. He turned on the edge of the kerb as the bus started again. For the first time in all the years he had known her she parted from him with no smile and no wave of her long arm.

IX

He stood on the kerb plunged in misery, looking after her as long as she remained in sight; but almost instantly with her disappearance he felt the heaviness lift a little from his spirit. She had given him his liberty; true, there was a sense in which he had never parted with it, but now was no time for splitting hairs; he was free to act, and all was clear ahead. Swiftly the sense of lightness grew on him: it became a positive rejoicing in his liberty; and before he was half-way home he had decided what must be done next.

The vicar of the parish in which his dwelling was situated lived within ten minutes of the square. To his house Oleron turned his steps. It was necessary that he should have all the information he could get about this old house with the insurance marks and the sloping "To Let" boards, and the vicar was the person most likely to be able to furnish it. This last preliminary out of the way, and—aha! Oleron chuckled—things might be expected to happen!

But he gained less information than he had hoped for. The house, the vicar said, was old—but there needed no vicar to tell Oleron that; it was reputed (Oleron pricked up his ears) to be haunted—but there were few old houses about which some such rumour did not circulate among the ignorant; and the deplorable lack of Faith of the modern world, the vicar thought, did not tend to dissipate these superstitions. For the rest, his manner was the soothing manner of one who prefers not to make statements without knowing how they will be taken by his hearer. Oleron smiled as he perceived this.

"You may leave my nerves out of the question," he said. "How long has the place been empty?"

"A dozen years, I should say," the vicar replied.

"And the last tenant—did you know him—or her?" Oleron was conscious of a tingling of his nerves as he offered the vicar the alternative of sex.

"Him," said the vicar. "A man. If I remember rightly, his name was Madley; an artist. He was a great recluse; seldom went out of the place, and"—the vicar hesitated and then broke into a little gush of candour—"and since you appear to have come for this information, and since it is better that the truth should be told than that garbled versions should get about, I don't mind saying that this man Madley died there, under somewhat unusual circumstances. It was ascertained at the post-mortem that there was not a particle of food in his stomach, although he was found to be not without money. And his frame was simply worn out. Suicide was spoken of, but you'll agree with me that deliberate starvation is, to say the least, an uncommon form of suicide. An open verdict was returned."

"Ah!" said Oleron. . . . "Does there happen to be any comprehensive history of this parish?"

"No; partial ones only. I myself am not guiltless of having made a number of notes on its purely ecclesiastical history, its registers and so forth, which I shall be happy to show you if you would care to see them; but it is a large parish, I have only one curate, and my leisure, as you will readily understand . . ."

The extent of the parish and the scantiness of the vicar's leisure occupied the remainder of the interview, and Oleron thanked the vicar, took his leave, and walked slowly home.

He walked slowly for a reason, twice turning away from the house within a stone's-throw of the gate and taking another turn of twenty minutes or so. He had a very ticklish piece of work now before him; it required the greatest mental concentration; it was nothing less than to bring his mind, if he might, into such a state of unpreoccupation and receptivity that he should see the place as he had seen it on that morning when, his removal accomplished, he had sat down to begin the sixteenth chapter of the first *Romilly*.

For, could he recapture that first impression, he now hoped for far more from it. Formerly, he had carried no end of mental lumber. Before the influence of the place had been able to find him out at all, it had had the inertia of those dreary chapters to overcome. No results had shown. The process had been one of slow saturation, charging, filling up to a brim. But now he was light, unburdened, rid at last both of that *Romilly* and of her prototype. Now for the new unknown, coy, jealous, bewitching, Beckoning Fair! . . .

At half-past two of the afternoon he put his key into the Yale lock, entered, and closed the door behind him. . . .

His fantastic attempt was instantly and astonishingly successful. He could have shouted with triumph as he entered the room; it was as if he had *escaped* into it. Once more, as in the days when his writing had had a daily freshness and wonder and promise for him, he was conscious of that new ease and mastery and exhilaration and release. The air of the place seemed to hold more oxygen; as if his own specific gravity had changed, his very tread seemed less ponderable. The flowers in the bowls, the fair proportions of the meadowsweet-coloured panels and mouldings, the polished floor, and the lofty and faintly starred ceiling, fairly laughed their welcome. Oleron actually laughed back, and spoke aloud.

"Oh, you're pretty, pretty!" he flattered it.

Then he lay down on his couch.

He spent that afternoon as a convalescent who expected a dear visitor might have spent it—in a delicious vacancy, smiling now and then as if in his sleep, and ever lifting drowsy and contented eyes to his alluring surroundings. He lay thus until darkness came, and, with darkness, the nocturnal noises of the old house. . . .

But if he waited for any specific happening, he waited in vain.

He waited similarly in vain on the morrow, maintaining, though with less ease, that sensitised-platelike condition of his mind. Nothing occurred to give it an impression. Whatever it was which he so patiently wooed, it seemed to be both shy and exacting.

Then on the third day he thought he understood. A look of gentle drollery and cunning came into his eyes, and he chuckled.

"Oho, oho! . . . Well, if the wind sits in *that* quarter we must see what else there is to be done. What is there, now? . . . No, I won't send for Elsie; we don't need a wheel to break the butterfly on; we won't go to those lengths, my butterfly. . . ."

He was standing musing, thumbing his lean jaw, looking aslant; suddenly he crossed to his hall, took down his hat, and went out.

"My lady is coquettish, is she? Well, we'll see what a little neglect will do," he chuckled as he went down the stairs.

He sought a railway station, got into a train, and spent the rest of the day in the country. Oh, yes: Oleron thought *he* was the man to deal with Fair Ones who beckoned, and invited, and then took refuge in shyness and hanging back!

He did not return until after eleven that night.

"*Now*, my Fair Beckoner!" he murmured as he walked along the alley and felt in his pocket for his keys. . . .

Inside his flat, he was perfectly composed, perfectly deliberate, exceedingly careful not to give himself away. As if to intimate that he intended to retire immediately, he lighted only a single candle; and as he set out with it on his nightly round he affected to yawn. He went first into his kitchen. There was a full moon, and a lozenge of moonlight, almost peacock-blue by contrast with his candle-frame, lay on the floor. The window was uncurtained, and he could see the reflection of the candle, and, faintly, that of his own face, as he moved about. The door of the powder-closet stood a little ajar, and he closed it before sitting down to remove his boots on the chair with the cushion made of the folded harpbag. From the kitchen he passed to the bathroom. There, another slant of blue moonlight cut the windowsill and lay across the pipes on the wall. He visited his seldom-used study, and stood for a moment gazing at the silvered roofs across the square. Then, walking straight through his sitting-room, his stockinged feet making no noise, he entered his bedroom and put the candle on the chest of drawers. His face all this time wore no expression save that of tiredness. He had never been wilier nor more alert.

His small bedroom fireplace was opposite the chest of drawers on which the mirror stood, and his bed and the window occupied the remaining sides of the room. Oleron drew down his blind, took off his coat, and then stooped to get his slippers from under the bed.

He could have given no reason for the conviction, but that the manifestation that for two days had been withheld was close at hand he never for an instant doubted. Nor, though he could not form the faintest guess of the shape it might take, did he experience fear. Startling or surprising it might be; he was prepared for that; but that was all; his scale of sensation had become depressed. His hand moved this way and that under the bed in search of his slippers. . . .

But for all his caution and method and preparedness, his heart all at once gave a leap and a pause that was almost horrid. His hand had found the slippers, but he was still on his knees; save for this circumstance he would have fallen. The bed was a low one; the groping for the slippers accounted for the turn of his head to one side; and he was careful to keep the attitude until he had partly recovered his self-possession. When presently he rose there was a drop of blood on his lower lip where he had caught at it with his teeth, and his watch had jerked out of the pocket of his waistcoat and was dangling at the end of its short leather guard. . . .

Then, before the watch had ceased its little oscillation, he was himself again.

In the middle of his mantel-piece there stood a picture, a portrait of his grandmother; he placed himself before this picture, so that he could see in the glass of it the steady flame of the candle that burned behind him on the chest of drawers. He could see also in the picture-glass the little glancings of light from the bevels and facets of the objects about the mirror and candle. But he could see more. These twinklings and reflections and re-reflections did not change their position; but there was one gleam that had motion. It was fainter than the rest, and it moved up and down through the air. It was the reflection of the candle on Oleron's black vulcanite comb, and each of its downward movements was accompanied by a silky and crackling rustle.

Oleron, watching what went on in the glass of his grandmother's portrait, continued to play his part. He felt for his dangling watch and began slowly to wind it up. Then, for a moment ceasing to watch, he began to empty his trousers pockets and to place methodically in a little row on the mantel-piece the pennies and halfpennies he took from them. The sweeping, minutely electric noise filled the whole bedroom, and had Oleron altered his point of observation he could have brought the dim gleam of the moving comb so into position that it would almost have outlined his grandmother's head.

Any other head of which it might have been following the outline was invisible.

Oleron finished the emptying of his pockets; then, under cover of another simulated yawn, not so much summoning his resolution as overmastered by an exorbitant curiosity, he swung suddenly round. That which was being combed was still not to be seen, but the comb did not stop. It had altered its angle a little, and had moved a little to the left. It was passing, in fairly regular sweeps, from a point rather more than five feet from the ground, in a direction roughly vertical, to another point a few inches below the level of the chest of drawers.

Oleron continued to act to admiration. He walked to his little washstand in the corner, poured out water, and began to wash his hands. He removed his waistcoat, and continued his preparations for bed. The combing did not cease, and he stood for a moment in thought. Again his eyes twinkled. The next was very cunning—

"Hm! . . . *I think I'll read for a quarter of an hour,*" he said aloud. . . .

He passed out of the room.

He was away a couple of minutes; when he returned again the room was suddenly quiet. He glanced at the chest of drawers; the comb lay still, between the collar he had removed and a pair of gloves. Without hesitation Oleron put out his hand and picked it up. It was an ordinary eighteen-penny comb, taken from a card in a chemist's shop, of a substance of a definite specific gravity, and no more capable of rebellion against the Laws by which it existed than are the worlds that keep their orbits through the void. Oleron put it down again; then he glanced at the bundle of papers he held in his hand. What he had gone to fetch had been the fifteen chapters of the original *Romilly*.

"Hm!" he muttered as he threw the manuscript into a chair. . . . "As I thought. . . . She's just blindly, ragingly, murderously jealous."

On the night after that, and on the following night, and for many nights and days, so many that he began to be uncertain about the count of them, Oleron, courting, cajoling, neglecting, threatening, beseeching, eaten out with unappeased curiosity and regardless that his life was becoming one consuming passion and desire, continued his search for the unknown co-numerator of his abode.

X

As time went on, it came to pass that few except the postman mounted Oleron's stairs; and since men who do not write letters receive few, even the postman's tread became so infrequent that it was not heard more than once or twice a week. There came a letter from Oleron's publishers, asking when they might expect to receive the manuscript of his new book; he delayed for some days to answer it, and finally forgot it. A second letter came, which also he failed to answer. He received no third.

The weather grew bright and warm. The privet bushes among the chopper-like notice-boards flowered, and in the streets where Oleron did his shopping the baskets of flower-women lined the kerbs. Oleron purchased flowers daily; his room clamoured for flowers, fresh and continually renewed; and Oleron did not stint its demands. Nevertheless, the necessity for going out to buy them began to irk him more and more, and it was with a greater and ever greater sense of relief that he returned home again. He began to be conscious that again his scale of sensation had suffered a subtle change—a change that was not restoration to its former capacity, but an extension and enlarging that once more included terror. It admitted it in an entirely new form. *Lux orco, tenebræ, Jovi.* The name of this terror was agoraphobia. Oleron had begun to dread air and space and the horror that might pounce upon the unguarded back.

Presently he so contrived it that his food and flowers were delivered daily at his door. He rubbed his hands when he had hit upon this expedient. That was better! Now he could please himself whether he went out or not. . . .

Quickly he was confirmed in his choice. It became his pleasure to remain immured.

But he was not happy—or, if he was, his happiness took an extraordinary turn. He fretted discontentedly, could sometimes have wept for mere weakness and misery; and yet he was dimly conscious that he would not have exchanged his sadness for all the noisy mirth of the world outside. And speaking of noise: noise, much noise, now caused him the acutest discomfort. It was hardly more to be endured than that new-born fear that kept him, on the increasingly rare occasions when he did go out, sidling close to walls and feeling friendly railings with his hand. He moved from room to room softly and in slippers, and sometimes stood for many seconds closing a door so gently that not a sound broke the stillness that was in itself a delight. Sunday now became an intolerable day to him, for, since the coming of the fine weather, there had begun to assemble in the square under his windows each Sunday morning certain members of the sect to which the long-nosed Barrett adhered. These came with a great drum and large brass-bellied instruments; men and women uplifted anguished voices, struggling with their God; and Barrett himself, with upraised face and closed eyes and working brows, prayed that the sound of his voice might penetrate the ears of all unbelievers—as it certainly did Oleron's. One day, in the middle of one of these rhapsodies, Oleron sprang to his blind and pulled it down, and heard as he did so, his own name made the object of a fresh torrent of outpouring.

And sometimes, but not as expecting a reply, Oleron stood still and called softly. Once or twice he called "Romilly!" and then waited; but more often his whispering did not take the shape of a name.

There was one spot in particular of his abode that he began to haunt with increasing persistency. This was just within the opening of his bedroom door. He had discovered one day that by opening every door in his place (always excepting the outer one, which he only opened unwillingly) and by placing himself on this particular spot, he could actually see to a greater or less extent into each of his five rooms without changing his position. He could see the whole of his sitting-room, all of his bedroom except the part hidden by the open door, and glimpses of his kitchen, bathroom, and of his rarely used study. He was often in this place, breathless and with his finger on his lip. One day, as he stood there, he suddenly found himself wondering whether this Madley, of whom the vicar had spoken, had ever discovered the strategic importance of the bedroom entry.

Light, moreover, now caused him greater disquietude than did darkness. Direct sunlight, of which, as the sun passed daily round the house, each of his rooms had now its share, was like a flame in his brain; and even diffused light was a dull and numbing ache. He began, at successive hours of the day, one after another, to lower his crimson blinds. He made short and daring excursions in order to do this; but he was ever careful to leave his retreat open, in case he should have sudden need of it. Presently this lowering of the blinds had become a daily methodical exercise, and his rooms, when he had been his round, had the blood-red half-light of a photographer's dark-room.

One day, as he drew down the blind of his little study and backed in good order out of the room again, he broke into a soft laugh.

"*That* bilks Mr. Barrett!" he said; and the baffling of Barrett continued to afford him mirth for an hour.

But on another day, soon after, he had a fright that left him trembling also for an hour. He had seized the cord to darken the window over the seat in which he had found the harp-bag, and was standing with his back well protected in the embrasure, when he thought he saw the tail of a black-and-white check skirt disappear round the corner of the house. He could not be sure—had he run to the window of the other wall, which was blinded, the skirt must have been already past—but he was *almost* sure that it was Elsie. He listened in an agony of suspense for her tread on the stairs. . . .

But no tread came, and after three or four minutes he drew a long breath of relief.

"By Jove, but that would have compromised me horribly!" he muttered. . . .

And he continued to mutter from time to time, "Horribly compromising . . . *no* woman would stand that . . . not *any* kind of woman . . . oh, compromising in the extreme!"

Yet he was not happy. He could not have assigned the cause of the fits of quiet weeping which took him sometimes; they came and went, like the fitful illumination of the clouds that travelled over the square; and perhaps, after all, if he was not happy, he was not unhappy. Before he could be unhappy something must have been withdrawn, and nothing had been granted. He was waiting for that granting, in that flower-laden, frightfully enticing apartment of his, with the pith-white walls tinged and subdued by the crimson blinds to a blood-like gloom.

He paid no heed to it that his stock of money was running perilously low, nor that he had ceased to work. Ceased to work? He had not ceased to work. They knew very little about it who supposed that Oleron had ceased to work! He was in truth only now beginning to work. He was preparing such a work . . . such a work . . . such a Mistress was a-making in the gestation of his Art . . . let him but get this period of probation and poignant waiting over and men should see. . . . How *should* men know her, this Fair One of Oleron's, until Oleron himself knew her? Lovely radiant creations are not thrown off like How-d'ye-do's. The men to whom it is committed to father them must weep wretched tears, as Oleron did, must swell with vain presumptuous hopes, as Oleron did, must pursue, as Oleron pursued, the capricious, fair, mocking, slippery, eager Spirit that, ever eluding, ever sees to it that the chase does not slacken. Let Oleron but hunt this Huntress a little longer . . . he would have her sparkling and panting in his arms yet. . . . Oh no: they were very far from the truth who supposed that Oleron had ceased to work!

And if all else was falling away from Oleron, gladly he was letting it go. So do we all when our Fair Ones beckon. Quite at the beginning we wink, and promise ourselves that we will put Her Ladyship through her paces, neglect her for a day, turn her own jealous wiles against her, flout and ignore her when she comes wheedling; perhaps there lurks within us all the time a heartless sprite who is never fooled; but in the end all falls away. She beckons, beckons, and all goes. . . .

And so Oleron kept his strategic post within the frame of his bedroom door, and watched, and waited, and smiled, with his finger on his lips. . . . It was his duteous service, his worship, his troth-plighting, all that he had ever known of Love. And when he found himself, as he now and then did, hating the dead man Madley, and wishing that he had never lived, he felt that that, too, was an acceptable service. . . .

But, as he thus prepared himself, as it were, for a Marriage, and moped and chafed more and more that the Bride made no sign, he made a discovery that he ought to have made weeks before.

It was through a thought of the dead Madley that he made it. Since that night when he had thought in his greenness that a little studied neglect would bring the lovely Beckoner to her knees, and had made use of her own jealousy to banish her, he had not set eyes on those fifteen discarded chapters of *Romilly*. He had thrown them back into the window-seat, forgotten their very existence. But his own jealousy of Madley put him in mind of hers of her jilted rival of flesh and blood, and he remembered them. . . . Fool that he had been! Had he, then, expected his Desire to manifest herself while there still existed the evidence of his divided allegiance? What, and she with a passion so fierce and centred that it had not hesitated at the destruction, twice attempted, of her rival? Fool that he had been! . . .

But if *that* was all the pledge and sacrifice she required she should have it—ah, yes, and quickly!

He took the manuscript from the window-seat, and brought it to the fire.

He kept his fire always burning now; the warmth brought

out the last vestige of odour of the flowers with which his room was banked. He did not know what time it was; long since he had allowed his clock to run down—it had seemed a foolish measurer of time in regard to the stupendous things that were happening to Oleron; but he knew it was late. He took the *Romilly* manuscript and knelt before the fire.

But he had not finished removing the fastening that held the sheets together before he suddenly gave a start, turned his head over his shoulder, and listened intently. The sound he had heard had not been loud—it had been, indeed, no more than a tap, twice or thrice repeated—but it had filled Oleron with alarm. His face grew dark as it came again.

He heard a voice outside on his landing.

"Paul! . . . Paul! . . . "

It was Elsie's voice.

"Paul! . . . I know you're in . . . I want to see you. . . ."

He cursed her under his breath, but kept perfectly still. He did not intend to admit her.

"Paul! . . . You're in trouble. . . . I believe you're in danger . . . at least come to the door! . . ."

Oleron smothered a low laugh. It somehow amused him that she, in such danger herself, should talk to him of *his* danger! . . . Well, if she was, serve her right; she knew, or said she knew, all about it. . . .

"Paul! . . . Paul! . . ."

"*Paul! . . . Paul!* . . . " He mimicked her under his breath.

"Oh, Paul, it's *horrible!* . . . "

Horrible, was it? thought Oleron. Then let her get away. . . .

"I only want to help you, Paul. . . . I didn't promise not to come if you needed me. . . ."

He was impervious to the pitiful sob that interrupted the low cry. The devil take the woman! Should he shout to her to go away and not come back? No: let her call and knock and sob. She had a gift for sobbing; she mustn't think her sobs would move him. They irritated him, so that he set his teeth and shook his fist at her, but that was all. Let her sob.

"Paul! . . . Paul! . . ."

With his teeth hard set, he dropped the first page of *Romilly* into the fire. Then he began to drop the rest in, sheet by sheet.

For many minutes the calling behind his door continued; then suddenly it ceased. He heard the sound of feet slowly descending the stairs. He listened for the noise of a fall or a cry or the crash of a piece of the handrail of the upper landing; but none of these things came. She was spared. Apparently her rival suffered her to crawl abject and beaten away. Oleron heard the passing of her steps under his window; then she was gone.

He dropped the last page into the fire, and then, with a low laugh rose. He looked fondly round his room.

"Lucky to get away like that," he remarked. "She wouldn't have got away if I'd given her as much as a word or a look! What devils these women are! . . . But no; I oughtn't to say that; one of 'em showed forbearance. . . ."

Who showed forbearance? And what was forborne? Ah, Oleron knew! . . . Contempt, no doubt, had been at the bottom of it, but that didn't matter: the pestering creature had been allowed to go unharmed. Yes, she was lucky; Oleron hoped she knew it. . . .

And now, now, now for his reward!

Oleron crossed the room. All his doors were open; his eyes shone as he placed himself within that of his bedroom.

Fool that he had been, not to think of destroying the manuscript sooner! . . .

How, in a houseful of shadows, should he know his own Shadow? How, in a houseful of noises, distinguish the summons he felt to be at hand? Ah, trust him! He would know! The place was full of a jugglery of dim lights. The blind at his elbow that allowed the light of a street lamp to struggle vaguely through—the glimpse of greeny blue moonlight seen through the distant kitchen door—the sulky glow of the fire under the black ashes of the burnt manuscript—the glimmering of the tulips and the moon-daisies and narcissi in bowls and jugs and jars—these did not so trick and bewilder his eyes that he would not know his

Own! It was he, not she, who had been delaying the shadowy Bridal; he hung his head for a moment in mute acknowledgment; then he bent his eyes on the deceiving, puzzling gloom again. He would have called her name had he known it—but now he would not ask her to share even a name with the other. . . .

His own face, within the frame of the door, glimmered white as the narcissi in the darkness. . . .

A shadow, light as fleece, seemed to take shape in the kitchen (the time had been when Oleron would have said that a cloud had passed over the unseen moon). The low illumination on the blind at his elbow grew dimmer (the time had been when Oleron would have concluded that the lamplighter going his rounds had turned low the flame of the lamp). The fire settled, letting down the black and charred papers; a flower fell from a bowl, and lay indistinct upon the floor; all was still; and then a stray draught moved through the old house, passing before Oleron's face. . . .

Suddenly, inclining his head, he withdrew a little from the door-jamb. The wandering draught caused the door to move a little on its hinges. Oleron trembled violently, stood for a moment longer, and then, putting his hand out to the knob, softly drew the door to, sat down on the nearest chair, and waited, as a man might await the calling of his name that should summon him to some weighty, high and privy Audience. . . .

XI

One knows not whether there can be human compassion for anæmia of the soul. When the pitch of Life is dropped, and the spirit is so put over and reversed that that only is horrible which before was sweet and worldly and of the day, the human relation disappears. The sane soul turns appalled away, lest not merely itself, but sanity should suffer. We are not gods. We cannot drive out devils. We must see selfishly to it that devils do not enter into ourselves.

And this we must do even though Love so transfuse us that we may well deem our nature to be half divine. We shall but speak of honour and duty in vain. The letter dropped within the dark door will lie unregarded, or, if regarded for a brief instant between two unspeakable lapses, left and forgotten again. The telegram will be undelivered, nor will the whistling messenger (wiselier guided than he knows to whistle) be conscious as he walks away of the drawn blind that is pushed aside an inch by a finger and then fearfully replaced again. No: let the miserable wrestle with his own shadows, let him, if indeed he be so mad, clip and strain and enfold and couch the succubus; but let him do so in a house into which not an air of Heaven penetrates, nor a bright finger of the sun pierces the filthy twilight. The lost must remain lost. Humanity has other business to attend to.

For the handwriting of the two letters that Oleron, stealing noiselessly one June day into his kitchen to rid his sitting-room of an armful of fætid and decaying flowers, had seen on the floor within his door, had had no more meaning for him than if it had belonged to some dim and far-away dream. And at the beating of the telegraph-boy upon the door, within a few feet of the bed where he lay, he had gnashed his teeth and stopped his ears. He had pictured the lad standing there, just beyond his partition, among packets of provisions and bundles of dead and dying flowers. For his outer landing was littered with these. Oleron had feared to open his door to take them in. After a week, the errand lads had reported that there must be some mistake about the order, and had left no more. Inside, in the red twilight, the old flowers turned brown and fell and decayed where they lay.

Gradually his power was draining away. The Abomination fastened on Oleron's power. The steady sapping sometimes left him for many hours of prostration gazing vacantly up at his red-tinged ceiling, idly suffering such fancies as came of themselves to have their way with him. Even the strongest of his memories had no more than a precarious hold upon his attention. Sometimes a flitting half-memory, of a novel to be written, a novel it was important that he should write, tantalised him for a space before vanishing again; and sometimes whole novels, perfect, splendid, established to endure, rose magically before him. And sometimes the memories were absurdly remote and trivial, of garrets he had inhabited and lodgings that had sheltered him, and so forth. Oleron had known a good deal about such things in his time, but all that was now past. He had at last found a place which he did not intend to leave until they fetched him out—a place that some might have thought a little on the green-sick side, that others might have considered to be a little too redolent of long-dead and morbid things for a living man to be mewed up in, but ah, so irresistible, with such an authority of its own, with such an associate of its own, and a place of such delights when once a man had ceased to struggle against its inexorable will! A novel? Somebody ought to write a novel about a place like that! There must be lots to write about in a place like that if one could but get to the bottom of it! It had probably already been painted, by a man called Madley who had lived there . . . but Oleron had not known this Madley—had a strong feeling that he wouldn't have liked him—would rather he had lived somewhere else—really couldn't stand the fellow—hated him, Madley, in fact. (Aha! That was a joke!) He seriously doubted whether the man had led the life he ought; Oleron was in two minds sometimes whether he wouldn't tell that long-nosed guardian of the public morals across the way about him; but probably he knew, and had made his praying hullabaloos for him also. That was his line. Why, Oleron himself had had a dust-up with him about something or other . . . some girl or other . . . Elsie Bengough her name was, he remembered. . . .

Oleron had moments of deep uneasiness about this Elsie Bengough. Or rather, he was not so much uneasy about her as restless about the things she did. Chief of these was the way in which she persisted in thrusting herself into his thoughts; and, whenever he was quick enough, he sent her packing the moment she made her appearance there. The truth was that she was not merely a bore; she had always been that; it had now come to the pitch when her very presence in his fancy was inimical to the full enjoyment of certain experiences. . . . She had no tact; really ought to have known that people are not at home to the thoughts of everybody all the time; ought in mere politeness to have allowed him certain seasons quite to himself; and was monstrously ignorant of things if she did not know, as she appeared not to know, that there were certain special hours when a man's veins ran with fire and daring and power, in which . . . well, in which he had a reasonable right to treat folk as he had treated that prying Barrett—to shut them out completely. . . . But no, up she popped: the thought of her, and ruined all. Bright towering fabrics, by the side of which even those perfect, magical novels of which he dreamed were dun and grey, vanished utterly at her intrusion. It was as if a fog should suddenly quench some fair-beaming star, as if at the threshold of some golden portal prepared for Oleron a pit should suddenly gape, as if a bat-like shadow should turn the growing dawn to mirk and darkness again. . . . Therefore, Oleron strove to stifle even the nascent thought of her.

Nevertheless, there came an occasion on which this woman Bengough absolutely refused to be suppressed. Oleron could not have told exactly when this happened; he only knew by the glimmer of the street lamp on his blind that it was some time during the night, and that for some time she had not presented herself.

He had no warning, none, of her coming; she just came—was there. Strive as he would, he could not shake off the thought of her nor the image of her face. She haunted him.

But for her to come at *that* moment of all moments! . . . Really, it was past belief! How *she* could endure it, Oleron could not conceive! Actually, to look on, as it were, at the triumph of a Rival. . . . Good God! It was monstrous! Tact—reticence—he had never credited her with an overwhelming amount of either: but he had never attributed mere—oh, there was no word for it! Monstrous—monstrous! Did she intend thenceforward. . . . Good God! To look on! . . .

Oleron felt the blood rush up to the roots of his hair with anger against her.

"Damnation take her!" he choked. . . .

But the next moment his heat and resentment had changed to a cold sweat of cowering fear. Panic-stricken, he strove to comprehend what he had done. For though he knew not what, he knew he had done something, something fatal, irreparable, blasting. Anger he had felt, but not *this* blaze of ire that suddenly flooded the twilight of his consciousness with a white infernal light. *That* appalling flash was not his—not his *that* open rift of bright and searing Hell—not his, not his! His had been the hand of a child, preparing a puny blow; but what was *this other* horrific hand that was drawn back to strike in the same place? Had *he* set that in motion? Had *he* provided the spark that had touched off the whole accumulated power of that formidable and relentless place? He did not know. He only knew that that poor igniting particle in himself was blown out, that—Oh, impossible!—a clinging kiss (how else to express it?) had changed on his very lips to a gnashing and a removal, and that for very pity of the awful odds he must cry out to her against whom he had lately raged to guard herself . . . guard herself. . . .

"*Look out!*" he shrieked aloud. . . .

The revulsion was instant. As if a cold slow billow had broken over him, he came to to find that he was lying in his bed, that the mist and horror that had for so long enwrapped him had departed, that he was Paul Oleron, and that he was sick, naked, helpless, and unutterably abandoned and alone. His faculties, though weak, answered at last to his calls upon them; and he knew that it must have been a hideous nightmare that had left him sweating and shaking thus.

Yes, he was himself, Paul Oleron, a tired novelist, already past the summit of his best work, and slipping downhill again empty-handed from it all. He had struck short in his life's aim. He had tried too much, had over-estimated his strength, and was a failure, a failure. . . .

It all came to him in the single word, enwrapped and complete; it needed no sequential thought; he was a failure. He had missed. . . .

And he had missed not one happiness, but two. He had missed the ease of this world, which men love, and he had missed also that other shining prize for which men forgo ease, the snatching and holding and triumphant bearing up aloft of which is the only justification of the mad adventurer who hazards the enterprise. And there was no second attempt. Fate has no morrow. Oleron's morrow must be to sit down to profitless, ill-done, unrequired work again, and so on the morrow after that, and the morrow after that, and as many morrows as there might be. . . .

He lay there, weakly yet sanely considering it. . . .

And since the whole attempt had failed, it was hardly worth while to consider whether a little might not be saved from the general wreck. No good would ever come of that half-finished novel. He had intended that it should appear in the autumn; was under contract that it should appear; no matter; it was better to pay forfeit to his publishiers than to waste what days were left. He was spent; age was not far off; and paths of wisdom and sadness were the properest for the remainder of the journey. . . .

If only he had chosen the wife, the child, the faithful friend at the fireside, and let them follow an *ignis fatuus* that list! . . .

In the meantime it began to puzzle him exceedingly why he should be so weak, that his room should smell so overpoweringly of decaying vegetable matter, and that his hand, chancing to stray to his face in the darkness, should encounter a beard.

"Most extraordinary!" he began to mutter to himself. "Have I been ill? Am I ill now? And if so, why have they left me alone? . . . Extraordinary! . . ."

He thought he heard a sound from the kitchen or bathroom. He rose a little on his pillow, and listened . . . Ah! He was not alone, then! It certainly would have been extraordinary if they had left him ill and alone—Alone? Oh no. He would be looked after. He wouldn't be left, ill, to shift for himself. If everybody else had forsaken him, he could trust Elsie Bengough, the dearest chum he had, for that . . . bless her faithful heart!

But suddenly a short, stifled, spluttering cry rang sharply out:

"Paul!"

It came from the kitchen.

And in the same moment it flashed upon Oleron, he knew not how, that two, three, five, he knew not how many minutes before, another sound, unmarked at the time but suddenly transfixing his attention now, had striven to reach his intelligence. This sound had been the slight touch of metal on metal—just such a sound as Oleron made when he put his key into the lock.

"Hallo! . . . Who's that?" he called sharply from his bed.

He had no answer.

He called again. "Hallo! . . . Who's there? . . . Who is it?"

This time he was sure he heard noises, soft and heavy, in the kitchen.

"This is a queer thing altogether," he muttered. "By Jove, I'm as weak as a kitten too. . . . Hallo, there! Somebody called, didn't they? . . . Elsie! Is that you? . . ."

Then he began to knock with his hand on the wall at the side of his bed.

"Elsie! . . . Elsie! . . . You called, didn't you? . . . Please come here, whoever it is! . . ."

There was a sound as of a closing door, and then silence. Oleron began to get rather alarmed.

"It may be a nurse," he muttered; "Elsie'd have to get me a nurse, of course. She'd sit with me as long as she could spare the time, brave lass, and she'd get a nurse for the rest. . . . But it was awfully like her voice. . . . Elsie, or whoever it is! . . . I can't make this out at all. I must go and see what's the matter. . . ."

He put one leg out of bed. Feeling its feebleness, he reached with his hand for the additional support of the wall. . . .

But before putting out the other leg he stopped and considered, picking at his new-found beard. He was suddenly wondering whether he *dared* go into the kitchen. It was such a frightfully long way; no man knew what horror might not leap and huddle on his shoulders if he went so far; when a man has an overmastering impulse to get back into bed he ought to take heed of the warning and obey it. Besides, why should he go? What was there to go for?

If it was that Bengough creature again, let her look after herself; Oleron was not going to have things cramp themselves on his defenceless back for the sake of such a spoilsport as *she!* . . . If she was in, let her let herself out again, and the sooner the better for her! Oleron simply couldn't be bothered. He had his work to do. On the morrow, he must set about the writing of a novel with a heroine so winsome, capricious, adorable, jealous, wicked, beautiful, inflaming, and altogether evil, that men should stand amazed. She was coming over him now; he knew by the alteration of the very air of the room when she was near him; and that soft thrill of bliss that had begun to stir in him never came unless she was beckoning, beckoning. . . .

He let go the wall and fell back into bed again as—oh, unthinkable!—the other half of that kiss that a gnash had interrupted was placed (how else convey it?) on his lips, robbing him of very breath. . . .

XII

In the bright June sunlight a crowd filled the square, and looked up at the windows of the old house with the antique insurance marks in its walls of red brick and the agents' notice-boards hanging like wooden choppers over the paling. Two constables stood at the broken gate of the narrow entrance-alley, keeping folk back. The women kept to the outskirts of the throng, moving now and then as if to see the drawn red blinds of the old house from a new angle, and talking in whispers. The children were in the houses, behind closed doors.

A long-nosed man had a little group about him, and he was telling some story over and over again; and another man, little and fat and wide-eyed, sought to capture the long-nosed man's audience with some relation in which a key figured.

". . . it was revealed to me that there'd been something that very afternoon," the long-nosed man was saying. "I was standing there, where Constable Saunders is—or rather, I was passing about my business, when they came out. There was no deceiving me, oh, no deceiving *me!* I saw her face. . . ."

"What was it like, Mr. Barrett?" a man asked.

"It was like hers whom our Lord said to, 'Woman, doth any man accuse thee?'—white as paper, and no mistake! Don't tell *me*! . . . And so I walks straight across to Mrs. Barrett, and 'Jane,' I says, 'this must stop, and stop at once; we are commanded to avoid evil,' I says, 'and it must come to an end now; let him get help elsewhere.' And she says to me, 'John,' she says, 'it's four-and-sixpence a week'—them was her words. 'Jane,' I says, 'if it was forty-six thousand pounds it should stop' . . . and from that day to this she hasn't set foot inside that gate."

There was a short silence: then,

"Did Mrs. Barrett ever . . . *see* anything, like?" somebody vaguely inquired.

Barrett turned austerely on the speaker.

"What Mrs. Barrett saw and Mrs. Barrett didn't see shall not pass these lips; even as it is written, keep thy tongue from speaking evil," he said.

Another man spoke.

"He was pretty near canned up in the Waggon and Horses that night, weren't he, Jim?"

"Yes, 'e 'adn't 'alf copped it. . . ."

"Not standing treat much, neither; he was in the bar, all on his own. . . ."

"So 'e was; we talked about it. . . ."

The fat, scared-eyed man made another attempt.

"She got the key off of me—she 'ad the number of it—she came into my shop of a Tuesday evening. . . ."

Nobody heeded him.

"Shut your heads," a heavy labourer commented gruffly, "she hasn't been found yet. 'Ere's the inspectors; we shall know more in a bit."

Two inspectors had come up and were talking to the constables who guarded the gate. The little fat man ran eagerly forward, saying that she had bought the key off him. "I remember the number, because of its being three one's and three three's—111333!" he exclaimed excitedly.

An inspector put him aside.

"Nobody's been in?" he asked of one of the constables.

"No, sir."

"Then you, Brackley, come with us; you, Smith, keep the gate. There's a squad on its way."

The two inspectors and the constable passed down the alley and entered the house. They mounted the wide carved staircase.

"This don't look as if he'd been out much lately," one of the inspectors muttered as he kicked aside a litter of dead leaves and paper that lay outside Oleron's door. "I don't think we need knock—break a pane, Brackley."

The door had two glazed panels; there was a sound of shattered glass; and Brackley put his hand through the hole his elbow had made and drew back the latch.

"Faugh! . . ." choked one of the inspectors as they entered. "Let some light and air in, quick. It stinks. Like a hearse—"

The assembly out in the square saw the red blinds go up and the windows of the old house flung open.

"That's better," said one of the inspectors, putting his head out of a window and drawing a deep breath. . . ."That seems to be the bedroom in there; will you go in, Simms, while I go over the rest? . . ."

They had drawn up the bedroom blind also, and the waxy-white, emaciated man on the bed had made a blinker of his hand against the torturing flood of brightness. Nor could he believe that his hearing was not playing tricks with him, for there were two policemen in his room, bending over him and asking where "she" was. He shook his head.

"This woman Bengough . . . goes by the name of Miss Elsie Bengough . . . d'ye hear? Where is she? . . . No good, Brackley; get him up; be careful with him; I'll just shove *my* head out of the window, I think. . . ."

The other inspector had been through Oleron's study and had found nothing, and was now in the kitchen, kicking aside an ankle-deep mass of vegetable refuse that cumbered the floor. The kitchen window had no blind, and was overshadowed by the blank end of the house across the alley. The kitchen appeared to be empty.

But the inspector, kicking aside the dead flowers, noticed that a shuffling track that was not of his making had been swept to a cupboard in the corner. In the upper part of the door of the cupboard was a square panel that looked as if it slid on runners. The door itself was closed.

The inspector advanced, put out his hand to the little knob, and slid the hatch along its groove.

Then he took an involuntary step back again.

Framed in the aperture, and falling forward a little before it jammed again in its frame, was something that resembled a large lumpy pudding, done up in a pudding-bag of faded browny red frieze.

"Ah!" said the inspector.

To close the hatch again he would have had to thrust that pudding back with his hand; and somehow he did not quite like the idea of touching it. Instead, he turned the handle of the cupboard itself. There was weight behind it, so much weight that, after opening the door three or four inches and peering inside, he had to put his shoulder to it in order to close it again. In closing it he left sticking out, a few inches from the floor, a triangle of black and white check skirt.

He went into the small hall.

"All right!" he called.

They had got Oleron into his clothes. He still used his hands as blinkers, and his brain was very confused. A number of things were happening that he couldn't understand. He couldn't understand the extraordinary mess of dead flowers there seemed to be everywhere; he couldn't understand why there should be police officers in his room; he couldn't understand why one of these should be sent for a four-wheeler and a stretcher; and he couldn't understand what heavy article they seemed to be moving about in the kitchen—his kitchen. . . .

"What's the matter?" he muttered sleepily. . . .

Then he heard a murmur in the square, and the stopping of

a four-wheeler outside. A police officer was at his elbow again, and Oleron wondered why, when he whispered something to him, he should run off a string of words—something about "used in evidence against you." They had lifted him to his feet, and were assisting him towards the door. . . .

No, Oleron couldn't understand it at all.

They got him down the stairs and along the alley. Oleron was aware of confused angry shoutings; he gathered that a number of people wanted to lynch somebody or other. Then his attention became fixed on a little fat frightened-eyed man who appeared to be making a statement that an officer was taking down in a notebook.

"I'd seen her with him . . . they was often together . . . she came into my shop and said it was for him . . . I thought it was all right . . . 111333 the number was," the man was saying.

The people seemed to be very angry; many police were keeping them back; but one of the inspectors had a voice that Oleron thought quite kind and friendly. He was telling somebody to get somebody else into the cab before something or other was brought out; and Oleron noticed that a four-wheeler was drawn up at the gate. It appeared that it was himself who was to be put into it; and as they lifted him up he saw that the inspector tried to stand between him and something that stood behind the cab, but was not quick enough to prevent Oleron seeing that this something was a hooded stretcher. The angry voices sounded like a sea; something hard, like a stone, hit the back of the cab; and the inspector followed Oleron in and stood with his back to the window nearer the side where the people were. The door they had put Oleron in at remained open, apparently till the other inspector should come; and through the opening Oleron had a glimpse of the hatchet-like "To Let" boards among the privet-trees. One of them said that the key was at Number Six. . . .

Suddenly the raging of voices was hushed. Along the entrance-alley shuffling steps were heard, and the other inspector appeared at the cab door.

"Right away," he said to the driver.

He entered, fastened the door after him, and blocked up the second window with his back. Between the two inspectors Oleron slept peacefully. The cab moved down the square, the other vehicle went up the hill. The mortuary lay that way.

THE CALL OF CTHULHU

H. P. Lovecraft

(1926)

Perhaps the greatest author of horror tales of the past hundred years, H. P. Lovecraft wrote a series of stories about encounters between unsuspecting humans and the horrific evil represented by the title character, the subject of the unearthly chant "In his house at R'lyeh dead Cthulhu waits dreaming."

I. The Horror in Clay

The most merciful thing in the world, I think, is the inability of the human mind to correlate all its contents. We live on a placid island of ignorance in the midst of black seas of infinity, and it was not meant that we should voyage far. The sciences, each straining in its own direction, have hitherto harmed us little; but some day the piecing together of dissociated knowledge will open up such terrifying vistas of reality, and of our frightful position therein, that we shall either go mad from the revelation or flee from the deadly light into the peace and safety of a new dark age.

Theosophists have guessed at the awesome grandeur of the cosmic cycle wherein our world and human race form transient incidents. They have hinted at strange survivals in terms which would freeze the blood if not masked by a bland optimism. But it is not from them that there came the single glimpse of forbidden aeons which chills me when I think of it and maddens me when I dream of it. That glimpse, like all dread glimpses of truth, flashed out from an accidental piecing together of separated things—in this case an old newspaper item and the notes of a dead professor. I hope that no one else will accomplish this piecing out; certainly, if I live, I shall never knowingly supply a link in so hideous a chain. I think that the professor, too, intended to keep silent regarding the part he knew, and that he would have destroyed his notes had not sudden death seized him.

My knowledge of the thing began in the winter of 1926-27 with the death of my grand-uncle George Gammell Angell, Professor Emeritus of Semitic Languages in Brown University, Providence, Rhode Island. Professor Angell was widely known as an authority on ancient inscriptions, and had frequently been resorted to by the heads of prominent museums; so that his passing at the age of ninety-two may be recalled by many. Locally, interest was intensified by the obscurity of the cause of death. The professor had been stricken whilst returning from the Newport boat; falling suddenly, as witnesses said, after having been jostled by a nautical-looking negro who had come from one of the queer dark courts on the precipitous hillside which formed a short cut from the waterfront to the deceased's home in Williams Street. Physicians were unable to find any visible disorder, but concluded after perplexed debate that some obscure lesion of the heart, induced by the brisk ascent of so steep a hill by so elderly a man, was responsible for the end. At the time I saw no reason to dissent from this dictum, but latterly I am inclined to wonder—and more than wonder.

As my grand-uncle's heir and executor, for he died a childless widower, I was expected to go over his papers with some thoroughness; and for that purpose moved his entire set of files and boxes to my quarters in Boston. Much of the material which I correlated will be later published by the American Archaeological Society, but there was one box which I found exceedingly puzzling, and which I felt much averse from shewing to other eyes. It had been locked, and I did not find the key till it occurred to me to examine the personal ring which the professor carried always in his pocket. Then indeed I succeeded in opening it, but when I did so seemed only to be confronted by a greater and more closely locked barrier. For what could be the meaning of the queer clay bas-relief and the disjointed jottings, ramblings, and cuttings which I found? Had my uncle, in his latter years, become credulous of the most superficial impostures? I resolved to search out the eccentric sculptor responsible for this apparent disturbance of an old man's peace of mind.

The bas-relief was a rough rectangle less than an inch thick and about five by six inches in area; obviously of modern origin. Its designs, however, were far from modern in atmosphere and suggestion; for although the vagaries of cubism and futurism are many and wild, they do not often reproduce that cryptic regularity which lurks in prehistoric writing. And writing of some kind the bulk of these designs seemed certainly to be; though my memory, despite much familiarity with the papers and collections of my uncle, failed in any way to identify this particular species, or even to hint at its remotest affiliations.

Above these apparent hieroglyphics was a figure of evidently pictorial intent, though its impressionistic execution forbade a very clear idea of its nature. It seemed to be a sort of monster, or symbol representing a monster, of a form which only a diseased fancy could conceive. If I say that my somewhat extravagant imagination yielded simultaneous pictures of an octopus, a dragon, and a human caricature, I shall not be unfaithful to the spirit of the thing. A pulpy, tentacled head surmounted a grotesque and scaly body with rudimentary wings; but it was the *general outline* of the whole which made it most shockingly frightful. Behind the figure was a vague suggestion of a Cyclopean architectural background.

The writing accompanying this oddity was, aside from a stack of press cuttings, in Professor Angell's most recent hand; and made no pretence to literary style. What seemed to be the main document was headed "CTHULHU CULT" in characters painstakingly printed to avoid the erroneous reading of a word so unheard-of. The manuscript was divided into two sections, the first of which was headed "1925—Dream and Dream Work of H. A. Wilcox, 7 Thomas St., Providence, R.I.", and the second, "Narrative of Inspector John R. Legrasse, 121 Bienville St., New Orleans, La., at 1908 A. A. S. Mtg.—Notes on Same, & Prof. Webb's Acct." The other manuscript papers were all brief notes, some of them accounts of the queer dreams of different persons, some of them citations from theosophical books and magazines (notably W. Scott-Elliot's *Atlantis and the Lost Lemuria*), and the rest comments on long-surviving secret societies and hidden cults, with references to passages in such mythological and anthropological source-books as Frazer's *Golden Bough* and Miss Murray's *Witch-Cult in Western Europe*. The cuttings largely alluded to outré mental illnesses and outbreaks of group folly or mania in the spring of 1925.

The first half of the principal manuscript told a very peculiar tale. It appears that on March 1st, 1925, a thin, dark young man of neurotic and excited aspect had called upon Professor Angell bearing the singular clay bas-relief, which was then exceedingly damp and fresh. His card bore the name of Henry Anthony Wilcox, and my uncle had recognised him as the youngest son of an excellent family slightly known to him, who had latterly been studying sculpture at the Rhode Island School of Design and living alone at the Fleur-de-Lys Building near that institution. Wilcox was a precocious youth of known genius but great eccentricity, and had from childhood excited attention through the strange stories and odd dreams he was in the habit of relating. He called himself "psychically hypersensitive," but the staid folk of the ancient commercial city dismissed him as merely "queer." Never mingling much with his kind, he had dropped gradually from social visibility, and was now known only to a small group of aesthetes from other towns. Even the Providence Art Club, anxious to preserve its conservatism, had found him quite hopeless.

On the occasion of the visit, ran the professor's manuscript, the sculptor abruptly asked for the benefit of his host's archaeological knowledge in identifying the hieroglyphics on the bas-relief. He spoke in a dreamy, stilted manner which suggested pose and alienated sympathy; and my uncle shewed some sharpness in replying, for the conspicuous freshness of the tablet implied kinship with anything but archaeology. Young Wilcox's rejoinder, which impressed my uncle enough to make him recall and record it verbatim, was of a fantastically poetic cast which must have typified his whole conversation, and which I have since found highly characteristic of him. He said, "It is new, indeed, for I made it last night in a dream of strange cities; and dreams are older then brooding Tyre, or the contemplative Sphinx, or garden-girdled Babylon."

It was then that he began that rambling tale which suddenly played upon a sleeping memory and won the fevered interest of my uncle. There had been a slight earthquake tremor the night before, the most considerable felt in New England for some years, and Wilcox's imagination had been keenly affected. Upon retiring, he had had an unprecedented dream of great Cyclopean cities of titan blocks and sky-flung monoliths, all dripping with green ooze and sinister with latent horror. Hieroglyphics had covered the walls and pillars, and from some undetermined point below had come a voice that was not a voice; a chaotic sensation which only fancy would transmute into sound, but which he attempted to render by the almost unpronounceable jumble of letters, "*Cthulhu fhtagn.*"

This verbal jumble was the key to the recollection which excited and disturbed Professor Angell. He questioned the sculptor with scientific minuteness; and studied with almost frantic intensity the bas-relief on which the youth had found himself working, chilled and clad only in his night-clothes, when waking had stolen bewilderingly over him. My uncle blamed his old age, Wilcox afterward said, for his slowness in recognising both hieroglyphics and pictorial design. Many of his questions seemed highly out-of-place to his visitor, especially those which tried to connect the latter with strange cults or societies; and Wilcox could not understand the repeated promises of silence which he was offered in exchange for an admission of membership in some widespread mystical or paganly religious body. When Professor Angell became convinced that the sculptor was indeed ignorant of any cult or system of cryptic lore, he besieged his visitor with demands for future reports of dreams. This bore regular fruit, for after the first interview the manuscript records daily calls of the young man, during which he related startling fragments of nocturnal imagery whose burden was always some terrible Cyclopean vista of dark and dripping stone, with a subterrene voice or intelligence shouting monotonously in enigmatical sense-impacts uninscribable save as gibberish. The two sounds most frequently repeated are those rendered by the letters *"Cthulhu"* and *"R'lyeh."*

On March 23d, the manuscript continued, Wilcox failed to appear; and inquiries at his quarters revealed that he had been stricken with an obscure sort of fever and taken to the home of his family in Waterman Street. He had cried out in the night, arousing several other artists in the building, and had manifested since then only alternations of unconsciousness and delirium. My uncle at once telephoned the family, and from that time forward kept close watch of the case; calling often at the Thayer Street office of Dr. Tobey, whom he learned to be in charge. The youth's febrile mind, apparently, was dwelling on strange things; and the doctor shuddered now and then as he spoke of them. They included not only a repetition of what he had formerly dreamed, but touched wildly on a gigantic thing "miles high" which walked or lumbered about. He at no time fully described this object, but occasional frantic words, as repeated by Dr. Tobey, convinced the professor that it must be identical with the nameless monstrosity he had sought to depict in his dream-sculpture. Reference to this object, the doctor added, was invariably a prelude to the young man's subsidence into lethargy. His temperature, oddly enough, was not greatly above normal; but his whole condition was otherwise such as to suggest true fever rather than mental disorder.

On April 2nd at about 3 p.m. every trace of Wilcox's malady suddenly ceased. He sat upright in bed, astonished to find himself at home and completely ignorant of what had happened in dream or reality since the night of March 22nd. Pronounced well by his physician, he returned to his quarters in three days; but to Professor Angell he was of no further assistance. All traces of strange dreaming had vanished with his recovery, and my uncle kept no record of his night-thoughts after a week of pointless and irrelevant accounts of thoroughly usual visions.

Here the first part of the manuscript ended, but references to certain of the scattered notes gave me much material for thought—so much, in fact, that only the ingrained scepticism then forming my philosophy can account for my continued distrust of the artist. The notes in question were those descriptive of the dreams of various persons covering the same period as that in which young Wilcox had had his strange visitations. My uncle, it seems, had quickly instituted a prodigiously far-flung body of inquiries amongst nearly all the friends whom he could question without impertinence, asking for nightly reports of their dreams, and the dates of any notable visions for some time past. The reception of his request seems to have been varied; but he must, at the very least, have received more responses than any ordinary man could have handled without a secretary. This original correspondence was not preserved, but his notes formed a thorough and really significant digest. Average people in society and business—New England's traditional "salt of the earth"—gave an almost completely negative result, though scattered cases of uneasy but formless nocturnal impressions appear here and there, always between March 23d and April 2nd—the period of young Wilcox's delirium. Scientific men were little more affected, though four cases of vague description suggest fugitive glimpses of strange landscapes, and in one case there is mentioned a dread of something abnormal.

It was from the artists and poets that the pertinent answers came, and I know that panic would have broken loose had they been able to compare notes. As it was, lacking their original letters, I half suspected the compiler of having asked leading questions, or of having edited the correspondence in corroboration of what he had latently resolved to see. That is why I continued to feel that Wilcox, somehow cognisant of the old data which my uncle had possessed, had been imposing on the veteran scientist. These responses from aesthetes told a disturbing tale. From February 28th to April 2nd a large proportion of them had dreamed very bizarre things, the intensity of the dreams being immeasurably the stronger during the period of the sculptor's delirium. Over a fourth of those who reported anything, reported scenes and half-sounds not unlike those which Wilcox had described; and some of the dreamers confessed acute fear of the gigantic nameless thing visible toward the last. One case, which the note describes with emphasis, was very sad. The subject, a widely known architect with leanings toward theosophy and occultism, went violently insane on the date of young Wilcox's seizure, and expired several months later after incessant screamings to be saved from some escaped denizen of hell. Had my uncle referred to these cases by name instead of merely by number, I should have attempted some corroboration and personal investigation; but as it was, I succeeded in tracing down only a few. All of these, however, bore out the notes in full. I have often wondered if all the objects of the professor's questioning felt as puzzled as did this fraction. It is well that no explanation shall ever reach them.

The press cuttings, as I have intimated, touched on cases of panic, mania, and eccentricity during the given period. Professor Angell must have employed a cutting bureau, for the number of extracts was tremendous and the sources scattered throughout the globe. Here was a nocturnal suicide in London, where a lone sleeper had leaped from a window after a shocking cry. Here likewise a rambling letter to the editor of a paper in South America where a fanatic deduces a dire future from visions he has seen. A despatch from California describes a theosophist colony as donning white robes en masse for some "glorious fulfilment" which never arrives, whilst items from India speak guardedly of serious native unrest toward the end of March. Voodoo orgies multiply in Hayti, and African outposts report ominous mutterings. American officers in the Philippines find certain tribes bothersome about this time, and New York policemen are mobbed by hysterical Levantines on the night of March 22–23. The west of Ireland, too, is full of wild rumour and legendry, and a fantastic painter named Ardois-Bonnot hangs a blasphemous "Dream Landscape" in the Paris spring salon of 1926. And so numerous are the recorded troubles in insane asylums, that only a miracle can have stopped the medical fraternity from noting strange parallelisms and drawing mystified conclusions. A weird bunch of cuttings, all told; and I can at this date scarcely envisage the callous rationalism with which I set them aside. But I was then convinced that young Wilcox had known of the older matters mentioned by the professor.

II. The Tale of Inspector Legrasse

The older matters which had made the sculptor's dream and bas-relief so significant to my uncle formed the subject of the second half of his long manuscript. Once before, it appears, Professor Angell had seen the hellish outlines of the nameless monstrosity, puzzled over the unknown hieroglyphics, and heard the ominous syllables which can be rendered only as "*Cthulhu*"; and all this in so stirring and horrible a connexion that it is small wonder he pursued young Wilcox with queries and demands for data.

The earlier experience had come in 1908, seventeen years before, when the American Archaeological Society held its annual meeting in St. Louis. Professor Angell, as befitted one of his authority and attainments, had had a prominent part in all the deliberations; and was one of the first to be approached by the several outsiders who took advantage of the convocation to offer questions for correct answering and problems for expert solution.

The chief of these outsiders, and in a short time the focus of interest for the entire meeting, was a commonplace-looking middle-aged man who had travelled all the way from New Orleans for certain special information unobtainable from any local source. His name was John Raymond Legrasse, and he was by profession an Inspector of Police. With him he bore the subject of his visit, a grotesque, repulsive, and apparently very ancient stone statuette whose origin he was at a loss to determine. It must not be fancied that Inspector Legrasse had the least interest in archaeology. On the contrary, his wish for enlightenment was prompted by purely professional considerations. The statuette, idol, fetish, or whatever it was, had been captured some months before in the wooded swamps south of New Orleans during a raid on a supposed voodoo meeting; and so singular and hideous were the rites connected with it, that the police could not but realise that they had stumbled on a dark cult totally unknown to them, and infinitely more diabolic than even the blackest of the African voodoo circles. Of its origin, apart from the erratic and unbelievable tales extorted from the captured members, absolutely nothing was to be discovered; hence the anxiety of the police for any antiquarian lore which might help them to place the frightful symbol, and through it track down the cult to its fountain-head.

Inspector Legrasse was scarcely prepared for the sensation which his offering created. One sight of the thing had been enough to throw the assembled men of science into a state of tense excitement, and they lost no time in crowding around him to gaze at the diminutive figure whose utter strangeness and air of genuinely abysmal antiquity hinted so potently at unopened and archaic vistas. No recognised school of sculpture had animated this terrible object, yet centuries and even thousands of years seemed recorded in its dim and greenish surface of unplaceable stone.

The figure, which was finally passed slowly from man to man for close and careful study, was between seven and eight inches in height, and of exquisitely artistic workmanship. It represented a monster of vaguely anthropoid outline, but with an octopus-like head whose face was a mass of feelers, a scaly, rubbery-looking body, prodigious claws on hind and fore feet, and long, narrow wings behind. This thing, which seemed instinct with a fearsome and unnatural malignancy, was of a somewhat bloated corpulence, and squatted evilly on a rectangular block or pedestal covered with undecipherable characters. The tips of the wings touched the back edge of the block, the seat occupied the centre, whilst the long, curved claws of the doubled-up, crouching hind legs gripped the front edge and extended a quarter of the way down toward the bottom of the pedestal. The cephalopod head was bent forward, so that the ends of the facial feelers brushed the backs of huge fore paws which clasped the croucher's elevated knees. The aspect of the whole was abnormally life-like, and the more subtly fearful because its source was so totally unknown. Its vast, awesome, and incalculable age was unmistakable; yet not one link did it shew with any known type of art belonging to civilisation's youth—or indeed to any other time. Totally separate and apart, its very material was a mystery; for the soapy, greenish-black stone with its golden or iridescent flecks and striations resembled nothing familiar to geology or mineralogy. The characters along the base were equally baffling; and no member present, despite a representation of half the world's expert learning in this field, could form the least notion of even the remotest linguistic kinship. They, like the subject and material, belonged to something horribly remote and distinct from mankind as we know it; something frightfully suggestive of old and unhallowed cycles of life in which our world and our conceptions have no part.

And yet, as the members severally shook their heads and confessed defeat at the Inspector's problem, there was one man in that gathering who suspected a touch of bizarre familiarity in the monstrous shape and writing, and who presently told with some diffidence of the odd trifle he knew. This person was the late William Channing Webb, Professor of Anthropology in Princeton University, and an explorer of no slight note. Professor Webb had been engaged, forty-eight years before, in a tour of Greenland and Iceland in search of some Runic inscriptions which he failed to unearth; and whilst high up on the West Greenland coast had encountered a singular tribe or cult of degenerate Esquimaux whose religion, a curious form of devil-worship, chilled him with its deliberate bloodthirstiness and repulsiveness. It was a faith of which other Esquimaux knew little, and which they mentioned only with shudders, saying that it had come down from horribly ancient aeons before ever the world was made. Besides nameless rites and human sacrifices there were certain queer hereditary rituals addressed to a supreme elder devil or *tornasuk*; and of this

Professor Webb had taken a careful phonetic copy from an aged *angekok* or wizard-priest, expressing the sounds in Roman letters as best he knew how. But just now of prime significance was the fetish which this cult had cherished, and around which they danced when the aurora leaped high over the ice cliffs. it was, the professor stated, a very crude bas-relief of stone, comprising a hideous picture and some cryptic writing. And so far as he could tell, it was a rough parallel in all essential features of the bestial thing now lying before the meeting.

This data, received with suspense and astonishment by the assembled members, proved doubly exciting to Inspector Legrasse; and he began at once to ply his informant with questions. Having noted and copied an oral ritual among the swamp cult-worshippers his men had arrested, he besought the professor to remember as best he might the syllables taken down amongst the diabolist Esquimaux. There then followed an exhaustive comparison of details, and a moment of really awed silence when both detective and scientist agreed on the virtual identity of the phrase common to two hellish rituals so many worlds of distance apart. What, in substance, both the Esquimau wizards and the Louisiana swamp-priests had chanted to their kindred idols was something very like this—the word-divisions being guessed at from traditional breaks in the phrase as chanted aloud:

"Ph'nglui mglw'nafh Cthulhu R'lyeh wgah'nagl fhtagn."

Legrasse had one point in advance of Professor Webb, for several among his mongrel prisoners had repeated to him what older celebrants had told them the words meant. This text, as given, ran something like this:

"In his house at R'lyeh dead Cthulhu waits dreaming."

And now, in response to a general and urgent demand, Inspector Legrasse related as fully as possible his experience with the swamp worshippers; telling a story to which I could see my uncle attached profound significance. It savoured of the wildest dreams of myth-maker and theosophist, and disclosed an astonishing degree of cosmic imagination among such half-castes and pariahs as might be expected to possess it.

On November 1st, 1907, there had come to the New Orleans police a frantic summons from the swamp and lagoon country to the south. The squatters there, mostly primitive but good-natured descendants of Lafitte's men, were in the grip of stark terror from an unknown thing which had stolen upon them in the night. It was voodoo, apparently, but voodoo of a more terrible sort than they had ever known; and some of their women and children had disappeared since the malevolent tom-tom had begun its incessant beating far within the black haunted woods where no dweller ventured. There were insane shouts and harrowing screams, soul-chilling chants and dancing devil-flames; and, the frightened messenger added, the people could stand it no more.

So a body of twenty police, filling two carriages and an automobile, had set out in the late afternoon with the shivering squatter as a guide. At the end of the passable road they alighted, and for miles splashed on in silence through the terrible cypress woods where day never came. Ugly roots and malignant hanging nooses of Spanish moss beset them, and now and then a pile of dank stones or fragment of a rotting wall intensified by its hint of morbid habitation a depression which every malformed tree and every fungous islet combined to create. At length the squatter settlement, a miserable huddle of huts, hove in sight; and hysterical dwellers ran out to cluster around the group of bobbing lanterns. The muffled beat of tom-toms was now faintly audible far, far ahead; and a curdling shriek came at infrequent intervals when the wind shifted. A reddish glare, too, seemed to filter through the pale undergrowth beyond endless avenues of forest night. Reluctant even to be left alone again, each one of the cowed squatters refused point-blank to advance another inch toward the scene of unholy worship, so Inspector Legrasse and his nineteen colleagues plunged on unguided into black arcades of horror that none of them had ever trod before.

The region now entered by the police was one of traditionally evil repute, substantially unknown and untraversed by white men. There were legends of a hidden lake unglimpsed by mortal sight, in which dwelt a huge, formless white polypous thing with luminous eyes; and squatters whispered that bat-winged devils flew up out of caverns in inner earth to worship it at midnight. They said it had been there before D'Iberville, before La Salle, before the Indians, and before even the wholesome beasts and birds of the woods. It was nightmare itself, and to see it was to die. But it made men dream, and so they knew enough to keep away. The present voodoo orgy was, indeed, on the merest fringe of this abhorred area, but that location was bad enough; hence perhaps the very place of the worship had terrified the squatters more than the shocking sounds and incidents.

Only poetry or madness could do justice to the noises heard by Legrasse's men as they ploughed on through the black morass toward the red glare and the muffled tom-toms. There are vocal qualities peculiar to men, and vocal qualities peculiar to beasts; and it is terrible to hear the one when the source should yield the other. Animal fury and orgiastic licence here whipped themselves to daemoniac heights by howls and squawking ecstasies that tore and reverberated through those nighted woods like pestilential tempests from the gulfs of hell. Now and then the less organised ululation would cease, and from what seemed a well-drilled chorus of hoarse voices would rise in sing-song chant that hideous phrase or ritual:

"Ph'nglui mglw'nafh Cthulhu R'lyeh wgah'nagl fhtagn."

Then the men, having reached a spot where the trees were thinner, came suddenly in sight of the spectacle itself. Four of them reeled, one fainted, and two were shaken into a frantic cry which the mad cacophony of the orgy fortunately deadened. Legrasse dashed swamp water on the face of the fainting man, and all stood trembling and nearly hypnotised with horror.

In a natural glade of the swamp stood a grassy island of perhaps an acre's extent, clear of trees and tolerably dry. On this now leaped and twisted a more indescribable horde of human abnormality than any but a Sime or an Angarola could paint. Void of clothing, this hybrid spawn were braying, bellowing, and writhing about a monstrous ring-shaped bonfire; in the centre of which, revealed by occasional rifts in the curtain of flame, stood a great granite monolith some eight feet in height; on top of which, incongruous with its diminutiveness, rested the noxious carven statuette. From a wide circle of ten scaffolds set up at regular intervals with the flame-girt monolith as a centre hung, head downward, the oddly marred bodies of the helpless squatters who had disappeared. It was inside this circle that the ring of worshippers jumped and roared, the general direction of the mass motion being from left to right in endless Bacchanal between the ring of bodies and the ring of fire.

It may have been only imagination and it may have been only echoes which induced one of the men, an excitable Spaniard, to fancy he heard antiphonal responses to the ritual from some far and unillumined spot deeper within the wood of ancient legendry and horror. This man, Joseph D. Galvez, I later met and questioned; and he proved distractingly imaginative. He indeed went so far as to hint of the faint beating of great wings, and of a glimpse of shining eyes and a mountainous white bulk beyond the remotest trees—but I suppose he had been hearing too much native superstition.

Actually, the horrified pause of the men was of comparatively brief duration. Duty came first; and although there must have been nearly a hundred mongrel celebrants in the throng, the police relied on their firearms and plunged determinedly into the nauseous rout. For five minutes the resultant din and chaos were beyond description. Wild blows were struck, shots were fired, and escapes were made; but in the end Legrasse was able to count some forty-seven sullen prisoners, whom he forced to dress in haste and fall into line between two rows of policemen. Five of the worshippers lay dead, and two severely wounded ones were carried away on improvised stretchers by their fellow-prisoners. The image on the monolith, of course, was carefully removed and carried back by Legrasse.

Examined at headquarters after a trip of intense strain and weariness, the prisoners all proved to be men of a very low, mixed-blooded, and mentally aberrant type. Most were seamen, and a sprinkling of negroes and mulattoes, largely West Indians or

Brava Portuguese from the Cape Verde Islands, gave a colouring of voodooism to the heterogeneous cult. But before many questions were asked, it became manifest that something far deeper and older than negro fetichism was involved. Degraded and ignorant as they were, the creatures held with surprising consistency to the central idea of their loathsome faith.

They worshipped, so they said, the Great Old Ones who lived ages before there were any men, and who came to the young world out of the sky. Those Old Ones were gone now, inside the earth and under the sea; but their dead bodies had told their secrets in dreams to the first men, who formed a cult which had never died. This was that cult, and the prisoners said it had always existed and always would exist, hidden in distant wastes and dark places all over the world until the time when the great priest Cthulhu, from his dark house in the mighty city of R'lyeh under the waters, should rise and bring the earth again beneath his sway. Some day he would call, when the stars were ready, and the secret cult would always be waiting to liberate him.

Meanwhile no more must be told. There was a secret which even torture could not extract. Mankind was not absolutely alone among the conscious things of earth, for shapes came out of the dark to visit the faithful few. But these were not the Great Old Ones. No man had ever seen the Old Ones. The carven idol was great Cthulhu, but none might say whether or not the others were precisely like him. No one could read the old writing now, but things were told by word of mouth. The chanted ritual was not the secret—that was never spoken aloud, only whispered. The chant meant only this: "In his house at R'lyeh dead Cthulhu waits dreaming."

Only two of the prisoners were found sane enough to be hanged, and the rest were committed to various institutions. All denied a part in the ritual murders, and averred that the killing had been done by Black Winged Ones which had come to them from their immemorial meeting-place in the haunted wood. But of those mysterious allies no coherent account could ever be gained. What the police did extract, came mainly from an immensely aged mestizo named Castro, who claimed to have sailed to strange ports and talked with undying leaders of the cult in the mountains of China.

Old Castro remembered bits of hideous legend that paled the speculations of theosophists and made man and the world seem recent and transient indeed. There had been aeons when other Things ruled on the earth, and They had had great cities. Remains of Them, he said the deathless Chinamen had told him, were still to be found as Cyclopean stones on islands in the Pacific. They all died vast epochs of time before men came, but there were arts which could revive Them when the stars had come round again to the right positions in the cycle of eternity. They had, indeed, come themselves from the stars, and brought Their images with Them.

These Great Old Ones, Castro continued, were not composed altogether of flesh and blood. They had shape—for did not this star-fashioned image prove it?—but that shape was not made of matter. When the stars were right, They could plunge from world to world through the sky; but when the stars were wrong, they could not live. But although They no longer lived, They would never really die. They all lay in stone houses in Their great city of R'lyeh, preserved by the spells of mighty Cthulhu for a glorious resurrection when the stars and the earth might once more be ready for Them. But at that time some force from outside must serve to liberate Their bodies. The spells that preserved Them intact likewise prevented Them from making an initial move, and They could only lie awake in the dark and think whilst uncounted millions of years rolled by. They knew all that was occurring in the universe, but Their mode of speech was transmitted thought. Even now They talked in Their tombs. When, after infinities of chaos, the first men came, the Great Old Ones spoke to the sensitive among them by moulding their dreams; for only thus could Their language reach the fleshly minds of mammals.

Then, whispered Castro, those first men formed the cult around small idols which the Great Ones shewed them; idols brought in dim aeras from dark stars. That cult would never die till the stars came right again, and the secret priests would take great Cthulhu from His tomb to revive His subjects and resume His rule of earth. The time would be easy to know, for then mankind would have become as the Great Old Ones; free and wild and beyond good and evil, with laws and morals thrown aside and all men shouting and killing and revelling in joy. Then the liberated Old Ones would teach them new ways to shout and kill and revel and enjoy themselves, and all the earth would flame with a holocaust of ecstasy and freedom. Meanwhile the cult, by appropriate rites, must keep alive the memory of those ancient ways and shadow forth the prophecy of their return.

In the elder time chosen men had talked with the entombed Old Ones in dreams, but then something had happened. The great stone city R'lyeh, with its monoliths and sepulchres, had sunk beneath the waves; and the deep waters, full of the one primal mystery through which not even thought can pass, had cut off the spectral intercourse. But memory never died, and high-priests said that the city would rise again when the stars were right. Then came out of the earth the black spirits of earth, mouldy and shadowy, and full of dim rumours picked up in caverns beneath forgotten sea-bottoms. But of them old Castro dared not speak much. He cut himself off hurriedly, and no amount of persuasion or subtlety could elicit more in this direction. The *size* of the Old Ones, too, he curiously declined to mention. Of the cult, he said that he thought the centre lay amid the pathless deserts of Arabia, where Irem, the City of Pillars, dreams hidden and untouched. It was not allied to the European witch-cult, and was virtually unknown beyond its members. No book had ever really hinted of it, though the deathless Chinamen said that there were double meanings in the *Necronomicon* of the mad Arab Abdul Alhazred which the initiated might read as they chose, especially the much-discussed couplet:

That is not dead which can eternal lie,
And with strange aeons even death may die.

Legrasse, deeply impressed and not a little bewildered, had inquired in vain concerning the historic affiliations of the cult. Castro, apparently, had told the truth when he said that it was wholly secret. The authorities at Tulane University could shed no light upon either cult or image, and now the detective had come to the highest authorities in the country and met with no more than the Greenland tale of Professor Webb.

The feverish interest aroused at the meeting by Legrasse's tale, corroborated as it was by the statuette, is echoed in the subsequent correspondence of those who attended; although scant mention occurs in the formal publications of the society. Caution is the first care of those accustomed to face occasional charlatanry and imposture. Legrasse for some time lent the image to Professor Webb, but at the latter's death it was returned to him and remains in his possession, where I viewed it not long ago. It is truly a terrible thing, and unmistakably akin to the dream-sculpture of young Wilcox.

That my uncle was excited by the tale of the sculptor I did not wonder, for what thoughts must arise upon hearing, after a knowledge of what Legrasse had learned of the cult, of a sensitive young man who had *dreamed* not only the figure and exact hieroglyphics of the swamp-found image and the Greenland devil tablet, but had come *in his dreams* upon at least three of the precise words of the formula uttered alike by Esquimau diabolists and mongrel Louisianans? Professor Angell's instant start on an investigation of the utmost thoroughness was eminently natural; though privately I suspected young Wilcox of having heard of the cult in some indirect way, and of having invented a series of dreams to heighten and continue the mystery at my uncle's expense. The dream-narratives and cuttings collected by the professor were, of course, strong corroboration; but the rationalism of my mind and the extravagance of the whole subject led me to adopt what I thought the most sensible conclusions. So, after thoroughly studying the manuscript again and correlating the theosophical and anthropological notes with the cult narrative of Legrasse, I made a trip to

Providence to see the sculptor and give him the rebuke I thought proper for so boldly imposing upon a learned and aged man.

Wilcox still lived alone in the Fleur-de-Lys Building in Thomas Street, a hideous Victorian imitation of seventeenth-century Breton architecture which flaunts its stuccoed front amidst the lovely colonial houses on the ancient hill, and under the very shadow of the finest Georgian steeple in America. I found him at work in his rooms, and at once conceded from the specimens scattered about that his genius is indeed profound and authentic. He will, I believe, some time be heard from as one of the great decadents; for he has crystallised in clay and will one day mirror in marble those nightmares and phantasies which Arthur Machen evokes in prose, and Clark Ashton Smith makes visible in verse and in painting.

Dark, frail, and somewhat unkempt in aspect, he turned languidly at my knock and asked me my business without rising. When I told him who I was, he displayed some interest; for my uncle had excited his curiosity in probing his strange dreams, yet had never explained the reason for the study. I did not enlarge his knowledge in this regard, but sought with some subtlety to draw him out. In a short time I became convinced of his absolute sincerity, for he spoke of the dreams in a manner none could mistake. They and their subconscious residuum had influenced his art profoundly, and he shewed me a morbid statue whose contours almost made me shake with the potency of its black suggestion. He could not recall having seen the original of this thing except in his own dream bas-relief, but the outlines had formed themselves insensibly under his hands. It was, no doubt, the giant shape he had raved of in delirium. That he really knew nothing of the hidden cult, save from what my uncle's relentless catechism had let fall, he soon made clear; and again I strove to think of some way in which he could possibly have received the weird impressions.

He talked of his dreams in a strangely poetic fashion; making me see with terrible vividness the damp Cyclopean city of slimy green stone—whose *geometry*, he oddly said, was *all wrong*—and hear with frighten expectancy the ceaseless, half-mental calling from underground: "*Cthulhu fhtagn*," "*Cthulhu fhtagn*." These words had formed part of that dread ritual which told of dead Cthulhu's dream-vigil in his stone vault at R'lyeh, and I felt deeply moved despite my rational beliefs. Wilcox, I was sure, had heard of the cult in some casual way, and had soon forgotten it amidst the mass of his equally weird reading and imagining. Later, by virtue of its sheer impressiveness, it had found subconscious expression in dreams, in the bas-relief, and in the terrible statue I now beheld; so that his imposture upon my uncle had been a very innocent one. The youth was of a type, at once slightly affected and slightly ill-mannered, which I could never like; but I was willing enough now to admit both his genius and his honesty. I took leave of him amicably, and wish him all the success his talent promises.

The matter of the cult still remained to fascinate me, and at times I had visions of personal fame from researches into its origin and connexions. I visited New Orleans, talked with Legrasse and others of that old-time raiding-party, saw the frightful image, and even questioned such of the mongrel prisoners as still survived. Old Castro, unfortunately, had been dead for some years. What I now heard so graphically at first-hand, though it was really no more than a detailed confirmation of what my uncle had written, excited me afresh; for I felt sure that I was on the track of a very real, very secret, and very ancient religion whose discovery would make me an anthropologist of note. My attitude was still one of absolute materialism, *as I wish it still were*, and I discounted with almost inexplicable perversity the coincidence of the dream notes and odd cuttings collected by Professor Angell.

One thing I began to suspect, and which I now fear I *know*, is that my uncle's death was far from natural. He fell on a narrow hill street leading up from an ancient waterfront swarming with foreign mongrels, after a careless push from a negro sailor. I did not forget the mixed blood and marine pursuits of the cult-members in Louisiana, and would not be surprised to learn of secret methods and poison needles as ruthless and as anciently known as the cryptic rites and beliefs. Legrasse and his men, it is true, have been let alone; but in Norway a certain seaman who saw things is dead. Might not the deeper inquiries of my uncle after encountering the sculptor's data have come to sinister ears? I think Professor Angell died because he knew too much, or because he was likely to learn too much. Whether I shall go as he did remains to be seen, for I have learned much now.

III. The Madness from the Sea

If heaven ever wishes to grant me a boon, it will be a total effacing of the results of a mere chance which fixed my eye on a certain stray piece of shelf-paper. It was nothing on which I would naturally have stumbled in the course of my daily round, for it was an old number of an Australian journal, the *Sydney Bulletin* for April 18, 1925. It had escaped even the cutting bureau which had at the time of its issuance been avidly collecting material for my uncle's research.

I had largely given over my inquiries into what Professor Angell called the "Cthulhu Cult," and was visiting a learned friend in Paterson, New Jersey; the curator of a local museum and a mineralogist of note. Examining one day the reserve specimens roughly set on the storage shelves in a rear room of the museum, my eye was caught by an odd picture in one of the old papers spread beneath the stones. It was the *Sydney Bulletin* I have mentioned, for my friend has wide affiliations in all conceivable foreign parts; and the picture was a half-tone cut of a hideous stone image almost identical with that which Legrasse had found in the swamp.

Eagerly clearing the sheet of its precious contents, I scanned the item in detail; and was disappointed to find it of only moderate length. What it suggested, however, was of portentous significance to my flagging quest; and I carefully tore it out for immediate action. It read as follows:

MYSTERY DERELICT FOUND AT SEA
Vigilant Arrives With Helpless Armed New Zealand Yacht in Tow.
One Survivor and Dead Man Found Aboard.
Tale of Desperate Battle and Deaths at Sea.
Rescued Seaman Refuses Particulars of Strange Experience.
Odd Idol Found in His Possession.
Inquiry to Follow.

The Morrison Co.'s freighter *Vigilant*, bound from Valparaiso, arrived this morning at its wharf in Darling Harbour, having in tow the battled and disabled but heavily armed steam yacht *Alert* of Dunedin, N. Z., which was sighted April 12th in S. Latitude 34°21', W. Longitude 152°17' with one living and one dead man aboard.

The *Vigilant* left Valparaiso March 25th, and on April 2nd was driven considerably south of her course by exceptionally heavy storms and monster waves. On April 12th the derelict was sighted; and though apparently deserted, was found upon boarding to contain one survivor in a half-delirious condition and one man who had evidently been dead for more than a week. The living man was clutching a horrible stone idol of unknown origin, about a foot in height, regarding whose nature authorities at Sydney University, the Royal Society, and the Museum in College Street all profess complete bafflement, and which the survivor says he found in the cabin of the yacht, in a small carved shrine of common pattern.

This man, after recovering his senses, told an exceedingly strange story of piracy and slaughter. He is Gustaf Johansen, a Norwegian of some intelligence, and had been second mate of the two-masted schooner Emma of Auckland, which sailed for Callao February 20th with a complement of eleven men. The *Emma*, he says, was delayed and thrown widely south of her course by the great storm of March 1st, and on March 22nd, in S. Latitude 49°51', W. Longitude 128°34', encountered the *Alert*, manned by a queer and evil-looking crew of Kanakas and half-castes. Being ordered peremptorily to turn back, Capt. Collins refused; whereupon the strange crew began to fire savagely and without warning upon the schooner with a peculiarly heavy battery of brass cannon forming part of the yacht's equipment. The *Emma*'s men shewed fight, says the survivor, and though the schooner began to sink from shots beneath the waterline they managed to heave alongside their enemy and board her, grappling with the savage crew on the yacht's deck, and being forced to kill them all, the number being slightly superior, because of their particularly abhorrent and desperate though rather clumsy mode of fighting.

Three of the *Emma*'s men, including Capt. Collins and First Mate Green, were killed; and the remaining eight under Second Mate Johansen proceeded to navigate the captured yacht, going ahead in their original direction to see if any reason for their ordering back had existed. The next day, it appears, they raised and landed on a small island, although none is known to exist in that part of the ocean; and six of the men somehow died ashore, though Johansen is queerly reticent about this part of his story, and speaks only of their falling into a rock chasm. Later, it seems, he and one companion boarded the yacht and tried to manage her, but were beaten about by the storm of April 2nd. From that time till his rescue on the 12th the man remembers little, and he does not even recall when William Briden, his companion, died. Briden's death reveals no apparent cause, and was probably due to excitement or exposure. Cable advices from Dunedin report that the *Alert* was well known there as an island trader, and bore an evil reputation along the waterfront. It was owned by a curious group of half-castes whose frequent meetings and night trips to the woods attracted no little curiosity; and it had set sail in great haste just after the storm and earth tremors of March 1st. Our Auckland correspondent gives the *Emma* and her crew an excellent reputation, and Johansen is described as a sober and worthy man. The admiralty will institute an inquiry on the whole matter beginning tomorrow at which every effort will be made to induce Johansen to speak more freely than he has done hitherto.

This was all, together with the picture of the hellish image; but what a train of ideas it started in my mind! Here were new treasuries of data on the Cthulhu Cult, and evidence that it had strange interests at sea as well as on land. What motive prompted the hybrid crew to order back the *Emma* as they sailed about with their hideous idol? What was the unknown island on which six of the *Emma*'s crew had died, and about which the mate Johansen was so secretive? What had the vice-admiralty's investigation brought out, and what was known of the noxious cult in Dunedin? And most marvellous of all, what deep and more than natural linkage of dates was this which gave a malign and now undeniable significance to the various turns of events so carefully noted by my uncle?

March 1st—our February 28th according to the International Date Line—the earthquake and storm had come. From Dunedin the *Alert* and her noisome crew had darted eagerly forth as if imperiously summoned, and on the other side of the earth poets and artists had begun to dream of a strange, dank Cyclopean city whilst a young sculptor had moulded in his sleep the form of the dreaded Cthulhu. March 23d the crew of the *Emma* landed on an unknown island and left six men dead; and on that date the dreams of sensitive men assumed a heightened vividness and darkened with dread of a giant monster's malign pursuit, whilst an architect had gone mad and a sculptor had lapsed suddenly into delirium! And what of this storm of April 2nd—the date on which all dreams of the dank city ceased, and Wilcox emerged unharmed from the bondage of strange fever? What of all this—and of those hints of old Castro about the sunken, star-born Old Ones and their coming reign; their faithful cult *and their mastery of dreams*? Was I tottering on the brink of cosmic horrors beyond man's power to bear? If so, they must be horrors of the mind alone, for in some way the second of April had put a stop to whatever monstrous menace had begun its siege of mankind's soul.

That evening, after a day of hurried cabling and arranging, I bade my host adieu and took a train for San Francisco. In less than a month I was in Dunedin; where, however, I found that little was known of the strange cult-members who had lingered in the old sea-taverns. Waterfront scum was far too common for special mention; though there was vague talk about one inland trip these mongrels had made, during which faint drumming and red flame were noted on the distant hills. In Auckland I learned that Johansen had returned *with yellow hair turned white* after a perfunctory and inconclusive questioning at Sydney, and had thereafter sold his cottage in West Street and sailed with his wife to his old home in Oslo. Of his stirring experience he would tell his friends no more than he had told the admiralty officials, and all they could do was to give me his Oslo address.

After that I went to Sydney and talked profitlessly with sea men and members of the vice-admiralty court. I saw the *Alert*, now sold and in commercial use, at Circular Quay in Sydney Cove, but gained nothing from its non-committal bulk. The crouching image with its cuttlefish head, dragon body, scaly wings, and hieroglyphed pedestal, was preserved in the Museum at Hyde Park; and I studied it long and well, finding it a thing of balefully exquisite workmanship, and with the same utter mystery, terrible antiquity, and unearthly strangeness of material which I had noted in Legrasse's smaller specimen. Geologists, the curator told me, had found it a monstrous puzzle; for they vowed that the world held no rock like it. Then I thought with a shudder of what old Castro had told Legrasse about the primal Great Ones: "They had come from the stars, and had brought Their images with Them."

Shaken with such a mental revolution as I had never before known, I now resolved to visit Mate Johansen in Oslo. Sailing for London, I reembarked at once for the Norwegian capital; and one autumn day landed at the trim wharves in the shadow of the Egeberg. Johansen's address, I discovered, lay in the Old Town of King Harold Haardrada, which kept alive the name of Oslo during all the centuries that the greater city masqueraded as "Christiana." I made the brief trip by taxicab, and knocked with palpitant heart at the door of a neat and ancient building with plastered front. A sad-faced woman in black answered my summons, and I was stung with disappointment when she told me in halting English that Gustaf Johansen was no more.

He had not survived his return, said his wife, for the doings at sea in 1925 had broken him. He had told her no more than he had told the public, but had left a long manuscript—of "technical matters" as he said—written in English, evidently in order to safeguard her from the peril of casual perusal. During a walk through a narrow lane near the Gothenburg dock, a bundle of papers falling from an attic window had knocked him down. Two Lascar sailors at once helped him to his feet, but before the ambulance could reach him he was dead. Physicians found no adequate cause for the end, and laid it to heart trouble and a weakened constitution.

I now felt gnawing at my vitals that dark terror which will never leave me till I, too, am at rest; "accidentally" or otherwise. Persuading the widow that my connexion with her husband's "technical matters" was sufficient to entitle me to his manuscript, I bore the document away and began to read it on the London boat. It was a simple, rambling thing—a naive sailor's effort at a post-facto diary—and strove to recall day by day that last awful voyage. I cannot attempt to transcribe it verbatim in all its cloudiness and redundance, but I will tell its gist enough to shew why the sound of the water against the vessel's sides became so unendurable to me that I stopped my ears with cotton.

Johansen, thank God, did not know quite all, even though he saw the city and the Thing, but I shall never sleep calmly again when I think of the horrors that lurk ceaselessly behind life in time and in space, and of those unhallowed blasphemies from elder stars which dream beneath the sea, known and favoured by a nightmare cult ready and eager to loose them on the world whenever another earthquake shall heave their monstrous stone city again to the sun and air.

Johansen's voyage had begun just as he told it to the vice-admiralty. The *Emma*, in ballast, had cleared Auckland on February 20th, and had felt the full force of that earthquake-born tempest which must have heaved up from the sea-bottom the horrors that filled men's dreams. Once more under control, the ship was making good progress when held up by the *Alert* on

March 22nd, and I could feel the mate's regret as he wrote of her bombardment and sinking. Of the swarthy cult-fiends on the *Alert* he speaks with significant horror. There was some peculiarly abominable quality about them which made their destruction seem almost a duty, and Johansen shews ingenuous wonder at the charge of ruthlessness brought against his party during the proceedings of the court of inquiry. Then, driven ahead by curiosity in their captured yacht under Johansen's command, the men sight a great stone pillar sticking out of the sea, and in S. Latitude 47°9', W. Longitude 126°43' come upon a coastline of mingled mud, ooze, and weedy Cyclopean masonry which can be nothing less than the tangible substance of earth's supreme terror—the nightmare corpse-city of R'lyeh, that was built in measureless aeons behind history by the vast, loathsome shapes that seeped down from the dark stars. There lay great Cthulhu and his hordes, hidden in green slimy vaults and sending out at last, after cycles incalculable, the thoughts that spread fear to the dreams of the sensitive and called imperiously to the faithful to come on a pilgrimage of liberation and restoration. All this Johansen did not suspect, but God knows he soon saw enough!

I suppose that only a single mountain-top, the hideous monolith-crowned citadel whereon great Cthulhu was buried, actually emerged from the waters. When I think of the *extent* of all that may be brooding down there I almost wish to kill myself forthwith. Johansen and his men were awed by the cosmic majesty of this dripping Babylon of elder daemons, and must have guessed without guidance that it was nothing of this or of any sane planet. Awe at the unbelievable size of the greenish stone blocks, at the dizzying height of the great carven monolith, and at the stupefying identity of the colossal statues and bas-reliefs with the queer image found in the shrine on the *Alert*, is poignantly visible in every line of the mate's frightened description.

Without knowing what futurism is like, Johansen achieved something very close to it when he spoke of the city; for instead of describing any definite structure or building, he dwells only on broad impressions of vast angles and stone surfaces—surfaces too great to belong to any thing right or proper for this earth, and impious with horrible images and hieroglyphs. I mention his talk about *angles* because it suggests something Wilcox had told me of his awful dreams. He has said that the *geometry* of the dream-place he saw was abnormal, non-Euclidean, and loathsomely redolent of spheres and dimensions apart from ours. Now an unlettered seaman felt the same thing whilst gazing at the terrible reality.

Johansen and his men landed at a sloping mud-bank on this monstrous Acropolis, and clambered slipperily up over titan oozy blocks which could have been no mortal staircase. The very sun of heaven seemed distorted when viewed through the polarising miasma welling out from this sea-soaked perversion, and twisted menace and suspense lurked leeringly in those crazily elusive angles of carven rock where a second glance shewed concavity after the first shewed convexity.

Something very like fright had come over all the explorers before anything more definite than rock and ooze and weed was seen. Each would have fled had he not feared the scorn of the others, and it was only half-heartedly that they searched—vainly, as it proved—for some portable souvenir to bear away.

It was Rodriguez the Portuguese who climbed up the foot of the monolith and shouted of what he had found. The rest followed him, and looked curiously at the immense carved door with the now familiar squid-dragon bas-relief. It was, Johansen said, like a great barn-door; and they all felt that it was a door because of the ornate lintel, threshold, and jambs around it, though they could not decide whether it lay flat like a trap-door or slantwise like an outside cellar-door. As Wilcox would have said, the geometry of the place was all wrong. One could not be sure that the sea and the ground were horizontal, hence the relative position of everything else seemed phantasmally variable.

Briden pushed at the stone in several places without result. Then Donovan felt over it delicately around the edge, pressing each point separately as he went. He climbed interminably along the grotesque stone moulding—that is, one would call it climbing if the thing was not after all horizontal—and the men wondered how any door in the universe could be so vast. Then, very softly and slowly, the acre-great panel began to give inward at the top; and they saw that it was balanced. Donovan slid or somehow propelled himself down or along the jamb and rejoined his fellows, and everyone watched the queer recession of the monstrously carven portal. In this phantasy of prismatic distortion it moved anomalously in a diagonal way, so that all the rule of matter and perspective seemed upset.

The aperture was black with a darkness almost material. That tenebrousness was indeed a *positive quality*; for it obscured such parts of the inner walls as ought to have been revealed, and actually burst forth like smoke from its aeon-long imprisonment, visibly darkening the sun as it slunk away into the shrunken and gibbous sky on flapping membraneous wings. The odour arising from the newly opened depths was intolerable, and at length the quick-eared Hawkins thought he heard a nasty, slopping sound down there. Everyone listened, and everyone was listening still when It lumbered slobberingly into sight and gropingly squeezed Its gelatinous green immensity through the black doorway into the tainted outside air of that poison city of madness.

Poor Johansen's handwriting almost gave out when he wrote of this. Of the six men who never reached the ship, he thinks two perished of pure fright in that accursed instant. The Thing cannot be described—there is no language for such abysms of shrieking and immemorial lunacy, such eldritch contradictions of all matter, force, and cosmic order. A mountain walked or stumbled. God! What wonder that across the earth a great architect went mad, and poor Wilcox raved with fever in that telepathc instant? The Thing of the idols, the green, sticky spawn of the stars, had awaked to claim his own. The stars were right again, and what an age-old cult had failed to do by design, a band of innocent sailors had done by accident. After vigintillions of years great Cthulhu was loose again, and ravening for delight.

Three men were swept up by the flabby claws before anybody turned. God rest them, if there be any rest in the universe. They were Donovan, Guerrera, and Angstrom. Parker slipped as the other three were plunging frenziedly over endless vistas of green-crusted rock to the boat, and Johansen swears he was swallowed up by an angle of masonry which shouldn't have been there; an angle which was acute, but behaved as if it were obtuse. So only Briden and Johansen reached the boat, and pulled desperately for the *Alert* as the mountainous monstrosity flopped down the slimy stones and hesitated floundering at the edge of the water.

Steam had not been suffered to go down entirely, despite the departure of all hands for the shore; and it was the work of only a few moments of feverish rushing up and down between wheel and engines to get the *Alert* under way. Slowly, amidst the distorted horrors of that indescribable scene, she began to churn the lethal waters; whilst on the masonry of that charnel shore that was not of earth the titan Thing from the stars slavered and gibbered like Polypheme cursing the fleeing ship of Odysseus. Then, bolder than the storied Cyclops, great Cthulhu slid greasily into the water and began to pursue with vast wave-raising strokes of cosmic potency. Briden looked back and went mad, laughing shrilly as he kept on laughing at intervals till death found him one night in the cabin whilst Johansen was wandering deliriously.

But Johansen had not given out yet. Knowing that the Thing could surely overtake the *Alert* until steam was fully up, he resolved on a desperate chance; and, setting the engine for full speed, ran lightning-like on deck and reversed the wheel. There was a mighty eddying and foaming in the noisome brine, and as the steam mounted higher and higher the brave Norwegian drove his vessel head on against the pursuing jelly which rose above the unclean froth like the stern of a daemon galleon. The awful squid-head with writhing feelers came nearly up to the bowsprit of the sturdy yacht, but Johansen drove on relentlessly. There was a bursting as of an exploding bladder, a slushy nastiness as of a cloven sunfish, a stench as of a thousand opened graves, and a sound that the chronicler would not put on paper. For an instant the ship was befouled by an acrid and blinding green cloud, and then there was only a venomous seething astern; where—God in heaven!—the scattered plasticity of that nameless sky-spawn was nebulously *recombining* in its hateful original form, whilst its distance widened every second as the *Alert* gained impetus from its mounting steam.

That was all. After that Johansen only brooded over the idol in the cabin and attended to a few matters of food for himself and the laughing maniac by his side. He did not try to navigate after the first bold flight, for the reaction had taken something out of his soul. Then came the storm of April 2nd, and a gathering of the clouds about his consciousness. There is a sense of spectral whirling through liquid gulfs of infinity, of dizzying rides through reeling universes on a comet's tail, and of hysterical plunges from the pit to the moon and from the moon back again to the pit, all livened by a cachinnating chorus of the distorted, hilarious elder gods and the green, bat-winged mocking imps of Tartarus.

Out of that dream came rescue—the *Vigilant*, the vice-admiralty court, the streets of Dunedin, and the long voyage back home to the old house by the Egeberg. He could not tell—they would think him mad. He would write of what he knew before death came, but his wife must not guess. Death would be a boon if only it could blot out the memories.

That was the document I read, and now I have placed it in the tin box beside the bas-relief and the papers of Professor Angell. With it shall go this record of mine—this test of my own sanity, wherein is pieced together that which I hope may never be pieced together again. I have looked upon all that the universe has to hold of horror, and even the skies of spring and the flowers of summer must ever afterward be poison to me. But I do not think my life will be long. As my uncle went, as poor Johansen went, so I shall go. I know too much, and the cult still lives.

Cthulhu still lives, too, I suppose, again in that chasm of stone which has shielded him since the sun was young. His accursed city is sunken once more, for the *Vigilant* sailed over the spot after the April storm; but his ministers on earth still bellow and prance and slay around idol-capped monoliths in lonely places. He must have been trapped by the sinking whilst within his black abyss, or the world would by now be screaming with fright and frenzy. Who knows the end? What has risen may sink, and what has sunk may rise. Loathsomeness waits and dreams in the deep, and decay spreads over the tottering cities of men. A time will come—but I must not and cannot think! Let me pray that, if I do not survive this manuscript, my executors may put caution before audacity and see that it meets no other eye.

THE LOTTERY

Shirley Jackson

(1948)

This story, published only a few years after the real-life horror of Nazism had become recorded fact, continues to shock readers with its all too plausible account of how a perfectly typical American small town can placidly accept a purposeful violent act as a natural extension of its community. No supernatural force is quite as disturbing as these cheerful neighbors at their annual gathering.

The morning of June 27th was clear and sunny, with the fresh warmth of a full-summer day; the flowers were blossoming profusely and the grass was richly green. The people of the village began to gather in the square, between the post office and the bank, around ten o'clock; in some towns there were so many people that the lottery took two days and had to be started on June 2th, but in this village, where there were only about three hundred people, the whole lottery took less than two hours, so it could begin at ten o'clock in the morning and still be through in time to allow the villagers to get home for noon dinner.

The children assembled first, of course. School was recently over for the summer, and the feeling of liberty sat uneasily on most of them; they tended to gather together quietly for a while before they broke into boisterous play, and their talk was still of the classroom and the teacher, of books and reprimands. Bobby Martin had already stuffed his pockets full of stones, and the other boys soon followed his example, selecting the smoothest and roundest stones: Bobby and Harry Jones and Dickie Delacroix—the villagers pronounced this name "Dellacroy"—eventually made a great pile of stones in one corner of the square and guarded it against the raids of the other boys. The girls stood aside, talking among themselves, looking over their shoulders at the boys, and the very small children rolled in the dust or clung to the hands of their older brothers or sisters.

Soon the men began to gather, surveying their own children, speaking of planting and rain, tractors and taxes. They stood together, away from the pile of stones in the corner, and their jokes were quiet and they smiled rather than laughed. The women, wearing faded house dresses and sweaters, came shortly after their menfolk. They greeted one another and exchanged bits of gossip as they went to join their husbands. Soon the women, standing by their husbands, began to call to their children, and the children came reluctantly, having to be called four or five times. Bobby Martin ducked under his mother's grasping hand and ran, laughing, back to the pile of stones. His father spoke up sharply, and Bobby came quickly and took his place between his father and his oldest brother.

The lottery was conducted—as were the square dances, the teen club, the Halloween program—by Mr. Summers, who had time and energy to devote to civic activities. He was a round-faced, jovial man and he ran the coal business, and people were sorry for him, because he had no children and his wife was a scold. When he arrived in the square, carrying the black wooden box, there was a murmur of conversation among the villagers, and he waved and called, "Little late today, folks." The postmaster, Mr. Graves, followed him, carrying a three-legged stool, and the stool was put in the center of the square and Mr. Summers set the black box down on it. The villagers kept their distance, leaving a space between themselves and the stool, and when Mr. Summers said, "Some of you fellows want to give me a hand?" there was a hesitation before two men, Mr. Martin and his oldest son, Baxter, came forward to hold the box steady on the stool while Mr. Summers stirred up the papers inside it.

The original paraphernalia for the lottery had been lost long ago, and the black box now resting on the stool had been put into use even before Old Man Warner, the oldest man in town, was born. Mr. Summers spoke frequently to the villagers about making a new box, but no one liked to upset even as much tradition as was represented by the black box. There was a story that the present box had been made with some pieces of the box that had preceded it, the one that had been constructed when the first people settled down to make a village here. Every year, after the lottery, Mr. Summers began talking again about a new box, but every year the subject was allowed to fade off without anything's being done. The black box grew shabbier each year: by now it was no longer completely black but splintered badly along one side to show the original wood color, and in some places faded or stained.

Mr. Martin and his oldest son, Baxter, held the black box securely on the stool until Mr. Summers had stirred the papers thoroughly with his hand. Because so much of the ritual had been forgotten or discarded, Mr. Summers had been successful in having slips of paper substituted for the chips of wood that had been used for generations. Chips of wood, Mr. Summers had argued, had been all very well when the village was tiny, but now that the population was more than three hundred and likely to keep on growing, it was necessary to use something that would fit more easily into the black box. The night before the lottery, Mr. Summers and Mr. Graves made up the slips of paper and put them in the box, and it was then taken to the safe of Mr. Summers' coal company and locked up until Mr. Summers was ready to take it to the square next morning. The rest of the year, the box was put way, sometimes one place, sometimes another; it had spent one year in Mr. Graves's barn and another year underfoot in the post office, and sometimes it was set on a shelf in the Martin grocery and left there.

There was a great deal of fussing to be done before Mr. Summers declared the lottery open. There were the lists to make up—of heads of families, heads of households in each family, members of each household in each family. There was the proper swearing-in of Mr. Summers by the postmaster, as the official of the lottery; at one time, some people remembered, there had been a recital of some sort, performed by the official of the lottery, a perfunctory, tuneless chant that had been rattled off duly each year; some people believed that the official of the lottery used to stand just so when he said or sang it, others believed that he was supposed to walk among the people, but years and years ago this part of the ritual had been allowed to lapse. There had been, also, a ritual salute, which the official of the lottery had had to use in addressing each person who came up to draw from the box, but this also had changed with time, until now it was felt necessary only for the official to speak to each person approaching. Mr. Summers was very good at all this; in his clean white shirt and blue jeans, with one hand resting carelessly on the black box, he seemed very proper and important as he talked interminably to Mr. Graves and the Martins.

Just as Mr. Summers finally left off talking and turned to the assembled villagers, Mrs. Hutchinson came hurriedly along the path to the square, her sweater thrown over her shoulders, and slid into place in the back of the crowd. "Clean forgot what day it was," she said to Mrs. Delacroix, who stood next to her, and they both laughed softly. "Thought my old man was out back stacking wood," Mrs. Hutchinson went on. "And then I looked out the window and the kids was gone, and then I remembered it was twenty-seventh and came a-running." She dried her hands on her apron, and Mrs. Delacroix said, "You're in time, though. They're still talking away up there."

Mrs. Hutchinson craned her neck to see through the crowd and found her husband and children standing near the front. She tapped Mrs. Delacroix on the arm as a farewell and began to make her way through the crowd. The people separated good-humoredly to let her through: two or three people said, in voices just loud enough to be heard across the crowd, "Here comes your Missus, Hutchinson," and "Bill, she made it after all." Mrs. Hutchinson reached her husband, and Mr. Summers, who had been waiting, said cheerfully, "Thought we were going to have to get on without you, Tessie." Mrs. Hutchinson said, grinning,

"Wouldn't have me leave m'dishes in the sink, now, would you, Joe?," and soft laughter ran through the crowd as the people stirred back into position after Mrs. Hutchinson's arrival.

"Well, now," Mr. Summers said soberly, "guess we better get started, get this over with, so's we can go back to work. Anybody ain't here?"

"Dunbar," several people said. "Dunbar. Dunbar."

Mr. Summers consulted his list. "Clyde Dunbar," he said. "That's right. He's broke his leg, hasn't he? Who's drawing for him?"

"Me, I guess," a woman said, and Mr. Summers turned to look at her. "Wife draws for her husband," Mr. Summers said. "Don't you have a grown boy to do it for you, Janey?" Although Mr. Summers and everyone else in the village knew the answer perfectly well, it was the business of the official of the lottery to ask such questions formally. Mr. Summers waited with an expression of polite interest while Mrs. Dunbar answered.

"Horace's not but sixteen yet," Mrs. Dunbar said regretfully. "Guess I gotta fill in for the old man this year."

"Right," Mr. Summers said. He made a note on the list he was holding. Then he asked, "Watson's boy drawing this year?"

A tall boy in the crowd raised his hand. "Here," he said. "I'm drawing for my mother and me." He blinked his eyes nervously and ducked his head as several voices in the crowd said things like "Good fellow, Jack," and "Glad to see your mother's got a man to do it."

"Well," Mr. Summers said, "guess that's everyone. Old Man Warner make it?"

"Here," a voice said, and Mr. Summers nodded.

A sudden hush fell on the crowd as Mr. Summers cleared his throat and looked at the list. "All ready?" he called. "Now, I'll read the names—heads of families first—and the men come up and take a paper out of the box. Keep the paper folded in your hand without looking at it until everyone has had a turn. Everything clear?"

The people had done it so many times that they only half listened to the directions: most of them were quiet, wetting their lips, not looking around. Then Mr. Summers raised one hand high and said, "Adams." A man disengaged himself from the crowd and came forward. "Hi, Steve," Mr. Summers said, and Mr. Adams said, "Hi, Joe." They grinned at one another humorlessly and nervously. Then Mr. Adams reached into the black box and took out a folded paper. He held it firmly by one corner as he turned and went hastily back to his place in the crowd, where he stood a little apart from his family, not looking down at his hand.

"Allen," Mr. Summers said. "Anderson . . . Bentham."

"Seems like there's no time at all between lotteries anymore," Mrs. Delacroix said to Mrs. Graves in the back row.

"Seems like we got through with the last one only last week."

"Time sure goes fast," Mrs. Graves said.

"Clark . . . Delacroix."

"There goes my old man," Mrs. Delacroix said. She held her breath while her husband went forward.

"Dunbar," Mr. Summers said, and Mrs. Dunbar went steadily to the box while one of the women said, "Go on, Janey," and another said, "There she goes."

"We're next," Mrs. Graves said. She watched while Mr. Graves came around from the side of the box, greeted Mr. Summers gravely, and selected a slip of paper from the box. By now, all through the crowd there were men holding the small folded papers in their large hands, turning them over and over nervously. Mrs. Dunbar and her two sons stood together, Mrs. Dunbar holding the slip of paper.

"Harburt . . . Hutchinson."

"Get up there, Bill," Mrs. Hutchinson said, and the people near her laughed.

"Jones."

"They do say," Mr. Adams said to Old Man Warner, who stood next to him, "that over in the north village they're talking of giving up the lottery."

Old Man Warner snorted. "Pack of crazy fools," he said. "Listening to the young folks, nothing's good enough for them.

Next thing you know, they'll be wanting to go back to living in caves, nobody work anymore, live that way for a while. Used to be a saying about 'Lottery in June, corn be heavy soon.' First thing you know, we'd all be eating stewed chickweed and acorns. There's always been a lottery," he added petulantly. "Bad enough to see young Joe Summers up there joking with everybody."

"Some places have already quit lotteries," Mrs. Adams said.

"Nothing but trouble in that," Old Man Warner said stoutly. "Pack of young fools."

"Martin." And Bobby Martin watched his father go forward. "Overdyke . . . Percy."

"I wish they'd hurry," Mrs. Dunbar said to her older son. "I wish they'd hurry."

"They're almost through," her son said.

"You get ready to run tell Dad," Mrs. Dunbar said.

Mr. Summers called his own name and then stepped forward precisely and selected a slip from the box. Then he called, "Warner."

"Seventy-seventh year I been in the lottery," Old Man Warner said as he went through the crowd. "Seventy-seventh time."

"Watson." The tall boy came awkwardly through the crowd. Someone said, "Don't be nervous, Jack," and Mr. Summers said, "Take your time, son."

"Zanini."

After that, there was a long pause, a breathless pause, until Mr. Summers, holding his slip of paper in the air, said, "All right, fellows." For a minute, no one moved, and then all the slips of paper were opened. Suddenly, all the women began to speak at once, saying, "Who is it?" "Who's got it?" "Is it the Dunbars?" "Is it the Watsons?" Then the voices began to say, "It's Hutchinson. It's Bill." "Bill Hutchinson's got it."

"Go tell your father," Mrs. Dunbar said to her older son.

People began to look around to see the Hutchinsons. Bill Hutchinson was standing quiet, staring down at the paper in his hand. Suddenly, Tessie Hutchinson shouted to Mr. Summers,

"You didn't give him time enough to take any paper he wanted. I saw you. It wasn't fair!"

"Be a good sport, Tessie," Mrs. Delacroix called, and Mrs. Graves said, "All of us took the same chance."

"Shut up, Tessie," Bill Hutchinson said.

"Well, everyone," Mr. Summers said, "that was done pretty fast, and now we've got to be hurrying a little more to get done in time." He consulted his next list. "Bill," he said, "you draw for the Hutchinson family. You got any other households in the Hutchinsons?"

"There's Don and Eva," Mrs. Hutchinson yelled. "Make them take their chance!"

"Daughters draw with their husbands' families, Tessie," Mr. Summers said gently. "You know that as well as anyone else."

"It wasn't fair," Tessie said.

"I guess not, Joe," Bill Hutchinson said regretfully. "My daughter draws with her husband's family; that's only fair. And I've got no other family except the kids."

"Then, as far as drawing for families is concerned, it's you," Mr. Summers said in explanation, "and as far as drawing for households is concerned, that's you, too. Right?"

"Right," Bill Hutchinson said.

"How many kids, Bill?" Mr. Summers asked formally.

"Three," Bill Hutchinson said.

"There's Bill Jr., and Nancy, and little Dave. And Tessie and me."

"All right, then," Mr. Summers said. "Harry, you got their tickets back?"

Mr. Graves nodded and held up the slips of paper. "Put them in the box, then," Mr. Summers directed. "Take Bill's and put it in."

"I think we ought to start over," Mrs. Hutchinson said, as quietly as she could. "I tell you it wasn't fair. You didn't give him time enough to choose. Everybody saw that."

Mr. Graves had selected the five slips and put them in the box, and he dropped all the papers but those onto the ground, where the breeze caught them and lifted them off.

"Listen, everybody," Mrs. Hutchinson was saying to the people around her.

"Ready, Bill?" Mr. Summers asked, and Bill Hutchinson, with one quick glance around at his wife and children, nodded.

"Remember," Mr. Summers said, "take the slips and keep them folded until each person has taken one. Harry, you help little Dave." Mr. Graves took the hand of the little boy, who came willingly with him up to the box. "Take a paper out of the box, Davy," Mr. Summers said. Davy put his hand into the box and laughed. "Take just one paper," Mr. Summers said. "Harry, you hold it for him." Mr. Graves took the child's hand and removed the folded paper from the tight fist and held it while little Dave stood next to him and looked up at him wonderingly.

"Nancy next," Mr. Summers said. Nancy was twelve, and her school friends breathed heavily as she went forward switching her skirt, and took a slip daintily from the box. "Bill Jr.," Mr. Summers said, and Billy, his face red and his feet overlarge, near knocked the box over as he got a paper out. "Tessie," Mr. Summers said. She hesitated for a minute, looking around defiantly, and then set her lips and went up to the box. She snatched a paper out and held it behind her.

"Bill," Mr. Summers said, and Bill Hutchinson reached into the box and felt around, bringing his hand out at last with the slip of paper in it.

The crowd was quiet. A girl whispered, "I hope it's not Nancy," and the sound of the whisper reached the edges of the crowd.

"It's not the way it used to be," Old Man Warner said clearly. "People ain't the way they used to be."

"All right," Mr. Summers said. "Open the papers. Harry, you open little Dave's."

Mr. Graves opened the slip of paper and there was a general sigh through the crowd as he held it up and everyone could see that it was blank. Nancy and Bill Jr. opened theirs at the same time, and both beamed and laughed, turning around to the crowd and holding their slips of paper above their heads.

"Tessie," Mr. Summers said. There was a pause, and then

Mr. Summers looked at Bill Hutchinson, and Bill unfolded his paper and showed it. It was blank.

"It's Tessie," Mr. Summers said, and his voice was hushed. "Show us her paper, Bill."

Bill Hutchinson went over to his wife and forced the slip of paper out of her hand. It had a black spot on it, the black spot Mr. Summers had made the night before with the heavy pencil in the coal company office. Bill Hutchinson held it up, and there was a stir in the crowd.

"All right, folks," Mr. Summers said. "Let's finish quickly."

Although the villagers had forgotten the ritual and lost the original black box, they still remembered to use stones. The pile of stones the boys had made earlier was ready; there were stones on the ground with the blowing scraps of paper that had come out of the box. Delacroix selected a stone so large she had to pick it up with both hands and turned to Mrs. Dunbar. "Come on," she said. "Hurry up."

Mrs. Dunbar had small stones in both hands, and she said, gasping for breath, "I can't run at all. You'll have to go ahead and I'll catch up with you."

The children had stones already. And someone gave little Davy Hutchinson a few pebbles.

Tessie Hutchinson was in the center of a cleared space by now, and she held her hands out desperately as the villagers moved in on her. "It isn't fair," she said. A stone hit her on the side of the head. Old Man Warner was saying, "Come on, come on, everyone." Steve Adams was in the front of the crowd of villagers, with Mrs. Graves beside him.

"It isn't fair, it isn't right," Mrs. Hutchinson screamed, and then they were upon her.